The Highlander's Promise

By Lynsay Sands

Lynsay Sands

The Highlander's Promise

AVONBOOKS

An Imprint of HarperCollinsPublishers

THE HIGHLANDER'S PROMISE. Copyright © 2018 by Lynsay Sands. All rights reserved. Printed in the United States of America. No part of this book may be used or reproduced in any manner whatsoever without written permission except in the case of brief quotations embodied in critical articles and reviews. For information, address HarperCollins Publishers, 195 Broadway, New York, NY 10007.

First Avon Books mass market printing: July 2018
First Avon Books hardcover printing: June 2018

Print Edition ISBN: 978-0-06-284267-1
Digital Edition ISBN: 978-0-06-246889-5

FIRST EDITION

18 19 20 21 22   LSC   10 9 8 7 6 5 4 3 2 1

The Highlander's Promise

Chapter 1

"*F*ISHING?"

Aulay noted the horror in his youngest brother's voice and felt his mouth twist with bitter humor. But, continuing toward the door to the hunting lodge, he merely growled, "That's what I said, Alick—fishing. I told ye I was coming here to relax."

"Aye, but I thought ye meant . . . relax, like . . . relaxing."

"Ye mean drinking and wenching and such," Aulay suggested dryly.

"Aye," Alick agreed eagerly.

"Nay." Aulay opened the door, allowing sunshine to cascade into the room. He then turned to face his brother, and drew away the long length of hair that he usually let drape over the ruined side of his face. He wasn't surprised when Alick swallowed and shifted his gaze away from him to the room at large. Aulay was sure the bright glare of sunlight merely highlighted the ugly scar that cleaved the side of his face.

"I'm no' interested in an aching head from drinking, or the irritation o' giggly bar wenches who shriek like babies when they see me face," he growled as he let the hair fall back into place. "I came to relax. Fishing relaxes me. 'Tis why I had the hunting lodge rebuilt close to the ocean after the fire, instead of where the original stood." Shifting his feet, he glanced out the door and then back before saying, "You're welcome to come do ye wish it. Otherwise, ye may as well return to Buchanan. For there will be no wenching or drinking here."

Alick didn't bother to hide his disappointment, but shook his head. "Fine, fishing it is then." Starting forward, he added, "But I'm no' staying the full two weeks with ye if all we're doing is fishing. A couple o' days, mayhap."

"As ye like," Aulay said with feigned disinterest as he headed out of the lodge. But, in truth, he was glad the lad didn't plan to stay long. He'd wanted to come on his own anyway. He always preferred to be alone when his black moods struck, and they always overtook him this time of year. Tomorrow was the anniversary of the battle that had taken his twin brother's life, and gifted him with the scar that had ruined his own. Aulay knew from experience that melancholy would soon drop over him like a cloak, and hang on him for a good week or two. It was why he'd planned this trip. He preferred to be alone to deal with his dark humors. His family tended to interfere and try to make him feel better. But, all they really managed to do was add to his misery by making him feel guilty for causing them worry.

"Fine. Where are we going fishing then?" Alick muttered, following him out of the lodge.

"The ocean," Aulay said dryly. "Where the devil do ye think I'd take ye to fish?"

"Oh. Right," Alick murmured.

"Right," Aulay agreed, and shook his head as he walked to where his horse was tethered with his fishing gear already waiting. He'd gathered fishing rods, nets and the other items they'd need and affixed them to his saddle while waiting for Alick to wake.

Any other time of year, Aulay would have walked to the beach. It wasn't that far. The new lodge was nestled in a clearing in a well-treed valley, so that it would be sheltered from the cold winter winds off the ocean. It made it a fair walk to the beach, but not far enough to necessitate riding a horse there . . . unless one found themselves exhausted at the very thought of traipsing that distance, lugging his net and fishing gear along with him, as he did now.

It was a quick jaunt by horseback and Aulay and Alick were soon in the small boat he kept on the beach and rowing away from shore.

"How far out are we going?" Alick asked after a few minutes.

"Not far," Aulay responded patiently.

Alick was silent for barely the count of ten before asking, "Are we nearly there?"

Aulay rolled his eyes, but then stopped rowing and raised his oars as he spotted something in the distance. Gaze narrowing, he peered past his brother's shoulder, trying to identify what he was seeing.

"What?" Alick asked, noting where his attention had gone and glancing over his shoulder to the water beyond the bow of the small craft. "There's something floating in the water."

"Aye." Aulay started to row again. He couldn't tell what they were looking at. It was large. At least, part of it was. Part of it was narrow too.

"What is it?" Alick asked, turning right around on his bench seat now, to face forward and better see what lay ahead.

"I'm no' sure," Aulay admitted.

They both squinted into the distance as the boat moved through the water, and then Alick said, "I think 'tis a ship's mast."

Aulay grunted, able now to see for himself that the large thing sticking out of the water was part of a crow's nest. It was on its side, with one half of it submerged, and the other half above water.

They both fell silent as he propelled them toward it and then Alick said, "I think there's a body laying across the far end. A woman."

"A woman?" Aulay asked dubiously and hoped it wasn't. Whatever lay ahead wasn't moving or crying out for help. Finding the bloated body of a dead woman floating in the water wasn't like to improve his mood any.

"I think I see bosoms," Alick explained.

"Of course ye do. Only you could make out bosoms from a hundred feet away," Aulay said acerbically, but as he rowed the boat closer, he could see what his brother was talking about. In the center at the far end of the mast, there did appear to be what could be bosoms pointing skyward.

"It *is* a woman," Alick said with certainty.

Aulay didn't comment. His attention was on the cloth of the sails he could see lying across the mast and floating in the water around it as they moved past the crow's nest. He shifted direction a bit to avoid getting caught up in it.

"A ship must have sunk," Alick said in a hushed voice as he moved forward in the small boat to get a better view. "But—"

"But what?" Aulay asked, putting more effort into the oars.

Alick leaned out over the bow, hanging far enough forward in an attempt to see that Aulay worried he'd fall out. Finally, Alick said, "She's tied to the mast. Why the devil would they tie her to the mast? Row faster, Aulay!"

"I am rowing as fast as I can," Aulay grunted, but dipped only one oar in the water this time to turn the boat slightly so he could get a better look at the angle of their approach and see how far they now were from the dead woman. He had no desire to ram into her.

"Was it to keep her from falling overboard in the storm, do ye think?" Alick asked.

Aulay was able to see the woman strapped to the far end of the mast now. He quickly scanned the surrounding water, but didn't see anything else floating nearby.

"It must have gone down in last night's storm," Alick commented.

Aulay nodded silently. The storm had started just after they'd arrived at the lodge. The wind had battered and torn at the log building so violently, he'd worried about losing the roof. That hadn't happened, but the storm had raged furiously for hours and he hadn't slept until it had ended.

His gaze skimmed the water around them again, but there was nothing to see. If a ship did sink, everything but this one mast with its sail had gone down . . . which didn't seem likely. There should be kegs floating, or crates, something. Not just a lone mast with a dead woman on it.

"Take us to the left a bit, Aulay," Alick said suddenly. "I won't be able to reach her and we'll just float right past her at this angle."

Aulay raised the right oar out of the water, and sank the left one in for a hard pull.

"Good, good, just a little closer and I'll be able to reach her," Alick said, his upper body disappearing from sight as he bent over the front of the boat.

Aulay gave one more pull on the oars, and then lifted them out of the water. Resting them inside the boat, he stood to move to the bow to help his brother, arriving just as the younger man cursed.

"What is it?" Aulay asked.

"Do you have a knife? I can't get the ropes untied. They're tight as the devil and must be knotted somewhere under the water."

Aulay leaned over the side of the boat to survey the situation. They were next to the woman. But Alick was right. The start of the rope was nowhere in sight. There would be no untying her. She'd have to be cut free.

"Move," he ordered, retrieving his dirk.

Alick shifted quickly out of the way and Aulay took his spot. He bent over to peer at the woman and paused, his eyes widening. She had been a beautiful lass, her face a pale white, her hair a deep, shiny black. The gown she wore was torn and tattered, presumably by the storm. It left the better part of her upper legs on display before they bent at the knee and disappeared over the end of the mast and into the water. She must have slid down the mast after the ship sank, he supposed, and then shifted his gaze to her upper body and the barely covered, and very generous bosoms Alick had noticed. The cloth there was as tattered as it was on her lower legs, leaving most of her on display. Everything else, however, was covered by rope that started under her breasts and was wrapped around and around her all the way down past her hips.

"I think she's alive," Alick said suddenly, sounding as shocked as Aulay felt at the suggestion when his brother pointed out, "Her breasts are rising and falling."

"Stop looking at her breasts," Aulay growled with disgust. "The lass needs help, not to have some young pillock ogling her breasts and—"

Aulay's words died abruptly when the woman opened her eyes, revealing that she was indeed alive. He stared into her sparkling bright green eyes, waiting for her to take fright at the sight of his scarred face and start in screaming, but she merely stared at him with dead calm. Finally, he said, "'Tis all right, lass. Ye're safe. We'll get ye off that mast and to shore quick as we can."

Her eyes widened then, and he took the time to notice that there was a circle of golden flecks floating in the green around each pupil, and then she breathed, "Angel."

Aulay tipped his head uncertainly. "Is that yer name, lass?"

"Nay." She shook her head on the mast, but then winced as if in horrible pain. Closing her eyes against it, she managed to get out, "You are the angel."

Aulay was sure she was delirious and nearly said, "Nay, I'm a highlander, no' an angel, when she added, "I thought sure I would die, but God sent you to save me."

He was just marveling over the words when Alick muttered, "Hmm, she must be delirious. Most ladies think ye a devil come straight out o' hell since—"

"Alick," Aulay growled as he slid his dirk under one of the strands of rope to begin sawing at it.

"Aye?"

"Shut it," he snapped as the first rope gave way to his blade and he moved on to work it under another.

Alick obeyed the order for all of a minute, before saying, "She's lucky the mast didn't land with her face down in the water. She'd have drowned fer sure."

The words actually made Aulay pause briefly and frown at the thought of this lovely creature coming to such an end, but then he gave his head a shake and continued to cut at the rope. The woman neither moved, nor opened her eyes again, and Aulay was quite certain she'd lost consciousness. He had to slice through six or seven lengths of rope before it all suddenly unraveled and fell away from her. The woman immediately began to slide off the log she lay on. A moan of protest slipped from her lips as she went, and Aulay quickly caught her upper arm with his free hand to prevent her sinking into the water.

"'Tis all right, lass. I've got ye," he said reassuringly as he quickly slid his dirk back into its sheath. Aulay then pulled the woman closer to the boat, and leaned out to scoop her from the water. She moaned as he lifted her, and he staggered under her weight. The lass was wee, but heavier than he expected. He hadn't taken into account that what was left of her long gown was now waterlogged.

Aulay paused briefly to adjust to the weight, and then turned to sit on the bench Alick had previously occupied. Once he had her settled in his lap, leaning against one arm, he was able to free his other hand to brush the damp strands of hair away from her face.

"Lass, are ye all right?" he asked, and was relieved when her eyes opened again. Smiling, Aulay murmured, "Good day to ye, lass. What's yer name? Tell us yer name and who yer people are and we'll get ye home safe to them."

"Nay," she said with alarm and winced in pain as if her own voice hurt her. Squeezing her eyes closed, she muttered, "He'll kill me."

"Who?" Aulay asked with a frown. "Who will kill ye, lass?"

She groaned, and mumbled a couple of words. Something about a cat and betrothed and his killing some Lady White?

"Yer betrothed?" Aulay asked with a frown. "Yer betrothed killed Lady White and will kill ye?"

"Nay," she groaned and instinctively shook her head, only to cry out and clutch it in both hands. After a moment, she got out, "Not my betrothed . . . make me marry him . . . will kill me like first wife."

Aulay frowned as he watched her struggle with the pain. Her face was completely bloodless now, her lips tight as she fought the agony apparently tearing at her head.

"All right, lass," he said soothingly. Rocking her from side to side as if comforting a wailing child, he promised, "All will be well. We'll no' tell anyone we have ye. We'll keep ye safe and see ye get healthy and strong again ere we worry about that. 'Twill all be fine."

Much to his surprise, the lass forced her eyes open again then. She stared at him through a world of agony, and then moved one hand to gently touch the scar that divided his face.

"Thank you," she whispered. She closed her eyes on a little sigh and her hands dropped away from both his face and her own head. Her expression then slackened, the pain slipping away and leaving serenity in its place as her head fell limply back.

"Is she dead?" Alick asked with concern.

"Nay, just unconscious," Aulay said and shifted his hand under her head, intending to lift it so he could better see her face. But feeling the lumps and abrasions there, he paused and felt around, trying to count the bumps. There were a lot of them. Most of them felt huge.

"Blood," Alick said with concern when Aulay took his fingers away.

Mouth tightening, Aulay noted the blood on his hand and clenched it shut. "She's several bumps on her head."

"She must have been tossed around by the storm, her head pounding on the mast repeatedly. 'Tis lucky she's alive at all."

"Aye. Row us ashore, Alick. She'll need tending," Aulay growled.

Alick took Aulay's place at the oars without argument and quickly set them to water.

"Once we're ashore, I'll ride to Buchanan and bring back Rory," Alick said as he paddled them back toward the beach.

Aulay nodded. Rory was the second youngest of the Buchanan brothers. He'd trained in healing for years and was quickly becoming known as the best damned healer in Scotland. If anyone could help the lass, Rory could. Aulay dropped his gaze to the woman in his arms, and then said, "Bring Conran, Geordie and Uncle Acair too. But do no' mention the lass to anyone else."

Aulay trusted his uncle, as well as his brothers Conran and Geordie, to keep their mouths shut, but wouldn't risk news of the lass getting out by telling anyone else of her presence.

"Right," Alick agreed firmly as he rowed.

Aulay continued to stare at the woman in his lap. She was so pale and fragile . . . and beautiful. He wished she'd open her eyes again and speak to him. She hadn't shown the least bit of fear on seeing his face. He'd expected her to scream her head off as most women did when they saw him. Instead, she'd caressed his scar and called him an angel. He could still feel her touch on his skin and wanted to feel it again. She gave him hope that he too could have a wife and partner who wouldn't shrink from him and—

The boat gave a jolt as the bottom ran up against the sand and was brought to an abrupt halt. Aulay waited a moment for it to settle and then stood with the woman in his arms, moved up to the front of the boat and stepped out. The minute he did, the boat rose in the water and slid off the sand. Alick quickly scrambled out after him, and pulled it up onto the beach a ways.

"Pull it right out," Aulay growled. "Back to where it was when we arrived, else the tide will take it."

Nodding, Alick put his back into the effort and Aulay watched until he managed the feat, before turning to walk to their horses. Once there though, he paused and glanced from the woman in his arms to his saddle.

"I'll hold her while ye mount."

Aulay glanced around to see Alick approaching. Nodding, he waited for the younger man to reach him and then handed the woman over, quickly mounted and then leaned down to take her back.

"Will you be all right getting her to the lodge alone?" Alick asked as he mounted his own horse.

"Aye," Aulay answered. "Ride to Buchanan and fetch the boys."

"I'll bring them back quick as I can," Alick assured him as he turned his horse and headed off.

Aulay watched until horse and man disappeared into the trees, and then turned to survey the coast. The mast seemed closer. It appeared to be slowly making its own way to shore. By his guess, she would have drifted up onto the beach by some time that afternoon, but there was still no sign of anything else left over from a shipwreck.

He shifted his gaze down to the woman in his arms and frowned. It would take a while for Alick to fetch Rory back, but he needed to get the woman to the lodge, replace her wet clothes with dry ones and put her in bed. He'd have to tend her head wounds too as best he could until Rory arrived. He'd clean away the blood at least.

Pressing the woman close to his chest, Aulay turned his horse and headed for the lodge. Moments later he was sliding from his mount. He held the lass high and tight in an effort to minimize her jostling as he landed, but it was a difficult task and he winced and glanced to her anxiously as he hit the ground with a jolt, but the lass didn't even stir.

Worried about that, he carried her quickly inside and straight up to the bedroom on the second floor.

The layout of the new lodge was much the same as the lodge that had burned down in an attempt to murder his sister-in-law, Murine, two years earlier. He'd had it built a little larger though, and had two bedrooms put on the upper floor rather than just the one. Despite that spare room, Aulay carried the lass to his bedchamber. It was the nicer of the two, and larger. It was also the only one properly set up with furniture just yet. The other held only a small bed, while his room had a larger one with bedside tables, and a small dining table and chairs set up by the fire.

Pausing beside the bed, he peered down at the woman in his arms and hesitated. She was still soaking wet, her gown dripping on the floor with each step he took. He really should have thought to remove the dress before bringing her inside, he supposed. It would have saved his having to clean up the mess he'd just trailed through the house.

Grimacing, Aulay turned and carried her to the table instead and sat her on it. Supporting her back with one hand so that she remained upright, he began to tug at her gown with the other, and soon realized that was not going to work. Wet as it was, the damned thing was clinging to her like a second skin, and, apparently, he had lost all dexterity at undressing a woman. There was a time he would have made short work of it. He used to get a lot of practice, but that had stopped some years ago.

Pushing the thought away, Aulay pulled out his dirk, slipped it carefully under the neckline of the gown and quickly sliced the front wide open. A surprised grunt slid from his lips when the dress gaped, leaving a display of pale flesh. The lass was white as a swan and covered in goose bumps from her time in the ocean and the wet clothes. The only splashes of color he noted were the two round, cinnamon nipples that were presently puckered and hard, also from being cold. Although he imagined they would look much the same from passion too.

Swallowing, Aulay forced his gaze away from her body and peered at her face as he began to work the gown off first one arm and then the other.

"My apologies, lass, but there are no ladies here to tend ye at the moment," he murmured, working quickly at her sleeves. Much to his relief, they came off relatively quickly and the top of the gown dropped away to gather around her waist. That was when he saw the bruising that started just below her breasts and continued down to disappear under the gown. They were marks left by the rope that had bound her to the mast. The dark lines ran around her stomach and sides, while her back was one large bruise, he saw when he leaned forward to look at it. A result of being cast about on the ocean waves while tied to the mast, he supposed. Grasping her by the waist just above the cloth of her ruined gown, he lifted her off the table. The tattered dress dropped off at once to land on the floor with a wet slap.

"There, that was no' so bad, was it? I expected more o' a fight to get it off and—Oh, Christ," Aulay ended on a mutter as he turned his attention from the wet cloth on the floor to the woman he held and noted that he'd lifted her high enough that her breasts were now directly in front of his mouth. Aulay closed his eyes at once and counted to ten . . . twice . . . and then again. It had been far too long since he'd enjoyed the company of a woman and this was just . . . well, it was like a starving man having the finest ale waved before his nose.

"Control yerself, ye idjit," he muttered to himself. "Just put her in the bed."

Aulay peeked one eye open to look around to see where the bed was in relation to where they stood. He then started toward it, still with just the one eye open. He had crossed half the distance when it occurred to him that he could lower the woman and remove the temptation presently waving in front of his salivating mouth. She was nearly a foot shorter than him after all, and he was presently holding her a good two feet off the floor. He didn't need to hold her that high.

Rolling his eyes at his own stupidity, Aulay lowered her several inches and then allowed his second eye to open as he navigated his way to the bed. He quickly laid her in it, and tried not to look at her as he swiftly pulled the linen and furs up to cover her.

"There!" he said, straightening with relief once he'd finished the task. Aulay then looked down at her with a satisfaction that quickly turned to a frown as he noted her perfect white and bare shoulders above the fur. Bending, he pulled the furs all the way to her chin and straightened again, but then considered the lass. Rory would want to examine her, of course. He'd come in, pull the furs down and—

Muttering under his breath, Aulay hurried to his chest and retrieved the spare white linen shirt he'd brought with him. It was a little wrinkled, but freshly laundered. Returning with it to the bed, he reached for the furs and then hesitated. As ashamed as he was to admit it, Aulay didn't think he could look at all that perfect white flesh and those hard nipples again without touching and possibly tasting them as he dressed her. There was only so much temptation a man could handle and the devil in him was already arguing that it would not hurt to just give them a quick lick or suckle. She'd never know.

It really had been a long time since he'd lain with a woman. Too long if he was having thoughts like this, Aulay decided with self-disgust.

Setting his jaw, he bent to reach for the top of the furs again, and then paused as he had an idea. Smiling at his own cleverness, he left the furs where they were for now and instead worked at getting her head into the shirt, a much more difficult task than you'd think. Or perhaps he did it wrong. He started with the hem, lifting her up slightly, furs and all, and pulling the hem of the shirt over her head and then tugging and tugging the material down until her head finally cleared the neck hole.

Easing her back to lay flat again, Aulay carefully withdrew one of her arms from under the furs and then the other. Leaving them lying on the furs that now reached just to her armpits, he quickly found one of the sleeves and then stuck the nearer arm into it, feeding the limb in with one hand, and pulling it out with the other. After doing the same with the other arm, he grasped the hem of the shirt in both hands, then gathered the top of the furs in each as well with the cloth and simply pulled downward, covering her with the linen shirt even as he withdrew the furs.

Aulay was just congratulating himself for his ingenuity and was pulling the furs back up when he noticed that the shirt was backward on her. Even worse, while the cloth on top covered her from neck to past her knees, the back was still up by her shoulders, leaving the shirt covering only most of her. He briefly considered righting the shirt and making sure the back went all the way down too, but then shook his head and pulled the furs up to her chin again. Nay. He'd managed to strip and dress the woman without doing anything to shame himself, and wasn't risking mucking it up now.

Sighing, Aulay straightened to peer at her. His mouth tightened when he noted the blood on the pillow. From her head wound, he realized, and there was a lot of it. He'd meant to take a look and clean away the blood while he waited for Rory, but had forgotten all about it after getting her gown off.

Turning, Aulay hurried from the room to fetch water and fresh linens to cut into bandages. Within moments he had her upright, slumped against his chest as he leaned over her and gently cleaned the wounds on the back of her head. It was a difficult task with her hair in the way. Aulay could barely see what he was trying to clean through the long, thick strands, and what he could see looked pretty nasty. So he was more than relieved when he heard the pounding of horse hooves approaching the lodge.

After easing her back onto the bed, Aulay balled up the scrap of linen with which he'd been trying to clean away the blood. Tossing it into the bowl of now red water on the bedside table, he then stood to walk to the window.

"Thank God," Aulay muttered when he spotted his uncle and brothers riding up to the lodge. He watched them dismount and tether their horses before he moved out of the room to watch from the landing as they entered below.

"Aulay," Rory said, sounding relieved when he spotted him. "Alick scared the devil out of us. He rushed us all out here without even slowing long enough to explain what was amiss. I thought ye must be direly wounded or some such to account for the urgency."

"Me too," Conran said grimly, glowering at their youngest brother.

"Ye said no' to let anyone else ken what was happening, and they were in the practice field at Buchanan with soldiers everywhere," Alick explained when Aulay glanced to him. "Each one o' them was fighting a Buchanan soldier, and I did no' think I should take the time to take each one o' them aside to explain what had happened. The lass looked to need help quickly."

"Aye," Aulay agreed solemnly.

"Lass?" Uncle Acair asked, glancing curiously from Alick to Aulay.

Turning away from the rail, Aulay merely waved for them to ascend and moved back into the room where the woman rested. The lodge was immediately filled with the sound of pounding feet as his brothers and uncle rushed upstairs to join him. When the sound stopped abruptly, Aulay glanced back to see that Uncle Acair and Rory had stumbled to a halt just inside the door as they spotted the woman in his bed. They were presently preventing everyone else from entering.

"Move, man! The lass needs help," Aulay growled impatiently, and the words had Rory continuing forward again at once.

"What's wrong with her?" Rory asked as he hurried around the bed.

"The back o' her head took a terrible beating," Aulay explained as Rory sat on the edge of the bed and leaned over her to lift her eyelids.

"Who is she?"

"Who beat her?"

"Is that blood?"

"What happened to her dress?"

Aulay turned at those questions from his brothers and uncle as they fanned out in the room, examining anything and everything they could find, including the woman in the bed.

When he noted the way his uncle was scowling as he examined the wet dress he'd picked up, Aulay ignored the other questions and answered his first. "I had to cut off her dress."

"Is that blood?" Geordie asked again, moving closer to the bed to get a better look.

"Aye," Aulay grunted, noting that blood now stained both the pillow and linens. "She took some terrible injuries to her head. I suspect from it bouncing off the mast we found her strapped to when we headed out fishing. The storm last night was fierce."

"Did she wake again after I left?" Alick asked as he stepped up beside him to peer down at her pale face.

Aulay shook his head.

"So we do no' ken who she is?" Alick asked.

"Nay," he admitted, watching Rory pull the furs down so that he could turn the woman onto her side away from them. The position made it much easier for him to examine her head, Aulay noted, and shook his head at himself for not thinking to do that himself when he was trying to clean the wound.

"She was awake when ye found her?" Rory asked sharply, his gaze moving from Aulay to Alick and back.

"Aye," they answered together, and then Aulay rumbled, "She spoke a bit ere passing out."

Shaking his head, Rory turned to poke and prod at the back of the lass's head. "I am amazed she was awake, let alone spoke. Dear God, she took a beating."

"Aye," Aulay agreed. What he'd been able to see had seemed bad.

"And this is from her head hitting the mast?" Rory asked with disbelief.

"As far as we ken," Aulay answered.

"It was a pretty bad storm here," Alick said, and then told Aulay, "Apparently, it mostly bypassed Buchanan keep. All they got there was a bit o' wind and some drizzle."

Aulay merely nodded. That happened sometimes.

"It must have been more than pretty bad for her to take this much damage," Rory said grimly.

Aulay grunted. "The mast was probably bobbing around on the water like a cork in rapids."

"What the devil was she doing strapped to a mast?" Uncle Acair asked with disgust, moving up on the other side of the bed to peer at her.

"Mayhap to keep her from falling overboard in the storm," Alick said, repeating his earlier suggestion.

"Making her stay below deck would ha'e done the job just as well, and wouldn't have left her bobbing around the ocean with her head pounding on the wood over and over," Geordie pointed out with displeasure.

"Ye say she spoke when ye first found her?" Uncle Acair asked.

Aulay merely nodded. It was Alick who told them, "Aye, Aulay asked her name and said he'd send word to her family, but she did no' like that idea at all. She started jabbering on about cats and white ladies and someone trying to kill her. Aulay had to promise he would no' find her family until she was healthy and well again just to calm her."

That wasn't exactly true, but it was close enough for now, so Aulay didn't comment and simply shifted his attention to Rory as the man sighed and straightened.

"Well?" Aulay barked, not liking the grim expression on his brother's face. He'd seen it before, usually when Rory didn't expect a patient to survive whatever wound they'd taken.

"She's in a bad way, Aulay, but I'll do me best to help her," he said solemnly. "I'll need to cut away her hair to better see and clean the wound, and then I need boiled water, clean linens, and my medicinals."

"Did ye no' bring them?" Aulay asked with alarm.

"Aye, but I set them down on the table below when I saw ye were well. I did no' ken about the lass here."

"I'll get yer medicinals," Alick said, leaving the room.

"I'll start some water boiling and find some clean linens fer ye to use," Geordie offered, following Alick.

Silence fell in the room briefly, and then Uncle Acair glanced to him and commented, "So we've another lass on our hands with someone trying to kill her?"

"So it would seem," Aulay said with a shrug. It did appear to be becoming something of a habit with the Buchanan men. Two of his brothers now had married lasses whose lives had been in threat and whom they'd kept safe. He had to wonder if it would happen a third time, and if so, which brother would be lucky enough to win the beautiful lass in his bed. Shifting, he said, "'Twas hard to follow some o' what she said. But it sounded like she was being forced to marry someone who was no' her betrothed and who had killed his first wife, and she thought would kill her."

"And the cat and white lady?" Conran asked.

Aulay shrugged. "Mayhap her cat and a Lady White went down with the ship."

The men nodded as if that made sense, and then glanced back to the lass.

"If ye promised no' to find her family ere she was well again, we'll have to keep the promise," Uncle Acair said solemnly after a minute.

"Aye," Aulay said firmly. That was the only thing he was clear on here.

"But it should no' be too hard to find out what ship went down in the storm and learn who she is that way," Conran pointed out. "We need no' approach her family to find out at least that much."

"True," Aulay agreed, and then added sternly, "but no one learns that she is here and alive until I say so."

Conran nodded, and then they all glanced to the door as Alick rushed back in with Rory's bag o' weeds.

"Thank ye, Alick." Rory took the bag and then ordered, "All but Aulay can leave now."

When the other men nodded and turned to exit the room, Rory added, "Have Geordie bring the linens up with the water when 'tis boiled."

"Aye," was the answer from all three men.

Once they'd left, Aulay turned to Rory and raised his eyebrows. "What do ye want me to do?"

"Ye're going to help me shave her head."

He glanced to her beautiful black tresses with alarm.

"Just the back. I need to see the injuries to clean them. It'll grow back," Rory said as he retrieved a wicked-looking knife from his medicinals bag. Turning back to the lass, he added under his breath, "if she survives."

Aulay's chest tightened at that last part. It verified his earlier suspicion that Rory didn't think the lass had much of a chance. The thought made him turn his gaze to the wee, pale lass in the bed. She looked delicate and weak, but he was quite certain she wasn't. The pain she'd seemed to be suffering, *and that she had withstood* long enough to ensure he wouldn't deliver her to her family, suggested a woman with spirit and a good deal of inner strength. She'd survive, Aulay decided. He'd do everything in his power to make sure she did.

Chapter 2

SHE OPENED HER EYES SLEEPILY AND PEERED CURIOUSLY AT the man who occupied the chair next to the bed. Her eyes felt dry and scratchy, her mouth was barren of any moisture, and her entire body felt achy and weak, but that was on the periphery of her mind at the moment. Mostly, her attention was on the man next to her. He seemed familiar to her, although she wasn't sure how. No name came to mind when she looked at him, but he was handsome, with long auburn hair and what would have been an almost too pretty face if not for the scar that ran from forehead to chin next to his nose, nearly cleaving it in half.

Eyes narrowing, she examined the scar with interest. It looked like someone had taken an ax to his face. Or perhaps the tip of a sword. The scar was relatively straight, and it wasn't puckered or angry-looking; so must be five or six years old at least. She examined it for a moment longer, and then shifted her attention to the rest of the man. He was big, at least twice as wide as her in the shoulders. Truly, he had a beautiful chest from what she could see. He also had long, muscular legs, she noted as her gaze slid downward. The man wore a plaid that was presently in disarray and showing more leg than was absolutely proper.

But then there was little that was proper about the man. He shouldn't be in her room at all . . . unless he was her father, brother or husband. The man was definitely too young to be her father. As for brother, she glanced from his chest to his legs and mentally shook her head. The feelings she was having were not very filial at the moment, so she was guessing he was not her brother. At least, she hoped not.

That thought made her frown. Should she not know? It certainly

seemed to her that she should know. But she didn't. She didn't even know
her own name, she realized with sudden alarm and began searching her
mind, trying to remember . . . something. Anything, really. But doing so
merely made her head hurt. A lot.

AULAY SHIFTED IN HIS SLEEP AND WINCED, WAKING UP AS HIS
neck gave a twinge of pain. Damn, he'd fallen asleep again, he realized
with a grimace, and opened his eyes only to freeze as he saw that Jetta's
eyes too were open. The thought made him frown to himself. He had no
idea of the woman's real name, but he and his brothers had been calling
her Jetta since shortly after finding her. He was the one who had suggested the name. It was her beautiful jet-black hair that had decided him
on it, and the name suited her despite the fact that she only had that long
beautiful hair on the sides and top of her head now. They'd shaved away
every last strand on the back of her head to clean her wounds.

She was awake now, though, and he would soon learn what her real
name was, Aulay told himself as he sat up straight. So long as she didn't
simply start shrieking the minute she saw his face. That possibility made
him glance to her face again. Frowning slightly, he wondered how long
she'd been awake. Had she looked at him? Had she noticed his terrible
scar? Probably, he decided. It was hard to miss. The damn thing was
all he saw when he looked in the polished silver mirror in the castle's
master bedroom. And it was all anyone else saw too. He knew that for a
certainty. His scar had been known to make women and children scream
or weep. Although the screaming had mostly happened when he was
first injured. The reactions recently had been much more discreet, a lip
curled with disgust, a shudder of revulsion, or simply turning away and
avoiding looking at him at all.

"Are you my husband?" she asked in a husky voice, and Aulay blinked
and glanced to the woman with surprise.

"What?"

"Well, only a husband or brother would be allowed in my room," she
explained, and then raised an eyebrow in question. "You are not my
brother?"

"Good God, nay," Aulay said at once. He'd been watching over the woman for three weeks now, tending her, constantly dribbling broth down her throat, and helping to turn her in the bed daily to prevent bedsores. During that time, none of his feelings could be called anything close to brotherly.

"Then you are my husband," she deduced with a smile, and Aulay stared at her blankly. It was not the reaction he would have expected. His own betrothed had refused to marry him, forfeiting a very rich bride price and walking away rather than spend her days *"having to look at his disgusting face for a lifetime,"* as she had put it. But this woman actually smiled at the thought that he was her husband, he noted with amazement.

"Have I been ill?"

Aulay noted that she looked curious and a little fretful, but not unduly alarmed. Nodding, he finally said, "Aye. Ye've been ill for three weeks now."

Her eyes widened. "Three weeks? What with?" she asked with a frown, and then guessed, "Fevers? There must have been fevers, I do not remember being ill and that only happens with fevers."

"Nay. Ye hit yer head and have been in a deep sleep since."

"Hit my head?" she asked, eyes widening. "Is that why I do not remember?"

Aulay frowned and sat forward in his chair. "What exactly do ye no' remember, lass?"

"Anything," she said almost plaintively, rising up in the bed. "I do not remember you, this room, or even my name. I—" Pausing, she shook her head helplessly, and then winced and squeezed her eyes closed as if in pain.

"Are ye all right?" Aulay stood at once, and moved closer to the bed to lean over her. "Is yer head paining ye?"

"A bit," she said weakly, and with, he was sure, little veracity. It obviously hurt more than just a bit.

"Here ye are, m'laird."

Aulay straightened abruptly and turned toward the door to see Mavis bustling into the room. A short, round woman with dark hair streaked liberally with gray, she carried a tray in hand and was chattering cheerfully away as she walked.

"I've brought some more broth fer our young Jetta. I made it from the quail ye caught yesterday. Ye just—Oh!" The woman paused abruptly, eyes widening as she saw that Jetta was sitting up. Sounding nonplussed, she said, "She's awake."

"Aye." Aulay smiled faintly at the woman's wide-eyed expression. It had been at Rory's suggestion that the maid be brought out to the lodge. She had helped them care for the lass. There were just some things a man had no business tending to when it came to women and Mavis had tended those matters alone.

"Thank ye fer the broth, Mavis," he said now.

"Ye're welcome, m'laird, o' course. Shall I fetch Master Rory?" the older woman asked, eyeing Jetta's still wincing face with concern as she hurried to set down the tray.

"Aye. Please." Aulay watched her rush from the room, and then turned back to Jetta, and frowned. Her eyes were still closed, but she was holding her head now. It seemed to him that rather than easing, her pain was increasing. Feeling helpless, he watched for a moment, and then turned and walked swiftly to the table where Mavis had set the tray. There were broth and a glass of cider on the tray, but Aulay's interest was the skin of uisge beatha that lay on the table next to it. Grabbing that, he returned to the bed.

"Here, lass," he murmured, settling on the bed next to her and quickly opening the skin. "Try this. Mayhap 'twill help."

Jetta moaned, but didn't open her eyes or even lift her head.

"Lass," he began, but paused and glanced toward the door at the sound of pounding feet coming up the stairs.

"Mavis said Jetta is awake," Rory said, rushing into the room a moment later.

"Aye." Aulay stood with relief, and gestured to her as she let her hands fall away from her head. "But she's in pain. Make it stop."

Rory's eyebrows rose at the demand, but he moved quickly to the bedside and leaned over their patient. It was only then that Aulay saw that she'd fallen back on the bed and appeared to once again be in her deep sleep.

"She was awake," he assured his brother with a frown.

"Did she say anything?" Rory asked, lifting her eyelids to peer at her eyes.

"Aye," Aulay murmured, wondering what he was looking for, or what he could learn from her eyes. "She does no' remember aught."

Rory glanced at him with surprise. "Nothing?"

"No' even her name," he rumbled.

"Hmm." Rory turned back to continue examining her, but said, "Perhaps no' so surprising. The back o' her head took a beating. In truth, I did no' think she'd even wake."

"Will she get her memories back, do ye think?" Aulay asked, his gaze sliding over her sleeping face.

Rory straightened and considered her for a moment, but then shook his head. "'Tis hard to say. She may, but she may not. Head wounds are a tricky business. She is lucky to be alive."

Aulay nodded, but then cleared his throat and said, "She thought I was her husband."

Rory turned to him, eyebrows raised. "Did ye explain that ye were no'?"

Aulay hesitated and then grimaced and shook his head. "She said only a husband or brother would be in her room and I did no' want to upset her, so I just . . ." He shrugged.

Rory eyed him briefly and then murmured, "Hmm," again and turned to peer at her once more.

"Should her head still hurt?" Aulay asked after a moment. "It has been three weeks since she was injured."

Rory sighed. "Head injuries are—"

"Tricky," Aulay interrupted dryly. It was a phrase he'd heard often since finding the lass. Any time he asked something his brother did not know the answer to, Rory said that head wounds were tricky and they would have to wait and see how this all played out. "In other words, ye do no' ken why her head is hurting."

"It could simply be because she's had little to eat or drink. Broth dribbled down her throat several times a day is no' ideal. 'Tis barely enough to keep her alive. As ye can see," he added, gesturing to her. "She's lost a good deal o' weight since ye found her."

"Aye," Aulay agreed unhappily and wondered how he had failed to notice that ere now. Oh, certainly, he'd noticed that she'd lost some weight, but he hadn't realized just how frail and thin she'd grown until this moment. Her face was slightly sunken with dark smudges under her eyes, and her skin was stretched tight over the bones in what he could see of her face, hands and wrists, leaving them almost skeletal-looking.

"I'll have solid food brought up, and cider for the next time she wakes," Aulay decided, and turned to head for the door.

"Brother," Rory said, bringing him to a halt.

Pausing at the door, Aulay glanced back. "Aye?"

"Ye might want to hold off on telling her ye're no' her husband when she wakes again. At least fer a little while," Rory suggested solemnly. "Just until we're sure she's recovering. She will be fragile at first, and it might be best no' to distress her too much until we are sure she is definitely on the mend. She will be upset enough by her memory loss. We will need to comfort her as much as possible, and thinking she is in the care of a loving, caring husband, rather than strangers, will give her that comfort."

"Aye," Aulay said solemnly, his gaze sliding to the woman. To Jetta, as they would have to continue to call her for now. At least, until she recalled her true name. If she recalled her true name. Part of him was hoping she wouldn't remember it. Then maybe she would continue to think him her husband and he could keep her.

The moment he had that thought, Aulay turned away and left the room. Of course, he couldn't keep her. She wasn't a pup who had followed him home after some adventure. Eventually, he'd have to tell her that he wasn't her husband, and the circumstances of her coming to be here. No doubt the news that they weren't married would be a big relief to her. Then she wouldn't have to look at his ugly face every morning. In fact, she would probably want to leave and get away from him the moment she knew she didn't have to stay.

Mouth tightening at the thought, Aulay strode quickly to the stairs and headed down to talk to Mavis and see about solid food for the lass. The next time Jetta woke up, there would be food and drink there waiting for her. He couldn't bear to stand by helplessly again while she suffered. If food and drink didn't work, he'd resort to those damned foul medicinals Rory was forever making, one that eased pain and put a body to sleep. Not that he wanted her to sleep. It seemed to him that he'd been waiting forever for her to wake. But he'd rather she slept than be in pain.

THE NEXT TIME SHE WOKE, THE ROOM WAS DARK. NOT COM-pletely, but there was no sunlight shining through the window. The only light in the room was coming from the fireplace. It was weak and cast shadows everywhere.

Recalling the pain that had assailed her shortly after waking the last time, she didn't sit up or move anything but her eyes at first. She remained still and simply peered around at what she could see of the room. A bedside table to her right held a goblet and an unlit candle. She could see a shuttered window beyond it. That made up the left side of the room, but directly across from the foot of the bed a table and two chairs were positioned before the fireplace. On the other side of the bed was an empty bedside table, two large chests against the wall and a chair next to the bed. The chair was empty this time, she noted. Her husband wasn't there, and she found herself disappointed by his absence. She would have liked to ask him questions. Things like, where was she? What was her name? What was his name?

Although, she realized suddenly, she had got some answers the last time she'd woken. She suspected she must be in Scotland. At least, her husband appeared to be Scottish. He wore Scottish dress, the traditional plaid that had shown off his legs quite nicely. He'd also definitely had a Scottish accent, as had the maid who had entered the room the last time she'd woken up. So . . . she must have married a Scot and now lived in Scotland. She didn't think she was Scottish herself. Her own accent when she'd spoken had sounded English to her ear, and even her thoughts had an English accent to them, rather than Scottish.

Other than that . . .

The maid had called her Jetta, she remembered suddenly, and was surprised she recalled it considering the pain that had been assaulting her at the time.

"Jetta," she murmured aloud, and grimaced at how scratchy her voice was. Her throat and mouth were terribly dry. Recalling a goblet on the bedside table, she glanced to it now and bit her lip. Had sitting up been what had triggered the pain the last time? If she sat up to see if there was anything in the goblet and to take a sip if there was, would she again be assaulted by the pain?

The possibility was enough to keep her prone for a moment or two longer, but then her thirst made her take the risk. She rolled to her side and reached for the goblet to lift it to see if it held anything first, though. There was no use risking that pain for nothing.

Finding the goblet heavy with liquid, Jetta set her mouth determinedly and struggled upright, swinging her legs to the floor as she did so that she sat on the side of the bed. Surprisingly, it was more of an effort than she'd expected. She didn't recall sitting up to be this much work the first time, but then she'd been distressed at the time, so perhaps that had aided her efforts to get upright.

Sighing, she reached for the drink, and then paused as she spotted the figure in the shadows on the floor. For a moment, fear leapt into her heart, but then she recognized her husband's scarred face and relaxed. A small smile tipped the corners of her mouth. What a sweet man. She'd been disappointed that he wasn't there before, but now realized he was sleeping on a pallet on the floor to ensure he didn't disturb her rest. The action was so thoughtful and kind . . .

Swallowing a sudden lump in her throat, she reached for the goblet once more, this time picking it up.

Jetta realized just how pathetically weak she was when she nearly dropped it. If she hadn't added her second hand to the effort, it would have slipped from her fingers. Holding it two-handed like a child, she lifted it to her lips and drank from the cup. It was apple cider, room temperature but sweet and rich and she gulped it eagerly down. Too eagerly, and too quickly. Jetta knew that the moment her stomach began to roil. For a moment, she thought she was going to heave it all back up.

But she sat completely still and held her breath as she waited and the sensation finally passed.

Letting her breath out on a little relieved sigh, Jetta set the cup back on the table and then peered at her husband as it occurred to her that she didn't know *his* name. That was another question she would like answered. Although, that might be a bit awkward. *"Excuse me, husband, could you tell me your name?"*

Jetta grimaced at the thought of it and then finally tore her gaze from him and glanced around the room again. There appeared to be food on the table, and she thought she should probably eat, but her upset tummy wasn't encouraging any kind of hunger. Besides, just the little bit she'd done so far was already tiring her and she wasn't at all sure she could make it to the table and back.

She should probably lie down and go back to sleep, Jetta thought, but her gaze slid back to her husband. He should really be in the bed with her and she was incredibly touched that he had taken on such discomfort on her behalf. The man didn't even have any furs to cover him. He'd just rolled himself up in his plaid, for heaven's sake. She glanced to the coverings on the bed and frowned when she noted that there was only the one fur on the bed itself. After a hesitation, she grabbed her pillow and dropped it on the pallet next to her husband's head, and then slid down to join him, dragging the fur from the bed with her.

Careful not to jostle him too much, Jetta managed to curl up into his side and cover them both with the fur from the bed. She'd barely managed the feat when her husband grumbled sleepily and rolled onto his side behind her, his arm wrapping around her as if to prevent her shifting about anymore. Jetta waited for some comment on what she'd done, but when nothing came except his deep breathing, she released the breath she'd been holding on a little sigh, and drifted off to sleep.

AULAY SHIFTED SLEEPILY AND CUDDLED INTO THE WARM FURS as morning light dragged him toward consciousness. But when the furs murmured and moved under his hand and arm, he opened his eyes with some confusion and found himself peering at the wee lass he'd pulled

from the water. Aulay froze and simply stared. He lay on his side on the
pallet with Jetta on her back next to him, and under him, he noted as he
became aware that he had one leg cast over both of hers and his arm was
resting on her stomach while his hand was quite happily cupping one of
her breasts. His fingers curved over it with a possessiveness and famil-
iarity it had no right to.

Even as Aulay thought that, his fingers unconsciously tightened slightly,
squeezing the soft flesh. Wee Jetta moaned and moved restlessly under
the caress, but he hardly noticed, his attention was on the fact that his
hand was the only covering her breast enjoyed. The front of the overlarge
shift Mavis had supplied to replace his shirt was wide open almost to her
waist, leaving one breast covered by his hand and the other simply bare.

Aulay eyed the bare breast and thought he had never seen anything
quite so perfect as that globe. God had been more than generous when it
came to fashioning Jetta's bosoms. They were full and rounded and her
nipples were a deep cinnamon color and presently puckered with excitement, he realized, and quickly pulled his hand away.

"Husband?" Jetta murmured sleepily.

"Aye," Aulay growled and when she smiled tremulously and put her
arms around him, hugging him tightly, he closed his arms around her in
return and hugged back. But when they eased apart, he couldn't resist
kissing her. He'd meant to just brush his lips over hers, but after first
stilling in surprise, Jetta started to kiss him back and the plan changed.
Aulay instead deepened the kiss, his tongue sliding between her lips to
delve inside. He tasted apple cider and smiled against her mouth as she
kissed him clumsily back. It seemed obvious that Jetta had no idea what
she was doing, but she was making a good effort, emulating his every
action. She was even squeezing his muscled chest as he wished to do to
her breast, and while he was hardening against her hip, she was pushing
herself up into the leg covering her lower body.

Growling in his throat, Aulay shifted his leg to urge her legs apart so
that his knee could rest between her thighs. He then pressed it against
the very core of her. She responded with a gasp of pleasure, her hands
clutching at his shoulders now and her efforts to emulate his kiss spiral-

ing down into simply sucking on his tongue as he thrust it in and out of her mouth. Her excitement was like fire to tinder, and Aulay had just covered her breast again, this time to caress and squeeze it, when he heard the bedroom door open.

"Aulay?"

Recognizing Rory's voice, Aulay stiffened and then moved quickly, dragging the fur up to cover Jetta on the floor, even as he pulled away from her and leapt to his feet.

"Aye," he said, his voice gruff as he bent quickly to scoop up Jetta, furs and all. Straightening, he growled, "I think she fell out o' bed." That was the only thing that made sense to him. How else had she wound up on the pallet with him?

"Fell out o'—" Rory began with surprise.

"Nay. I did not fall, husband," Jetta interrupted, peering up earnestly at Aulay. "When I saw you were there on the floor without even a fur to cover you, I joined you to share the fur from the bed."

"Oh." Aulay stared at her, nonplussed, and then turned to set her on the bed.

"Ye're awake." Rory crossed the room to peer at Jetta as Aulay straightened. "Well, ye've more color this morning. That's good."

Aulay glanced to Jetta and noticed that she did indeed have more color in her face. He couldn't tell if it was a result of their passion, or embarrassment at the interruption. Either way, her cheeks were quite pink, he noted before she shyly ducked her head.

"You drank all of your cider," Rory said next.

Aulay glanced to the empty mug just as his brother set it back on the table.

"And ye were able to keep it down?" Rory asked next.

"Aye," Jetta said in a shy whisper, and then cleared her throat and admitted, "I feared I might not for a moment, but then my stomach settled and I was able to keep it down."

"That's a good sign," Rory said, and leaned forward to press an ear to her chest.

When Jetta stiffened in shock and sent a wide-eyed look his way,

Aulay managed a reassuring smile. "He's just listening to yer heart, lass," he explained and then noted the frown on his brother's face and asked with concern, "What is it?"

"Her heart is racing," Rory muttered, straightening to look at her face again, eyebrows rising when she flushed a bright red. Turning slowly, Rory peered at Aulay with suspicion.

"I'm sure yer entering without knocking merely startled her," Aulay muttered, avoiding his gaze.

"Aye. I'm sure," Rory said dryly, and then turned to offer a gentle smile to Jetta. "Do ye remember anything today? Yer name or where ye come from?"

"I . . . my name is Jetta," she answered.

Aulay gave a start, surprised that the name he'd given her was the same as her true name, but then she admitted, "I heard the maid call me that yesterday."

"Ah," Rory said solemnly. "So, ye do no' remember anything ere waking up here the first time?"

She shook her head apologetically. "Do you think I will? Remember things, I mean."

Rory hesitated, but then apparently decided that honesty was the best policy . . . in this instance, at least. "I do no' ken, lass. Ye took some terrible damage to the back o' yer head. In truth, I'm surprised ye survived it at all, and apparently with all o' yer faculties intact, other than yer memory." That made him frown and he asked, "*Are* all yer faculties intact?"

"I think so," Jetta said slowly and then shrugged helplessly. "How would I know if they were not?"

Rory smiled faintly. "Well, is yer vision blurry at all?"

"Nay," she said at once, appearing relieved to be able to say it.

"What about smell or taste? When ye drank the cider did—?"

"It smelled and tasted fine to me," she said.

"And yer speech does no' seem impeded at all," he pointed out. "So I would say yer memory is the only thing that was affected by the injury."

"Aye," she agreed, but looked dissatisfied and said, "I know I should be grateful for that, but there is so much I do not remember. For instance, how did I injure my head?"

Rory turned to glance at Aulay, obviously leaving it to him, and he cleared his throat and said, "Shipwreck."

Jetta blinked at the words. "I hit my head in a shipwreck? How?"

Aulay frowned at the question, but said, "Ye were strapped to the mast. When the ship broke apart, you and the mast ye were on bobbed about on the water's surface. Ye ended up banging yer head repeatedly on it." At least, that was what he'd decided must have happened. It was the only thing that made sense. And unfortunately, they hadn't been able to find out anything else. His brothers had made discreet inquiries, but had not been able to find out the name of the ship that she'd been on. In fact, as far as they could tell, no ships had sunk during the whole week when she appeared.

"And you saved me?"

Aulay blinked his thoughts away and glanced to her at that question, but it was Rory who said, "Aye, Aulay and Alick cut ye free o' the mast and got ye to shore."

"Alick?" Jetta asked, her expression uncertain.

"Our youngest brother," Rory explained.

Her eyes widened. "There are three of you?"

"Nine," Rory said, even as Aulay said, "Eight."

"Sorry," Rory muttered, and corrected himself. "Eight. There used to be nine of us, eight brothers and one sister. But one o' our brothers died some years back so now there are only the eight of us."

"*Only* eight?" she asked with mild amusement. "That seems a lot to me."

"I suppose," Rory agreed with a smile and then asked lightly, "So ye did no' have a lot o' brothers and sisters?"

"I . . ." Jetta frowned, her thoughts obviously turning inward as she tried to find the answer.

Aulay watched, waiting to see if she would remember, but when she raised a hand and began to rub at her forehead as if it were paining her, he said, "Let it go, lass. Ye'll remember it all soon enough."

"Aye," she said on a sigh, and then pointed out, "Or you could just tell me yourself and save me the effort of trying to remember."

Aulay stiffened, but was saved from having to respond by Rory who said, "'Tis better ye remember on yer own, lass. That way we'll ken 'tis a true memory and no' just something ye think ye recall because ye were told."

"Oh," Jetta murmured, and Aulay wasn't surprised to see the confusion the suggestion caused in her. Rory's attempt to save him from having to admit that he didn't have any of the answers she was seeking had been a little less than logical to his mind. Surely she'd know the difference between memories and stories she'd been told?

Shaking his head, Aulay whirled away from the bed, muttering, "I'll fetch Mavis up to change yer bed and help ye bathe while I see to hunting up something for the sup."

"Oh, but I do not want you to leave."

That soft cry brought Aulay to a halt at the door. Turning slowly, he peered at her. Jetta's cheeks were still flushed, not as flushed as they had been directly after his kissing her, but flushed just the same. Her hair was a glorious disarray of black waves around her face that begged for attention. She was clutching the furs to her chest, hiding what he knew were bared breasts from view, and her expression was as forlorn as an abandoned bairn's. It was all enough to make him want to stride straight back to the bed, climb in with her and kiss that expression off her face.

Unfortunately, he wasn't in the newly-roused-from-sleep-and-not-thinking-straight stage he'd been in when he'd found her cuddled up to him on the pallet of furs earlier and begun to kiss her. Now he was wide awake, and so was his conscience. Jetta might be under the mistaken impression that they were husband and wife and that kind of behavior was perfectly acceptable, but he was more than aware that they weren't, and it wasn't. He had no right to kiss and touch her like that. No matter how much he wanted to. And he really, really wanted to. Hell, if Rory had arrived even a couple minutes later, Aulay very well might have taken the lass right there on the floor. That being the case, he knew the best thing he could now do was to stay away from the temptation she offered and let her heal in peace.

Unfortunately, when Aulay opened his mouth to give some excuse as to why he could not remain with her, he instead found himself saying, "I'll no' be gone long. I'll return to break me fast with ye after Mavis has seen to yer bath and such."

Jetta didn't seem overly pleased with his response, and he suspected she was about to protest his leaving again, but then she suddenly took a deep breath and forced herself to relax and nod. "Very well. Thank you."

She sounded calm and composed, but Aulay noted the way her lip trembled before she bit on it. Frowning, he glanced to Rory in question, suspecting something was going on here he did not understand.

Murmuring an excuse to Jetta, Rory stood and crossed the room to follow him out the door.

"What is—?" Aulay began, but Rory raised a hand to silence him and pulled the door closed. He then ushered him several feet away before speaking.

"She will be emotional for the first little while," he said solemnly once they were out of earshot of the room. "And ye can expect her to be clingy."

"Clingy?" he asked with dismay. In the last three weeks that he'd watched over the woman in his bed, Aulay had found himself drifting into fantasies about what they would be doing if she were awake. Those had ranged from her running screaming from his room on first sight, to their enjoying games of chess, having picnics by the loch and making love before a roaring fire. They had not included an emotional and clingy woman.

"Her mind has betrayed her. She has no memory of anything to do with herself or her past," Rory pointed out. "She will naturally be feeling frightened and want you, as the man she thinks to be her husband, to stick close."

"Aye," Aulay said slowly, starting to understand. "Mayhap I should send Alick and Geordie out again to ask around about a ship that may have sunk three weeks ago so that we can at least find out her real name."

"That might be a good idea," Rory agreed solemnly. "Knowing her true name may help with her memory."

"Aye," Aulay murmured and then frowned as he considered the problem. His brothers would have to be careful again as they had the first time and not reveal her presence here, he thought, and then realized Rory was still talking.

"—but right now, all she knows, and wrongly so, is that ye're her husband. Whether she admits it or not—even to herself—she will be anxious and needy. We must be patient with her, and make her feel safe and secure. That is why I suggested ye not correct her about ye no' being her husband. She needs things that will comfort her right now, and believing she is at home and has a loving and caring husband will be more comforting than thinking she is weak, alone and without her memory among strangers."

"Ah," Aulay murmured, relaxing a bit.

"Once she has regained some strength, and some confidence in herself and her ability to cope, we can explain that ye're no' her husband," Rory assured him. "By then she will ken we ha'e no plans to harm her and she is safe with us."

Aulay nodded.

"I trust ye'll remember that ye're *not* her husband, though?" Rory added quietly.

"O' course," Aulay growled, scowling at him. "She is under me protection. I'll no' take advantage o' that."

"I am glad to hear it." Rory said with a nod, but then added, "Because when I came in it looked like ye might be."

When Aulay merely stared at him, not deigning to respond to his comment, he said, "It looked like ye were kissing her and more, brother. And when ye set her in the bed her cheeks were flushed, her heart pounding like a drum, and I could tell the gown Mavis put her in was wide open under that fur she was clutching to her chest."

"'Tis none o' yer business, Rory," Aulay said coldly.

Rory hesitated, and then straightened his shoulders and said, "Aye, 'tis. She's me patient, and judging by her speech and the quality o' the gown she wore, or what was left o' it," he added dryly, "she is a lady. If ye ruin her, ye will have to marry her, Aulay. I'll no' let ye take advantage of the poor lass in her state and treat her like she was naught but some light skirt. She thinks ye're her husband."

Aulay just stared at Rory, the words reverberating through his head. *"If ye ruin her, ye will have to marry her."* For some reason, they didn't hold the horror Rory seemed to expect they would . . . and *that* scared the hell out of him.

Chapter 3

*J*ETTA SHIFTED IMPATIENTLY WHERE SHE SAT UP IN BED, AND glanced around the room again. Shortly after her husband and his brother had left, they'd returned carrying a tub and had been followed by Mavis carrying two pails of water. The men had quickly left after depositing the tub, only to return several times with more water.

Once the men had filled the tub to Mavis's satisfaction, the old woman had shooed them from the room and then had helped Jetta from the bed, urged her out of the ridiculously large gown she was wearing and ushered her into the water. Leaving her there to wash up, Mavis had turned her attention to stripping the bed and then making it up with fresh linens before returning to Jetta.

Mavis was a very efficient woman. She'd helped Jetta with the bath, washing her back and her hair for her, tsking over the yellow bruising covering her body and then chattering away about this and that and nothing at all as she'd helped her dry off and dress in yet another overlarge shift before tucking her back into bed.

Jetta peered down at the gown she wore and gave a depressed sigh. Mavis had said she'd lost a good deal of weight while ill, and the shift proved that out. Truly, it hung on her something awful. It made her worry what her dresses would look like on her. If they gaped at the chest as her shift did, they would be positively indecent, she supposed, and thought perhaps she should ask for a needle and thread and start to work now on taking in the gowns.

Her gaze slid to the chests along the wall at that thought, and she was just wondering which was hers when the bedroom door opened and Aulay entered, carrying a tray with food on it. Jetta brightened at once at his arrival and smiled in greeting.

"All done with hunting?" she asked as she watched him set the tray on the table by the fire.

"Aye. We brought back a fine fat rabbit, a couple o' pheasants and a deer," he announced as he crossed to the bed. "Rory is cleaning them as we speak and Mavis is planning a venison stew for the sup. In the meantime, she sent ye some other offerings. Are ye hungry?"

"Aye. I—Oh!" Jetta gasped with surprise and grabbed for his shoulders when he suddenly bent to scoop her up into his arms.

"Relax," he chided, as he carried her to the table. "I'll no' drop ye."

"Aye," Jetta breathed and forced herself to settle in his arms. He was her husband after all. He could carry her around if he liked. She even began to enjoy being in his arms again, but then they reached the table and he set her in one of the chairs.

"Thank you," she murmured as he straightened, and then flushed and tugged at the neckline of her shift when she saw how much skin it was exposing. It sagged so low that the tops of her nipples were on display, which merely reminded her of his kissing and caressing her that morning and flustered her even more. Trying to make the material cover her more decently, she glanced toward her husband to be sure he hadn't noticed, but of course he had. And judging from his expression he was recalling that morning as well.

Swallowing nervously, Jetta licked her suddenly dry lips and shyly lowered her eyes. Unfortunately, her gaze landed squarely on the front of his plaid, which was poking out in front like some sort of queer sideways tent. She stared at it blankly until he suddenly shifted and dropped to sit across from her.

"Food," Aulay said firmly, but his voice was husky and he was avoiding looking at her now, she noted.

Jetta peered at the tray he'd carried in and her mouth promptly dropped open. "Dear God, husband!"

"What?" he asked with concern.

"I—Well, just look at how much food you brought," she said with dismay.

Relaxing, he began to remove items from the tray and set them before her. "Ye need to eat well to regain yer strength."

"Aye, but—Goodness, 'tis no wonder my gowns are so big if this is how I ate ere hitting my head." By her reckoning there was enough food on the tray to feed ten people and he was placing most of it before her.

"Yer gowns?" he asked with a frown.

"Aye." She raised a hand self-consciously to her neckline again, and grimaced. "I must have been much bigger ere the injury."

For some reason that caused a short, deep laugh to slip from his lips, and she eyed him uncertainly, not sure what the joke was.

Catching her confusion, he explained, "That is no' yer shift, lass. Mavis was kind enough to loan it to ye. The dress ye were wearing was ruined in the storm. I at first put ye in one o' me shirts, but Mavis thought ye'd do better in one o' her shifts instead."

"Oh," Jetta said with relief, and then frowned. "But where are my gowns then?" she asked, and then answered herself before he could. "Oh, of course, they must have gone down with the ship."

"Aye," Aulay muttered.

"So," Jetta sighed, closing her eyes. "I have lost not only my memory, but all of my clothes too."

The touch of his hand on hers brought her eyes open.

"Never fear. We'll get ye new gowns," he said, squeezing her hand gently.

"Thank you, husband," Jetta said with a crooked smile and then found she had to fight a sudden bout of tears at his kindness. Blinking rapidly, she tried to force the tears back, and then dashed them impatiently away when her efforts failed.

"Are ye all right?" Aulay asked, his eyes narrowing on her.

"Aye. I am just—" She shook her head irritably. "I appear to be overly emotional. Every kindness makes me want to weep. 'Tis ridiculous."

"Ye're mending from a terrible injury, Jetta. Be patient with yerself. Rory said ye would be emotional fer a bit. 'Twill pass."

Jetta was relieved by his words, for truly she had nearly burst into tears at least three times while Mavis was helping her earlier, and she found it all just a bit overwhelming. Jetta was quite sure she wasn't normally such a weeping willow. Forcing herself to take a deep breath, she calmed herself and then managed a half smile and considered the food set out before her, but then shook her head. "I cannot possibly eat all of this."

"I do no' expect ye to," he said with amusement. "I just was no' sure what ye would feel like eating, or might be able to stomach after so long without food, so brought ye a selection to choose from."

"Oh," she breathed, and felt her eyes flood again at the considerate action.

Much to her relief, Aulay ignored her emotional response and merely suggested, "Mayhap ye should start with the soup. Yer stomach may no' be up to anything too heavy just yet."

"Aye." Jetta dashed away her tears again with one hand, while pulling the soup nearer with the other. They ate in silence at first, Jetta concentrating on her soup and Aulay gobbling up almost everything else. Good Lord, she'd thought it enough food for ten, but it wouldn't even have fed two Aulays, she thought with amusement. The man had a huge appetite.

"Stop watching me and eat yer soup," Aulay ordered suddenly and Jetta realized she had stopped eating to gape at him.

Grinning, she turned her attention back to her soup, but then shook her head. "I cannot eat another spoonful. I am done."

"Ye need to eat more than that, lass," Aulay said with a frown. "Ye're far too skinny and need to build yer strength back up."

Jetta hunched her shoulders a little self-consciously. She had gasped aloud when Mavis had helped her out of her borrowed sleeping gown to get in the bath and she'd first seen herself naked. Truly, other than her breasts, she was all bones and tightly stretched skin. It hadn't looked very attractive and had made her wonder what had moved Aulay to kiss her the way he had that morning. She'd decided then that theirs must be a love match, for she was sure only love could move someone to want to kiss and caress her as he had when she looked like a walking skeleton.

"Mayhap ye'll feel like having something else later," Aulay said solemnly when she simply stared at the remains of her cooling soup. She'd managed almost half of it, but just couldn't stomach any more.

Smiling with relief, she lifted her head and nodded. "Mayhap."

Aulay eyed her for a minute and then began to set the remains of their meal back on the tray. "Would ye like to play chess or something then? Or would ye rather rest?"

"Chess please," Jetta said at once and began to help him clear the food from the table. Within moments they had finished the task. Aulay then retrieved a finely carved chess game from one of the chests against the wall and they took a moment to set it up on the table.

"'Tis beautiful," Jetta murmured, pausing to examine a knight. The horse's head was so detailed it almost looked real.

"Aye," Aulay said in a soft rumble, examining his own knight. "Me brother Ewan carved them years ago as a gift to me parents."

"Ewan?" she asked curiously. "Is he here too?"

"Nay." Aulay set the horse's head on the board. "He is dead."

"He was the eighth brother and the reason there are only seven when there were eight," she murmured, remembering what he and Rory had said earlier.

"Aye. But actually, Ewan was the second brother, not the eighth," Aulay corrected her. "He was me twin, born right after me."

"Really?" she asked curiously. "Then you were close?"

"Close as two brothers can be," he said solemnly.

Jetta hesitated, but then asked, "How did he die?"

"In battle." His voice was low, and there was something in his expression that told her that talking about Ewan still pained him terribly. Letting that topic go, she asked, "So you are the older twin . . . and laird?"

Aulay nodded, and continued to set out pieces.

"Oh." Jetta glanced toward the window, but all she could see were trees. Turning her gaze back to her husband, she watched him, and then cleared her throat and said tentatively, "Husband?"

"Aye?" he said absently.

"Where exactly are we?" she asked apologetically.

Aulay jerked a blank gaze up to hers.

Grimacing, she pointed out, "I do not remember anything. Not even which castle I am lady of."

"Buchanan." The word was almost a growl. "I am clan chief and laird o' Buchanan." Clearing his throat, he added, "However, that is no' where we are at the moment. We are in me hunting lodge. I brought ye here after we fished ye out o' the water . . . to heal."

Jetta nodded. She supposed that explained why it was so quiet here. Which, when she thought about it, was probably why he'd brought her here to heal. Castles were rarely quiet.

"Buchanan," she breathed and turned her attention to setting out the rest of her own pieces as she murmured, "Jetta Buchanan. Lady Jetta Buchanan. Lady Buchanan."

Finishing with her pieces, she raised her head, and paused when she saw that Aulay hadn't returned to arranging his own pieces, but was just staring at her.

"Is there something amiss, my lord husband?" she asked uncertainly.

He opened his mouth, hesitated, and then closed his mouth again and returned to setting up his men with a shake of the head. "Nay. The board is set. Yer move first, lass."

Nodding, Jetta surveyed the board, and then picked up one of her pawns and moved it.

"Ye ken how to play," Aulay commented after they'd both made several moves.

"Aye." She smiled at him with a combination of pride and relief. "Apparently I have not forgotten everything."

She watched him move his bishop, moved her knight and then asked, "What is your sister like?"

Aulay glanced to her with surprise. "Saidh?"

"Is that her name?" Jetta asked.

"Aye." He watched her move her knight again and contemplated the board as he asked, "Why do ye ask?"

Jetta shrugged. "I find it hard to imagine having so many brothers and suspect she was either spoiled rotten by the lot of you, or—" She paused briefly to raise her eyebrows when he burst out laughing.

"It would definitely be the *or*, lass," he assured her with amusement. "Saidh is no' spoiled."

"Nay?" she asked with a smile.

"Nay," Aulay said firmly. "She's a fighter. She had to be to survive the lot o' us harassing her through the years."

Jetta smiled at the affection she heard in his voice, and asked, "How old is she?"

"I was eleven when she was born," Aulay announced. "She is twenty-two or-three now."

"So, a year or two younger than me," Jetta murmured and then froze and lifted a shocked face to him. "I remember my age!"

Aulay's eyes widened. "Do ye remember yer birthday?"

Jetta paused to think, scanning her mind briefly. It had to be in there somewhere. She knew it. If she remembered her age, her birthday had to be in her memory too. If she could just—

"Lass?" Aulay said solemnly.

Jetta lifted her head and looked at him with confusion. "Aye. What?"

"Ye're rubbing yer forehead. Is it starting to pain ye?" he asked quietly.

Jetta frowned. Actually, her head was *pounding*. It had come on suddenly, and was quickly getting worse, but she really wanted to remember—

Aulay watched Jetta closely, noting the deepening lines of pain on her face as she tried to recall the date of her birth. He was about to insist she stop trying, when she suddenly swayed in her seat. He leapt up just in time to catch her as she started to fall out of her chair.

Mouth tight, he carried her to the bed, laid her in it and then moved to the door and opened it to bellow for Rory.

"What's happened?" his brother asked a moment later as he stepped off the stairs and hurried toward him.

"She remembered how old she is," Aulay announced, turning back into the room and leading the way to the bed. "But then she tried to remember her birthday and—" Aulay shook his head as they reached the bed. "The effort seemed to bring on terrible pain, and then she just collapsed."

Rory bent to lift Jetta's eyelids and checked her eyes. He then leaned his head down to listen to her heart. "How was she prior to that?"

"Good," Aulay said. "She was sitting up in bed when I came in. I carried her to the table. She ate almost half a bowl of soup. We started to play chess, and then . . ." He shrugged.

"How did she remember how old she is?" Rory asked, straightening next to him.

"I do no' ken," he said with a frown. "She was asking about Saidh, asked how old she was. I told her she was about twenty-two or twenty-three and she said, 'so a year or two younger than me,' and then she got excited that she remembered and I asked if she knew her birthday, and . . ." He gestured to her unconscious form.

Pursing his lips, Rory turned back to Jetta and murmured, "So the memory came naturally, almost as a side thought."

"A side thought?" Aulay asked, raising his eyebrows.

"I mean, she wasn't trying to remember. It just came out when she thought of Saidh's age. Some part of her automatically compared it to her own age and the memory naturally cropped up to allow it," he explained, and then added, "But when she deliberately set out to try to remember something else, her head started to hurt and she fainted."

"Aye," Aulay said thoughtfully, and then added, "she was trying to remember things when the pain struck her the first time as well."

"Hmm." Rory frowned and shook his head. "She may be awake and walking about now, Aulay, but her mind must still be healing. 'Tis the only explanation I can think of for the pain her trying to force memories brings on." Expression solemn, he added, "She could do herself great damage trying to force the memories before her mind is completely healed."

"So, ye're thinking 'tis like walking too soon on a leg that was broken and has no' completely mended," he suggested. "She could just damage it all over again?"

"Aye, exactly like that," Rory said with a sigh. "Ye need to tell her to just let it come naturally and no' to try to force the memories to return."

Aulay snorted at the suggestion. "Would ye stop trying to remember were ye in her situation?"

"Nay," he admitted with a grimace, and considered the problem briefly. Finally, Rory just shook his head. "I do no' ken what ye can do. But do whatever ye can to keep her from trying to force the memories. Maybe distract her or something anytime she tries. Otherwise, I shall have to start feeding her sleeping drafts to send her back to sleep every time she wakens. In fact, mayhap I should just do that anyway. We have no idea how much damage she does every time she tries to force it. Aye, I will go get—"

"Nay," Aulay said at once, not happy with the thought of keeping the woman drugged and sleeping. When Rory turned to him in question, Aulay said, "I will try distracting her first. If that does no' work, then ye can resort to the sleeping drafts, but let me try first."

Rory frowned, but then nodded. "Very well. But if ye can no' distract her, send fer me and I'll mix her up a sleeping draft."

Aulay grunted agreement and watched him leave the room before turning to look down at Jetta. Judging by her expression, the pain had followed her into unconsciousness. But he was determined it would be the last time it plagued her.

JETTA OPENED HER EYES AND THEN LET THEM FLUTTER CLOSED again when bright sunlight pierced the woolly sleepiness she'd been enjoying. Goodness, it was bright in the room, which meant it must be twice as bright outside. A warm, sunny day then, she thought. There were few enough of those where she came from. Most days either started rainy, or quickly became rainy where she grew up in Northern England.

"Oh," Jetta gasped, her eyes popping open again with surprise.

"Are ye all right, lass?"

Turning her head, she stared blankly at her husband for a moment and then smiled widely and blurted, "I just remembered I grew up in Northern England."

His eyes widened slightly at the news, but she hardly noticed. Jetta was already frowning and trying to remember where in Northern England.

"Lass," Aulay said.

"Aye?" she asked absently, still searching for more memories.

"Are ye hungry?" he asked. "Can ye eat some more soup if I have some brought up?"

Did she know the names of any of the castles or villages in Northern England perhaps? she asked herself.

"Jetta."

That would be a start, she decided. She would make a list of all the villages and castles in Northern England that she could think of. If she could think of any. At the moment nothing was—Her thoughts died abruptly when Aulay suddenly kissed her. One moment she was lying there with her eyes closed, trying to think, and the next his mouth closed warm and firm over hers, completely washing away every thought in her head.

For a moment, Jetta was so startled that she didn't respond to the caress, but then as her earlier passion stirred in her once again, she opened to him and kissed him eagerly back. The moment she did, Aulay broke the kiss and smiled crookedly at her. "Do ye want some soup, lass?"

"Aye," she breathed, although, frankly, Jetta suspected she would have said yes to anything he asked at that moment. All she really wanted was for him to keep kissing her. Unfortunately, the moment she said yes, he straightened away from her and walked to the door. Mavis or Rory must have been out in the hall for some reason, because rather than leave the room or shout an order, she heard him murmuring to someone.

Sighing, she closed her eyes briefly, and then opened them just as quickly.

"Northern England," Jetta murmured, recalling what she'd been thinking about before he'd kissed her. She knew her age and she knew she'd grown up in Northern England, somewhere it rained a lot. Her memories were coming back. Slowly, and in bits and pieces, but still they were returning. That had to be a good thing, didn't it?

"Do ye want to sit at the table to eat?"

Jetta opened her eyes at that question and saw that Aulay had finished giving his instructions and was now crossing back to the bed. She glanced to the table, and sat up with a nod, but barely got the furs and linen tossed aside before he was there scooping her up into his arms.

Jetta didn't struggle, but merely settled into his hold and wrapped her own arms around his neck as she admitted, "I like it when ye carry me."

"Do ye?" he asked with amusement.

"Mmm-hmm," Jetta murmured, leaning up slightly to press a kiss to his chin. "It makes me feel small and cared for."

"Ye *are* small and cared for," he said gruffly.

"Aye," she agreed. "Mavis told me that you are the one who repeatedly spooned broth down my throat to keep me from starving to death while I slept. She said she offered to do it for you, but you insisted on doing it yourself and only gave up the task to her when you had castle business to tend to and could not do it yourself. She said the times that happened would not even equal all the fingers on her hand." She pressed another kiss to his chin and whispered, "Thank you."

"Ye're welcome," he said, his voice a low husky growl that sent shivers down her back.

When he paused then, she glanced around to see that they'd reached the table. Knowing he was about to set her down, she gave him a quick hard hug and whispered, "I think I must be the luckiest wife in the world having you to husband." Releasing him then, she leaned back and added, "And I bet I fell in love with you the moment I saw your handsome face."

Jetta felt him stiffen, and tipped her head to eye him with curiosity. "What?"

"Are ye mocking me, lass?" he growled, spearing her with his eyes.

"Mocking you?" she asked with confusion.

"I ken I am no' a handsome man," Aulay said grimly. "I was at one time, but no' anymore, no' since the battle where Ewan was killed and where I gained the scar on me face."

Jetta shifted her gaze to his scar and saw her husband flinch as he realized she was looking at it. Aulay was incredibly stiff now, as if awaiting a blow, and it made her wonder if they had never had this discussion before. Had she never reassured him that his scar did not detract from his attractiveness in her eyes? Truly? Had she been that stupid ere the wound that took her memory?

"I do not know what you see when you look at your reflection, husband," she said solemnly. "But I see a handsome man. In fact, I like the scar. It keeps you from looking too pretty and makes it appear that you have a bit of a devil in you."

"Ye think I look like the devil?" he asked stiffly, completely taking her words the wrong way.

Frowning, Jetta caught his face in her hands and turned him until his eyes were straight on to hers, and then she said firmly, "Not *the devil*, a *bit of a* devil. It makes you look a little dangerous, like a Viking come to raid and pillage, or a bandit looking to rob and rape, or a warrior come to kidnap and have his way with me."

Much to her relief, her words seemed to amuse him somewhat for he smiled suddenly and commented, "There appears to be a theme in there, lass."

"Aye, well . . ." Jetta hesitated, but then decided if her husband did not realize she found him attractive she had failed as a wife and needed to correct that right away. The man had cared for her himself while she was ill rather than leave her to the care of a servant, and he had treated her with nothing but kindness and concern since she'd first awoke. He deserved to know he was a good, attractive man and that she felt lucky to be his wife.

Clearing her throat, she said, "I find you very handsome, husband. I also like your kisses and touch . . ." Swallowing, she continued bravely, "And the idea of you having your way with me sends shivers all through me and leaves me wanting."

Much to Jetta's embarrassment, her admission at first seemed to make the man freeze. It made her wonder how their married life had been before the accident that had stolen her memories. Had she shunned him because of the scar? Or had he taken her possible shyness with her new husband for revulsion? Worried that she might have hurt him in the past, Jetta began to search her mind for memories that might clear up the matter for her. Determined to know what she'd done so she could fix it, she concentrated hard on the task, searching her mind and wincing as the effort immediately started her head pounding. She had just raised a hand to rub her pounding forehead when Aulay suddenly released her legs.

Jetta gasped, thinking at first that he was dropping her, but it was only her legs Aulay released. Allowing them to drop, he caught her at the waist with both hands and lowered his mouth to hers.

"Oh," she breathed just before his lips covered her own. The kiss was so passionate, demanding and all-consuming that Jetta hardly noticed when he set her on top of the table. At least, not until his hands began to move over her body and she realized he was no longer holding her up. They moved over her back, caressing and massaging and pressing her tighter against his chest and then slid lower, gliding down and under her bottom to cup and urge her forward on the tabletop as he moved between her legs and ground against her.

Gasping at the unfamiliar sensation that sent shooting through her, Jetta clutched at his shoulders and kissed him back with an almost frantic eagerness. She even wrapped her legs around him to pull him tighter as she shifted her own hips, trying to move against him as he was doing with her.

"Husband," Jetta cried in protest when he suddenly broke their kiss and pulled back. She then felt a tug, and glanced down to see that the overlarge shift no longer covered her breasts, but had been pulled under them. Even as she noted that, he tugged the sleeves down her arms so that the gown fell to pool around her hips, leaving her bare from the waist up. Before she could try to cover herself, Aulay covered one breast with his warm, firm hand and began to knead. With one hand on her breast and the other at her shoulder to support her, he urged her back until Jetta was almost lying on the tabletop. Aulay had leaned forward as he'd eased her down, and the moment he had her at the position he wanted, he claimed one of her breasts, taking almost half of it into his mouth and suckling as he slowly drew back until only the now hard tip remained between his lips. He nipped her lightly then before turning his attention to the other breast and removing his hand so he could repeat the action.

Groaning, Jetta shifted and almost struggled in his arms briefly under the passionate teasing, and then she couldn't take it anymore and tangled her hands in his hair to pull his face to hers for another kiss. This time she was the aggressor, thrusting her own tongue forward to duel with his.

Jetta even got so bold as to let one hand creep down toward the hardness pressing against her so intimately. The moment she neared it, however, Aulay broke their kiss, dragged a chair over with one foot and then dropped to sit in it.

Jetta stared at him with confusion, unsure what was happening. Was all that lovely passion over? Was she supposed to slip off the table and take the other seat as if nothing had hap—

"Husband!" she cried with shock when he suddenly caught her by each leg, drew her forward until her bottom was almost off the table, and then ducked his head under the hem of her shift and began to press kisses up along first one thigh and then the other. "Husband, please," she muttered, unsure herself if she were begging him to stop or to continue, and then he spread her wider and buried his head between her legs, his mouth finding the core of her. Gasping, Jetta did a little hop on the tabletop, her legs closing like a vise around his head and her hands reaching to clutch at him through the cloth of her shift as his tongue rasped over her most tender skin.

"Oh God!" Jetta cried, her eyes wide open one moment and squeezed shut the next as he did things she had never imagined could be done. Things she was also sure shouldn't be done in the eyes of the church. Jetta was aware that he had pushed her legs open again and was holding them that way as he devoured her with his lips, teeth and tongue. But mostly she was aware only of the sensations now ripping through her as Aulay licked, suckled and nipped at her tender flesh, causing such exquisite pleasure.

It was a revelation to her, and Jetta could not believe that it was possible to forget something so incredibly powerful as this. Family and loved ones? Aye, perhaps they could be lost to memory, but this mad passion? How had she forgotten this? How had she not begged for it the moment she opened her eyes? Dear God, it felt as if he were drawing her very soul out of her. Her entire body was taut as a bow and quivering with the need he was producing in her. She was panting for breath, her heart thudding wildly. Jetta felt as if she might lose her mind if he continued, but was sure she would surely die if he stopped . . . and then something shattered within her. Some fine string that he was pulling just snapped under the strain, and pleasure exploded within her, drawing a scream from her lips and making her body convulse as she was overwhelmed with a sweet release.

When Jetta regained some small semblance of herself and opened her eyes, she was no longer on the tabletop. She was again in Aulay's arms and he was carrying her to the bed. In fact, they'd reached it, she realized when he stopped and bent to lay her in it. Jetta immediately slid her arms around his neck, pulling on him and urging him to kiss her when he would have straightened. Aulay hesitated, but then pressed a quick kiss to her lips even as he caught her hands and said, "Someone is at the door."

As if to prove his words, a loud knock sounded at the door then. Knowing it probably wasn't the first round of knocking and that she had simply been too overwhelmed by her release to hear the first, Jetta reluctantly lay back on the bed and allowed him to disentangle himself and straighten.

"'Tis probably Mavis with the soup I sent for," he said with a smile, and then squeezed her hands before releasing them and turning to head for the door.

Jetta closed her eyes and listened drowsily as Aulay answered the door and began to speak with who she was sure was Rory. At least, it sounded to her like it was Rory's voice she was hearing. She couldn't make out what was being said, but the younger man seemed agitated, she thought with a complete lack of curiosity just before sleep pulled her down into its gentle folds.

Chapter 4

"WHAT THE DEVIL ARE YE DOING TO THE POOR LASS? I HEARD her screaming all the way out at the well."

Aulay scowled at Rory and stepped into the hall to pull the door closed so that Jetta wouldn't hear. As he shut it, he wondered, though, if Mavis too had heard Jetta's passionate cries. The lass was a very vocal lover, which he'd found vastly satisfying at the time, but now realized could be something of a problem.

"Thank God, Mavis didn't hear," Rory said now, answering that question. "At least I do no' think so. She is out hunting up wild herbs and spices to cook with and said she would bring up the soup once I'd watered it down a bit with water from the well. Which is fortunate," he assured him. "Had she been here she probably would have rushed into the room to stop ye from killing the poor lass. What the devil was going on? Is she having nightmares?"

Aulay raised his eyebrows at that and then shook his head with disgust. "The very fact that ye'd ask that tells me ye really need to set yer medicinal studies aside once in a while and visit the local light skirt, brother."

Rory stiffened at the words and then narrowed his eyes. "Aulay, ye did no'—?"

"Nay," he interrupted firmly, and shifted to ease his discomfort as he added, "I just . . . distracted her." That wasn't strictly true, of course, he admitted to himself. He'd originally intended to distract her by moving her to the table and making her eat. But when she'd said she found him attractive and enjoyed the idea of his having his way with her, Aulay had been . . . well, frankly he'd been shocked, amazed and so damned happy and turned on he'd wanted to—

"Aulay," Rory snapped, and if he was to judge by the level of irritation in his brother's tone, not for the first time. "When I said distract her, I did no' mean that ye should make free with her virtue. I—"

"Her virtue is intact," Aulay interrupted stiffly, and then spotted Mavis coming up the hall behind Rory and gave him a warning look before nodding at the woman and saying, "Ye're back."

"Aye." She smiled. "I found what I needed pretty quick. I think there must ha'e been a garden near here at one time. I found a variety o' herbs and spices nearby."

"That's helpful," Aulay murmured.

"Aye." Mavis smiled and then glanced to Rory and smiled at him as well. "Thank ye fer adding the water. The soup was already bubbling again when I came back in."

Aulay's eyebrows rose at the guilt-stricken expression that now claimed Rory's face. Obviously, he hadn't added the water in the end. No doubt Jetta's screams had distracted him from his purpose. To keep the maid from noticing his brother's reaction, Aulay said, "Thank ye, Mavis. The lass is too thin and needs to eat as much and as often as she can to regain her strength."

"Aye, she is frightfully skinny," the woman agreed solemnly as she reached them and Aulay took the tray. "I'll have a try at making some o' those sweet pastries Cook is always making up at the castle. Everyone loves those and they'll help put some weight on the girl."

"Good idea," Aulay said with approval as she turned and headed back the way she'd come. Once she had reached the stairs and was again out of ear-shot, Aulay shifted his gaze back to his brother. Noting the anger still burn-ing in the younger man's eyes, he said, "Her virtue is intact. She is under me care and protection. I would no' betray her trust by taking advantage."

Rory arched one eyebrow grimly. "She thinks ye're her husband, Au-lay. Do ye think she'd let ye kiss her, or anything else, if she knew ye were no' married? Even kissing her is betraying her trust in this situa-tion. At least it is until ye tell her the truth."

"Ye're the one who told me no' to tell her the truth," he pointed out with irritation. "Ye said it might set back her recovery."

"Aye, I did," he agreed. "And I still believe that. Head wounds are a tricky business and until she is fully recovered I think she needs to rest as much as possible, feel as safe and comfortable as possible, and avoid excitement *of any kind*."

"Christ," Aulay muttered through clenched teeth, and then took a calming breath and said, "Fine. I'll no' get her excited *in any way*."

Rory nodded with satisfaction. "Good."

Shaking his head, Aulay started to turn back toward the door.

"Oh, I almost forgot."

"What?" Aulay asked impatiently, pausing.

"Alick arrived earlier," he announced.

Aulay raised an eyebrow. "What did he want?"

"Just to let ye ken that Conran and Geordie set out yesterday to ask about any boats that may have sunk three weeks ago."

"Conran?" Aulay said with a frown. "My message instructed Alick and Geordie to do it."

"Aye, but then apparently Conran got thinking on it and felt he and Geordie should do it so Alick could continue on with their plans for him to visit Saidh," Rory explained. Mouth twisting, he added, "No doubt, Conran did no' wish to be stuck with that particular chore himself, so took Alick's task so Alick could still head to MacDonnell."

Aulay arched his eyebrows at that. "Alick planned to visit Saidh?"

Rory nodded. "Aye, the boys were talking after they got the message from ye that Jetta had awoken and decided Alick should visit Saidh and see if she had any spare dresses that might fit Jetta. They all felt she might soon want to wear more than Mavis's borrowed shifts and such now that she is awake."

"Good God, nay!" Aulay said at once.

"Nay?" Rory asked with surprise.

"If Saidh finds out about Jetta she will ride straight here to find out what is about. That is the last thing we need right now. Tell Alick to go find a cloth merchant instead. Some of them also carry already sewn gowns. But even if he can no' find one who carries them, he should buy cloth and we could set several of the women at Buchanan to sewing."

"Ah," Rory murmured, suddenly looking down at his feet and appearing uncomfortable in general.

"What is it?" Aulay asked, his eyes narrowing.

"Actually, ye misunderstood me. Alick has already been *and left* here. He is on his way to Saidh's as we speak."

"What?" Aulay growled the word.

"Aye," Rory said apologetically. "He arrived just after we returned from hunting and ye came back upstairs to break yer fast with Jetta."

"And ye're only telling me this now?" he snapped.

Rory shrugged. "I forgot."

"God's teeth, Rory! Saidh'll be headed here by dawn," Aulay said with exasperation.

"Maybe no'," Rory said. "Mayhap ye'll be lucky and when Alick gets to MacDonnell it will only be to learn that Saidh is off visiting Edith or Murine, or Jo."

"When have I ever been that lucky?" Aulay asked with disgust.

"Hmm," Rory said and then grinned. "Ye're right. She'll be here by dawn."

Cursing, Aulay turned away and nudged the door open. He then stepped into the room and used one foot to push the door closed on his brother's laughing face.

"Bastard," he muttered to himself as he started toward the bed. His footsteps slowed, though, and he then stopped and grimaced at the tray he held when Aulay realized that Jetta was sound asleep and snoring softly.

JETTA WRINKLED HER ITCHY NOSE AND REACHED UP SLEEPILY TO scratch it, managing to poke herself in the eye instead. Fortunately, it was closed, but the action brought it open and she peered blearily around at the dim room and then glanced to the window to see the weak predawn light slipping around the shutters. It was early yet, she saw and closed her eyes, intending to go back to sleep, but a soft snore made them pop open again and she sat up to peer down at the floor beside the bed.

A smile curved Jetta's lips when she spotted her husband there, still sound asleep. The man had been up and out of the room every morning since their tryst on the table nine long days ago. Mavis had been the first face she'd seen this last week and two days, when she'd arrived to help her with her morning ablutions. Aulay had only rejoined her once she was up and seated at the table, ready to break her fast. Aside from his no longer being there when she woke up, another change was that he hadn't kissed her even once since then, or done any of those other delicious things that had given her such pleasure.

Her smile faded at the thought. Jetta had no idea what had happened. Was he angry with her? Did he not find her attractive anymore? Her hand moved self-consciously to the bald spot on the back of her head. It seemed they'd shaved away the hair there to tend to her wounds. Those were healed now, but the hair hadn't grown back more than an inch or so and felt strange when she touched it. It probably looked strange too, Jetta thought with a frown.

Still, she'd had that hair missing since before waking and it hadn't seemed to stop him from kissing her and . . . er . . . stuff on the table then. Jetta had no idea why he hadn't touched her since, but was beginning to worry about what that might mean for her marriage. Not that he wasn't still kind and attentive. Aulay spent all of his time with her once Mavis had helped her with her ablutions and such and left the room. He returned then and played chess and other games with her, or told her tales about his brothers and sisters and growing up. He also took every meal with her, and was constantly fetching sweets and other snacks for her in an effort to make her eat more.

In truth, Jetta didn't think she could ask for a better husband. He was most kind and attentive. It was just his refusal to kiss and touch her that was different, and she found it worrisome. Jetta didn't think she could bear living with him for the rest of her life if she never again got to enjoy the pleasure he'd shown her. In fact, she now found she craved it constantly. If his hand brushed hers, or his arm, or if he even looked at her lips, her heart tripped and started pounding with excitement and anticipation. And all she had to do was look at him and she wanted him to kiss or touch her. But he didn't, and she was hurt and confused by the fact that he no longer seemed to want to.

Jetta peered at him silently, trying to sort out why and suddenly realized that while he had shown her great pleasure that time at the table, and even the time before, she had done little but moan and groan and cry out in response. She'd barely even kissed him back properly, let alone touch him in return. Not only had that been incredibly selfish, but it may have made him think she did not wish him to do the things he'd done to her. She needed to let him know that she did enjoy and desire his attentions that way, and the best way she could think to do that was to show him.

Letting out the little breath she'd been holding, Jetta straightened her shoulders and slid her feet to the floor, only to pause and simply sit on the bed, contemplating her husband. He was lying on his side, cocooned in his plaid, which might be a problem. She would surely wake him up did she try to unwrap him, and Jetta suspected that if he woke up before she at least did something to rouse his interest, he would bring an end to her efforts before they had even started.

Biting her lip, she considered him briefly and then smiled and turned to pull the largest fur off the bed and into her lap. Grasping it firmly in hand, she then stood and let it drop to the floor between her and her husband before gently and carefully laying it over him. Straightening then, she backed up and sat on the edge of the bed to wait. It seemed to take forever, and Jetta was beginning to fear that it wouldn't work, and then he murmured sleepily and shifted onto his back, pushing the furs and plaid restlessly away from his overheated body.

Jetta almost leapt to her feet and clapped and squealed over the fact that her plan had worked, but she managed to restrain herself and then she lost the urge as she took in what her actions had revealed.

Aulay hadn't just pushed away the fur, he'd pushed off the plaid too. He was now covered only by a linen shirt that was presently tangled around his stomach, leaving him completely on display from the waist down.

Jetta had thought she'd known what to expect. She instinctively knew she'd seen naked babies, both male and female. But the little jigglies she'd seen on baby boys bore no resemblance to the monster sleeping in its nest of curls that she was presently staring at. And she had absolutely no recollection of seeing that before.

Good Lord! What was she supposed to do with it?

The question echoed in her head briefly. Unfortunately, no answer came to her mind and Jetta actually considered lying back in bed and pretending to sleep until he woke up and left the room. But then she steeled herself and shook her head. If she wished to enjoy the pleasure he showed her, it did seem she should show him some too. Besides, she would just do to him what he had done to her. That should work . . . shouldn't it?

Grimacing, Jetta slid off the bed to kneel beside him and glanced nervously from his sleeping member to his sleeping face and back as she tried to figure out how to start. Aulay had begun by kissing his way up her thighs, and then . . . well, she wasn't quite sure what he'd done once he'd reached the spot between her legs. She felt sure he'd licked and nibbled and . . . well, frankly, she'd been so excited and wound up, she'd concentrated on the sensations he was causing rather than what exactly he was doing.

So, kissing, nibbling and licking it would be, Jetta thought. That was what she would do. How hard could it be?

Kneeling next to him, she pressed a kiss to the skin just inside of one of his knees, and then the other, and then a little higher on each leg, and then a little higher still, and then she raised her head and blinked as she noted that the sleeping monster had woken and was slowly stretching. She bit her lip briefly, but then straightened her shoulders again and began to press kisses along the length of the monster itself, her eyes widening as it grew longer and began to stand under her attention. It was becoming quite impressive by the time she kissed the tip, but when she experimentally closed her mouth over it Jetta learned just how hard it could be as it swelled even more and pushed against the back of her throat.

Eyes widening, Jetta clasped her hand around the base and withdrew her lips somewhat until a more comfortable amount remained inside, and was startled when the action drew a long moan from her husband.

Glancing to him sharply, she saw with relief that he was still sleeping, but his expression was almost pained and his head and hands were shifting restlessly. So were his legs, she noted as they moved too. Encouraged by this clue that she might be doing something right, Jetta eased more of him into her mouth before pulling back again and smiled with satisfaction around the monster when Aulay groaned what sounded like her name.

That had to be a good sign. Certainly, it would have been distressing had he groaned another woman's name, she thought and decided to step up her game. Letting him slide from her mouth, Jetta used her hold to shift the member so that it was positioned like a cob of corn before her mouth. She then began to press little nibbling kisses along its length. Much to her disappointment, however, that didn't seem to work as well. At least, her husband didn't moan again under the attention. Frowning, she pulled his erection upright and tried sliding her mouth over the tip once more, relieved when it brought another one of his deep, hungry groans.

All right then. This was what he liked best. Good. She could do this, she thought, sliding her mouth up and down on the tip in long, slow strokes. Jetta was concentrating so hard on what she was doing that when Aulay suddenly growled her name and tangled his hand in her hair, she gave a start and unintentionally bit down. Realizing what she'd done when he suddenly roared in pain, Jetta released him at once and leapt back to peer at him wide-eyed.

"Oh, husband, I am sorry," she cried anxiously as he curled into a fetal position with his hands covering his maltreated organ. His roar turned into a long string of curses. "Truly, you just startled me. Please, I am so sorry. I did not mean to bite you. Did I hurt you?"

"Oh God," he groaned, his face pressed into the pallet of furs.

"I mean, I know I hurt you," she said quickly. "But did I break the skin or—" Pausing, she bit her lip and peered at where his hands and upper legs now hid him from her view. "Mayhap ye should let me look and see how much damage was done."

"Nay," Aulay growled, the word muffled by the furs he was pressing his face into.

"But—"

"Get into bed, wife," he said, and even lifted his head to say it.

His voice was as hard as stone, she noted and stared at him helplessly for a moment, but then climbed dejectedly back into bed and crawled under the linen. She had thoroughly messed that up, Jetta acknowledged to herself. He would never want to touch her again now. She would spend the rest of her life in a marriage where her husband was kind and gentle with her, but would not share his passion, and she didn't know why.

Jetta sniffled as tears began pooling in her eyes and spilling over to run down the sides of her face and into her hair. The worst part was that she had almost the perfect marriage. She might not have a lot of memories, but she knew in her heart that few women were lucky enough to have a husband as wonderful and considerate as Aulay. She knew without a doubt that he was much more attentive and sweet than most men, and if she had just been able to sort out this business of why he wasn't bedding her, her marriage would have been as close to perfect as she thought was possible. But she'd failed, Jetta acknowledged, snuffling as the tears began to pour out of her eyes in earnest.

She'd failed and would never again know the pleasure of his sweet lips on hers and his hand and mouth on her body and whatever else it was happy couples did in the bedroom. This time a soft hiccupping sob followed the thought and Jetta squeezed her eyes closed with misery.

"Jetta? What's the matter? Why are ye crying?"

Blinking her eyes open, she stared in surprise at Aulay as she saw that he was off the floor and now bent over the bed, eyeing her with concern. She'd hurt him and he was worried about her. He was so sweet, she thought, and cried all the harder.

"Jetta." Aulay sounded alarmed now as he sat on the bed beside her and scooped her up into his lap. Pressing her to his chest, he rubbed her back and asked, "What is it, lass? Did I hurt ye when ye bit me?"

Jetta blinked her eyes open at the ridiculous question, and then released a small watery laugh and shook her head. "Nay, of course not. I just—I really did not mean to bite you, husband."

"Aye," he said on what sounded like a relieved sigh. "I ken."

"I am so sorry."

"I ken, ye are," he murmured, rubbing little circles on her back. "'Twas an accident."

"Aye, and now I have ruined everything," she said unhappily and felt his hand pause.

"What have ye ruined, lass? What were ye trying to do exactly?" he asked and Jetta could hear the frown in his voice now.

"I was trying to please you," she admitted shyly. "I thought mayhap you have not kissed or touched me again because you thought I did not want it because when you . . . did what you did, I just lay there like a dead fish and I wanted to show you—"

"Ye did no' lie there like a dead fish," Aulay interrupted, sounding amused. "Ye responded as passionately as any man could wish."

"I did?" she asked, pulling back to peer at him with surprise.

He nodded solemnly.

"Then did I do something to anger you?" Jetta asked with a frown.

His eyebrows rose at the question. "Nay. What would make ye think that?"

"Because you have not kissed nor touched me again since then. I thought either you believed I did not want you to, or that I had somehow angered you, or that you simply tired of me and did not want me anymore because of my shorn head and my being too thin."

"Oh, lass," Aulay said softly, cupping her cheek with his hand. "Ye've no' angered me, and I am definitely no' tired o' ye. In fact, nothing could be further from the truth. Every minute I am with ye I have to fight no' to kiss and touch ye," he admitted, his eyes dropping to her mouth and his face moving closer.

"Truly?" Jetta whispered uncertainly.

"Aye, truly. All I think of all the day long is kissing ye senseless, stripping yer shift off so that I can look at all o' ye without it in the way, and then cupping and caressing yer beautiful breasts before claiming them with me mouth and suckling at them until ye groan me name with need."

"Oh," Jetta breathed weakly, her body tingling at the thought.

"I want ye, lass," Aulay admitted on a growl, although he really needn't bother saying it now. She could feel that he wanted her. He was presently hard and pressing against her bottom where she sat in his lap. "I truly do. I've never wanted anyone so much in me life. All I can think about is laying ye across the bed, spreading yer legs and tasting yer sweet passion again until ye scream and then driving meself into ye and—" His words died when she suddenly leaned up and kissed him.

Jetta hadn't been able to take it anymore. His words and the pictures they were creating in her mind had her body tingling and wet and she wanted what he was describing. She wanted more. She wanted to make him groan again as she had with her mouth. She wanted his body naked and covering hers everywhere. She wanted . . . well, she wanted it all. And she put all that want into her kiss. This time she was the one urging his lips open and sliding her tongue into his mouth, and this time it was her hands moving over his body, caressing his arms and chest and then reaching around and down to cup his bottom.

Aulay had frozen the moment she kissed him, but when she squeezed his behind and rubbed her chest against his, he was suddenly all passion and motion. His tongue thrust forward to tangle with hers, and his hands made short work of tugging her shift down and claiming her breasts.

Jetta moaned as he kneaded them and then plucked at her nipples. She then gasped in surprise when she found herself suddenly on her back on the bed with him over her.

Tearing his mouth from hers, Aulay pressed kisses along her cheek to her ear and growled, "Spread yer legs."

Jetta obeyed at once, and then groaned when he lowered himself to rest against her and ground into her very core with only the thin cloth of the shift between them. Aulay groaned too, and then his mouth was on hers again, his kiss a fiercely demanding one as he ground his hips into her again. A sound much like a sob came from her throat then and Jetta shifted restlessly and then wrapped her legs around his hips, urging him on. The move shifted the cloth between them, and when he next ground against her she felt his flesh against hers. He was hard and hot and the feel of him sliding against her slick heat made her moan into his mouth and tighten her fingers on his arms where she was now clutching him. But it made Aulay freeze again.

Afraid he was going to stop, Jetta tore her mouth from his and cried, "Husband, please."

Rather than urge him to continue, the words made him close his eyes and lean his forehead on hers. "Lass, ye're killing me."

Jetta stilled now too and frowned with confusion. "I do not understand. Why are you stopping?"

"Why indeed," Aulay muttered, sounding bitter, and then said almost wearily, "We can no' do this, lass."

"But I want to," she said, bewildered by his refusal. "And we are married. I—" Her words died and they both glanced sharply toward the door when it opened. Rory started into the room, paused abruptly as he took in their position, and then turned a sharp angry look on Aulay and snapped, "A word, brother," before turning away and stepping out of the room. He pulled the door closed silently behind him.

"Well, hell," Aulay muttered, rolling off her and flopping onto his back on the bed.

Jetta hesitated and then sat up and tugged her shift down to cover herself before pulling it back onto her arms. Once she was decently covered, she looked uncertainly to Aulay.

"Your brother seemed . . ."

"Angry?" Aulay suggested when she hesitated to say it.

"Aye," she admitted, and then cleared her throat and asked, "do you know why?"

"Oh aye, I ken why," he assured her dryly. "He's upset at me for what we were doing."

Jetta frowned. "Well, that is just ridiculous. We are husband and wife. Besides, we should be angry at him for entering without knocking."

Aulay was silent for a minute and then sat up and slid his feet to the floor. Standing up then, he knelt to begin pleating his plaid and murmured, "I should not have been kissing and caressing ye or anything else."

"Why?" she asked with dismay. They were husband and wife . . . and she liked it. She wanted him to do it again, and more. "We are married, bedding is part of that, and if we want to we can—Well, at least I want to," she added uncertainly.

"Lass, I want to as well," he assured her, raising his head to eye her solemnly. "Surely ye ken that?"

Her gaze dropped to his still very erect member and she blushed and nodded.

"But the fact is, ye do no' ken everything," he said solemnly.

"What do I not know?" Jetta asked with a frown.

Aulay hesitated long enough that he was finished with his pleating before he said, "He warned me no' to excite ye until ye've recovered. He fears it can hamper and even set back yer healing."

Eyes widening, Jetta watched him don his plaid, and asked, "Is that why you have not touched or kissed me since—?" Her question died when he stood and then bent and pressed a quick, hard kiss to her lips.

Straightening then, he strode to the door, saying, "I will send Mavis to ye."

Jetta watched him go with a sigh, disappointed that the passionate interlude was over.

Chapter 5

"If ye can no' control yerself, I will ha'e to insist ye avoid spending time alone with the lass," Rory snapped the minute Aulay stepped out into the hall and pulled the door closed again. "She is me patient, Aulay. I—"

"I can control meself," Aulay snapped, cutting him off. "I *was* controlling meself. I have no' even kissed the lass since ye warned me no' to more than a week ago, but this morning she—" He cut himself off abruptly, unwilling to tell his brother that he'd woken up to find Jetta kneeling next to him with his cock in her mouth.

God's teeth, just the thought of it made Aulay hard as a rock. He still couldn't believe she'd done that. Well, he could since she'd explained why she'd done it, but . . . no, he couldn't believe it. It had certainly been a lovely way to start the day . . . right up until she'd chomped down on him like he was a tasty side of beef. The memory made him wince. He'd only been half-awake at that point. Awash in the pleasure she was giving him, he'd been swimming toward full consciousness and then, pow! He was wide awake and howling and the pleasure wasn't even a memory, but had been pushed out by the pain.

Sighing, he glanced at his brother and said, "She was hurt that I had not kissed her again and thought it meant I no longer found her attractive so tried to rouse my interest."

"And obviously succeeded," Rory said grimly.

"Aye, but I only kissed her. I did not take her innocence. Her virtue is still intact. And after ye left I explained that ye did no' think it was a good thing fer her to get excited until she'd healed, so all is well. She'll no' do that again, and I will continue to control meself."

Rory eyed him solemnly for a minute, and then sighed and nodded. "Very well. But I will warn you one last time, brother. If you take her innocence, you will have to marry her."

Aulay scowled at him with irritation. "Brother, I understand ye're only looking out fer the lass, but I am the eldest brother. I am laird at Buchanan and you can no' make me do anything I do no' wish to do." Mouth tight, he added, "And I'll no' let ye force *her* into doing anything she does no' wish to do either."

He fell silent for a moment, allowing that to sink in, and then asked, "Now, why did ye come to the room? Is something amiss?"

Rory grimaced, and then admitted, "Nay. Well, aye. I thought I heard ye shout and howl. 'Tis what woke me. So I came to be sure all was well."

Now it was Aulay's turn to grimace. He could hardly tell Rory what had happened. So he continued to remain silent, searching his mind for some excuse for his shout and howl that didn't involve Jetta, her teeth and his cock.

"It was probably just a dream I had," Rory offered suddenly.

"Aye," he said at once with relief. "A dream."

Nodding, Rory turned toward the stairs, but as he walked away, he added, "Odd Mavis had the same dream wake her up though."

Aulay closed his eyes on a sigh. Really, he should have put more care into building this place. Sound carried as if the walls were parchment thin. However, he hadn't considered sound an issue when he'd set the men to building it. There had been no woman in his life then, and in truth, he hadn't expected there ever to be, or considered the sound issues a woman's presence might cause.

"I'll send Mavis up to help Jetta with her ablutions."

Aulay opened his eyes in time to see his brother jog lightly down the steps, and then turned to re-enter the bedchamber. He stepped inside and closed the door, and then paused when he saw that the bed was empty. Blinking in surprise, he glanced swiftly around the room, finding Jetta at the window. She'd pulled the shutters open and was leaning out to peer at the clearing around the lodge in the dawning light.

"Careful, lass," he said, moving quickly to her side. "We would no' want ye falling out the window."

The caution made her chuckle softly. "I will not fall out, husband. I just . . . the fresh air is so lovely. And I wanted to see something besides this room."

Aulay frowned slightly and peered out at the trees surrounding the lodge. It was a lovely sight, the tall, strong trees waving in a light breeze, the sound of birds chirping, the grass as green and bright as Jetta's eyes. He himself had spent most of the last more than four weeks now in this room watching over Jetta, but had made the occasional excursion outside. He had returned to Buchanan a handful of times to handle castle business too, but they had been short trips before she'd woken. Since Jetta had regained consciousness he hadn't left the lodge, although he had gone outside early in the mornings while Mavis had helped with her ablutions, often hunting up some game for their meals, or riding to a nearby loch for a morning dip to clean up. The ocean was closer than the loch, but the fresh water was better for his purposes than the salt water the ocean offered. Besides, Aulay had enjoyed the brisk ride in the morning air after the hours inside.

Jetta, however, hadn't been out of this room at all. A change of scenery and the fresh air might do her a world of good, he thought suddenly.

"If ye're feeling up to it mayhap we could go for a short walk, or a ride today," he said impulsively. "Mayhap we could even ride out and break our fast by the ocean."

"Really?" She turned a face full of excitement to him, her eyes wide and happy.

"Aye," Aulay said, smiling at her expression, and then he frowned and added, "Well, if Rory says 'tis all right. I would no' wish to do anything to set back yer healing."

"Oh aye," Jetta said her smile fading and worry taking its place now. "Do you think he will allow it?"

Aulay opened his mouth to answer, but then paused and glanced to the door as a soft knock preceded Mavis entering. He nodded in greeting to the woman, and then turned back to Jetta and took her arm to urge her away from the window.

"I'll ask him while Mavis attends ye," he promised, and, noting the way she was now worrying her lip with her teeth, added, "I'm sure he'll think it a fine idea."

"ABSOLUTELY NOT."

Aulay rolled his eyes at Rory's firm words and said, "But she has been cooped up in the room upstairs for weeks now. Surely some fresh air will only do her good?"

"She has been unconscious most of that time," Rory pointed out with a scowl. "The lass only woke up little more than a week and a half ago. She's been very ill, Aulay. And she is still ill."

"Not really," Aulay argued. "I mean, I ken she has no memory ere waking here, but otherwise she is fine. There is no fever, no open wound, the back of her head has mostly healed and while she is weak still, she grows stronger every day. She has even put some weight back on."

"Not nearly enough," Rory said at once. "The lass is still far too thin and frail. She needs to build more strength before we risk outings."

"She is hardly going to gain strength lounging about in a bed," Aulay pointed out with exasperation. "She needs to be up and about."

Rory was silent for a moment, and Aulay could tell by his expression that he was considering it, so said, "A compromise then. A picnic by the ocean. She will need only walk below and to the horse, and then from the horse to a blanket on the beach and back. That way she can get fresh air, a very little bit of exercise, and the sight of the ocean might even spark a memory for her. Perhaps she'll recall the ship she was on and its sinking."

Rory eyed him curiously. "Ye want her to remember she is no yer wife?"

Aulay hesitated, his mind torn on the subject. Part of him wanted her to remember everything. The part that found hope in her response to his kisses and in her admission that she was attracted to him. That part wanted her to know they weren't really married so that he could ask her to marry him for real. Because that part was daring to hope that she might agree, and that he could have the wife and children that he'd always taken for granted that he would have before he'd taken the injury to his face.

But another part, the one that still ached from his fiancée's rejection as well as the horrified response of others to his battered face . . . that part would rather she never know. It would rather they continue in this limbo of being married, but not married. Of having her, but not being able to have her. That part feared she would be relieved by the news that they were not man and wife, and would admit she'd just been making the best of a bad situation, but would be happy to escape having to look at him every day. In truth, he'd rather have this strange half relationship than risk losing her altogether. But what he said in the end was, "The sooner she remembers who she is, the better able we will be to keep her safe from whatever threat she was afraid of before she lost her memory."

Rory stared at him so hard for so long that Aulay suspected his brother knew about his other hopes and fears, but finally he said, "Very well. We will take her to the beach to break her fast."

"Good," Aulay said with a grin, not even minding that Rory would accompany them. In truth, he knew that it was probably for the best. It would make it easier for him to behave himself, which was becoming harder to do all the time. This morning's antics certainly weren't helping him any. He couldn't get the image of waking up to find Jetta taking him into her mouth out of his mind, and even the pain that had followed was no longer detracting from his body's response to the memory. Nay, it was better they have a chaperone from now on.

"'TIS BEAUTIFUL," JETTA BREATHED, PEERING OVER THE WIND-swept beach.

"Does it look at all familiar?" Aulay asked as he urged his mount down the sloping path to the shore, and regretted it almost at once. If she had seen shore at all from her position on the mast, it would have been from the opposite angle, from the water. Besides, a glance down showed her frowning as she now tried to find some memory of the beach. "Do no' try to force the memories, lass. Just relax and let whatever comes, come."

"Aye," she said on a sigh.

Aulay hesitated, and then asked, "Were ye saying aye to—?"

"To just relaxing and letting the memories come," Jetta said on a laugh, and then added apologetically, "I do not recognize anything."

"'Tis fine," Aulay assured her, and then looked over his shoulder toward Rory, who was following them on his own mount. "I thought close to shore might be nice. We can walk a little way along the beach in the surf after we eat. 'Twill be easier than trying to walk in the dry sand."

"Aye," Rory agreed easily and followed when they reached the sand and Aulay urged his horse toward shore.

He stopped a good ten feet short of the surf. While it would be easier to walk in the wet sand than the dry, he didn't want to picnic on it. Aulay lifted Jetta from where she sat before him on the mount and leaned to set her on her feet in the sand. He then quickly dismounted himself. Noting the way Jetta was self-consciously plucking at the plaid she wore over her borrowed shift, he smiled and assured her, "Ye look fine, lass."

Jetta peered down at herself with a slight grimace, but nodded, and he felt bad that he hadn't had a dress to offer her. This was the best he could come up with, pleating a spare plaid he had and fashioning a sort of overdress for her to wear with the somewhat indecent shift. She was swimming in cloth, but decently covered at least. Still, Aulay decided he really needed to arrange for clothing for her if they were going to start leaving the lodge more often. Besides, he had to return to Buchanan soon. While he knew that, between his uncle and his brothers, the keep and its people were in good hands, he still felt guilty for not being there himself. He was the laird, after all, and should be tending to his people, not delegating it to others.

The worry over clothing for Jetta made him wonder about Alick and what was taking him so long. He should have been back with any gowns Saidh might have been able to loan them by now, if not with his sister herself. Hell, he expected Geordie and Conran to return with their report anytime, and they'd had to ride both up and down the coast, stopping at every port as far away as England in the south and all the way up the Scottish coast to the north.

"This should be good."

Aulay glanced around to see Rory unfolding and shaking out a plaid to lay it on the sand.

"Oh, lovely, I am starving," Jetta said, moving toward the picnic spot Rory had chosen.

"Well, seat yerself then, lass," Rory said lightly. "Mavis packed this basket full. She sent some lovely pastries, some fruit, some cheese, some boiled eggs and even some meat."

"Goodness, she must have thought she was feeding an army," Jetta said, settling on the plaid and watching wide-eyed as Rory began pulling out the offerings. Turning to grin at Aulay then, she added mischievously, "That or two Buchanan brothers."

"Har har," Aulay said dryly as he settled next to her on the plaid, but he couldn't hold back the grin her teasing caused. Catching Rory's confused expression, Aulay explained, "She thinks I ha'e an exceptionally large appetite."

"Ah," Rory said and then smiled at Jetta and told her with certainty, "He doesna. Dougall eats more than him, and our youngest brother, Alick, eats more than he and Dougall combined."

"Nay!" Jetta cried with disbelief. "'Tis impossible that anyone could eat twice what Aulay does."

"Men eat more than women," Aulay said with amusement. "Surely ye ken that from yer father?"

"Nay. My father never ate like you do. He preferred his drink," she assured him.

Aulay stilled at the words, just a heartbeat before she gasped and cried, "Oh! I remember my father preferred drink to food!"

Exchanging a glance with Rory, Aulay reached out to cover her hand with his own and said soothingly, "Aye. Ye do. Now, remember no' to force it, but did ye recall anything else just now? Did ye picture someone in yer mind? Or think o' yer uncle's name or anything?"

"I . . ." Jetta frowned, but when he squeezed her hand gently, she relaxed her forehead and breathed out before saying, "I got a quick impression of a small man. Not muscular or tall like you and your brothers.

He was slender and not much taller than me and his head was balding," she said slowly and then shook her head and met his gaze. "That is all."

"But that is good," he assured her, squeezing her hand again. "Every memory that comes back, no matter how small, is a good thing. It means the rest will most like follow, does it no', Rory?" he asked, turning to his brother.

Rory smiled and nodded, but Aulay could read his brother and knew he didn't really think it was all that good. A frown tried to claim Aulay's mouth then, but not wanting to alert and alarm Jetta, he forced it away with a smile and squeezed her hand again. "Come. You said you were starving. We should eat."

The three of them began to eat, Rory and Jetta chatting and laughing as they did, but Aulay was quieter, his gaze slipping between Jetta and his brother as he worried about the man's expression when he'd asked him if her remembering was not good. It troubled him, and he wanted to ask him about it, so he was incredibly relieved when Jetta decided she'd had enough to eat and walked down to the surf. Watching her hitch up her plaid and wade into the water a ways until she could wash her hands, Aulay asked solemnly, "Is it not good that she is remembering?"

"Of course, any memory is good," Rory said solemnly. "But it troubles me that she is not getting full-on memories, just bits and pieces. I should think her memory would be coming back on its own by now if it ever truly will."

"You told her no' to try to remember," Aulay pointed out with a frown. "And so ha'e I because you advised it. She has stopped trying to remember and is just letting whatever come, come."

"Aye, I ken," Rory said solemnly. "But I expected by no' trying, she would relax and the memories would shake loose o' their own accord. That does no' appear to be happening."

"Ye want her to try now," Aulay realized.

Rory nodded, and then said quickly, "But only to see if trying still brings on the pain. If it does, she should stop at once. If not . . ."

"If not, what?"

Aulay turned his head swiftly to see that Jetta had returned. She was smiling, her expression curious. While she'd obviously caught Rory's last couple of words, she hadn't heard much before them. If she had, he didn't think she'd be smiling.

"All cleaned up?" he asked, getting to his feet.

"Aye. Mavis's pastries are lovely, but do get me all sticky," she said on a laugh, and then looked around as the sound of horse hooves caught her ear.

"Someone's approaching," Rory said, standing up next to them.

"Aye," Aulay murmured, his hand on his sword. He watched tensely for a moment and then relaxed when a rider came into view, heading down the path they'd taken to the beach. "'Tis young Simon."

"Who is that?" Aulay heard Jetta ask Rory as he started toward where the path ended at the beach.

"One o' the Buchanan soldiers," Rory answered. "Rest here. We will see what is about."

Aulay glanced around in time to see Jetta nod solemnly and settle on the plaid to wait patiently.

"What do you think is about?" Rory asked, moving up beside him.

"I'm no' sure," Aulay admitted. "Trouble, probably. But there is only one man, so hopefully it is no' too terribly serious trouble."

"Hopefully," Rory agreed dryly and then fell silent until the rider had reached them.

"M'laird," Simon said in greeting as he reined in. "I went to the lodge and Mavis said ye were here."

"Aye," Aulay responded. "What's amiss, Simon?"

"Yer uncle sent me to fetch Rory," Simon said almost apologetically. "Young Katie was shot with an arrow and needs tending."

"Katie the maid?" Aulay asked with surprise.

"Aye," Simon said grimly.

"I'll fetch me horse," Rory said at once and turned to hurry back to where their horses waited.

"What happened?" Aulay asked. "How did a maid take an arrow? Was it an accident in the practice yard?"

Simon shook his head. "From what I understand, she was out collecting fresh lavender to mix in with the rushes. Laird Geordie came across her on his return to Buchanan from that task ye sent he and Conran on and offered her a ride to the keep. She was seated behind him on the horse and was hit in the back."

Aulay frowned. He knew Geordie had been frolicking with the lass of late and would be upset at this turn of events.

"Who shot her?" he asked. "Was it a hunting arrow gone astray, or—?"

"I do no' ken, m'laird," Simon admitted unhappily. "I'm sure yer uncle is looking into that, but as soon as Katie was brought in, he sent me to fetch Rory."

Aulay nodded and turned to glance at his brother as Rory leapt on his horse and rode him quickly back to them. "All set?"

"Aye. Fortunately, I brought me medicinals with me today just in case the outing was too much fer Jetta," Rory said, patting the bag hanging from his saddle. He glanced toward the beach then, and said, "Mayhap ye and Jetta should return with me. Simon could go fetch Mavis and follow us."

Aulay seriously considered doing that, but then shook his head. "We would just slow ye down. Besides, the lass has no clothes to wear."

"Oh aye," Rory said, but instead of leaving, just sat there frowning.

"I promise she is safe with me," Aulay said solemnly. "I will no' take advantage o' her while ye're gone."

Sighing, Rory nodded and waited as Simon urged his horse to walk around Aulay and return to the path heading back the way he'd come. "Send for me if Jetta has a setback or ye need me."

"Aye. Safe journey," Aulay murmured and watched his brother follow Simon up the trail. Once the two men were out of sight, he returned to Jetta. Much to his surprise, she was already packing away the food. By the time he reached her, she'd finished with that and moved on to gathering the plaid Rory had laid out for them to sit on for their picnic.

"We need not leave right away if ye wish a walk or something," he said mildly as he reached her.

Jetta paused and peered at him with surprise. "I assumed something was wrong at Buchanan and you were needed."

Aulay shook his head. "Rory is the one who was needed. One o' the maids took a stray arrow in the back while outside the gates. Uncle Acair sent for Rory to tend her."

"Oh, the poor thing," Jetta said with a frown as she began to fold the plaid. "Arrows can be so difficult to remove. Pulling them back out the way they went in can do more damage than the initial injury. I found 'tis often better to snap off the end with the fletching and push the arrow through and out if possible, but if 'tis in her back . . ." She shook her head. "You can kill them trying to save them."

Aulay raised an eyebrow as he watched her fold the plaid in half and then in half again. "So ye've tended many arrow wounds."

"Aye, well, my mother taught my sister and me all she knew about healing ere she died and . . ." Jetta paused and blinked in surprise, the plaid held in her hand, folded into a fourth of its original size. Eyes wide with wonder, she whispered, "I have a sister."

"Do ye remember her name?" Aulay asked.

"I . . ." She narrowed her gaze in concentration as she tried to recall.

"If trying to remember causes ye pain, stop at once," he said with concern. "I just hoped mayhap ye'd remembered her name as ye thought on her and yer mother."

"Nay," she said on a sigh, but then brightened and smiled at him. "But you know her name and can tell me."

Aulay froze briefly, but then made himself relax and shook his head. "Ye ken Rory thought it best if ye remember things on yer own."

"Oh aye," Jetta said on a sigh and then argued, "But I do remember I *have* a sister. You would only be telling me her actual name."

Aulay looked away and struggled briefly with his conscience. He couldn't tell Jetta her sister's name. He didn't know it, and that was what he was struggling with. He wanted to be honest with her and tell her that he didn't know. Yet, he didn't want to tell her that, and not just because Rory thought it better she not be distressed. He also didn't want to tell her because then he would have to admit they were not married and the moment he did, he feared she would wish to leave him . . . and he didn't want to lose her.

Taking the folded blanket from her, Aulay bent and picked up the basket with the remains of their meal and murmured, "We should return to the lodge."

Jetta looked disappointed, but nodded solemnly. "The sun has gone anyway. It looks like a storm is coming."

Aulay glanced skyward to see that she was right. Storm clouds were rolling across the sky, quickly blocking out the sunlight. The day was growing chilly and by his estimation they'd be lucky to make it off the beach before the clouds opened up and dropped rain on them. Laying the plaid on the basket, Aulay carried it in one hand and with his other hand took Jetta's arm and walked her as swiftly as he dared to his horse. He would have liked to move at a jog or even a run, but walking through the shifting sands was hard work and the lass was just fresh from her sickbed.

He wasn't terribly surprised when the rain started just as they reached his mount. Aulay was surprised, however, at how hard the downpour was. Cursing, he reached for the plaid he'd set on top of the basket, and then glanced around with dismay when he saw that it was missing. Spotting it back by where they'd started, he realized it must have fallen off the basket the moment they started to walk. He almost retrieved it, but then just left it. He'd hoped to drape it over Jetta to keep her as dry as possible, but by the time he got to the plaid and back she'd no doubt be drenched through anyway, so he left it where it lay and simply handed her the basket so that he could mount. Aulay then leaned down to catch Jetta under the arms and lifted her up before him, basket and all.

The ride back was made much faster than the ride out had been. Probably faster than it should have been even. Aulay knew he should ride with more care. A horse could lose its footing in such a storm, but Jetta had been sick for so long and was still weak enough that he was concerned getting caught out like this might set back her healing. He wanted desperately to get her back to the lodge, out of her wet clothes and in front of a nice fire as quickly as he could. He did his best to shelter Jetta with his body as they rode, but it was a futile effort and they were both soaked through by the time he reined in his mount in front of the lodge.

Scooping her up into his arms, Aulay dropped off his mount and then carried her to the door of the lodge. Fortunately, she had the presence of mind to reach out and open it for him, since his hands were full. He was able to carry her straight in. Setting her down, Aulay glanced around the main floor with a scowl. Not seeing Mavis anywhere around, and not wishing Jetta to try to take the stairs on her own, he suggested she warm herself by the cooking stove and then hurried back out to tend to his horse.

The beast was huffing and stamping his feet in the pouring rain, obviously not happy at being stuck in it. He followed eagerly when Aulay caught his reins and jogged to the small stables. Both of them were relieved to be out of the storm once in the small building. As worried as he was about Jetta, Aulay did not neglect his mount. He took the time to remove his saddle and dry the beast down before putting him in his stall.

Moving to the stable doors then, Aulay opened one and paused briefly in surprise when he saw that the storm had moved on. Thunder was still vibrating overhead, and he could see shafts of lightning in the distance, but the rain itself had died or now continued elsewhere. Releasing a relieved breath, he stepped outside and closed the stable doors, then headed for the lodge.

Aulay was halfway across the clearing to the lodge when the sight of Mavis coming out of the woods with a basket over her arm made him slow. She was a bit damp, but not soaking, so he supposed she must have found shelter from the worst of the storm. Aulay waited for her and nodded in greeting when she glanced up and noticed him.

"Ye're back, m'laird," she said solemnly as she approached. "Got caught in the storm I see."

"Aye. It hit just as we started back," he admitted.

Mavis nodded. "Fortunately, I was on me way back and near a large old oak when the storm started. It kept the worst of the rain off of me," she told him and then gestured to the basket she carried. "I went to see if I could find some eggs for lunch," she explained, drawing his gaze to the eggs nestled in the basket she carried. "I happened on a quail's nest and thought I'd make some papyns for the lass, and then I found several more nests so there is enough fer all o' us."

Despite having just eaten, Aulay smiled faintly at the thought of poached eggs in a golden sauce.

"I take it Simon found ye?" she commented, regaining his attention.

"Aye. He said ye told him where to find us?"

Mavis nodded. "He arrived just as I was leaving to look fer eggs. I refused to tell him where ye were at first. Did no' want him to ruin the lass's first excursion out o' the lodge, but when he told me what had happened, I kenned I had to send him yer way. Did Rory leave with him?"

"Aye," Aulay murmured. "Simon arrived just after we finished breaking our fast and Rory left right away with him."

Mavis nodded and then sighed wearily as she led the way to the lodge door. "'Tis a terrible thing about young Katie."

"Aye," he agreed solemnly, following her inside and pulling the door closed behind them.

"Is the lass back in her room?" Mavis asked, glancing around as she crossed to the cookstove.

"She must be," Aulay murmured, noting that the main floor was empty. He glanced toward the upper landing and saw that the door to their room was closed.

"Did she get as wet as ye are?" Mavis asked with a narrowing gaze.

"Unfortunately, aye," Aulay admitted, not happy at the fact. "I told her to warm herself by the cookstove, but—"

"She probably wanted to get out o' her wet clothes quick as she could," Mavis said, bringing him to a halt. Aulay had been heading for the stairs intending to check on her, but paused at that, quite sure walking in on her naked would not aid him in keeping his promise to his brother.

"I'll just set these aside for now and go check on the lass ere I cook 'em. She may want a bath to warm her up after her soaking," Mavis said, placing the basket on the table. She turned toward the stairs, and then paused and shook her head sadly. "Poor, wee Katie. Such a pretty lass with all that long black hair, and such a sweet girl too. Hard to believe anyone would want her dead."

"I'm sure 'twas an accident," Aulay said, surprised that she'd think otherwise. "A stray arrow from a hunter."

Mavis turned to peer at him with amazement. "A stray arrow from a hunter? She was shot just as they reached the drawbridge. What hunting would anyone be doing there?"

Aulay stiffened at this news. "The drawbridge?"

"Aye, that's what young Simon said," she announced firmly. "And whoever shot could no' be aiming at young Geordie either . . . unless they thought to shoot right through young Katie and into him. She was hit midback and straight on, Simon said." Mavis shook her head again and started up the stairs, muttering, "Nay, someone has it in fer our Katie. Someone who kens their way around a bow and arrow too. Lord help us, I do no' ken what the world is coming to when sweet young lasses like Katie are . . ."

Aulay didn't catch the rest. The woman had continued up the stairs as she spoke, her voice fading with each step. Frowning, he turned and moved to peer out the window, thinking that if what Mavis said was true, then Katie's getting shot was attempted murder. And, as laird, he should be looking into it right that moment. He should be finding the culprit and seeing them punished. The safety of the people of Buchanan was his responsibility, and he should be on his way back right that minute. Not loafing about at the lodge, trying not to make love to a woman who thought she was his wife, but wasn't.

Hands clenching into fists, Aulay whirled from the window and hurried upstairs, arranging things in his mind as he went. He couldn't take Jetta with him. She had no clothes. But he wouldn't leave her alone out here either. He'd leave Mavis with her for now, but he'd also send his uncle and half a dozen soldiers to guard them both until he could return. Or until he could find some damned dresses for the lass and bring her to join him at Buchanan. And he'd be quick about finding the culprit behind shooting Katie with the arrow. It shouldn't be that hard. As he recalled, she was a sweet young girl. In fact, the only motive he could think of for anyone wishing her harm was jealousy, either of her beauty, or of the attention Geordie showed her. His brother had proven himself quite taken with the lass these last couple months. In fact, he wouldn't be surprised if Geordie told him he wished to marry the girl.

Aulay frowned at the thought as he stepped off the stairs and started along the landing. He wasn't sure what he would do if and when that time finally came. Geordie was a nobleman, son of a baron, and Katie was the bastard daughter of a kitchen maid. That kind of union simply wasn't considered acceptable as a rule. At least not by most. The idea didn't bother him, though, but he did have to consider Geordie's future and how others would accept such a union.

Pondering that as he reached the bedroom door, Aulay opened it, strode inside and then came to an abrupt halt as he recalled why he'd been waiting below in the first place. Because Mavis was helping Jetta change. They weren't done with that task. Jetta was standing completely naked by the bed. The shift and plaid she'd been wearing were a soggy heap on the floor at her feet, and Mavis was approaching with a clean, dry shift for her to don. For one moment, Aulay let his gaze travel over all that beautiful naked flesh. He noted that she'd filled out a bit this last week and a half since she'd woken up, and that the bruises that had still been a faded nasty yellow when last he'd seen them were now completely gone, and then his gaze lifted to her face and he saw that she had spotted him and was staring at him wide-eyed and obviously embarrassed.

Jetta wasn't trying to cover herself though, he noted. And why should she? She thought him her husband with every right to look on her naked, he realized.

"I have to go," he said finally.

"Oh, m'laird," Mavis said with surprise. She peered at him wide-eyed and then glanced from him to Jetta and back, and simply dropped the shift over the lass's head and helped her get her arms through the arm holes. The maid then turned to him and asked politely, "Ye were saying?"

"I have to go," Aulay repeated, still staring at Jetta. In his mind he could still see her standing there gloriously nude.

"And where're ye going, m'laird?" Mavis asked patiently.

Aulay finally shifted his gaze to the maid. Only then was he able to regather his thoughts. Giving his head a shake, he cleared his throat and said, "I am returning to Buchanan to look into this matter with Katie. But I'll send Uncle Acair and some soldiers back to guard ye until I return."

Risking a look at Jetta, he noted her upset, and sighed. "I'm sorry, lass. I'd take ye with me, but we have no clothes fer ye yet. I'll see to that too while I'm there and bring ye back some pretty dresses to wear so ye're no' stuck here."

He watched several emotions cross her face; upset, worry, even fear and disappointment, but then she schooled her features into a calm expression, straightened her shoulders and nodded. "Very well, husband. Safe travels."

Aulay nodded and turned to the door, but then hesitated. It simply didn't feel right leaving her like this. Whirling back, he crossed the room and bent, intending to press a quick kiss to her forehead. She, however, tipped her head up at the last moment and his kiss landed on her mouth. The moment his lips met hers, Aulay gave up the idea of a quick kiss, and instead claimed her mouth properly.

Jetta needed no coaxing. Her mouth opened at once on a little sigh and when he felt her hands creep around his neck, he slid his own around her waist and pulled her close, then let his hands glide down her body until they cupped her bottom. Squeezing, Aulay lifted her slightly and straightened a bit, the action rubbing her groin against his, and then he eased her back to the floor and reluctantly broke their kiss.

"I have to go," he murmured again. "The safety of me people is me responsibility."

"Aye," she whispered solemnly. "Be safe, husband."

"And you, wife, stay safe until I return," he ordered huskily, and then, ignoring Mavis's raised eyebrows, he turned and strode quickly from the room before he changed his mind and took her to his bed instead. The woman was like some kind of madness in his blood. He walked around wanting her all the time. These last days of refusing to allow himself to touch her had been an agony. He really needed to find out who she was and set things to rights there. If he didn't soon do that, he feared that—despite his promises to Rory—he would end up bedding the lass and trapping her into having to marry him.

And don't think that idea didn't hold a hell of a lot of appeal to him. Having Jetta in his life always. A warm, welcoming wife who seemed blind to his scars and greeted him with eagerness. The only problem was, he suspected all of that would disappear did she learn they weren't really married. He suspected she was just making the best of the situation she found herself in, and that if she learned they weren't married and she could leave . . . she would.

It was what Adaira had done. Betrothed since birth, they'd grown up as neighbors, always knowing they would someday marry. They'd both been perfectly happy with it. They'd even loved each other, or so she'd said and he'd believed. But when he'd returned home scarred from battle, she'd taken one look at his ruined face and screamed in horror . . . and then she claimed him more monster than man and refused to marry him.

When her father had tried to force the marriage, announcing that it would go on as planned, she'd threatened to kill herself or flee to take the veil. Much to Aulay's relief, her father had relented then and broken the contract. By that point, he'd had no interest in marrying the woman himself. She wasn't, after all, the woman he'd thought her to be and he didn't want a wife who saw him as a monster. Even so, he would have married her to fulfill the contract if the father hadn't broken it. His honor would have demanded it.

Striding outside, Aulay walked to the small stable they'd built at the edge of the clearing to fetch and saddle his mount. He then led the beast out into the yard. His gaze slid to the bedroom window as he mounted. Spotting Jetta in the window, watching him as he settled in his saddle, he paused briefly and peered back at her for a moment. But then he raised his hand in a wave, turned his mount and headed off. It was surprisingly wrenching to leave her.

He'd pulled her from the water more than four weeks ago, but she hadn't been awake for more than twelve days, and yet he felt as if she'd been a part of his life for much longer. In fact, it was hard to recall his life before her arrival in it. Aulay didn't know how that had happened, but he needed to do something about it. He needed to toughen his heart against her . . . else he wouldn't survive when she finally left him.

Chapter 6

"THERE NOW, HE'S GONE," MAVIS SAID GENTLY AS THEY watched Aulay disappear into the trees. "Come sit yerself down and let me dry yer hair by the fire, lass. Then ye can come below with me and I'll make ye some lovely papyns fer the nooning."

"We just broke our fast," Jetta protested with amusement as she allowed Mavis to urge her away from the window.

"Aye, but by the time I get yer hair dry and make the papyns, 'twill be the nooning," the old servant assured her as she positioned her before the fire. Leaving her there, Mavis moved off to drag over one of the chairs from the table.

Jetta settled obediently in the chair and then closed her eyes as the woman set to work. First, Mavis used a fresh linen to soak up the worst of the water from her hair, and then she tossed that aside and set to work brushing the still-damp strands. She used long repetitive strokes, drawing the brush through Jetta's hair and lifting the damp tresses away from her scalp and neck so that the strands rose with the brush and then dropped to lay flat again, the action helping to dry it. It was oddly soothing, and Jetta nearly fell asleep in her chair before Mavis decided her hair was dry enough.

"There we are, that should do," Mavis announced, setting the brush aside. She turned back to survey her then and frowned slightly. "Ye look a bit tired, lass. Did ye still want to come below with me or would ye rather nap?"

"Oh nay! No nap." Jetta stood up at once, and tried to look more alert as she assured her, "I shall come below." It would be her second time out of the room since waking, and both in the same day. It wasn't something she wanted to give up on. Just the thought of it brightened her mood considerably.

"Verra well. Ye can sit at the table and keep me company while I cook," Mavis said brightly as she led her to the door. "And I'll tell ye all about wee Katie while I cook."

"The girl who was shot with the arrow?" Jetta asked. The maid had mentioned it as she'd helped her undress before Aulay had arrived.

"Aye, poor wee lass," Mavis said with a shake of the head as they started up the hall. "Ye remind me a bit o' her, actually. She's tiny and has long black hair too. O' course, she has it all o'er whereas Rory had to shave the back o' yer head. Still, otherwise, the two o' ye are quite alike."

Grimacing, Jetta raised a hand self-consciously to the back of her head.

Catching the action, Mavis clucked her tongue. "Oh, now, do no' fret, it'll grow back quick enough. Besides, it obviously does no' bother the laird. Just look at how he sticks close and rarely leaves yer side. Why I've never seen the man so happy. At least, no' since that Stuart bitch broke his heart."

Jetta's eyes widened in surprise at the curse, and she asked, "The Stuart . . . ?"

"Bitch," Mavis said helpfully as they started down the stairs, and then shook her head with disgust. "I do no' often cuss, and I do dislike calling another woman such a name, but that lass is one deserving o' it. She was a piece o' work, that one. I was no' at all surprised when she refused to marry our Aulay after he was scarred."

"She refused to marry him because of the scar?" Jetta asked with outrage.

"Aye, and no' kindly. Said he was a monster, she did, and that she'd rather die than have to look at his face all the rest o' her days. And him still in his sickbed, barely alive when she did it too," she added grimly.

"Bitch," Jetta breathed, horrified that anyone could be so cruel to such a kind man.

"There now, I told ye, did I no'?" Mavis said with satisfaction. "Aye, Adaira Stuart was a true bitch. She had most o' the nobles fooled thinking her sweet and kind, but no' me or any other servant she encountered. Adaira was sweet as honey on the tongue to all the men and any noble lady about, but get her alone in a room with a servant and she showed her true colors quick enough."

"She was unkind to the servants?" Jetta asked with a scowl. Her mother had taught her that one should always be kind to servants. She'd taught her to be kind to everyone, but especially peasants and servants. She'd said that their lives were hard, their days long and full of back-breaking labor, and they should be shown every kindness by those they worked so hard for. Of course, her father had never—

Jetta stopped walking abruptly as she suddenly realized she was re-membering something. Of course, the moment she realized that she was remembering something, the thoughts in her head dried up like a puddle under a hot sun.

"What is it, lass? Are ye all right?" Mavis asked with concern.

"Aye," Jetta sighed, and then forced a smile and continued down the stairs with her as she admitted, "Your words just made me remember something my mother once said."

"Ye got a memory back?" Mavis asked, obviously happy for her at the thought.

"Aye, a small one," she admitted, smiling faintly, and then squeezing the maid's hand, she suggested, "Mayhap if ye keep talking I'll remem-ber more."

"Oh, well then, I'll talk til I'm blue in the face, m'lady. That I will," she assured her cheerfully as they reached the bottom of the stairs and stepped off. Ushering her to a large wooden table with benches on either side, she said, "Now you just sit yerself down and I'll tell ye all about the nasty cow what broke our laird's heart."

Nodding, Jetta settled at the table to watch as Mavis started puttering about. After a moment though, she paused and lifted her head to sniff the air with a small frown. "Is something burning?"

Mavis stilled at the question, her own nose rising and beginning to twitch, and then her head turned sharply toward the fire and she rushed to it with an alarmed cry. "Me stew!"

Standing, Jetta followed and peered over the woman's shoulder as she cursed under her breath and began to poke at the stew over the fire with a wooden spoon.

"I suspected Rory had no' remembered the water and I did plan to check on it," she muttered with irritation. "That lad is always forgetting to do what I ask him. Ye'd think a lad bright as that could hold on to a thought fer more than a minute." Clucking, she added on a sigh, "But then mayhap he has too many thoughts in his head to hold on to a one." Shaking her head, she muttered, "I ken I should ha'e checked it, and I did plan to, but he said he had added the water, and then what with Simon arriving and me heading out to find eggs, and then the storm, I plum forgot . . ."

Tsking with irritation, she set the spoon aside and moved off to grab a bit of cloth to protect her hands as she lifted the pot off the hook over the fire. "Get the door for me, please lass."

Hurrying ahead of her, Jetta opened the door so Mavis could carry the pot out, but as the woman passed, she suggested, "Mayhap it can still be saved. Perhaps if ye scooped out the burned bits and—"

"Nay, lass. The charred flavor will be all through the stew. 'Tis fine though. I planned on papyns for the nooning meal, and there's still plenty o' time fer me to get some more stew going fer the sup. Now, just you go sit down, I will no' be a minute getting rid of this."

Jetta watched her walk off toward the stables. At least, she thought she was headed to the stables, but the maid paused and tipped the heavy pot to dump its contents on the ground at the base of a tree next to the stables. Sighing, Jetta pushed the door closed and moved to sit at the table again and wait as she'd been instructed.

JETTA WOKE WITH A START AND SAT UP SHARPLY IN BED, HER eyes darting around for the source of the sound that had roused her from sleep. For a moment she was confused and befuddled, not recognizing the strange room she was in. Certainly, it wasn't her bedchamber at Fitton. That room was much larger, the bed having a canopy and curtains you could use to close out light and sound. This room was—

At the lodge, Jetta realized suddenly, her mind clearing as she swung her feet over the side of the bed and they landed on the pallet still lying beside it. The pallet her husband usually slept on. Or had, she supposed, since he'd left for Buchanan and would not be sleeping there this night. She'd have the room all to herself, Jetta thought, and glanced around as the last of her confusion drifted away.

She'd stayed below with Mavis while the woman cooked the papyns, but once they'd eaten the delicious eggs in a rich sauce, Jetta had suddenly found herself exhausted. So much so, she hadn't even argued when Mavis had suggested she have a little lie down and rest a bit. The woman had seen her up here and tucked her in, and that was the last thing Jetta recalled. She couldn't have slept too, too long though, Jetta decided as she noted the bright sunlight streaming through the open shutters at the window.

"He was poisoned I tell ye!"

Frowning at the shouted words from outside, Jetta pushed herself off the bed and moved to the window to peer out. Her eyes widened as she looked down at the half a dozen or so men gathered near the tree by the stables. They were standing around something lying at the base of the tree where Mavis had dumped the stew. All of them were now talking at the same time so that Jetta couldn't tell what was being said anymore.

"What the devil's going on?"

Jetta's gaze shifted quickly to a man who had just come out of the lodge. At first she was sure it was Aulay. His height, size, stride, even his voice were so similar to her husband's that she was sure it was him, but then she noted the gray streaks in the man's hair and decided it must be the Uncle Acair that Aulay had assured them he'd send out to stay with them while he was at Buchanan. She knew she was right when Mavis suddenly hurried out of the lodge and rushed toward the man, crying, "What is it, Acair? What's amiss?"

Jetta's eyebrows widened slightly as she watched the maid. Mavis wasn't looking her usual self. Her clothes were a bit awry, her face flushed, and the way she was looking at and addressing Aulay's uncle was . . . well, frankly it was far more like he was a beau than a lord. The way Acair was looking at Mavis told a story of its own too. The two of them were obviously lovers, Jetta decided as Acair broke away from the men and moved to intercept Mavis. Taking her arm, he gently ushered her back toward the cottage, murmuring in her ear as he did and bringing a look of dismay to her face.

Jetta watched until they disappeared inside again, and then shifted her gaze back to the men by the tree. Several of them had moved away now and she could see one was sitting on the ground, holding what appeared to be a dead dog in his lap. He was rocking it back and forth, his face full of sorrow.

Frowning, Jetta started to withdraw from the window, intending to go below and find out what was going on, but then a splash of color in the trees caught her eye. Pausing, she searched the woods beyond the stables and could have sworn she saw someone moving away through the woods. Someone in colorful clothing and moving swiftly. That was all she saw though before whoever it was moved completely out of sight.

One of the men, Jetta told herself. Perhaps looking for a spot to relieve himself or a place to bury the dog, she thought as she headed for the door. Although none of the other men were wearing bright colors, Jetta considered as she opened the door and stepped out onto the landing.

"Oh, lass, I was just coming to check on ye. I was afraid all the foofaraw may have woken ye."

Jetta paused and smiled with concern at Mavis as the older woman rushed toward her from the stairs. "What happened?"

"Oh, 'tis an awful thing. Young Robbie's dog was poisoned," she said unhappily, catching her arm, and urging her back the way she'd come. "Poor thing. He was a good dog too. All the lads liked him. But he ate that burned stew I threw out and . . ." She shook her head unhappily. "There must have been some kind o' poisonous plant at the base o' the tree where I threw out the stew and he ate some o' it along with the stew. 'Tis the only thing I can think could ha'e happened. But the poor beast is dead."

"Oh no," Jetta said with dismay, despite having seen the dead dog. Somehow hearing what had happened was worse than seeing the dog lying in the man's lap. In truth, he'd looked as if he could have been sleeping when she'd seen him. But hearing about it, well, she recalled how upset she'd been when her own dog, Jezebel, had died and—

"Aye, I'm afraid so, and I feel just awful about it. Had I tossed the stew somewhere else, or . . ." She shook her head. "Poor beast. He really was a good dog."

Deciding now was not the time to talk about her having another memory returned to her, Jetta merely nodded and allowed herself to be drawn back into the bedchamber. But this new memory reminded her that she'd had another memory when she'd first woken up. Of her bedroom back at . . . damn, where had it been? She was sure a name had come to her as she'd thought of her bedchamber at home. Now all that remained was a vague idea of a curtained bed or something, and she couldn't recall the name that had come to her mind with the image. The memory had faded like the remnants of a dream from her mind.

"Poor beast," Mavis murmured again as she closed the door behind them. "Come along, the plaid ye were wearing should be dry by now. Let's get it on ye so ye can go below. Acair's curious to speak with ye now ye're awake."

"That *was* Uncle Acair I saw outside, then?" Jetta asked, pleased that she'd guessed right.

"Aye. He and the boys arrived just after ye fell asleep. The laird sent them to guard us until he can return," Mavis explained as she felt the plaid she'd laid over a chair by the fire, and—apparently finding it dry—retrieved it and laid it out on the floor to begin putting pleats into the material.

Jetta crossed the room to join her. "Let me do that, Mavis. I need to learn how."

"So, there still is no news on a ship that sank?" Aulay asked with a frown. This was the first chance he'd got to ask his brother what he and Geordie had learned while out looking for news of the ship Jetta had been on. He hadn't felt right about asking Geordie when he'd gone to see him in the room where Rory was tending Katie. His brother had been so pale and upset over the maid, he'd let the matter go and asked Conran to follow him below to talk to him instead. This, however, was not the news he'd hoped to get from his brother, Aulay thought, as he watched Conran shake his head.

"Nay. I did no' learn anything more than Geordie and Alick did the first time. Neither did Geordie," he added, and then explained, "We met on the ride back and talked. We rode together the last part o' the way until we encountered Katie." Mouth tightening, he added, "I should ne'er ha'e taken the lead. I should have ridden behind them to watch their backs."

"Ye could no' ha'e kenned that was going to happen," Aulay said firmly. "And yer being behind them probably would no' ha'e changed anything."

"Mayhap," Conran said unhappily, and then breathed out a sigh and said, "Anyway, neither Geordie nor I found even a whisper o' news about a ship that sank in that storm three weeks ago. Well, almost five weeks now," he said grimly. "It just did no' happen."

"Well, Jetta had to come from somewhere," Aulay growled with frustration.

"Aye," Conran agreed and then asked, "Ye're sure it was the mast o' a ship she was strapped to?"

"Aye. The crow's nest was mostly still intact, and the sail still attached. It was definitely a mast," he assured him.

"What the devil happened to the ship, then?" Conran was beginning to sound frustrated too.

Aulay scowled, but then stilled.

"What?" Conran asked at once. "Have ye an idea?"

Aulay was silent for a minute, considering the thought that had just popped into his head. Finally, he nodded. "I'm thinkin' mayhap the ship did no' sink."

Conran raised his eyebrows at the suggestion. "So 'twas no' a mast ye found her tied to?"

"Aye, it was," Aulay assured him.

"Well then—"

"Da told me once about a ship he traveled on, and a storm that came on so fast and rough the wind snapped the mast just below the crow's nest ere they could lower the sails."

Conran considered that briefly. "And ye're thinking mayhap the same thing happened here, only much lower on the mast?"

"Aye," Aulay growled. "The mast could have had a weakness at the base that snapped when the storm struck."

"Taking Jetta with it," Conran said slowly.

"But leaving the ship afloat," Aulay finished grimly.

"We did hear mention o' a ship or two taking damage in the storm and limping into one port or another fer repairs," Conran told him.

"Had any lost their masts?" he asked sharply.

Conran shook his head. "I do no' ken. I did no' ask what kind o' damage. We were looking for a boat we'd thought had sunk."

Aulay cursed.

"We can ride out again and ask about ships with damage," Conran offered.

"Nay. Ye can't," he said abruptly. "I need ye here to sit with Geordie."

When Conran's eyebrows rose, Aulay frowned and considered the situation briefly. He hadn't yet had a chance to talk to the men who were on the wall when Katie took the arrow. By the time he got back to Buchanan, sent Uncle Acair back to the lodge with some men, and talked to Geordie, the men who had been on the wall had all finished their shift. But if they'd seen anything of import, they'd have told Acair, so he didn't expect to learn much from them anyway. And he had men out searching the woods, but wasn't holding out much hope there either. As far as he could tell, his only hope of catching Katie's attacker was if they tried again to kill her.

"To comfort Geordie, or protect Kate?" Conran asked finally, when Aulay remained lost in his thoughts.

Aulay considered explaining his thinking, but in the end, merely said, "Both."

"So ye *do* think Kate's attacker may try again," Conran said with a frown. "Does Geordie know?"

"Nay." Aulay saw no reason to worry Geordie with this added issue.

He was concerned enough about the lass. "I do no' want him or anyone else to ken ye're guarding them. That way, should Geordie leave the room to visit the garderobe, Kate's attacker will think the way clear to make another attempt."

"How are we to manage me guarding them without Geordie knowing?" Conran asked with a frown.

"The passages," Aulay said. "Ye'll ride out on a supposed chore for me, and take the passages back in. Ye can watch the room from there."

"Ahhh," Conran said with sudden understanding. "That would be why ye had Katie moved to Saidh's old room when ye got back this morn. The guest chamber she was in could no' be reached by the tunnels."

"Aye."

"What if Katie dies ere another attempt is made?" Conran asked. "Rory has no' held out much hope o' her recovering. Whoever shot the arrow at her may just be waiting to see if she dies from her injuries from the first attempt."

Aulay scowled over that. There was a good possibility that might happen. And then once the lass died, another attempt would be unnecessary and they would never find out who had killed her. He didn't like that thought at all. Young Katie deserved justice.

"I'll have Rory suggest she's improving," Aulay said, thinking he'd have to have him say it in the Great Hall in front of a crowd of their people. He'd ask how the lass was, and Rory could say she was much stronger than expected and improving.

"That should work," Conran said with a nod. "Whoever shot her with the arrow is more likely to make a second attempt if they think she is getting better." Conran picked up his ale and took a long swallow. Setting his drink down then, he nodded again and said, "Verra well. I'll head out right away."

Aulay shook his head. "'Tis nearly the sup. Ye'd never set out on a journey this late in the day. Ye can set out in the morn."

Conran frowned and shook his head. "I do no' like the idea o' leaving Geordie and Katie unprotected all night. I'll say I'm retiring early to rest up for my trip tomorrow, and then slip into the passage from me room tonight. Then I'll ride out in the morn and slip back through the passages to continue watching the room."

Aulay shook his head at once. Conran couldn't watch all night and tomorrow too. "I'll watch the room tonight, so ye can rest up to watch tomorrow."

"Truly?" Conran asked with surprise.

Aulay arched his eyebrows. "Ye need no' sound so surprised. I do do things around here too."

"Well, aye, usually," he agreed. "But this will leave you missing out on rest, fer I ken ye'll no' be left to sleep the morn away tomorrow. Half the population o' Buchanan seems ready to pester you with complaints now ye're back after having been away this past month."

"Aye," Aulay said dryly. It was part of the reason it had taken him so long to get his uncle off on his way to the lodge and then to get up to see Geordie. He'd been constantly stopped by people with one problem or another he needed to sort out for them. In fact, Aulay was rather amazed he'd managed to have this conversation with Conran without interruption. As if he'd jinxed himself with the thought, the keep doors opened, and the stable master entered, looked around, spotted him at the table and hurried toward them.

"Do no' worry about me and sleep," Aulay said finally as he got to his feet. "I had four weeks o' little but sleep. I'll survive a night or two without."

Leaving Conran at the table, he walked to meet the stable master and see what was wrong.

Chapter 7

*A*ULAY WAS IN A DEEP SLUMBER WHEN A SOFT KNOCK AT THE door stirred him. Blinking sleepily, he glanced toward the window to see the weak early morning light seeping through. The sun wasn't even fully up, he noted with a frown and sat up in the bed, finding it odd to be in one after nearly five weeks on the pallet on the floor that he'd been calling bed since Jetta's arrival in his life. Actually, he recalled suddenly, he hadn't really slept in this one. At least, not for long. Conran had only relieved him from watching Geordie and Katie moments ago from what he could tell. By his guess, he'd got perhaps ten minutes of sleep.

Groaning at the thought, Aulay climbed from the bed and crossed the room in his bed shirt, thinking Jetta would probably tease him did she see him in it. He followed the thought with a shake of the head meant to remove thoughts of his wee counterfeit wife.

Aulay had been doing his best not to think of Jetta since leaving the lodge. But that was something he was finding ridiculously hard to do. From the moment he'd ridden away from the lodge, everything had seemed to remind him of her. His horse's tail, he'd noted, was the same jet black as her hair. The grass under the bright sunlight was the same sparkling green as her eyes. The fluffy white clouds filling the sky overhead after the storm had made him think of her porcelain skin . . . and that had just been during the first few minutes of his journey back. It had continued all the way here and still continued.

When he'd had Rory take him to see Katie on his arrival here, the dark-haired maid lying pale and still in the bed had reminded Aulay of Jetta when she'd still been unconscious. The maid was petite like her, and had the same dark hair as well. Knowing she probably didn't look all that much like Jetta, and that it was just his infatuated mind seeing Jetta everywhere, Aulay had then gone below to talk to his uncle and find out what they'd learned about the attack. Servants had immediately brought pastries for him to break his fast with and he'd thought that, as nice as Mavis's pastries had been, Cook's were better and he should take some back for Jetta when he returned.

Truly, he did not seem able to have a single thought enter his head without it somehow leading to thoughts of Jetta. That realization had led Aulay to acknowledging that he was never going to break this attraction he had for her. Knowing that, he'd also quite plainly seen his future. Jetta would somehow find out they were not married and leave him, and he would be a broken man. It was that simple. Aulay had thought he was broken after the injury he took and Adaira's leaving him, but suspected that would be nothing next to his losing Jetta. This loss, he feared, was one he would not recover from.

Made irritable by the thought, he pulled his door open and scowled at the knocker. When Aulay realized it was Alick, his scowl merely deepened. "Where the devil ha'e you been?"

Eyes widening with surprise, his younger brother frowned. "Did Rory no' tell ye? I went to see Saidh and Greer."

"Aye, he told me," Aulay admitted. "But that was two weeks ago. What the devil took ye so long?"

"They were away when I arrived at MacDonnell," he explained. "Off visiting Niels and Edith on their way north. So I rested overnight at MacDonnell and then followed them to Drummond. But by the time I arrived, they'd left Drummond for Carmichael, to see Dougall and Murine. Well," he said with apparent exasperation. "O' course, Edith insisted I rest the night before continuing on and . . ."

Aulay listened absently to his brother's long, drawn-out explanation, or perhaps he didn't really listen at all. Mostly he was wondering to himself if Jetta would like Edith, Murine, Jo and Saidh. His sister was thick as thieves with her friends, which was a good thing since two of them were now married to two of his brothers. But he suspected Jetta would like them. She'd probably like their friend Jo, too, and fit in easily with the group of women. And they, of course, would love her, he decided. She was clever and sweet with a wonderful sense of humor. How could they help but love her?

They couldn't, Aulay decided firmly and returned his attention to his brother as he concluded, "We finally caught up with them as they returned home to MacDonnell, but the minute I finished explaining about Jetta, Saidh insisted on heading here. O' course, she first had to pack fresh clothes and Greer had to take care o' some business, so we did no' leave right away, but, finally, here we are," Alick finished.

"Here ye are," Aulay agreed dryly. "But why are ye knocking on me door so early in the morning?"

Alick grimaced. "Well, ye ken what Saidh is like. She was threatening to come up here and wake ye herself, but I thought it best to warn ye first."

"Warn me o' what?" Aulay asked with grim suspicion.

"Oh . . . er . . ."

Aulay narrowed his eyes. "Ye did no' just tell her we rescued the lass from the water, did ye?" he accused. "What else did ye tell her?"

Alick grimaced. "I did no' mean to tell her anything. It just slipped out."

Snorting with disgust, Aulay turned and strode back across his room to snatch up his plaid and begin pleating it. "What does she ken?"

"Er . . . well . . ." Alick hesitated, and licked his lips nervously as he watched Aulay finish his pleating and then don the plaid and fasten it in place.

"Well?" Aulay prompted, turning to spear his brother with a look.

Alick winced and then admitted apologetically, "Everything."

"Damn ye, Alick," Aulay growled, and strode past him to head out of the room.

"Well, ye ken how she can be," Alick muttered, hard on his heels. "Once Saidh knew about Jetta, she insisted on picking at me until she got every last detail."

Aulay snorted, knowing it wouldn't have taken all that much picking to get Alick to talk. The lad gossiped like an old woman.

"But 'tis fine," Alick assured him. "'Tis no' like ye're doing anything wrong. Ye saved the lass's life, and yer taking care o' her, nursing her back to health yerself and everything. I told Saidh how ye've been feeding her and entertaining her and not left her side. I'm sure she's just curious."

"Aye," Aulay muttered dryly, not believing that for a second. He didn't doubt for a minute that it was more than mere curiosity. His sister was here to ask him questions he had no desire to answer, or even think about. Things like why had he not tried harder to find out who Jetta might be and where she belonged or who her family was? And how and when did he intend to tell Jetta that they were not really husband and wife?

Cursing under his breath, Aulay straightened his shoulders as he descended the stairs. His sister could be a royal pain when she wanted to be, and he suspected she would want to be in this case. She was a protector by nature, standing up for others and fighting for their rights whenever she felt it necessary. He had no doubt she would feel the right thing to do here was tell Jetta everything and do all they could to find out who she was and where she belonged. The problem was, he wasn't eager to do that. He knew he should be. He even felt he should be. But he didn't want to. Besides, doing so might endanger the woman. They needed to find out what the situation was before they even considered revealing to her family that she was alive.

Which meant finding out who she was and where she was from, something he hadn't managed to do so far, he admitted guiltily. The guilt was because he hadn't really tried all that hard. While there not being a ship that sank was a stumbling block, there were other ways to find out where she came from and what her name was. He simply hadn't bothered to try any of them.

And why hadn't he done that? Because Aulay liked Jetta. He liked talking to her and he liked the way she looked at him. There was no fear or revulsion in her expression when she peered at his face. It was as if it wasn't just her memory she'd lost, but her vision as well, and Aulay had even suspected that was the case until Rory had tested her vision and assured him that she saw just fine. So she simply didn't appear to be horrified by the scar on his face, which was a miracle to his mind. The woman was beautiful, and grew more so every day as she regained some of the weight she'd lost while unconscious. And she seemed to like him, to truly like him.

"What are ye doing to find Jetta's people and learn her real name and situation?"

Aulay tore himself from his thoughts and scowled at his sister at that question. He hadn't even yet reached the table and she was already on her feet and marching toward him, grilling him like he was a naughty lad up to mischief. Which was exactly what he'd expected. He supposed it was good that he knew her so well.

"And good morn to ye too, sister. I hope yer journey here was uneventful," Aulay said mildly as he reached her and bent to press a kiss to her cheek. Straightening, he then offered a nod of greeting to her husband, Greer MacDonnell, who was still seated at the trestle tables, chewing on a pastry. The sight made his stomach growl with hunger.

"Aulay," Saidh said in warning, dragging his attention back to her. "Alick said the girl does no' remember a thing and thinks ye're married and that she *sleeps in yer bed with ye*. How could ye take advantage o' the lass like that? Ye—"

"I suggest ye stop there ere ye say something we shall both regret," Aulay said coldly, interrupting her diatribe. She did stop, but she also eyed him with anger and disappointment. Ignoring that for the moment, he turned to scowl at Alick and said, "Ye did no' bother to mention that I am sleeping on a pallet on the floor, while Jetta occupies me bed?"

"How could I tell her that?" Alick asked with surprise. "I did no' ken it."

Aulay blinked at the claim and then frowned as he realized he hadn't really discussed the sleeping arrangements with anyone but Rory. Actually, he hadn't discussed much of anything with anyone since Jetta had arrived. He'd been at the lodge with her for weeks, passing the hours at her bedside, at first just watching her sleep and looking for any sign she might wake. Once she did wake, he'd then spent his time at her side, plying her with food and drink and answering her questions about Buchanan and its people as she tried to find memories of her life here and the people in it that simply didn't exist.

"So ye ha'e no' taken advantage?" Saidh asked.

"O' course no'," Aulay snapped, turning his attention to Saidh again and noting the relief rushing over her. Rather than being pleased that she believed him, Aulay was actually even more annoyed at this proof that she'd thought so poorly of him. Forget that he'd come quite close to taking advantage of Jetta a time or two, the fact was, he hadn't. And wouldn't. And Saidh should know that.

"Ye ken me, Saidh," he said grimly. "How could ye think fer a minute that I'd take advantage o' a wee, beautiful lass in such a sad state?"

"Well, I did no' at first," she assured him apologetically. "But Alick said—"

Aulay waved away her words and moved around her to settle at the table and pour himself some cider. He'd barely finished the task when a tray with several pastries on it was set before him. Taking one of the still-warm treats, he popped it in his mouth and began to chew.

"I'm sorry, Aulay," Saidh said on a sigh, settling next to him and placing a hand on his arm. "I do ken better than that. I should ha'e realized Alick had it all wrong. He usually does."

"Hey!" Alick protested. "I was no' wrong . . . exactly. I said she was in his bed and she is. I just did no' ken he was on the floor rather than in bed with her. And she *does* think he's her husband," he pointed out.

"Aye. About that," Saidh murmured and arched her eyebrows at him.

"She came to that conclusion herself when she first woke," Aulay said. "She thought only a husband would be in her bedroom. She was even dismayed to have Rory in there, despite his being a healer. And Rory suggested we no' correct her. He does no' wish us to upset her any more than necessary lest we set back her healing."

"Aye, Alick explained that," Saidh said diffidently. "But surely she's past the delicate stage now and could be told. Do ye no' think?"

"Rory thinks not," he said with a shrug. "Ye shall ha'e to talk to him about that."

"Verra well." Saidh patted his arm gently, as if she thought he needed soothing, and then she cleared her throat and said, "And what of finding her family?"

Aulay stiffened and then turned to glare at Saidh's husband, Greer, as if her words were somehow his brother-in-law's fault.

"Do no' look at me that way," the MacDonnell said dryly and then pointed out, "She is *your* sister and was full-grown when I met her. I did no' make her this way. I just love her the way she is."

Clucking with disgust at the soft sentiment, Aulay picked up his cider and took a swig.

"Aulay?" Saidh said firmly. "What have ye done about trying to find out who she is and where she comes from?"

"I told her that ye sent us out to ask about what ship might have sunk in that storm," Alick assured him quickly, and then turned to Saidh and reminded her, "And I told you that as far as anyone knew, none had."

"Aye. At that time, mayhap," Saidh said solemnly. "But have ye sent men to ask since? Surely, someone will realize by now that her ship did no' arrive where it was headed?"

Aulay turned another glare on Alick, and the younger man made a face.

"I did try to tell ye about that too, Saidh," Alick said with disgust. "I tried to tell ye that ere I left Buchanan, Geordie and Conran had headed out to try again."

"And?" Saidh asked, spearing Aulay with her eyes. "What happened?"

"Still no news o' a ship that sank," Aulay growled.

"Then mayhap the ship did no' sink," Saidh said at once. "Alick did mention that there was no debris in the water besides the mast. Mayhap the mast was claimed by the storm, but the ship survived."

She looked so damned pleased with herself for the suggestion that Aulay almost felt bad for the pleasure it gave him to say, "That thought had occurred to me, Saidh. And I did plan to send Conran and Geordie out again, eventually. But Geordie is no' likely to want to leave Katie just now and Conran is . . . away at the moment."

"Then send someone else," she said at once. "One of the soldiers can ask questions as easily as Geordie and Conran."

"Nay," Aulay said abruptly as Rory approached the table.

"Why not?" she demanded.

"The situation is much too tricky to trust to just anyone, Saidh," Rory explained when Aulay couldn't be bothered to, and then frowned and asked, "Did Alick no' tell ye that there is some concern fer the lass's life?"

"Aye, he mentioned that she said something about a cat, a white lady and a betrothed who wasn't a betrothed, who would kill her," Saidh admitted, and then added, "but since none of that makes any sense, is it no' possible that 'twas just a fevered dream she was telling ye about?"

Aulay stiffened at the suggestion. It was not something he'd considered, and it did seem possible, but after contemplating it briefly, he shook his head. "It matters little. She was terrified at the mention o' her family and I'll no' risk returning her to people who might be sending her to her death." Eyeing her coldly, he added, "And ye should no' expect me to. Ye certainly did no wish us to send Murine back to her brother, or leave Edith to the care o' her murderous family."

"That was different," Saidh said at once.

"Was it?" her husband asked gently.

Biting her lip uncertainly, Saidh turned to peer at Greer, and asked, "Ye think she really may have a family like Murine or Edith's?"

Greer considered the matter and then said, "I think Aulay is right to move cautiously here until we ken if that is no' the case fer this poor lass. It would be a shame if he and Alick rescued her and then he and Rory put such time and care into healing her, only to hand her over to a family who would see her dead anyway."

Saidh's shoulders slumped slightly as she released a sigh, and then she turned to peer at Aulay for a moment, before finally saying, "Well then, we shall ha'e to figure a way to find out who she is without giving away that she is here until we ken that 'tis safe to do so."

Aulay merely grunted and picked up a pastry. It was exactly what he'd been saying. He bit into his pastry with a little sigh of pleasure.

"I would like to meet her," Saidh announced, standing up. "I presume she is up in yer room?"

Shaking his head, Aulay swallowed the food in his mouth, intending to answer, but Rory did it first.

"She is still at the lodge."

"Ye left her alone when she may have a murderous family out to get her?" she asked with dismay.

"She's no' alone. Uncle Acair and a retinue of soldiers are there with her. As is Mavis. Besides, her family do no' ken she is there," Aulay said at once. "They can't. We do no' even ken who *they* are," he pointed out with exasperation. "Besides, I could no' bring her back. She has no clothes."

"Oh aye," Saidh said, her expression clearing. "Alick mentioned that."

Aulay was just relaxing again, when she suddenly nodded and headed for the keep doors. "Well, that can be fixed quickly enough. We brought some dresses fer her. I'll head to the lodge now and give them to her. That way I can meet her too."

"Men!" Greer barked, grabbing several pastries to take with him as he got to his feet.

Aulay raised his eyebrows as a dozen MacDonnell soldiers immediately stood at the far end of the trestle tables and started to follow their lady. Turning his gaze back to his brother-in-law, he asked, "Is there something ye've no' told us?"

Greer paused and glanced to him in question. "What do ye mean?"

"Well, 'tis no' a long trip. Ye really do no' need yer men to ride to the lodge and back," he pointed out. "Is someone out to harm me sister? Again?"

"Oh." He smiled. "Nay. The men are needed to drive and guard the wagons with the chests o' dresses in them."

The MacDonnell hurried off then, leaving Aulay staring after him.

"Just how many chests and wagons are there?" he muttered to himself.

"Six chests, three wagons," Alick answered, bringing Aulay's head around his way.

"Six?" he asked with disbelief.

The younger man clucked his tongue with disgust. "I knew ye were no' listening to me up in yer room when I was telling ye o' me trials trying to find Saidh."

"Six?" Aulay repeated.

"I told ye!" he said with exasperation. "I'd just missed Saidh and Greer when I got to MacDonnell. They'd already left to see Niels and Edith at Drummond, but were gone from there too when I reached Drummond. They'd left there for Carmichael to see Dougall and Murine. But I stopped the night at Drummond and when Edith heard about poor wee Jetta, she decided she'd send some dresses and managed to fill a whole chest for me to take," he explained. "She e'en gave me a wagon to harness to me horse to cart it in. O' course, dragging the wagon with the chest in it slowed me down further and by the time I got to Carmichael, Saidh and Greer had already left there as well. They were headed for Sinclair. I stayed the night at Carmichael and when Murine heard Jetta's sad tale, she filled a chest for me to take in the wagon too. And then—"

"Let me guess," Aulay interrupted dryly. "Saidh and Greer had already left Sinclair by the time ye got there too, but Jo and Campbell Sinclair insisted ye stay the night, heard the tale, and gave ye a chest as well."

"Three chests," Alick corrected him, his expression grim.

"Three?" Aulay echoed with surprise.

"Aye, one with dresses in it, and two with bolts o' fabric she thought Jetta might use to make gowns in a fashion she preferred," he explained, and then added with disgust, "I needed a bigger wagon and another horse to help pull it, and now I was going ridiculously slowly."

"Aye, I can imagine," Aulay growled.

"Me next stop was MacDonnell again, where I finally caught up with Saidh and Greer, and she supplied a chest o' dresses as well. But they decided on three midsized carts rather than the large one in hopes we could travel more quickly."

"So ye went all the way up to Sinclair," Aulay muttered, shaking his head.

"I ha'e been everywhere this past week," Alick said with disgust, and then accused him, "Ye truly did no' listen to a word I said in yer bedchamber, did ye?"

Aulay stared at him for a minute, and then rather than answer the question, growled, "And ye told all o' them about Jetta?"

"Uh," Alick said weakly. "Well . . ."

Aulay closed his eyes.

"I suspect that means we'll be having more company within the week," Rory put in, sounding cheerful.

"More like within the next hour," Alick said apologetically. "They were all eager to come meet Jetta and sent messengers to MacDonnell yester eve with news they'd be arriving at Buchanan this morning. 'Tis why we left so early. Saidh wanted to be here to greet them."

"God's teeth," Aulay muttered with disgust. His home was about to be invaded by three more very beautiful, very kind and very sweet busy-bodies who would help his sister interfere horribly in his life, he thought and then frowned as a thought struck him. Scowling at Alick, he asked shortly, "If Edith gave ye a chest o' damned dresses, why did ye no' just return to Buchanan then? Why continue to hunt down Saidh? The dresses were what were wanted."

"Aye, but I kenned ye'd want Saidh and the others here for the wedding," he pointed out as if that should be obvious, and then added, "Finding them all now saved me having to find them later."

"What wedding?" Aulay asked with bewilderment.

"Yours . . . to Jetta. I felt sure ye'd want to marry her now that ye've taken her to yer bed."

"I didn't take her—she is alone in me bed," Aulay growled furiously. "Her honor is safe."

"Aye, but no one else kens that, and she's obviously a noble lady. Ye can't just tell her ye're her husband, let people think ye've bedded her, and then not marry her. She's ruined now whether ye've slept with her or no'," he pointed out, and Aulay suddenly understood. Alick had continued to hunt Saidh because it allowed him to call in reinforcements. The rest of the family had been dragged into it, to force him to marry Jetta if he didn't agree to do so willingly. Dear God, they would force Jetta to marry him whether she wanted to or not if he didn't do something to prevent it.

Glancing toward the keep doors, Aulay stood abruptly, thinking only that he needed to beat Saidh to the lodge, collect Jetta and flee. Where to, he didn't know, but fleeing was the only way to save her from being forced to marry him when she might not want to.

"Did ye no' mention to me last night that ye wanted to question the men who were on the gate about what they may or may no' ha'e seen when Katie was shot with the arrow?" Rory asked solemnly.

Aulay paused and turned on him with a scowl. Leave it to Rory to be his conscience. His younger brother had been doing that for the last five weeks when it came to his interactions with Jetta and he was growing heartily sick of it. Besides, that was before he'd learned the four horsewomen of the Apocalypse were about to descend on him. Well, three, he supposed. One of them was already here.

"Saidh loves ye," Rory said solemnly. "So do Murine and Edith, and Jo likes ye too. And all four o' them are kind. They'll no' harm Jetta or do anything to hurt you." He allowed that to sink in and then added, "And Geordie and Katie need ye here."

Aulay hesitated, but then sank back in his seat with a sigh. Four horsewomen of the Apocalypse or not, he had responsibilities to attend.

Chapter 8

"*O*H AYE, AULAY WAS A LIGHTHEARTED AND CHARMING DEVIL ere the wound he took to the face," Acair Buchanan assured Jetta. "Went all solemn and quiet afterward though. I blame that whor—lass," he corrected himself quickly and rushed on, "that lass he was betrothed to. Tossed him over like bad ale once he was scarred, she did."

Jetta nodded solemnly. "Mavis told me about Adaira."

"Aye, Adaira," Uncle Acair said with disgust and then shook his head and added, "she always seemed like such a nice wee lass. But once he was scarred . . ." Acair's mouth tightened.

"Do you know what became of her?" Jetta asked with curiosity. Mavis hadn't said. "Did she ever marry?"

"Aye." His mouth twisted angrily. "The wedding was barely canceled when we got word she'd run off to marry some heir to a marquis or something. She ended up in France o' all places if ye can imagine. Probably suits her. The French all think they're better than everyone else anyway, and so did Adaira. But then, her mother was French, so I suppose she came by it natural-like."

Jetta's eyebrows drew together as she considered what he'd said. His words had twigged something in her memory. Obviously, she'd heard this story before from Mavis, at least parts of it. Or she may have heard it all ere her head injury, she thought and waited briefly for the twig to surface fully enough for her to grab at it, but that small twigging was all she got.

Sighing, she let go of it and asked Acair the questions she hadn't thought to ask Mavis. "Then how did my husband and I become betrothed? Did my parents not arrange a betrothal for me at birth, or shortly afterward, as is the custom? I mean, I could not have been betrothed to him from birth if he was already betrothed to Adaira. Did my own betrothed die as a child, leaving me available to be betrothed to Aulay?"

"Oh . . . er . . ." Uncle Acair glanced around as if for aid, but he and Mavis were the only ones there besides Jetta. All of his men were outside, guarding the cabin in shifts with half standing guard while the other half slept in a small tent they'd set up next to the stables. Uncle Acair himself had taken the second bedroom in the lodge, and Mavis had slept on a pallet in Jetta's room. She had offered the old woman the other half of the bed, not seeing any need for her to sleep on pallets on the cold hard floor, but the maid had refused, insisting she was used to it and wouldn't sleep well in the "soft, hot" bed.

"What's got yer attention there, Mavis?" Uncle Acair asked suddenly, apparently distracted from her question.

Jetta followed his gaze to the maid, growing curious herself when she noted the still and alert stance the woman had taken at the window.

"I thought I heard laughing," Mavis murmured, not taking her eyes off the scene beyond the open window shutters.

Uncle Acair shared a wry smile with Jetta. "Aye, well, the men do laugh on occasion."

"Nay, no' the men. I thought I heard women's laughter," Mavis said quietly, obviously still listening. "Oh! 'Tis m'lady Saidh!"

Jetta's eyes widened with sudden alarm and she glanced down at the plaid she wore over her shift. She'd woken up before Mavis this morn and had pleated and donned it herself ere slipping from the room and coming below. Her lack of practice at the task showed. The plaid was crooked, the pleats less than uniform with one large, then the next small, and the next somewhat askew. The whole thing probably looked a sacklike mess on her, but she hadn't minded when it had just been her, Mavis and Uncle Acair here. However, now her husband's sister had arrived . . .

"Oh dear," Jetta murmured, thinking she would embarrass her husband looking so shabby. "I should—"

"Sit, lass," Acair said firmly, when she started to rise, ready to flee to her room. "Saidh was never one to fuss o'er fashion. Ye'll look just fine to her."

"Oh look! Lady Murine and Lady Edith are with her too!" Mavis said with mounting excitement.

"Niels's and Dougall's wives?" Jetta asked with alarm, recognizing the names from tales Aulay had told her. While he'd obeyed Rory's orders and spoken precious little about their life together, he had told her stories about his childhood and life before her, telling her about his brothers and even about how two of them had met their mates, Edith and Murine.

"They're family, lass," Acair said firmly, placing a hand over hers in a way that might be meant to offer support, but also ensured she couldn't flee. "Murine and Edith'll no' fuss o'er what ye're wearing either."

"And that friend o' theirs, Lady Jo Sinclair is with them too," Mavis added with glee. "And oh look! Dougall, Niels, Greer, and the Sinclair are all with them as well." Pausing, she glanced toward the cooking area and said, "Thank goodness I made those pasties. But I'd best double the rabbit stew I was making for lunch."

Moaning, Jetta closed her eyes as the woman bustled back to the stove. She was contemplating what she feared was her coming humiliation when their guests entered, but then Acair released her hand and said, "All right then, lass. Go on with ye."

Breathing out her relief, Jetta stood abruptly, and then grabbed at the table when a wave of dizziness rolled over her.

Uncle Acair stood at once and scooped her up into his arms. "Ye're still not fully recovered, are ye, lass?"

"I just stood up too quickly," she assured him faintly.

"Hmm," he grunted. "I'll take ye to yer room. But fair warning," Acair added as he headed for the stairs. "The lassies'll most like head straight up to see ye once they're inside. So we're just delaying the inevitable."

"So long as their husbands do not follow," Jetta murmured, wrapping her arms around Uncle Acair's shoulders and then offering him a crooked smile.

"What are ye thinking, lass?" he asked curiously as he carried her up the stairs.

"That looking at you I see how my husband will look in twenty years. You are remarkably similar in looks to Aulay. As is Rory."

"Aye." He grinned. "'Tis the Buchanan blood. It runs strong. All male Buchanans look similar."

"And does Saidh too?" she asked curiously, glancing back over his shoulder toward the door below.

"Nay, thank the good Lord," he said dryly. "Buchanan features do no' sit well on a female's face as our poor sister Maighread proved. I love her dearly, but a more unattractive woman I've never seen. Her own be-trothed took one look at her face and refused to have her. Said it would be like waking up to me in his bed every morn."

Jetta's eyes widened in dismay at this news. "What happened to Maighread?"

"Oh, she took the veil when her betrothed insulted her so. Said she'd rather be a nun than deal with unfeeling bastard men. Which was a crying shame if ye ask me. She may ha'e looked like another Buchanan lad, but she took after our mother to be sure. She was sweet-natured and nurturing. She would have made a good wife and mother." Acair sighed at the memory and then added more cheerfully, "Fortunately, our Saidh turned out the opposite. She inherited her mother's long black hair and good looks, but her father, my brother's, personality. She's pretty as a picture she is. Just acts like one o' the boys instead o' looking like them."

"Oh," Jetta said weakly, not sure what else to say. The picture Acair had put in her head was of a prettier version of Aulay with black hair and bosoms, stomping around with a sword in hand.

"Here we are," Uncle Acair announced cheerfully as he carried her into her bedchamber. He'd barely stepped inside when they heard the lodge door opening below and the sound of laughter and chatter burst into the small building. Smiling wryly, Acair set her on her feet beside the bed and added, "And there they are. I'm guessing ye have about two minutes ere the lassies come bursting in here to see ye, so—" Pausing, he tilted his head and listened at the sudden rush of feet on the stairs. It sounded like a stampede.

"Make that less than a minute," he said dryly, and moved quickly aside just as several women rushed into the room, tugging a beaming Mavis along with them.

Well, tugging and hugging. It looked to Jetta as if they simply swept the woman up on entry and passed her around, each hugging and greeting her as they bustled her up to the bedchamber. Now the greetings died and the room fell silent as four women paused to take her in.

Jetta peered back, probably looking much like a frightened doe, and then her gaze sought out Mavis. Noting the affection with which the maid was taking it all in, Jetta made herself relax. These were members of her family. Well, three of the four newcomers were. The fourth was a friend, but she presumed a friend to her too, else why would the woman travel all this way?

Pasting a welcoming smile to her face, Jetta straightened and surveyed the women. Two blondes, a redhead, and one with long pure black hair, much like her own, Jetta realized and smiled faintly at the thought. It was exactly how her husband had described his sister. *"Long black hair like yers, but hers tends toward being straight, while yers has nice waves to it."*

"Saidh," she said, smiling at the woman with long black hair, and then turning to the redhead, she said, "Edith," and finally, she turned her gaze to the two blondes and said solemnly, "and Murine and Jo."

"Ye ken who we are?" Edith asked with surprise.

Jetta bit her lip and wrinkled her nose, but then sighed.

"Nay," she admitted. "I mean, if you are asking do I recall you, I fear not," she said apologetically. "But my sweet Aulay has told me a lot about each of you so I knew Saidh has black hair, while yours is red," she added to Edith, and then turned to the last two women to say, "he said Murine and Jo both had blond hair, so I know you are Murine and Lady Sinclair, but am not sure which of you ladies is Murine and which is Lady Sinclair."

"Oh," Edith murmured, a soft smile curving her lips as she turned to the others and said, "She called him her sweet Aulay."

"Aye." One of the blondes sighed. "Is that not wonderful?"

Jetta flushed, a bit embarrassed, and then glanced to Saidh as Aulay's sister moved toward her. When the woman took her arms in hand and peered at her solemnly, though, her expression became uncertain.

"Does his scar no' bother ye?" Saidh asked bluntly.

Jetta's eyes widened, but she answered promptly and firmly. "Nay."

"Nay?" Saidh prodded insistently and now Jetta frowned as she recalled her earlier worries on the matter.

"Did it bother me ere the accident?" she asked anxiously. "Was I unkind or cruel to him about the scar before I lost my memory? Because if I was . . ."

"If ye were?" Saidh prompted when she fell silent.

"Then I was a fool," she said sadly. "My husband is the kindest, most considerate man alive, and the scar does not take away from that. He is handsome. The scar merely adds a rakish air to his good looks. If I was too blind or foolish to see that ere hitting my head, then I was a stupid, shallow child."

Much to Jetta's confusion, Saidh suddenly beamed and tugged her into a firm hug, saying, "Welcome, sister," as she did.

The two of them were then immediately beset by the other three women, all of whom rushed forward to surround and embrace them both as well. Mavis soon joined in too so that it became just a large pile of hugging and cries of welcome. Confused though she was, Jetta was touched and found her eyes dampening with tears at the acceptance. Before those teardrops could become a waterfall, it ended just as suddenly as it began, and the women all began to pull away, chattering excitedly as they did.

"I will tell the men to have the chests brought up!" one of the blondes announced firmly, heading for the door.

"I shall fetch me brush. We must do her hair ere we take her back," the other said, sounding excited.

"I'll order a bath," Edith announced, and then glanced to Mavis. "There is a tub here?"

"Aye, aye." Mavis headed for the door. "I'll order the boys to bring it in and fetch water."

"Do no' be silly, Mavis," Edith said, chasing after her. "I shall tend that. I did no' mean to make more work fer ye. What is it ye're cooking? It smells divine."

"'Tis a fine stew for yer noon repast," Mavis said proudly. "Speaking o' which, I needs must double it now there are so many more here for the meal."

"Well, you tend that while I take care of the bath then," Edith said firmly.

"I'll need more rabbits," Mavis said with concern.

"I guess that means I'm going hunting," Acair said wryly, reminding Jetta that he was still there. Heading for the door now he added, "I suppose I'll need enough for lunch and supper too, so I'll take a few o' the men with me."

"No need to bother about supper," Saidh announced, bringing him to a halt at the door. "We'll all be back at Buchanan by the sup I should think."

"Really?" he asked with interest. "Does Aulay ken yer plan?"

Saidh shrugged. "I'm sure he's guessed I'll bring her back. After all, the only thing keeping her here was her lack o' dress. Now we can fix that. Besides," she added with a somewhat sly smile, "I'm sure the people o' Buchanan will be glad to see their laird's wife is alive and well."

Acair grinned at the comment and nodded approval before turning to Jetta and saying, "The lassies'll take good care o' ye, girl, and their men'll be here to stand guard while I'm away hunting up another rabbit. But send one o' the soldiers fer me do ye need me."

"Thank you," she whispered.

Smiling, he gave her a wink and headed out the door.

Jetta watched him go and then glanced to Saidh and asked, "Are we really going to Buchanan today?"

"Aye," Saidh said firmly. "I think it is the best thing we can do under the circumstances."

Jetta nodded solemnly, but taking in the spark of something in the woman's eyes and suspecting she understood what Saidh was hoping would happen, Jetta sighed and cautioned, "I will be glad to see my husband again. I missed him almost the moment he left. But I hope you are not thinking that being there will help spark some memories in me."

Saidh tilted her head and eyed her curiously. "Ye do no' think it will?"

Jetta shook her head. "If seeing and being with the man I obviously love dearly did not spark memories, I do not see how a building could."

Saidh paused briefly and swallowed, her eyes shimmering with what looked suspiciously like tears, before she asked, "Ye love him?"

"How could I not? He is wonderful," Jetta said with a wide smile, happy to talk about her husband. "He cared for me all through my illness with such patience and concern, and truly every time he kisses or touches me—" Realizing what she was saying, Jetta paused and was sure by the heat in her face that she was blushing.

"Kisses and touches and . . . ?" Saidh murmured, and then asked delicately, "You two have no' . . . ?"

Jetta shook her head quickly, grateful when the woman didn't finish her question. Positive she was now as red as a tomato, Jetta explained, "Rory insists I should not have excitement of any kind until I am healed, so other than that one time when he . . ." Pausing, she swallowed and shivered as she recalled him pleasuring her on the table. After a moment though, she shook her head and cleared her throat before continuing, "Well, and that was not the actual bedding or anything, but I was very excited, but Aulay has not done anything like that since because of Rory's orders I not be excited."

"Ah." Saidh grinned in a way that made Jetta sure the woman had a good idea what the "not the actual bedding" had entailed. Tempering her grin now, she asked, "But ye like his kisses and touches?"

"Oh aye," Jetta admitted on a sigh. "Aulay is truly wonderful in all ways. I find it hard to believe I was so lucky as to have him to husband."

"But ye do," Saidh announced firmly. "And I'm going to see it stays that way."

Jetta glanced at her uncertainly. "See that it stays that way?"

"Here we are!" Edith burst into the room with a passel of soldiers in tow. As they trudged in with their burdens, she announced, "The tub and the cold water are here, and there are several pots of water warming over the fire. A few minutes and they should be ready too!"

"I'll go check on them and tell Greer we plan to return to Buchanan ere day's end," Saidh announced, hurrying for the door. "He'll want to send one o' the men back to warn Cook so he kens he has extra mouths to feed."

Jetta watched her go with a frown. She knew from the tales Aulay had told her that Greer was Saidh's husband, and she understood that the woman probably did need to let him know they weren't staying so that the men could prepare to leave rather than settle in here, but she wished Saidh would stay so she could question her about the "see that it stays that way," bit. The words didn't even make sense to her. Why would Saidh need to see it stayed that way? Was there some question that it wouldn't? Was her husband considering setting her aside because of her head injury? Perhaps he didn't like that she couldn't remember him. Perhaps he feared this memory affliction could be passed on to their children when they had them. Dear God, surely he wouldn't set her aside?

"Here we go!"

Jetta glanced toward the blonde who entered the room on that announcement. Her eyes widened as she saw the men following the woman, carrying chests. She could see three at first, but as the first men entered, she saw more behind them and it turned out there were six chests in all, each needing two men to carry them.

"What . . . ?" she asked faintly, eyeing the chests with curiosity.

"Dresses," Edith announced with excitement.

"Well, most of them have dresses," the blonde corrected her. "There are also two chests of cloth for you to have new gowns made to your taste."

"True," Edith agreed with a grin. "Jo had scads of cloth sent to her by her uncle and she kindly piled two chests full of it fer ye."

"Jo," Jetta murmured, smiling at the woman, both out of gratitude and because she now knew which blonde was which. Expression sincere, she smiled at the women and said, "Thank you. This is so very kind of you." Her smile fading a bit, she shifted her gaze to the chests as each one was set down and added, "I could hardly believe it when my husband said all of my belongings had been lost when the ship sank."

When no one commented, she frowned and shifted her gaze back to the women. "Where were we going?"

"Oh, well . . ." Edith hesitated and looked to the other two women as if for help.

"I fear we do no' ken the answer to that," Murine said quietly. "Dougall mentioned that Aulay liked to take a bit o' break this time o' year, but I do no' recall his saying where he planned to go."

"Me neither," Edith and Jo said at the same time.

Jetta frowned with dissatisfaction at that and peered back to the chests as she thought aloud, "It must have been a long break for me to pack every last gown I owned." She considered that briefly, and then glanced to the two chests that had been in the room since her waking there and her frown deepened as she added, "And why were Aulay's chests not lost as well?"

"Oh, those chests have been here since they rebuilt the lodge," Murine said easily.

"Rebuilt it?" Jetta asked, and then gave her head a shake as she recalled Aulay telling her about the fire. "Oh, yes, the first one burned down while Dougall was courting you."

"Aye. Compliments o' me cousin and half brother," Murine said dryly, and then shook her own head. "Dougall and I offered to pay fer the new lodge to be built, but Aulay would no' hear o' it." Clucking her tongue with something like exasperation, she then added, "Anyway, those chests have been here since the day the lodge was finished. Aulay kept spare plaids and such in them so he need no' drag a lot of cloth and weapons with him when he came to the lodge."

Jetta nodded, but asked, "Why did I not do the same?"

The women all exchanged somewhat panicked gazes, and then turned to the door with relief when Saidh rushed in saying, "The water is almost boiled, but I thought while we waited we could go through the dresses in the chests . . . in case whatever you choose to wear needs airing to let out any wrinkles."

The women seized on the suggestion like it was a bit of water in the desert, all of them talking and moving at once. Jetta soon found her questions pushed from her mind as the women set upon the chests and began lifting out gown after gown for her consideration.

Chapter 9

"I TAKE IT FROM YER EXPRESSION THAT TALKING TO THE MEN on the wall was no' very helpful," Rory commented.

Aulay shook his head. "Nay. No' one o' them saw anything o' use," he admitted as he dropped to sit at the trestle table next to his brother.

"They did no' see anything at all?" Rory asked with a frown.

Aulay shrugged. "The archer must have been in the cover o' the woods. Not one o' them realized anything was amiss until Geordie reached back to catch the lass as she started to fall off his mount and one o' them noted the arrow sticking out o' her back."

"Damn," Rory murmured.

"Aye," Aulay agreed grimly despite it being exactly what he'd expected. While he had feared he wouldn't learn anything useful, there had still been that little bit of hope that he might. Sighing, he caught the eye of a nearby maid, and gestured to his brother's ale and then himself, letting her know he wanted some. As the maid nodded and hurried away, he added, "And I sent the men out again to search the woods surrounding the castle, but in a wider area this time. Still nothing. Whoever it was left nothing behind to hint at who they might be."

Rory frowned. "So we have no idea who may have shot the arrow?"

"No idea at all, and no real way to find out unless they make a second attempt," Aulay admitted.

"I presume that's why Conran is up in the passage outside Katie's room?" Rory asked. "In case a second attempt is made?"

Aulay glanced at him sharply. "How did ye ken he was there?"

"I heard him," Rory said dryly. "And I heard who I presume was you last night. The two o' ye tromp around like bulls."

Grimacing, Aulay nodded. "Good to ken. I'll warn him to be quieter, and try to be quieter myself."

"That is probably for the best," Rory said mildly.

"Aye, well, do no' mention his being there to anyone," Aulay murmured. "As far as everyone here kens I sent Conran out on a chore."

"Ye're actually hoping whoever it is makes a second attempt," Rory said solemnly.

"'Tis the only way I can think to catch them and give Katie and Geordie some justice," Aulay admitted. "If whoever shot her does no' make a second attempt, I've no idea where to even start looking."

Rory nodded. "I'll make sure there is no reason for anyone to enter the room. No' even a maid. If anyone enters, 'twill no' be fer a good purpose."

"Good," Aulay grunted, and then asked, "How is the lass?"

Rory shook his head silently.

Taking that to mean the lass was alive, but that his brother didn't expect her to remain so for long, Aulay rubbed one hand wearily over the back of his neck. He'd intended to ask the question and instruct Rory to say the girl was healing well at the sup last night. Unfortunately, he'd forgotten until it was too late. By the time he'd recalled talking about that with Conran, Aulay had already been installed in the passage outside the room where Katie lay. Grimacing, he said, "Next time I ask that will be in front o' a lot o' people. When I do, lie and say she is recovering surprisingly well and ye expect her to be up and about soon."

Rory didn't ask for an explanation. Apparently he understood why Aulay said that, because he merely nodded.

Aulay asked next, "How is Geordie?"

"Stuck to her bedside and praying," Rory said solemnly, and then added, "He's no' going to take it well when she finally goes."

"I'll ha'e to think o' something to get his mind off o' her when she passes," Aulay said quietly.

"Mayhap we'll get lucky and Jetta will turn out to have three or four sisters in need o' rescuing," Rory said dryly and when Aulay glanced to him in question, he shrugged and pointed out, "Saidh has run out o' friends in need o' rescuing, yet we still have three brothers in need o' brides."

"Jetta has at least one sister," Aulay informed him. "She recalled that after ye left fer Buchanan. And we ha'e four brothers in need o' brides, no' three," Aulay corrected him.

"I was considering you already attached thanks to Jetta's arrival," Rory said with amusement.

"So was I," Aulay said dryly. "Ye're leaving yerself out."

"Oh." His eyes widened. "Well, I never . . . I mean, I do no' need . . ." Pausing, he frowned and then changed the subject. "Speaking o' Jetta, Saidh and the girls have arrived at the lodge and are bringing her back today."

"What?" Aulay stared at him with surprise.

Rory nodded. "Uncle Acair sent one o' the men ahead with the news so Cook could prepare for the added company for the evening repast. The soldier arrived while ye were talking to the men who were standing guard when Katie was shot, so he spoke to me. He said the women are presently bathing, and preparing Jetta, but they intend to bring her back in time for the sup."

"Damn," Aulay breathed. While he wanted her there at his side, and had even known that Saidh planned to bring her, now that Jetta's arrival was imminent, every single problem that her presence at Buchanan could cause was marching across his mind. Problems like the possibility that someone would tell her they weren't married.

"What the devil is Saidh thinking bringing her here?" he said with dismay. "She kens the lass thinks me her husband."

"Aye, well, that may be what she's thinking of," Rory said mildly. "If Jetta arrives and—in front of witnesses here—greets ye by calling ye husband and ye call her wife, or even if ye do no' call her wife, but do no' deny being her husband, ye'll be handfasted, brother. As good as married in the eyes o' the law."

Aulay blinked as the words reverberated in his head and he softly breathed, "Damn."

He hadn't thought of that. Just her greeting him could seal her fate and make her his wife by law. He could keep her. They would be considered by both church and state to be married by consent. A ceremony and priest weren't even needed.

The thought was an enticing one. Handfasted to Jetta. To have her as his wife for real. He'd be able to bed her and . . .

And if she ever found out that she hadn't really been married to him in the first place, but had basically been tricked into handfasting to him . . . The thought made him frown and shake his head.

"Why not?" Rory asked. "Ye obviously like the lass."

"Aye," Aulay agreed solemnly.

"And am I right in guessing ye would welcome her being yer wife fer real?"

Aulay peered out over the nearly empty Great Hall. There were only a few people around, a handful of men on break seated at the far end of the trestle tables, a couple maids cleaning and the lass bringing him his ale. His gaze caught on the woman briefly, something about her reminding him of Jetta. He couldn't say what. Her face was smudged with dirt and he couldn't see her hair—it was secured on her head and covered with a kerchief—and she certainly didn't walk like Jetta. This woman's stride was confident and quick, while Jetta tended to walk slowly and cautiously if she walked at all. She hadn't walked much yet and wouldn't until she'd regained more strength.

Deciding it was just another case of everything reminding him of Jetta, Aulay turned his attention back to his brother and nodded silently. Aye, he'd welcome Jetta being his wife for real. She was . . . well, he'd never thought he'd be lucky enough to find a woman who would marry him willingly. Actually, the idea of a willing woman was so attractive he probably would have made do with nearly any woman who agreed, but Jetta . . . Well, with her it wouldn't be making do at all. She was smart, sweet, funny, kind, passionate, beautiful . . . And she genuinely seemed to like and want him. She wasn't repulsed by his scar at all. She was perfect, and he wished with all his heart that she truly was his wife. But . . .

"She'd be safe then from marrying whoever she feared was such a threat when she still had her memory," Rory pointed out. "And she seems to like ye too, brother. She seems perfectly content believing she is married to ye as it is."

"Aye, but we're *no'* married," Aulay pointed out. "I'd be tricking her into the union. I can no' do that to her. She deserves better."

Rory nodded solemnly. "Then ye'd best sort out a way to greet her where no one can witness her calling ye husband. Else she could claim marriage later."

Aulay smiled faintly at the suggestion. "I did no' say I'd mind being her true husband. Just that I do no' wish to force *her* into it. If she forces me 'twould be a different story," he said with a wry smile.

"Ah." Rory smiled as well. "So ye *do* want her to wife. Ye just do no' want to feel like ye forced *her* into taking ye as husband?"

"Aye," Aulay admitted and then noting someone hovering behind him, turned to glance at the maid waiting there.

"Yer ale, m'laird," she said and set the drink down in front of him.

"Thank ye," he murmured, and then stiffened as he noted the way her lip curled with disgust as her gaze slid over his scar before she turned away. Mouth tightening, he swiveled back to the table and picked up his ale. That reaction was something he hadn't had to suffer in a month. Even before that he'd seen it less and less as time had passed since the injury. Mostly because if Mavis saw a maid react at all to his scars, she either got rid of them or reassigned them to somewhere they wouldn't have contact with him. Aulay had never ordered her to do that, never even asked her to, but he knew she did it. The action had meant the maids in the castle had changed quite frequently at first. They still changed often enough that he didn't always recognize the women in the Great Hall. For instance, while the one who had sneered at him seemed vaguely familiar, Aulay didn't at all recognize at least three of the other maids tidying the Great Hall.

"She is lucky Mavis was no' here to see that," Rory said quietly.

"Aye," Aulay murmured, staring down into his drink, and then, glancing to his brother, he asked, "Do ye really think Jetta does no' mind me scar? Or is she just better at hiding it?"

"I think if yer scar bothered Jetta in the least, Mavis would ha'e sussed it out right quick and found a way to be rid o' her," Rory said honestly.

"Aye . . . mayhap," Aulay muttered, but turned his gaze back to his ale, wondering if that were really true. Perhaps Jetta was better at hiding her disgust. Or perhaps the repeated blows she'd taken had damaged her brain.

"Conran told me yer theory about the ship not sinking and the mast being all that was lost to the storm last night at sup," Rory said suddenly.

"Aye," Aulay said wearily, suddenly feeling his lack of sleep.

"I think 'tis a good theory," Rory informed him. "And I think ye should send some men out to ask around about any ships having taken that type o' damage. We could find out who she was that way."

"Aye," Aulay agreed, but without much enthusiasm. Learning who she was might be one step closer to losing her. Or it might mean she'd willingly marry him to save herself. The problem was he didn't want Jetta to marry him for that reason. He wanted her to want to be his wife, not to see him as the lesser of two evils. But he was finding it harder to believe that might be possible after the maid's response to seeing his face. The last two weeks with Jetta, he'd managed to forget how monstrous most people found him. The maid had reminded him nicely.

Clearing his throat, he straightened a bit and said, "Alick can go now he's back, but Geordie will no' go, and I can no' send Conran either. I need him to keep an eye on Katie and Geordie to help us catch her attacker," he pointed out.

"What about Uncle Acair?" Rory suggested.

Aulay frowned at the suggestion. "He's too old to ride as far and fast as we need."

"But he could guard Geordie in Conran's stead," Rory pointed out.

Aulay considered that and then shook his head and ran a weary hand through his hair. "He's no' as young as he used to be, Rory. I fear he'd doze off in the passage within an hour o' starting his shift and the killer could strike again and take both Katie and Geordie this time."

Rory frowned, but didn't argue the point. He merely asked, "So ye'll no' look into it?"

Aulay was silent for a minute, considering. Finding out who she was might mean losing her. But was it not better to find out and get it over and done with sooner rather than later? The longer he was around her, the more it would hurt to lose her. Straightening his shoulders, he said, "Aye. I'll look into it. I just need to sort out whom among the soldiers I can send. I need someone I can trust to approach the matter delicately, and keep his mouth shut."

"Do we have anyone like that?" Rory asked with uncertainty.

"That is the problem. I do no' ken. We probably do, but I usually depend on our uncle, or one o' our brothers to handle matters like this, so . . ."

"So you're no' sure who among the men are as trustworthy," Rory said with understanding, and then smiled wryly. "Having so many brothers to count on has always been useful, but now that our numbers are dwindling . . ."

Aulay gave a soundless laugh and shook his head. "Ye make it sound like Dougall and Niels are dead. They are still among our numbers."

"But they are no' here anymore," Rory pointed out. "They have wives and their own homes to watch out for."

"Aye," Aulay agreed. "And they manage without us always at their beck and call now. I will too," he assured him. "I just need to consider whom I might best be able to trust and who would make a good first in future once all o' ye have married and moved away."

Rory's eyebrows rose at the words. "Pushing us out the door, Aulay?"

"Nay," he assured him. "Ye'll always have a home here, brother. But seeing Dougall and Niels so happy makes me hope fer a wife, family and home o' yer own in future fer each o' the rest o' ye. Ye're all fine men and deserve it."

"As do you," Rory said solemnly. "And greeting Jetta as yer wife when she arrives would see that ye have it."

"Aye, well . . ." He peered down at his drink briefly, and then lifted his head and said, "I shall just ha'e to hope I can convince her to marry me

without trickery once I can tell her the truth that we are no' married."
Arching his eyebrows, he added, "When do ye think that'll be?"

Rory grimaced at the question. "In truth, I do no' ken. I'd feel better
did she regain her memories and realize that on her own."

"And if she ne'er does?" Aulay asked solemnly.

Rory frowned. "I do no' ken why ye just do no' let her handfast with
ye and keep her. Then we could openly look for her family and her name.
And I do no' think she'd mind. She likes ye, Aulay. She does no' e'en
mind yer face."

Rather than encourage him as Aulay believed his brother intended,
Rory's words made him close his eyes to hide the flicker of pain they sent
through him. *"She does no' e'en mind yer face."* Whether Rory realized
it or not, those words told Aulay that his brother found his face as distressing as every one of the maids Mavis had removed from his presence.
And that he was surprised that Jetta didn't.

"Nay," he said finally. "I'll no' trick her into marriage. I'll ride out and
meet the party ere they reach Buchanan."

Rory scowled at him with frustration, then predicted, "She'll still
likely call ye husband when she sees ye."

"Aye, but then it will be in front o' friends and family," Aulay pointed
out, positive none of them would do anything he did not wish.

"And Greer's men," Rory countered.

"Aye," Aulay murmured with a small frown.

They were both silent for a moment and then Rory asked, "What will
ye do about sleeping arrangements? She will expect to share a room here
as ye did at the lodge."

Aulay considered the issue and then pointed out, "The master bedroom and the room next to it are connected."

Rory smiled faintly. "Father said it was the only way to keep from
having a babe in the bed with him and mother. He said he got the idea
after three miserable months o' sharing their bed with you and Ewan.
Mother would no' dream o' leaving ye in a room on yer own when first
born. She wanted ye both close where she could keep an eye on ye. So
he connected the two rooms as a compromise. The two o' ye were in yer

own room, but the door was left open so she could hear ye cry and get to ye quickly."

"And it came in handy what with seven more bairns following us. It will also come in handy now. I will put her in the master, and as far as everyone else is concerned, I will take the smaller room meself."

"But ye'll really be in the master with her?" Rory guessed.

"Aye. I'll sleep on a pallet on the floor as I did at the lodge, but no one will ever see me enter the master bedchamber."

"That should work," Rory said with a nod.

Aulay raised his eyebrows. "Ye're no' going to protest me sleeping in the master chamber with her, or warn me no' to take her innocence?"

"I do no' have to," Rory said looking slightly irritated. "If ye're unwilling to trick her into handfasting with ye, then ye're no' likely to try to force her into marriage by taking her innocence. She is probably safer with you than any man here."

Aulay smiled wryly. The irony was, he wanted her more than ever, but was also more determined than ever not to claim her because he wanted her for life, not for one sweet night of pleasure. "My, how the tables ha'e turned."

Rory glanced at him curiously when he murmured that. "What do ye mean?"

"At the lodge ye were harping on me behaving and protecting her virtue, and now ye seem eager fer me to trick the lass into me bed and I am the one resisting."

"True," Rory admitted with a faint smile, and then his expression grew solemn and he said, "I have never known ye to be as happy as ye have been these two weeks since Jetta woke, Aulay. At least not since ye were wounded. Ye actually laughed when we took Jetta to the beach to break our fast, and the way ye look at her . . ." He lowered his head slightly, and peered at his hands where they rested on the tabletop. "I believe ye could be happy with her, Aulay, and I'd like to see that. We all would."

Aulay lowered his head and stared into his own drink. There was nothing he could say. He thought he could be happy with Jetta too, and it was definitely something he'd like to see.

"Well, ye've a lot to consider and I should go check on Katie," Rory said, standing up. "I'll let ye ken when she . . ."

"Aye," Aulay murmured, not needing him to finish the sentence. He would let him know when Katie died. Rory was positive she would. But then, he'd been sure Jetta wouldn't survive her wounds either and she had. Life was full of surprises. If Katie had a strong enough will, she'd survive and surprise them all as well, he thought as he watched Rory head for the stairs.

Once his brother had disappeared upstairs, Aulay turned his gaze back to his drink with a sigh. He did have a lot to consider. Whom he could trust here as much as he trusted his brothers and uncle. How he would tell Jetta that they weren't married when he was finally able to. How he could convince her to marry him.

Unfortunately, the moment Jetta entered his mind, his thoughts began meandering down another path. Rory had said Saidh and the other women were presently "preparing" her to come to Buchanan. He supposed that meant they were bathing and dressing her and so on, which made him wonder where they were in the preparations at that moment. Was she stepping naked into a steaming bath? Or had she already bathed and was now standing naked as they lifted one gown or another over her head? Mostly in his mind, she was just standing there naked as she had been when he'd last seen her. With that image filling his mind, any attempt at sensible thinking was pretty much useless at that point.

Aulay tried though. He considered all his issues—from finding justice for Katie and Geordie, to whom among his men he could trust as much as his brothers, and even whom he should send out to ask around about the ship that Jetta had been on. He thought and thought and thought, and when thoughts of Jetta distracted him, he forced them away and continued thinking, right up until he judged it was time to head out if he wished to meet up with Jetta and the others ere they arrived at Buchanan.

His timing was pretty good as it turned out. Aulay met up with the group no more than ten minutes away from the keep. Spotting them as he rode around a bend, he reined in to wait for them, his gaze sliding over each person in turn as he instinctively searched for Jetta. Not finding her, he began to scowl and consider where the devil she could be. Aside from his sister, her husband and their men, as well as his two brothers Dougall and Niels, their wives and their men, the party also contained Mavis, his uncle and the men he'd sent with his uncle. This meant they couldn't have left the lass behind. Mavis and his uncle wouldn't do that. Still, there was no Jetta that he could see, not even in the wagons carrying the chests of gowns.

"Where the devil is she?" Aulay barked the moment the party reached him and came to a halt. He glanced to his uncle when all eyes turned his way, his eyebrows rising when his uncle lifted the plaid he had draped over the front of himself and revealed Jetta curled up against his chest, sound asleep.

"I fear we forgot she is still healing and tires easily," Saidh explained apologetically. "We plumb wore her out with our fussing. She was sound asleep in Uncle Acair's lap ere we left the clearing around the lodge."

Relaxing at once, Aulay urged his horse closer to his uncle and peered at Jetta silently, torn between a desire to drag her away from his uncle to rest in his own lap, and leaving her to sleep peacefully where she was for the rest of the short journey.

"Ye can take her if ye like," Uncle Acair murmured, glancing affectionately down at the lass. "She'll no' wake. She's slept peaceful as a lamb the whole way, no' waking to sounds or the jostling she's taken. Yer shifting her to yer horse probably will no' even stir her."

When Aulay merely nodded and reached for her, his uncle shifted the plaid out of the way and lifted her carefully in his arms to hand her over. He was right. Jetta barely stirred at the transferal. She murmured sleepily, inhaled as her head rested against his chest, and then smiled and without ever opening her eyes whispered "husband" with recognition.

Smiling over the fact that she apparently recognized his scent, Aulay took the plaid his uncle now offered and draped it over her, murmuring, "Aye wife. Rest now, we'll be home soon."

When Jetta murmured something unintelligible and then seemed to fall into a deeper sleep, Aulay tucked the plaid around her and then lifted his head and froze. His uncle, his siblings and their mates had all urged their horses closer and were watching him with smiles on their faces. It made his own soft smile morph into a scowl and he growled, "She's been verra ill. Ye should no' have worn her out so."

Aulay didn't then wait for a response, but urged his mount to turn and headed back toward Buchanan, leaving his family to follow. He rode his horse into Buchanan and straight up to the keep doors. Holding Jetta close, he then slid off his mount and nodded at the lad who rushed forward to take his horse's reins. Leaving the lad to it, he carried Jetta up the steps, only to pause when he reached the doors.

"Shall I get that fer ye, m'laird?"

Aulay glanced around to see Cullen, one of his soldiers, hurrying up the stairs behind him. "Thank ye," he murmured as the man reached past him to open the door.

Cullen nodded and held the door as he carried Jetta in. Aulay heard the door close behind him and assumed Cullen had remained outside until he got above stairs and reached the closed door of the master bedchamber. Cullen proved he hadn't left him to his own devices when he suddenly moved in front of him to open that door as well.

"Thank ye," Aulay said with surprise.

"I thought ye might need a hand once ye got up here," the man said with a wry smile.

"Ye were right," Aulay said quietly, and made a note that the man had forethought.

"I'll close the door behind ye, and go back to me business then, m'laird," Cullen said solemnly.

"Aye," Aulay murmured and finally stepped into the room. Cullen eased the door closed as he'd said he would and Aulay carried Jetta to the bed.

She barely stirred when he laid her in it. He took the time to cover her up, and then straightened and eyed her for a minute. She looked so sweet in sleep, a peaceful smile on her face. Aulay brushed one finger gently down her cheek.

His touch made her stir and blink her eyes open.

"Husband?" she murmured sleepily.

"Aye. Rest, lass," he said quietly. When she closed her eyes again, he straightened and left the room to head below stairs. The Great Hall was relatively empty as he made his way toward the trestle tables, with just a few men seated at the far end nearest the Great Hall doors.

Chapter 10

"*A* DRINK, M'LAIRD?" ONE OF THE MAIDS ASKED AS HE AP-proached the trestle tables.

"Aye. Ale, please, Maggie," he murmured, recognizing the woman and smiling in passing. Her eyes widened briefly at the smile, but then she bobbed a nod and hurried off to fetch it, leaving Aulay to take his seat at the head of the trestle tables. It seemed he'd barely sat down when the keep doors opened to allow the large crowd that was his family to enter. The group was chattering as they came in, and continued to do so as they crossed the Great Hall and made their way upstairs. Aulay watched them go, a bit surprised that the men were going above stairs. But while the women all headed off to the doors to their rooms, no doubt to settle in and unpack, the men all went as one to the chamber Katie, Geordie and Rory were presently in. They were checking on Geordie and the lass, he realized.

Aulay briefly considered going up to Katie's room as well, but then let the idea go. He was exhausted after being up all night and simply didn't have the energy to chase after his guests. No doubt they'd make their way back here in search of drinks to wash away the dust of the journey when they finished talking to Geordie and Rory.

"Yer ale, m'laird."

Aulay glanced up and sat back as the maid set it before him. "Thank ye, Maggie."

"Me pleasure, m'laird," she said and smiled brightly before moving off.

Aulay watched her go and then peered toward the upper landing, wondering how long Jetta would sleep. She had spent a good deal of time sleeping during her first week after regaining consciousness, but had done better this last week. However, he was guessing the arrival of his sister, sisters-in-law and Jo Sinclair had probably been a lot more excitement than she was used to. He just hoped she did not sleep through the sup. While she'd gained back some of her weight, she was still far thinner than she'd been when they'd pulled her from the water. She couldn't really afford to miss meals. On the other hand, he supposed the sleep would do her good and he could have Cook prepare a tray for her later.

"Rory says ye want to send out men to ask around about the ship Jetta was on, but do no' ken whom ye can trust with the job among yer men."

Aulay looked up with a start to see Dougall settling at the table next to him. Noticing movement beyond him, he watched as Niels, Uncle Acair, Greer MacDonnell and Campbell Sinclair all settled at the trestle tables around him. It seemed they were done with their visit with Rory and Geordie.

"Rory talks too much," Aulay said dryly as he caught the eye of the nearest maid and gestured for her to bring more ale.

"Aye. He always did," Dougall said with a chuckle, and then added seriously, "But I understand yer problem."

Turning to him in surprise, Aulay raised an eyebrow in question.

Shrugging, Dougall admitted, "I found meself with the same issue at Carmichael. I knew none o' the men there, so at first did no' ken whom I could trust when it came to delicate situations."

"As I found it was fer me at Drummond, at first," Niels put in solemnly. "It'll take a while to suss out who can be trusted, but ye will."

"I do no' have a while," Aulay said, shifting impatiently. "I need men I ken I can trust right now if I wish to learn who Jetta is and the situation she is in."

"Or the boys and I could take turns above stairs in Conran's stead, and ye could send out him and Alick," the Sinclair said mildly. "With the four o' us doing it, 'twould mean shorter shifts."

"Five," Aulay corrected him. "I'll take a shift too."

"Six," Uncle Acair countered firmly. "I'm no' so old I can no' stand watch fer an hour or two." Grimacing, he added, "Any more than that and I might fall asleep, but I can manage a couple hours at least."

Aulay considered him briefly and then nodded. Glancing from man to man, he pointed out, "It could take a while. Mayhap a couple o' weeks. Ye'd be willing to stay that long?"

The Sinclair shrugged mildly. "We did no' travel all this way just to turn around and head home. We planned to stay a few days at least, but can easily extend it."

"Aye," Greer agreed. "Besides, I'll no' be able to get Saidh to leave here until the situation between you and Jetta is resolved. She likes her, by the by. She'll be doing all she can to make yer marriage a real one."

"If ye expect me to be upset by that news, ye're bound to be disappointed, for I wish Saidh good luck with the endeavor," Aulay admitted.

"There is no luck needed. Jetta loves ye."

Aulay turned sharply in his seat to look over his shoulder at that announcement, his eyebrows rising when he saw his sister approaching the table. She took the last few steps, paused behind and between him and her husband, Greer, who had taken the seat on his left, and then waited expectantly. The MacDonnell smiled faintly and turned to look at Campbell Sinclair, who immediately slid along the bench seat, giving him room to make way for Saidh.

"Ye think she loves me?" Aulay asked with interest once his sister was seated.

"I do no' think it, I ken it," she assured him solemnly. "She told me she did."

Aulay stared at her for a moment, his mind slow to accept what she said, and then sure he must have misheard, he asked, "She told ye that she loved me?"

"Aye," she said softly, a smile curving her lips. "She loves ye, Aulay. She thinks ye're wonderful. She thinks ye're kind and smart and sweet, and ye're kisses and touch leave her wanting. She loves ye, Aul. She says she does, and there's no doubt in me heart at all that she was no' telling the truth. Jetta loves ye."

While Aulay stared at his sister, trying to accept what she said, the men at the table, his uncle, brothers, brother-in-law and friend, broke out in whoops and congratulations, all of them standing to approach and pat his shoulders as they did.

"Ye've found yer bride, nephew."

"Congratulations, brother. I'm happy fer ye."

"Congratulations. She's a fine woman."

"She's a lucky woman. I'm happy fer ye both, brother."

Aulay swallowed and even managed a smile as they thumped his back, but his mind was racing. She loved him. She'd told Saidh she loved him. Mayhap he wouldn't lose her after all when she found out they were not married as she'd assumed.

"What are ye all so happy about?"

The men all paused and turned to smile at the women crossing the hall toward the tables. It seemed the other girls were finished organizing their rooms to their satisfaction as well. Edith, Murine and Jo were joining them.

"I just told Aulay that Jetta loves him," Saidh said with a smile.

"Aye." Edith grinned. "She called ye her *'sweet Aulay.'*"

Murine nodded. "And she said ye were the kindest, most considerate man alive."

"And she thinks ye handsome too," Jo added. "She thinks yer scar merely adds a rakish air to yer good looks."

"Oh ho," Dougall said with a grin, punching him lightly in the shoulder. "Did ye hear that? Handsome and rakish."

"She wants ye, Aulay," Niels said smiling widely. "It must be love. Ye're as good as done fer now. Ye'll be sending fer the priest any day now."

"Aye," Saidh said at once. "And the sooner ye do, the better, if ye want to avoid losing her."

Stiffening, Aulay turned to her in question. "Losing her?"

"Trust is part o' love, brother," she pointed out solemnly. "Ye need to tell her the truth about yer no' being married ere she finds out from another source. Else ye risk her finding out on her own, and mayhap fleeing or some such thing."

"Fleeing?" he said sharply.

"I would," Saidh said grimly.

"Ye'd flee?" he asked with dismay.

"Well, aye. If I found out on me own I would," she assured him. "Because it would no' just mean that you lied to me, but that everyone I knew, the *only* people I knew, had all been lying to me." Shaking her head she said firmly, "Mark me words, does she find out on her own, she will no' longer trust a single one o' us, or feel at all safe here."

Aulay stared at her with openmouthed dismay, and after a moment, Saidh arched an eyebrow and asked, "What would ye do if ye woke up somewhere with no memories and then after weeks o' living with whom ye thought were yer family, ye learned the people whom ye've been trusting and believing in were no' who they claimed to be and had been lying to ye the whole time?"

Aulay's jaw snapped closed, his teeth grinding viciously together. He was in an impossible situation. Rory was telling him he shouldn't tell her and had a good reason for it, and Saidh was giving him a good reason why he should. He felt like he was being torn in two directions. He didn't want to set back Jetta's healing, but on the other hand, he definitely didn't want her feeling she could not trust him or anyone else here, and Saidh was right, that could happen if he didn't tell Jetta they were not married, and she found out from another source.

The worst part about all of this was that he hadn't really lied at all. He wasn't the one who'd claimed to be her husband. She'd assumed he was. He just hadn't corrected her. He hadn't corrected her at first because . . . well, he hadn't really got the chance. But then Rory had told him not to and he'd been happy to let her think he was her husband. He'd actually enjoyed pretending she was his wife. Too much. Now he wanted it to be true. But that wasn't likely to happen if she found out they weren't married from someone else, and felt so betrayed she ran off.

"Ye're putting him in a tough spot, Saidh," Uncle Acair said when Aulay remained silent. "Rory is advising him no' to tell her, at risk o' damaging her health, and yer telling him to tell her or risk her ne'er trusting him and perhaps losing any future with her. Ye're asking him to choose between her health and their future. How can he choose? He loves her. He'll neither wish to harm her health, nor lose her."

Aulay stiffened. He hadn't said he loved her . . . had he? Nay, he was sure he hadn't. He'd admitted he liked her and would like to really have her to wife, but he didn't think he'd mentioned love.

"Aye, ye're right," Saidh agreed with a sigh. "'Tis impossible."

"Well, mayhap he could tell her without telling her," Edith suggested tentatively and then turned to Aulay and said, "Mayhap ye can tell her ye love her, and that there are some things Rory wished ye no' to tell her, but ye're concerned she may learn before he allows ye to tell her, and that should that happen, she should remember that ye love her."

"That'll just drive her mad with curiosity," Dougall predicted, and shook his head. "And she might get angry that he will no' tell her what he's no' telling her."

"Aye," Murine agreed pensively, and after a pause suggested, "instead, mayhap ye should just tell her ye love her and that ye want her to ken ye'd marry her all o'er again, any day she chose, because ye want to spend the rest o' yer life with her."

"That might work," Jo commented. "Then if she learns ye're no' married, she'll ken ye *will* marry her if she wishes."

"Aye," the other women agreed together.

Aulay stared at them, and shook his head. He'd known the women wouldn't be able to keep from interfering in his life. This was all their fault. They were the ones who had brought Jetta here to Buchanan, raising the risk of her finding out they weren't married.

"Oh, there she is," Edith warned in a hushed tone.

His thoughts scattering, Aulay glanced to Edith to see her looking toward the stairs. Following her gaze, he spotted Rory descending the steps. His brother was perhaps a third of the way down them, and even as Aulay looked, Rory's eyebrows rose as he noted them all staring his way. Shifting his gaze past the man, Aulay saw Jetta on the landing, walking toward the top of the stairs, and stopped breathing as he took her in. She looked absolutely beautiful.

Aulay had been so happy to see her and so intent on her face earlier that he'd hardly noted the gown she wore. It was a lovely deep green dress that he suspected would have fit her beautifully when he and Alick had first found her, but was presently just a touch too big after the weight she'd lost while unconscious. Jetta had gained back some of the weight, but not enough to properly fill out the dress. Even so, she looked beautiful in it. She was wearing a crispin or caul that gathered the hair from the front and sides and pulled it back behind her head where it hung down, encased and partially hidden in a veil as dark as her remaining hair.

Aulay didn't doubt for a minute that his sister and the other women had either made or given it to her to hide the fact that she was missing a good deal of hair on the back of the head. And he was grateful for it, for while the missing hair hadn't bothered him, it had obviously bothered Jetta. Or perhaps it was a combination of the missing hair and not having proper clothes that had affected her, because she had been tentative and self-conscious at the lodge, but was now walking with much more confidence, and a happy smile claimed her lips as she spotted him.

The corners of his mouth lifting in return, Aulay immediately stood and headed for the stairs. Jetta was still recovering her strength and he worried the stairs might be too much for her. He had just opened his mouth to tell her to wait and he would carry her down, when she reached the top of the steps and a dark figure suddenly came from the side and shoved her.

It happened so fast, Aulay could barely believe his eyes, but an enraged roar burst from his mouth as Jetta fell forward, and Aulay lunged for the stairs.

Rory, who had been descending, paused abruptly at his bellow and turned to see what had upset him. Spotting Jetta tumbling toward him, he started back up the stairs, but even he was not close enough to prevent her slamming her head into the steps at least two or three times before he reached her and brought her fall to a halt.

By the time Aulay reached them, Rory had helped her to a sitting position on the stairs and was crouched down beside her on the steps.

"Jetta?" Aulay said with concern, crouching on her other side.

"I am fine," she murmured, lifting her head and managing a smile. "As I was just telling Rory, my ankle hurts a bit, but my hair and the crispin cushioned my head."

"I still think I should take a look," Rory said with a frown. "Ye're just recovering from a serious head injury, and—"

"Fine." Jetta sounded a bit exasperated, but resigned.

"Let us get ye back up to yer room then," Rory said, and started to help her to her feet.

"Wait here a minute, Rory. I need to go up before ye," Aulay said grimly.

"Ye do? Why?" Rory asked with surprise.

"Because someone pushed her down the stairs," Cam Sinclair said grimly, following Aulay when he moved past Rory and Jetta to make his way up to the landing.

"What?" Rory asked with shock.

"Aye," Aulay heard Jetta say. "Someone shoved me. I did not see who, though."

"Someone did shove her, Rory. I saw someone come up behind her and give her a shove," Saidh growled, sounding angry.

"Who was it?" Rory asked at once.

There was a pause and then Saidh admitted unhappily, "I did no' see. It happened so fast, and the figure was in shadow and wearing dark clothes. All I really got was an impression of someone."

"Me too," Edith announced. "But 'tis dark on the landing."

"The torches are out up there," Uncle Acair commented.

"Aye," Murine put in. "I noticed that as we came down. Why are the torches no' lit?"

Aulay surveyed the upper hall with narrowed eyes as he reached the landing. What Murine said was true. The torches were not lit, at least not the ones by the stairs. There were some still lit at the end of the hall, but the ones that might have revealed who pushed her were all out.

"There's no one in the hall," Cam said behind him and Aulay turned to see that the Sinclair wasn't the only one who had followed him. Dougall, Niels and Greer were behind him as well. Uncle Acair had stayed with Jetta and Rory.

"Nay," Aulay said finally, casting another glance along the hall. "But this is the only way below so whoever pushed her is still here. 'Tis why I did no' rush right up, but first stopped to see that Jetta was all right."

"Ye want to search the rooms?" Greer asked.

"We'll all help," Dougall put in.

Aulay nodded. "But I want one man to stay at the top o' the stairs so whoever pushed Jetta does no' slip from an unsearched room, to one already searched to avoid us."

"I'll wait out here and watch the stairs," Niels offered. "And I'll check the chests of dresses the men left in the hall while I do."

"Thank ye," Aulay murmured. "Then Dougall and Cam can take the rooms to the right o' the stairs, and Greer and I'll take the rooms on the left."

He waited just long enough to see the men all nod, and then turned to head to the left. Greer followed, but continued past him when he opened the door to the room where Katie was resting with Geordie watching over her. Aulay's gaze slid to the woman in the bed with her long, black hair fanned out on the pillow around her pale face and for a moment it was like being back at the lodge, peering at Jetta in her sickbed.

Shaking the thought away, he glanced to his brother and his expression softened slightly as he noted the way Geordie sat sprawled in the chair. His eyes were closed, his head nodding and soft snores slipping from his lips. Aulay had no doubt Rory had walked in on exactly this scene several times at the lodge before Jetta had regained consciousness. Only he had been the one sprawled asleep in the chair.

Shifting his gaze away from his brother, he surveyed the rest of the room just to be sure whoever had pushed Jetta hadn't risked slipping in here to hide, and then eased the door silently closed and moved on to the next door just as Greer stepped out. His brother-in-law met his gaze and shook his head to indicate he'd found nothing in the chamber and they moved on to the next rooms. They made quick work of their end of the hall. Even so, Cam and Dougall were quicker and came to join them as they reached the last door on their end of the hall.

"Nothing?" Aulay asked as Greer opened the door and entered the room he and Saidh had been given to sleep in. They normally stayed in Saidh's old room when they visited, but that was where Katie was at the moment, so they had taken one of the guest rooms.

"Nothing," Cam Sinclair confirmed solemnly.

That made Aulay turn narrowed eyes into this, the last room. Pushing away from the door, he followed Greer inside and then paused to look around, but could tell at a glance that there was really nowhere to hide.

"I see our Saidh still keeps her room a mess," Dougall said with amusement behind him.

Aulay didn't comment, but did peer around at the gowns tossed everywhere.

"Saidh's maid, Joyce, usually tidies up after yer sister at home, but we left her behind to watch Rhona, Sorcha and Ailsa," Greer explained, moving around the bed and then bending to look under it. "Saidh was loath to leave them behind, but me squire, Alpin, insisted the triplets should no' be exposed to the rigors o' travel at only six months old," he added dryly, and then straightening from looking under the bed, smiled grimly and announced, "So we left him to help Joyce with the lasses while we're gone."

"I'm sure he was no' well pleased by that," Dougall said with amusement.

"Actually, I think the opposite is true," Greer admitted wryly as he shifted some of the dresses to be sure all they were was dresses. "I thought he'd be upset, but he's taken quite a shine to the girls. He's verra protective o' them and often volunteers to entertain them. He seemed content to remain behind with the lasses."

"Alpin's a good lad," Cam murmured, moving another pile of dresses aside. "And he had it right. Traveling with bairns is a trial. 'Tis why we left Bearnard with me mother and father. Jo and I are missing him, but while he's out o' nappies now, he's teething and fussing with it, which is a terrible trial for him when traveling. Fortunately, me mother enjoys her grandson, teething or no'." Glancing to Greer, he added, "I can no' imagine three bairns teething at the same time though. Ye're in fer a treat, me friend."

"Every day with me lasses is a treat," Greer said. He sounded sincere, and they knew he was. Greer adored all four of the females in his life. Saidh, and the three beautiful little girls she'd given him.

"There is no one in this chamber," Dougall said solemnly, once they'd searched every possible hiding spot in the room.

"Then we must have missed something," Aulay said grimly. "Someone pushed Jetta down the stairs."

"Aye," Cam said, and then raised his eyebrows. "We search again?"

"Aye," they all said as one.

"I'm thinkin' we should switch sides this time," Aulay said as they left Saidh and Greer's room. "Greer and I'll take the bedchambers Dougall and Cam searched the first go round, and they check the ones we did."

"That sounds a good idea," Cam said with a nod. "One o' us might catch something the other missed."

Greer and Dougall murmured agreement and they broke up again to search the rooms.

This time, they met by Niels at the top of the stairs when they'd finished. No one had to say they hadn't found anything. None of them had a culprit in hand. They gathered in a loose half circle in front of Niels and exchanged questioning looks.

"I did see someone behind Jetta," Aulay said grimly. "They came from the side, reaching to push her."

"I saw it too," Cam assured him.

"And I," Greer agreed.

Niels and Dougall nodded.

"If ye did no' find them in one o' the chambers, ye ken what that means," Dougall said quietly.

"The passages," Aulay growled.

"But only the family kens about the passages," Niels protested with a frown, and then added wryly, "And o' course, Sinclair and MacDonnell."

They'd had to tell the two men about the passages so that they could help guard Katie's room. Of course, they didn't know where the entrance was outside, or where and how to open the passage at the top of the stairs leading down to the tunnel to the caves. They only knew how to enter the passages from their respective rooms and access the entrance to the room Katie was in.

"Aye, but all o' us were below when someone pushed Jetta," Dougall pointed out. "So it was no' one o' us, and yet whoever it was managed to leave the floor without using the stairs. If ye can think o' another way to do that besides the passages, I'd be interested to hear it."

"Geordie was no' with us," Niels pointed out. "Nor Alick, nor Conran."

"Alick is hunting up more meat fer Cook," Aulay said quietly. "We expected ye to stay a couple days at least, so Cook needed more meat fer the meals. And Conran is already in position watching Geordie and Katie."

"He's in the passages?" Cam asked with interest and then pointed out, "If he is, he may ha'e seen who pushed Jetta if they used the passages to escape."

Aulay was turning to hurry back into Katie's room before Cam had even finished speaking.

Chapter 11

GEORDIE WAS STILL SPRAWLED IN THE CHAIR, SOUND ASLEEP, when Aulay rushed into the bedchamber where Katie lay. Ignoring his brother as well as the men following him, Aulay moved to the wall next to the fireplace, and pushed on three rocks at the same time using one foot and both hands. He then stepped back as a click was followed by a section of the stone wall swinging inward toward him. Aulay waited for it to come to a halt, and then pulled it further open and stared at the empty space beyond.

"What is it?" Dougall asked moving up behind him. Seeing the empty passage, he said with bewilderment, "Where is he?"

Aulay shook his head, his expression grim. Conran was not the type to neglect his duties. He should have been right there, watching the room . . . unless someone made him leave. Turning away, he moved to grab a candle off the mantel and lit it from the flames in the fireplace.

"I'll check the passage," Dougall said, stepping up next to him. "Ye might be needed here."

"And I'll go with him," Niels added, joining them.

When Aulay merely nodded and handed the candle over, Dougall took it and then headed into the passage with Niels on his heels.

Once the two men had disappeared from sight, Aulay turned his attention to Geordie. The man's not waking at their entrance was suddenly suspicious and he moved to Geordie's side and bent to press an ear to his chest.

"Is he alive?" Greer asked with concern.

"Aye." Aulay turned toward Katie. After the briefest hesitation, he bent and pressed an ear to her chest as well. At first there was nothing, and then he heard a weak thud. He waited to hear another before straightening. "She's alive. But Rory should check them both."

"I'll fetch him," Greer offered and headed out of the room.

"Why is Geordie no' waking up?" Cam asked with a frown, moving closer to the man.

Aulay was hoping it was simply because the man was exhausted from lack of sleep. He'd been in the room watching over Kate since she was wounded. But it was possible that he'd been drugged. Returning to his brother's side, he tapped him on the shoulder firmly. Geordie moaned and reached out to push away his hand the first time, but when Aulay tapped again, he slowly forced his eyes open, and scowled.

"Aulay. What's about?" he asked, looking and sounding irritated, and then he suddenly sprung upright and glanced toward Katie.

"She's fine," Aulay growled.

Geordie slumped back in his seat with a sigh, and ran weary hands over his face, trying to wake up fully. "Why did ye wake me then?"

"To be sure ye yet lived," Aulay said dryly.

"Aye. I'm fine. I was no' the one who took an arrow to the back," Geordie said bitterly, and then frowned and glanced from Aulay to Cam and then to the open passage entrance. "What's happened?"

"Someone pushed Jetta down the stairs and Conran is missing," Aulay said bluntly.

"What?" Geordie asked with an amazement that quickly turned to concern. "Is Jetta all right? Who pushed her?"

"We do no' ken who did it. But aye, she seems fine. Rory is with her now." Aulay glanced to the passage, wondering if he shouldn't join his brothers in the dark and narrow pathway within the walls. If they ran into trouble—

"And ye say Conran is missing?" Geordie asked, dragging Aulay's gaze back again.

When he merely nodded, it was Cam who explained, "Conran was in the passage, keeping an eye on ye and Katie in case the person who shot an arrow at her tried to harm her again. He's missing now, which we found out when we were searching for the culprit who pushed Jetta down the stairs."

"Her attacker is up here somewhere?" Geordie asked with concern.

"Aye. Or they were," Aulay growled as it occurred to him that Niels was no longer watching the stairs. The culprit could be fleeing down them even now.

"Ye think they forced Conran out o' here with them?" Geordie asked, bringing his attention back.

"I do no' ken," Aulay admitted as he strode toward the door. "He—" Pausing, he turned toward the passage as Conran rushed into the room with Dougall and Niels on his heels. His first reaction was relief. It was followed quickly by anger for the scare they'd all had. A scowl starting, he demanded, "Where the devil were ye?"

"I had to relieve meself," Conran said apologetically and then glanced around the room. "Rory and Geordie were both here with the lass when I left, and I thought I'd only be a minute, so it would be all right. The next thing I ken, Dougall and Niels were scaring the hell out o' me in the passage as I returned."

Aulay sighed and shook his head. He could hardly be angry with his brother for slipping away to relieve himself.

"Sorry, Aulay. Bad timing, I guess," Conran said now. "But is it true? Dougall and Niels said someone pushed Jetta down the stairs?"

"Aye," he muttered. "But don't apologize. I should ha'e thought to give ye breaks. I had to visit the garderobe a time or two meself last night." Arching an eyebrow now, he asked, "I do no' suppose ye saw anyone or heard anything while on yer way there, or back?"

"Nay. Well, I spotted Jetta digging through the gowns in one of the chests in the hall when I slipped from the passage entrance there next to the garderobe, but she did no' see me."

"That must ha'e been just before she started down the stairs," Cam muttered and Aulay nodded.

"Most like," Conran agreed. "She was gone when I headed back, and other than that I did no' see anyone or anything out o' the ordinary."

Aulay's mouth tightened at the news. It would have been too much to hope that Conran had seen anything useful, he supposed, and then shifted his gaze to the door to the hall when it opened. Rory entered with a sour look on his face, and Greer on his heels.

"I was just wrapping Jetta's ankle when Greer came to fetch me. What's happened now?" the healer asked irritably and then spotted Conran and the open entrance to the passage. "I thought yer presence in the passage was supposed to be a secret?"

"Aye, well, now it's no' a secret," Aulay pointed out with a scowl. "Is Jetta all right?"

"She twisted her ankle," Rory said with disgust. "She'll be limping fer a bit, but should be able to walk on it now it's wrapped." Raising his eyebrows, he then asked, "What's happened here? Who else is hurt?"

"Mayhap no one," Aulay admitted. "Greer fetched ye back to check on Katie and Geordie, and possibly Conran we thought at the time, though he is fine."

"When we got here, Conran was missing and Geordie seemed in a deep sleep. We feared the worst," Cam explained. "But Conran had just stepped away to visit the garderobe, and Geordie woke up in the end, so Kate's probably fine too, or as fine as she was ere this," he added.

"Just check her to be sure, Ror," Aulay growled.

Rory nodded and moved to the bedside at once.

"Why was Conran's being in the passage a secret?" Geordie asked with a frown as he watched Rory examine Katie.

"I did no' want ye to fret any more than ye already were," Aulay admitted. "And with Conran keeping an eye from the passage there was no need fer ye to."

"Mayhap ye should have two men in the passage at a time to make sure the room is covered despite garderobe breaks," Greer said with a frown.

Aulay shook his head. "No need. Now that Geordie kens someone is watching, the person can sit in the room with him, and only slip into the passage to watch when neither Geordie nor Rory are in the room." Shifting his attention to Geordie he added, "While Rory has left a time or two, ye've yet to do so. Ye should probably leave the room, brother.

I ken ye do no' want to, but our watching up until now has been a waste of time since ye've no' left her side except when Rory was with her and that just to visit the garderobe. No one is like to try to harm her with ye both here to witness."

Geordie scowled. "Ye're going to use her as bait?"

"Someone will be watching her at all times," Aulay assured him, and then arched an eyebrow and asked, "Can ye think o' another way to capture whoever shot the arrow into her?"

Geordie frowned briefly, but then rubbed his hands over his face and shook his head. "Nay. I can no' imagine anyone wanting to hurt wee Katie. She's sweet as can be."

"There is no change. She does no' appear to have been harmed in any way," Rory announced, straightening. "In fact, if anything, she's slightly improved."

"Really?" Geordie asked, perking up substantially.

"Aye," Rory said and smiled wryly. "We may ha'e another lass survive when I did no' think she would."

Aulay considered that as he peered at Katie, and once again it struck him that she could easily be mistaken for Jetta. The black hair, the pale face and petite figure with generous breasts . . . Their facial features differed. Jetta's eyes were larger, her lips a little fuller, and her face was oval while Katie's was heart-shaped. Other than that though, the two women could have been sisters.

"If we are done in here, we should let Geordie and Katie rest," Rory said suddenly.

Aulay knew from his expression that his brother wanted a word with him, away from Geordie. Nodding, he headed for the door, but paused once he reached it and turned back to tell Conran, "The men ha'e offered to take shifts watching Katie and Geordie. I'll come talk to ye after we sort out the who and when."

Appearing relieved at this news, Conran nodded and Aulay led the others out of the room. He walked nearly to the stairs before pausing to face Rory. Raising his eyebrows, he said, "I got the feeling ye had something ye wanted to discuss with me?"

"Aye," Rory said quietly, and glanced around to include the other men as he said, "I ha'e to tell ye, Aulay, every time I go into that room, I think 'tis just like entering the bedchamber at the lodge has been this last two month. I mean, Katie almost looks like Jetta lying in that bed," he pointed out. "And we brothers all resemble each other a great deal. In fact, Geordie is just a younger version o' ye."

"Younger and unscarred," Aulay muttered.

"Aye. But from a distance and on horseback, the two could easily have been mistaken fer you and Jetta," he pointed out solemnly.

"Ye're thinking Jetta was really the target when Katie was shot?" Cam suggested quietly, not appearing surprised.

Rory hesitated, and then said, "Mayhap. Although, Jetta was no' even here. And I can't think that anyone here would wish to harm Jetta?"

"The archer who loosed that arrow does no' have to be from here," Cam pointed out and then reminded them, "there is that business about her family and someone she feared who would kill her."

"Aye, but her family do no' ken she's here. No one does," Rory pointed out, seeming now to want to argue against what his own words had suggested.

"*As far as we ken* her family has no' learned she's here," Aulay corrected him solemnly, feeling he had to at least consider the possibility. But then he shook his head. "The only thing we ken fer certain is that Katie was shot with the arrow, and Jetta was pushed down the stairs."

"Aye, but Katie does resemble Jetta and might have been mistaken fer her from a distance," Dougall said solemnly. "And Rory's right, Geordie could ha'e been mistaken fer ye from a distance as well. Probably we all could."

"And Katie's getting shot brought you and Rory and then Jetta home to Buchanan, where she was pushed down the stairs," Niels pointed out.

Aulay glanced from man to man with surprise. "Ye're now all thinking the two attacks are connected?"

"Nay, I'm sure they're no' thinking that," Rory assured him. "They're just considering this from every angle."

"Although," Cam said now, "it does seem more likely that Katie was mistaken fer Jetta, than that ye have two murderous bastards on yer hands. I mean, we already ken the lass was afraid o' someone she felt sure would kill her."

"Aye," Dougall said now, "but how would anyone from her family find out she was here? Or about the passages if that's how they escaped?"

"They would no'," Aulay assured them. "At least, they should no' ken about the passages. Besides, from what I could tell, she was no' afraid o' her family so much as the man they were forcing her to marry."

"Do we ken anything about him?" Cam asked with interest.

Aulay shook his head. "Nay, from what we could understand, he was no' her betrothed, but she was being forced to marry him anyway, and she feared he would kill her." After a pause, he added, "Which puts paid to the attacker being a member o' Jetta's family. Even if they ha'e some-how tracked her here to Buchanan, they can hardly force her to marry anyone if she is dead."

"Aye, ye're right," Rory acknowledged, and then said, "so we've two separate attackers, one after Katie and one after Jetta."

"Unless it was the other way around and Jetta was mistaken fer Katie when she was pushed down the stairs," Dougall suggested.

Aulay was just blinking in surprise at that suggestion when Niels said, "What about the poisoned stew?"

"What?" Aulay peered at him with amazement. "What poisoned stew?"

"Oh, I forgot to tell ye about that." Dougall scowled with consterna-tion and quickly explained about Robbie's dog dying after eating the charred soup Mavis had thrown out. He ended with, "Mavis feared she'd dumped the stew on some sort o' poisonous plant and the dog just gob-bled that up with the stew, but . . ."

"But now ye're wondering if Robbie was no' right and the stew was poisoned," Aulay said quietly.

Dougall looked uncomfortable. "I just think everything should be considered."

Aulay began to rub his temples as he considered what he'd learned. "Right, so, here are the facts as we ken them. Katie was shot with an arrow. A dog died from eating stew that was meant for Jetta and Mavis, and may or may no' have been poisoned. And now Jetta was pushed down the stairs."

"Aye, but we are no' sure who the arrow was meant for. Katie may ha'e been the target, or she could have been mistaken for Jetta," Dougall added.

"And the stew is less certain," Greer added. "There could have been a poisonous plant at the base o' the tree where Mavis tossed the stew, or the stew could ha'e been poisoned and Mavis and Jetta escaped dying simply because Rory forgot to water down the stew as Mavis asked him to."

"But I do no' think Jetta was mistaken fer Katie when she was pushed down the stairs," Cam said solemnly. "The attacker was too close to mistake her for anyone else."

Blowing out a breath, Aulay turned and walked to the railing to peer at the tables below. The Great Hall was bustling now with activity, the tables full of people arriving for the evening meal, but his eyes immediately found and settled on the women at the head table. They were gathered in a group, surrounding Jetta where she sat on the bench seat, and appearing to fuss with her hair.

"Rory took Jetta's caul off to examine her head," Niels murmured, moving to stand next to him. "The ladies are now replacing it."

"I thought she said her caul cushioned her head and saved her from harm?" Aulay said with sudden concern. He wouldn't have left her had he thought her wounded.

"She did, and it did," Niels assured him. "But Rory checked to be sure."

"Oh." He relaxed a little.

"And she did no' get away completely without injury," Niels added, alarming him all over again, until he added, "she twisted and banged her ankle in the fall. Rory thought at first it was broken, but then decided nay. It hurts her to walk on it though. Uncle Acair had to carry her to the table."

Despite having already known this news, Aulay scowled as he moved to the top of the stairs.

Before he could start down, Niels asked, "What are we going to do about this latest attack?"

"Aye," Dougall said, and added, "and how are we going to sort out whether Katie or Jetta was the target o' the arrow, and whether the stew was poisoned?"

"None o' that matters," Aulay said firmly and swore every single one of the men gasped at his words like old women. Turning to face them, he pointed out, "Someone shot Katie with an arrow and attacked Jetta. Both of those are certainties. I want both women guarded night and day. I also want the passages and tunnel locked off."

"Ye can do that?" Cam asked with interest.

"Aye," Aulay said simply, not bothering to explain that the entrance at the cave could be locked, as could the entrance to the stairs from the tunnels as well as the entrance to the passages from the stairs. The ancestor who had built the castle and its tunnels had been no fool. He knew secrets got out and it was best to be able to lock off the entrances should anyone discover that particular secret.

"We can split up," Cam suggested. "Half can help guard Katie and half to watch Jetta."

Aulay shook his head. "I'll put four soldiers on me wife, and watch her meself as well. The rest o' ye stick to the original plans to guard Katie."

When no one commented and they all just stared at him wide-eyed, Aulay frowned. "What?"

"Ye called her yer wife, brother," Dougall said solemnly.

Aulay stiffened and tried to think if he had, but then didn't care. "Mayhap I did, but it matters little, she is going to be me wife on the morrow if I can convince her to have me. I'm telling her the truth and asking her to marry me this night."

"Aulay," Rory said with a frown.

"I ken ye fear it could set back her healing," he growled, "but her being dead would set it back a hell o' a lot further."

Rory's mouth grew tight. "And ye think marrying her will help keep her safe?"

"It can no' hurt," he said grimly. "And if her family is somehow behind this, then aye, it might keep her safe."

Rory raised his eyebrows. "I thought ye had no wish for her to marry ye merely to save herself."

"I am hoping 'twill no' be for that reason," Aulay admitted solemnly. "But if 'tis . . ." He sighed and shrugged. "I would rather see her alive than hold on to me pride and see her dead."

"But ye do no' even ken if marrying her will save her," Rory pointed out. "These attacks may no' be by her family. How could they ken she was here?"

"They could have overheard Alick or Geordie asking questions about a ship that sank and suspected the mast she was on was found," he pointed out.

"That's possible," Dougall said thoughtfully. "And then they need only have followed them home here to Buchanan to find Jetta."

Cam snorted at the suggestion. "They would no' need to follow them anywhere. You boys all look alike, and what with yer mercenary work over the years, and ye each having financial interests that are so varied—Dougall with his horses, Niels with his sheep, Rory with his healing and so on," he said for example. "Everyone in Scotland kens a Buchanan when they see him."

"There ye ha'e it," Aulay said quietly. "It could verra well be Jetta's family behind the attacks. Although I do no' ken why they'd want her dead if they were trying to marry her off to some murderous bastard," he added with frustration. Shaking his head, he continued on, "And I'll no' ken that until Jetta remembers. Mayhap telling her that her name is no' Jetta and reminding her o' what she said when we first found her will help her regain her memories."

"Well I'd suggest ye wait to ha'e that talk with her until after the sup," Uncle Acair said, drawing their attention to the fact that he now stood on the top step of the stairs.

Aulay glanced at him with surprise, wondering how much he'd heard.

"Because Alick and the other men are back from the hunt, the maids are bringing out the sup as we speak and wee Jetta is hungry enough she asked me to come fetch ye," he announced and then arched an eyebrow. "Ye ken the lass needs to eat to regain her strength, and I'm thinking she'll need strength fer the conversation ye're planning to have with her."

Aulay shifted his gaze to the table below and noted that the women had all sat down now. He could clearly see Jetta peering his way and the encouraging smile she was giving him.

"Aye," he said, "I'll hold off until after the sup."

"Warn me before ye talk to her," Rory said quietly. "And call me if ye need me."

When Aulay nodded, Rory turned to go back into the room where Katie, Geordie and Conran were.

The moment the door closed, Aulay turned to the other men and raised his eyebrows. "Is there anything else anyone can think o' that we need to discuss before we go down?"

When everyone shook their heads, Aulay started down the stairs, his gaze seeking out Jetta as he went. She was listening to something Murine was saying now, and smiling widely. She had a beautiful smile. It was one he hoped to enjoy the rest of his life. If Jetta would have him. Unfortunately, he wasn't at all sure she would, and the worry that she might not was making his stomach roil. He had no appetite at all just now and would have preferred to drag her above stairs and get the coming conversation over with. But he would wait until after she'd eaten. She needed to eat.

Chapter 12

"So your maid, Joyce, stayed behind to watch the girls?"

Jetta glanced up from her food to peer curiously at Saidh when Edith asked her that question.

"Aye," Saidh said. "I wanted to bring them, but Alpin was harping on about dragging the babes across the country while so young, and what if there was danger and so on, so I finally gave in and agreed to leave them at MacDonnell with him and Joyce." She grimaced now and admitted, "It has only been a day and I already miss them."

Murine grinned and admitted, "There was a day I was thinking 'twould be better were ye graced with lads only and no lasses." She shook her head and then added, "And then ye had trip—"

"Just a minute," Saidh interrupted. "What do ye mean ye were thinking 'twould be better did I ha'e only lads?"

Murine arched her eyebrows. "Do ye no' recall how ye explained the bedding to me the night Dougall and I married?"

"Aye," Saidh said at once. "What was wrong with it? I thought 'twas brilliant."

"Brilliant?" she asked with a snort.

"How did she explain it?" Edith asked curiously from the other side of Jetta and Aulay.

"She—Just a minute," Murine said suddenly and stood up to hurry away from the table.

Jetta watched her go and then noticed that the men had all stopped speaking to stare after her too. She also noticed that Murine's husband, Dougall, was looking amused. It made Jetta suspect he had already heard how his sister had explained the bedding to his young wife.

"Here we are!"

Jetta glanced around at that announcement to find that Murine had returned. She had not reclaimed her seat, however, but had approached from the other side of the table so that they could all see her. The woman was carrying a loaf of bread and the biggest carrot she had ever seen, one that was so dirty it looked fresh from the ground. It was also incredibly knobby and twisted, Jetta noted with curiosity.

"Right, I shall explain it to Jetta, just as Saidh explained it to me," Murine announced with a wicked grin that suggested this would be fun. She then set down the carrot and bread and instead picked up her own and Jetta's wine. Handing Jetta hers, Murine lifted her own and announced, "Saidh seemed terribly thirsty and downed her own wine in one gulp that day, so . . ."

Murine downed the drink in one long gulp and then set it down on the table with a grimace and said, "All right."

Jetta merely held her wine and watched uncertainly as Murine picked up the carrot and loaf of bread. Holding up the loaf, Murine turned with it so everyone in the family could see, and then turned back to Jetta and announced, "This is you."

"It is?" Jetta asked uncertainly.

"Exactly what I said," Murine announced with amusement. "At which point, Saidh frowned at the bread, and then she did this." Setting the loaf on the tabletop, Murine took Dougall's *sgian-dubh* when he held it out and used it to slice the loaf in half. Setting one half aside, Murine then sliced a slit down the center of the soft part of the other where it had been separated from the first.

Apparently finished, Murine straightened and held the half loaf up with the crusty side against her palm and the soft center with the slit facing Jetta as she announced, "*This* is you, and this—" she held up the rather large, knobby and very dirty carrot "—is Aulay."

"Looks like Aulay could use a bath," Cam said with amusement.

"Looks like he's spent time with one too many light skirts," Greer countered. "Are those knobby things supposed to be sores?"

Murine grimaced and then glanced to Aulay and said apologetically,

"The one Saidh used for Dougall wasn't quite as big, but it was even dirtier and knobbier."

"As it should be," Aulay said mildly.

Cam chuckled, and then raised and lowered his eyebrows suggestively and asked, "Aye, but how did Saidh ken how big a carrot she should use?"

"She used to spy on us when we were skinny dipping as lads," Niels tattled with amusement.

"I did no' pick the carrot," Saidh said with exasperation. "I just asked me maid to bring me a loaf o' bread and a carrot."

"Enough," Murine interrupted the teasing and laughter. "No interruptions, please. As Saidh said, this is difficult enough."

When they all fell silent then, Murine nodded and then paused as if trying to recall what came next. After a moment, she muttered, "Oh aye," and stuck the carrot down the neckline of her gown to nestle between her breasts.

"Oh, say," Niels said with surprise. "Saidh was giving ye some advanced instruction."

Murine glanced to Niels with confusion, which Jetta thoroughly understood. She was a bit confused by his comment as well. However, while she remained confused, Murine peered down at the carrot between her breasts and quite suddenly seemed to understand, because her cheeks immediately turned a bright crimson and she reached as if to withdraw the carrot.

"Don't," Dougall said, making her pause. "Ignore my idiot brother, wife, and continue with it just as Saidh did."

Smiling gratefully at her husband, Murine nodded and let her hand drop from the carrot. Leaving it tucked snugly between her breasts, she soldiered on, "As I mentioned, Saidh was verra thirsty, and at this point tucked the carrot just there while she poured herself another goblet o' wine."

Murine picked up her empty goblet, pretended to down another glass full and then moved in front of Jetta again, and held up the bread and empty goblet. "Right. This is you, and this is—oh hell." Murine made an exaggerated face of exasperation that suggested she was still mimicking

Saidh, and set down the goblet to retrieve the carrot instead, before starting again, "This is you, and this is Aulay. And this is what will happen
tonight," she announced, and pushed the larger end of the carrot into the
slit in the bread. Although, of course, the carrot was much larger than
the slit, and what she was really doing was mashing the bread dough
with the carrot head, hammering it over and over again as she repeatedly
drove the carrot into the dough and pulled it out.

"Dear God in heaven."

Jetta heard Aulay breathe those horrified words as she gaped at what
Murine was doing to the poor bread, and then Murine announced, "But
it's much nicer than it looks. He'll kiss ye and such, and ye'll get all excited and want to punch him hard in the face."

"What?" Jetta gasped, her eyes wide.

"That is what Saidh told me," Murine assured her cheerfully as she
jammed the carrot into the bread as if the orange vegetable was her fist
and the loaf Aulay's face.

Jetta turned to Saidh askance. "Punch him?"

"That's how I feel," Saidh said with a shrug. "That if he does no' end
this sweet torture and give me my release soon I will have to punch him."

The men around them were divided in their responses. Saidh's brothers burst out laughing, Uncle Acair rolled his eyes and shook his head,
Cam looked startled at the words and Greer just grinned.

"But," Murine continued, "Saidh said that ye'd then feel like an ex-
plosion has gone off inside ye, and 'twould be so nice." Murine glanced
skyward and released a long, starry-eyed sigh as if pondering the release,
but she was obviously still portraying Saidh's conversation with her, because in the blink of an eye the expression was replaced with an inquisi-
tive expression as she turned to Jetta and asked, "Understand?"

Unable to speak at the moment, Jetta nodded weakly.

"Oh, thank God," Murine muttered and tossed her props over her
shoulder and then eyed Jetta's wine and asked, "Are ye going to drink
that?"

Jetta shook her head.

Murine smiled. "Which was my answer as well, and as I watched,

Saidh grabbed it up and chugged it down. It was at that point I thought it might be best all around did Saidh have all sons and no daughters with Greer. For surely, no young lass should have to hear the marriage bed described that way," she finished and then signaled the end of her little show with a curtsy.

"Bravo!" Niels said on a laugh, beginning to clap.

"Aye, fer a minute there, I actually believed ye to be Saidh," Cam said with a grin as he too clapped.

"This is the second time I've seen it and it still amuses me." Jo chuckled.

Beaming, Murine gave another curtsy and then hurried around the table to reclaim her seat.

Biting her lip, Jetta glanced to Saidh then to see how she was taking all of this, but Saidh was sitting and looking completely unperturbed. Catching Jetta's concerned gaze, she shrugged mildly and said, "'Tis what happens."

Her words brought a groan from Aulay that drew Jetta around to see the dismay on his face. Frowning, she shifted her gaze uncertainly toward Dougall.

Her brother-in-law gave her a reassuring smile, and patted Aulay on the back. "Relax, brother. 'Tis fine."

"I do no' see what everyone finds so funny," Saidh said, drawing Jetta's attention away from her husband. "There was nothing wrong with me instruction to Murine. That is exactly what happens."

Jetta bit her lip to hide her amusement and then heard Aulay mutter in response to Dougall, "Aye, ye can say that. Ye'd already bedded Murine when she was given that horrible instruction. But Jetta is still untried and like to stay that way forever after that display."

No one else heard the words. Jetta barely caught them herself, and yet, for a moment, the entire room went silent around her. It took a moment for her to realize that it was her. The room hadn't gone silent at all. She could see people moving and talking, but could hear nothing. There was no clinking of metal, no lighthearted chatter, no laughter. Everything was suddenly silent, which left her mind screaming as it rushed madly about like a mouse loose in a pantry full of food.

She was still untried? Had they never consummated their marriage? Why? Did he not find her attractive enough? Had he not wanted to marry her? Or was it the other way around? Had she refused him her bed? Perhaps, as she had feared, she'd been repulsed by his scar before losing her memories.

Jetta could not imagine that though. He was an attractive man despite the scar. But perhaps she had been understandably shy and reticent on their wedding night and he had taken that as rejection. Perhaps the shipwreck and her head injuries were the chance they'd needed to repair a marriage that had been limping along under misunderstandings and misperceptions. Aye, that seemed possible, and if so, she would grasp that chance with both hands and fix everything, for she had a good man, and was quite sure she could have an amazing marriage if she just worked at it.

That decision seemed to act like a switch, turning the sound back on for Jetta as Murine said, "I love ye, Saidh, and ye ken it. And much to me surprise, while I thought it might be best did ye have lads and no' lassies, now ye've had the triplets, I see how lucky they are."

"Triplets?" Jetta echoed with surprise, briefly distracted from her worries.

"Aye," Murine told her, leaning forward to see her past Saidh and Greer. "Saidh gave birth to triplets just six months ago."

"Oh my God! I am an aunt thrice over?" Jetta gasped, eyes wide. She then frowned as she wondered if she was still an aunt if her marriage had not yet been consummated. Were she and Aulay even legally married without the consummation?

"We all are," Edith said excitedly, reclaiming her attention. "Well, except for Jo, but she is their Godmother."

Jo nodded with a smile. "And we are going to betroth my Bearnard to the eldest girl, little Rhona."

"And then ye'll be family too," Edith said with a grin. "We'll all be related!"

Jetta smiled faintly as the women all grinned at each other, and then commented, "Rhona is a lovely name. What names did ye give the other girls?"

"Sorcha and Ailsa," Saidh said at once.

Jetta's eyes widened incredulously. "You named one after me?"

Aulay froze when Jetta said that. He was not the only one. There was a sudden and complete silence among the people seated around him, and no one at the high table was now moving or speaking. All sat gaping at Jetta with wide eyes, even himself. He sat still, watching her eyes round with realization and then flood with emotion as she turned to stare at him. He saw confusion, heartbreak, fear and grief, and then pain. Eyebrows drawing together in concentration, she stared at him briefly and then stood up, as if wanting to escape the knowledge filling her. But the moment she put weight on her foot, she cried out in pain and then tumbled sideways over the trestle table bench, her head plummeting toward the Great Hall floor.

"Jetta!" Aulay roared, leaping to his feet, but was not quick enough to catch her before she hit the floor. Cursing himself for failing her, he knelt to gather her into his arms.

"She hit her head again," Alick said with dismay, kneeling across her body from him.

"The crispin cushioned her head when she fell down the stairs. I am sure it did it this time too," Saidh said, joining them.

"Then why has she lost consciousness again?" Aulay asked grimly.

"I do no' ken," Saidh admitted, eyeing Jetta unhappily.

"I'll fetch Rory," Alick said straightening.

"Have him come to my room," Aulay ordered, standing up and carrying Jetta toward the stairs on his brother's heels. He peered down at Jetta as he took the stairs, noting the pallor of her face and the pained wince her brows were forming. He suspected she'd regained her memory, or at least part of it. Something about her expression after she'd said *"You named one after me?"* had told him she was remembering something, probably who she was, and more important to him, who she wasn't. Aulay was quite sure she now knew he was not her husband, and he was scared to death about what that might mean for him. He'd not got to tell her himself, or to explain. And if Saidh was right, that was a very bad thing.

"Pull back the linen and furs so he can lay her in the bed."

Aulay glanced around at that order from Saidh, somewhat surprised to find that he'd reached the master bedchamber while distracted by his thoughts. Well, *they'd* reached the master bedchamber, he realized as he noted that his entire family had followed him, from Uncle Acair on down to Jo and Cam Sinclair, who weren't strictly family yet, but would be someday if their son married young Rhona. The only ones missing were Rory, Alick, Conran and Geordie.

Aulay had barely had the thought when Rory rushed into the room with Conran and Alick on his heels.

"Alick said Jetta hit her head. Again," Rory growled, rushing to the bed. "What happened?"

"What happened is she remembered her name was no' Jetta, but Sorcha or Ailsa," Cam announced solemnly.

Rory's eyebrows rose. "Which is it? Sorcha or Ailsa?"

"We do no ken," Saidh admitted, eyeing Jetta with concern. "We were talking about Rhona marrying Bearnard someday. Jetta asked what my other two daughters' names were. I told her and she said, 'Ye named one after me?'"

"And then she fainted," Edith added worriedly.

"I do no' think she fainted," Murine argued. "She tried to stand up, and when she put weight on her injured ankle, she cried out and fell, hitting her head."

"Either way, it would seem her name is either Sorcha or Ailsa," Jo pointed out.

Much to Aulay's relief, Rory ignored the women and moved up beside him to examine Jetta.

"I pulled back the linens and furs," Dougall said. "Ye can lay her in the bed."

"Just let me remove her caul first," Rory muttered, working on the headpiece. "'Twould be harder to remove with her lying down."

Aulay grunted agreement, and shifted his arm a little lower on Jetta's back to keep it out of the way as his brother fussed with the headpiece.

"Do ye want me to do it?" Murine offered, moving up beside them.

Rory did not answer at first, but after struggling briefly with the crispin, gave up and stepped back. "Aye. Please."

Murine immediately took his place and made short work of removing the headpiece. She then stepped away so that Rory could step up again and examine Jetta's head, first visually and then by running his hands over it.

"So her name is Sorcha or Ailsa," Edith murmured. "Can ye imagine? She has the same name as one o' yer daughters, Saidh. 'Tis like it was meant to be."

"Aye," Jo agreed, and then added, "but 'tis strange. Her accent is English, but both Sorcha and Ailsa are good Scots names."

"Mayhap her mother was Scottish, but her father English so that she was raised there," Murine suggested.

"She has no new bumps or injuries," Rory announced, drawing his attention again. "Lay her down and tell me what happened. She remembered her name. Is that all?"

"I do no' think so," Aulay admitted as he set her gently in the bed. "I think she remembered a lot more than her name."

"What makes ye think that?" Alick asked with surprise as they watched Rory lift her eyelids and peer at her eyes.

"Her expression when she turned to me. She looked . . ." Aulay paused and frowned as he recalled the gamut of emotions that had rushed across her face. "Verra upset," he said finally, if a little lamely. Considering the matter, he frowned and added, "Although, she did get that pained face she gets whenever she tries to remember something, so she may no' ha'e remembered everything. She appeared to be trying to remember more."

"In other words, ye do no' ken what she remembered," Rory said, finishing with his examination and straightening to eye Aulay as he said, "Her name may be all she did remember, and is upset because we have not been calling her by it."

"Which probably told her we ha'e been lying to her all this time," Saidh pointed out grimly, and then scowled at Aulay. "I warned ye. I told ye ye needed to tell her the truth ere she discovered it for herself. Now she'll no' ken what to think, and will no' trust us when all we want is to keep her safe."

"I was going to tell her," Aulay assured her defensively.

"He was," Rory admitted, his tone sharp as he added, "despite my insistence that he should not and that she needed to feel safe and loved in the bosom of her family to heal. He was going to ignore that advice and tell her after the sup."

"I was going to ask her to marry me too, though," Aulay pointed out, glowering at him. "That should have let her know she was cared for and would be kept safe."

"Safe from what?"

Aulay's gaze jerked from Rory down to Jetta, where she lay with her eyes now open.

Chapter 13

"Jetta. Ye're awake," Aulay said with relief, settling on the side of the bed and taking her hand.

"Sorcha," she said tightly. Avoiding meeting his gaze, she tugged her hand free of his and repeated. "Safe from what?"

"The man yer family was sending ye to marry and whoever pushed ye down the stairs," Aulay said quietly. Trying not to be hurt by her pulling away from him, he let his own hand rest in his lap.

She met his gaze then, her eyes wide. "I am to marry someone else and you allowed me to think we were husband and wife? You let me betray my own betrothed?"

"Nay," he said at once. "He was no' yer betrothed."

Confusion immediately filled her face. "But you said—"

"Ye were somewhat conscious when we found ye, and seemed to still ha'e yer memories then," Aulay interrupted to explain. "And when I tried to soothe ye and said we'd find yer family and see ye safely to them, ye got quite upset."

"Aye," Alick put in, moving closer. "Ye fashed something awful at the thought o' our taking ye to yer family. Ye seemed terrified and said something about a cat, and a white lady and a betrothed who was no' yer betrothed, but ye were being forced to marry him, and how he'd kill ye like his last wife." Nodding to emphasize his words, he added, "Aulay had to promise ye we'd no' take ye to yer family until ye were hale and healthy again to calm ye down."

Jetta frowned, her gaze sliding between Alick and Aulay now.

"But when ye woke up ye did no' remember anything," Aulay added solemnly. "Even who ye were. And ye asked me was I yer brother, and when I said nay, ye decided I was yer husband and—"

"And you did not bother to correct me," she said, her voice sharp.

"I did no' really get the chance," he said and reminded her, "Mavis came in and then Rory, and—"

"And," Rory interrupted, "when he told me ye'd mistaken him fer yer husband, I told him it was better to let ye think that fer a bit."

"Why?" she asked with amazement.

"Because it soothed ye to think ye were among loved ones, and I felt sure ye'd heal faster were ye feeling safe and cared for. Ye were still very ill at the time," he reminded her. "Ye'd no' had anything but broth dribbled down yer throat fer three weeks. Ye were rail thin, and so weak, I was no' even sure ye'd survive. But I thought ye'd ha'e a better chance at survivin' did ye think ye were safe and home, rather than kenning that ye were in a strange place among strangers."

Jetta breathed out a sigh and closed her eyes wearily.

"Jetta. I mean, Sorcha," Rory began.

"Jetta," she interrupted quietly, knowing she was probably confusing them. She'd just corrected Aulay when he'd called her Jetta moments ago and referred to herself as Sorcha and was now doing the opposite. But she was confused too. While she knew her name was Sorcha, she'd become used to being called Jetta. Besides, she had no idea who Sorcha was and wouldn't until she regained her memories. Now, she felt like Jetta Buchanan. But she wasn't Jetta Buchanan, she thought unhappily.

"Jetta then," Rory said solemnly, before continuing, "I'm sorry if my decision to withhold the truth upsets ye. But I stand by that decision, lass. Despite the trouble it caused in the family. I think it did help ye."

"Trouble?" she asked with surprise, her eyes blinking open.

Rory hesitated and then said, "I'll explain the trouble in a minute, but first, ye ha'e to tell us, did ye remember anything else but ye're first name? Do ye recall yer family name? Or where ye're from? Or . . . anything?" he asked.

Aulay watched her expression change and knew the answer to Rory's question before she spoke.

"Nay," she admitted unhappily. "Just that I am Sorcha and that my mother named me that because she knew from the moment I came squalling into the world that I would be a bright light in her life. She told me that just ere dying in my arms," she admitted, the grief he'd seen earlier washing over her face again. Forcing it back, she said, "I tried to remember more. I tried to force it, but the pain got so bad I could not bear it anymore and then I put weight on my ankle and fell."

Everyone was silent for a minute and then Aulay patted her hand and murmured, "I'm sure the rest will come."

Much to his relief, she didn't pull away from his touch this time. He didn't push though, merely patted her hand and then withdrew his own.

Peering at Rory, Jetta raised her eyebrows in question. "The troubles caused in the family by not telling me who I really was? Ye were going to explain."

"Oh aye." Clearing his throat, Rory said, "First, Aulay and I came to loggerheads several times o'er his behavior around ye. He appeared to ha'e trouble remembering that the two o' ye were no' really married."

Jetta immediately began to blush and Aulay suspected she was recalling those times in question. He certainly was now that Rory had mentioned them, and for a moment he basked in the memory of the taste of her, the sound of her excited cries, the way she'd responded to his kisses . . . and waking to find her mouth on him. That memory was particularly piquant, he thought and then grunted and looked around with surprise when someone punched him in the arm. Spotting Saidh standing next to him, scowling ferociously, he frowned and raised his eyebrows in question. His sister gave him a meaningful look and then nodded toward Jetta.

Turning, he glanced at her and saw that she was not experiencing quite the same joy in the memories as he had been before Saidh punched him. In fact, she was bright red and nearly squirming in the bed with apparent embarrassment and what might be shame.

Scowling, he patted her hand again and said, "Ye've naught to be ashamed o', lass. Ye believed we were married. Besides, yer innocence is still intact."

Rather than soothe her, that made her blush deepen and she looked more distressed than ever. Aulay was relieved when Rory continued, "The other trouble it caused was with Saidh. She was most upset that we were no' telling ye the truth, and took both Aulay and me to task for it. She e'en tried to convince us to tell ye everything."

"I did," Saidh assured her. "Unfortunately, men are stupid. At least me brothers are. They would no' listen to me."

Jetta offered Saidh a crooked smile.

"The fact that they're sitting here telling ye this instead o' telling ye what's most important proves it," Saidh added, turning to scowl at Aulay briefly.

Not having a clue what she was referring to, Aulay glowered back.

Apparently recognizing that he didn't know what she was talking about, Saidh said with exasperation, "Greer told me ye planned to tell Jetta everything after the sup and to ask her to marry ye?"

"Oh aye," he agreed quickly and turned to Jetta, nodding his head firmly. "I planned to tell ye tonight."

"Why?" she asked at once.

Nonplussed, Aulay stared at her. "Why what?"

She hesitated and then asked, "Why were you going to tell me now after so long leaving me in the dark?"

Aulay paused to consider before answering, suspecting he was treading on uneven ground here, and then he said, "I wanted to tell ye from the first, but did no' wish to risk yer healing. However, what with someone pushing ye down the stairs and whatnot we began to worry this may ha'e something to do with yer family or who they were trying to make ye marry and it did seem ye'd be safer if ye were married, and ye had to ken ye were no' married before I could ask ye to marry me."

"So you were going to tell me so that you could ask me to marry you, and you want to marry me to keep me safe?" she asked with a small frown.

"Aye," Aulay said, and then glanced around when one of the women gasped. His eyebrows rose as he took in the various reactions of his family. His brothers, as well as Cam and Greer, were all nodding as if he was making perfect sense. The women, however, at least Edith, Murine and Jo, all looked horrified. But it was the reactions of Uncle Acair, Rory and Saidh that troubled him most. Rory was wincing, Uncle Acair was shaking his head and rolling his eyes skyward as if silently asking his dead brother, Aulay's father, how he had managed to raise such an idiot, and Saidh had her lips pursed and a somewhat confounded expression, as if she thought his answer made sense, but also thought it was not quite right and she could not for the life of her figure out why. That was most troubling to him. He understood ladies expected sweet words and romantic gestures, but he was not that kind of man. However, if his own sister, who was—in his estimation—as far from a romantic as could be found . . . well, if she thought his answer lacking, that was bad.

Scratching the back of his head, he peered back at Jetta and noted her dejected pose. She was peering at her hands where they lay on her chest, and she looked disappointed. Wounded even, he thought.

"Tell the lass how ye feel about her, ye dolt," Uncle Acair hissed.

Aulay took a moment to scowl at the man, and then turned back to Jetta to see that she'd raised her eyes and was watching him hopefully. That was when it suddenly occurred to him that he'd never given any indication that he even had feelings for her, which he supposed wasn't fair. After all, Jetta had said how she felt about him repeatedly since waking. She'd told him she wanted him, that she felt lucky to have him to husband, even that she loved him. Of course, that had all been influenced by her belief that they were married, but that didn't make it any less true. He, however . . . well, he had not even told her he liked her, Aulay realized now. He had a vague recollection of saying she was wee and cared for in response to a comment of hers once, but other than that he'd not said one word about his own feelings for her. And it seemed to him that he probably should.

Slipping off the bed to kneel on the floor beside it, Aulay took her hands in his and said solemnly, "Lass, I thought ye beautiful the minute I laid eyes on yer face. I've wanted ye from the minute we dragged ye out o' the ocean and onto me boat. And I decided to keep ye the minute ye saw me face and did no' flinch, weep or scream at the scar, but instead called me yer angel."

"Did she?" Edith asked eagerly.

"Aye," Alick said. "She said he was an angel sent by God to save her, and touched his cheek as if he were a precious gift."

"Oh," the women sighed together.

Ignoring them, Aulay continued, "Fer the three weeks I tended ye, I worried every minute o' every day that ye'd no' survive, and the thought distressed me something terrible. But ye did survive. Ye woke and thought me yer husband and . . ." He shook his head and then took a deep breath, let it out and said, "I do no' ken if what I feel is love. But I think o' ye all the time, even when ye're no' with me. And these days since ye've woken have been the happiest o' me life."

When her smile widened, he added, "And not only that. I see ye everywhere, lass. Every maid I see with long black hair reminds me o' ye. Even some without hair, or well, with their hair covered," he explained and shook his head before continuing, "I worry about ye constantly too. I hated being away from ye when I had to return to Buchanan without ye. I like spending time with ye. I like playing chess with ye, and Nine Men's Morris, and I like talking to ye. I just enjoy yer company. But I like kissing and touching ye best o' all, and I'm aching to bed ye. I want ye fer me wife, lass. I want to wake every day to yer smiling face, I want to ha'e beautiful bairns with ye that we can raise together to be fine, strong men and women, and I want to live to be an old man and die in yer arms, for 'tis as close to heaven as I've ever been."

Someone snuffled behind him, and Aulay glanced around, scowling when he saw that the women were all weeping like bairns. Christ, even Alick was weeping like a girl, but not Saidh. Her eyes were glassy, but she was manfully keeping her tears from dropping. He could always count on Saidh.

Turning back to Jetta, he blew out a breath and said solemnly, "But I do no' want ye to marry me only fer the safety it offers. I'll keep ye safe, married or no'. But I'd rather ye only marry me if ye have soft feelings fer me too, and want to spend yer life with me the way I do you."

"Aye," she said softly.

Aulay hesitated, and then asked uncertainly, "Aye, what?"

"Aye, I want to marry you for you," she said on a soft laugh, and then tugged her hands from his and framed his face with them. "Have I not already told you I love you? Mayhap at first it was because I thought you my husband, and assumed that I had loved you ere the shipwreck where I lost my memories, but I quickly came to see why I *would* love you. You are all I could wish for in a husband, Aulay. In truth, you are probably more than I ever dared hope for. I would consider myself lucky to be your wife, bear your bairns and die an old woman in your arms. I see a happy future with you."

Aulay grinned, but hearing more sniffling behind him, asked, "Even if marrying me means ye'll be stuck with me large, nosy and interfering family?"

Glancing past him, she grinned as she took in the people surrounding them and nodded. "Aye. Even then, husband. I mean, Aulay." Grimacing, she added, "Sorry. I am so used to calling you that, I just—"

"Well, in truth, ye've every right to call him that, lass," Uncle Acair said now. "Ye may no' ha'e had benefit o' a priest, but yer married by habit and repute now." When she peered at him uncertainly, he explained, "Ye've lived together as a couple, ye calling him husband, and him even calling ye wife a time or two. Ye presented yerselves as a couple to society, or at least to us." He shrugged. "Ye're handfasted, which is as good as married here in Scotland. The courts would say that legally, ye *are* wed."

"Oh," she murmured, but then frowned.

Certain he knew what she was thinking, Aulay assured her, "We will have a priest marry us all good and proper though. In fact—" Turning, he glanced to Alick, who was still looking wet-eyed, and said, "Alick, go fetch—"

"Damn! The priest," Niels said suddenly, interrupting Aulay.

Noting his expression, Aulay narrowed his eyes. "What? Is there something wrong with Father Archibald?"

"Not wrong exactly," Niels assured him. "But Edith wanted to have a word with him when we arrived, and Alick said—"

"The stable master told me he rode out this morning just ere I arrived with Saidh and Greer and the chests," Alick said, interrupting Niels.

"Damn," Aulay breathed with a frown.

"Aye. That's how we lost Father MacKenna," Dougall reminded him grimly.

"What?" Cam asked with confusion.

"Our last priest was Father MacKenna," Niels explained. "But when Dougall brought Murine here and they hoped to marry, he suddenly rode off, never to be heard from again."

"We suspect Murine's brother and cousin had something to do with it," Dougall said grimly. "They would no' ha'e wanted him to marry us and ruin their plans."

"I'm sure this is no' the same as MacKenna," Greer said soothingly. "Archibald is fine and will return tonight or in the morn."

"And if he does no', Drummond is no' far from here," Edith pointed out.

"Aye." Niels smiled. "Our priest could marry ye."

"MacDonnell is close too," Saidh added. "If we held the wedding there, ye could meet Alpin and see yer nieces."

"Failing that there is Carmichael," Dougall put in.

"Or Sinclair," Cam added. "We'd be pleased to host yer wedding."

Aulay stared at them all, his heart warmed by all the offers, but panic setting into his brain at the thought of having to accept one over the others.

"I'm thinking we should just give Father Archibald a chance to return," Uncle Acair said before Aulay could be forced to choose between the many offers. "If he does no' return tonight, we can send some men out after him first thing in the morn. If they do no' bring him back, then we'll have to consider an alternative. But at least here, we could all attend," he pointed out. "Including the people o' Buchanan she will become lady of."

"Aye," Dougall said with a nod. "That would be best."

"Let us hope Father Archibald returns, then," Niels murmured.

"Aye," Uncle Acair agreed. "Now, why do we no' let these two get some rest. It has been a long day, and tomorrow may be even longer fer them if Father Archibald returns."

No one argued. Everyone turned and made their way from the room, murmuring good-nights and sleep-wells as they went.

Jetta watched Aulay walk the others out, her thoughts a bit confused.

She was having trouble adjusting to the thought that he was not really her husband. Yet, she reminded herself, they would marry on the morrow, or as soon as they could find a priest. Still, she had thought of him as husband for . . . well, for the entire history that she could remember.

Sighing, she gave her head a little shake. According to Uncle Acair—Jetta stopped the thought as she realized he wasn't her uncle yet. Although, maybe he was. According to Uncle Acair she and Aulay were married by something and repute. She couldn't remember what he'd said. She did remember his saying they were handfasted, considered married by law. So, Aulay was her husband after all, and these people who had treated her like family, *were* her family. But she'd feel better if they had a proper marriage, blessed by a priest.

The sound of the door closing caught her ear and Jetta glanced up as Aulay turned back to the room. She bit her lip briefly, and then asked, "Do you think Father Archibald will return tomorrow?"

"If we're lucky he will," Aulay muttered as he crossed to the bed. "I've no desire to offend anyone by choosing where to marry if he does no'."

"Oh aye, that could be tricky, could it not?" she agreed and lowered her head to peer at her hands as she considered the problem. If they chose MacDonnell as the spot to wed—and that would be her preference since she'd like to meet her soon-to-be nieces—it might leave Niels, Dougall and even the Sinclairs offended.

"Aye, very tricky," Aulay agreed. "I've no desire to inadvertently hurt anyone's feelings, so we shall have to hope luck is with us this time."

Nodding, she glanced around only to frown when she did not see him anywhere in the room.

"Unfortunately, while I hate to admit this to ye fer fear ye'll change yer mind about marrying me," he continued, his voice the only proof of his presence, "I am no' the luckiest o' men, me love."

Following the sound of his voice, Jetta peered over the side of the bed to see him lying on a pallet there, one arm over his face. She was frowning at his words, until the last two sank in. *"Me love."* It was the first time he'd used an endearment when addressing her, and it made her heart melt. She enjoyed the feeling for a moment, and then scowled at the man on the floor, and said, "I do not understand how you can say that. You seem to me to be a very lucky man indeed."

Aulay shifted his arm aside and blinked up at her in surprise. Probably partially because he didn't expect to see her there, hanging over the side of the bed above him, but also because of her words.

"What?" he asked with disbelief. "How can ye say I'm lucky?"

"How can you say you are not?" she countered at once.

"Have ye seen me face?" he asked dryly.

"Oh piffle," Jetta said, pulling back and dropping to lie on the bed with disgust.

"What the devil does that mean?" Aulay asked, sitting up so he could see her again. When she didn't respond except to shrug, he asked, "How would ye like to walk around with a face so ugly bairns run away crying and women scream in horror when they see ye?"

"Oh, they did not do that," she said turning to eye him with disbelief.

"They did," he assured her bitterly.

Frowning at this news, Jetta examined his scar more closely, and then admitted, "I suppose, at first, when the scar was still red and raw, it might have caused a stir."

"Damned right it did," he growled resentfully. "The first year I hardly left the keep to avoid the reactions it caused."

"And the second?" she asked.

"It was a little better," he admitted reluctantly.

"And no doubt it was better still the year after that," she suggested.

He shrugged unhappily.

Jetta considered him briefly and then asked, "Would ye really rather never have been scarred and be married to Adaira Stuart, then?"

"Who told ye about Adaira?" Aulay asked with surprise.

"A couple of people have mentioned her," she said evasively. "Now answer the question. Would you rather be unscarred and married to Adaira?"

"Good God, nay," he growled. "She was no' at all the woman I thought her. I found out things about her after the betrothal was broken that . . ." He shook his head. "I made a lucky escape there."

"Lucky?" she asked innocently.

"Aye. Do ye ken she tried to seduce Sinclair at court?" he asked with outrage, not catching the *lucky* bit. "And that was ere I was ever injured. He said he refused her offer because he kenned she was betrothed to another, though he did no' ken it was me at the time. That was ere we knew each other so well, but I am sure there were others she offered herself to who had less honor."

Mouth tight, he said, "And, she beat her maid. Mavis told me that after the betrothal was broken too. Beat her something fierce once, right in front o' Mavis, for merely dropping her brush. Had we married, she may ha'e tried to beat the servants here. Nay, that wench was no' the lady I had always thought her to be."

"Hmm. A lucky escape indeed then that ye were scarred and she broke the betrothal," she murmured.

"Aye." He nodded, and then glanced to her sharply. His eyes narrowed. "Ye're saying had I no' been scarred, I'd be married to the wench."

"And stuck with her for a lifetime," Jetta pointed out solemnly. "I think two or three years of misery as your scar healed was a good exchange for avoiding a lifetime of misery with Lady Adaira Stuart."

"Aye," he muttered. "When ye put it that way, mayhap I did get off lucky." Gaze softening, he added, "Especially since I now get to marry you instead."

"Your luck was my luck as well, m'laird, for I get to have you to husband," she assured him with a smile, and then added, "and I get your very large, very loving and caring family as my own too."

Aulay smiled crookedly at that. "They may be nosy, and interfering, but mean well."

"Aye, and there is another example of your good luck," she assured him.

"Mostly," he said solemnly, and she knew he was thinking of Ewan, the brother he'd lost.

"Nay, not mostly," Jetta insisted gently. "Husband, you have six brothers and a sister who all love you and have rushed here to be of aid if they can. Just their having survived to this stage in life is lucky. Your family has lost only one of nine children. Do you not know how rare that is? Most families lose thrice that number ere their children are out of britches. But your family lost only the one and you have six brothers and one sister who are not only still healthy and well, but who love and care about you and are here when you need them," she said, and felt her eyes tear up as she said it, for she knew she had not been so lucky else her family would not have been trying to send her off to someone she wasn't even betrothed to and whom she apparently had feared would kill her. Jetta knew she would have done everything in her power to prevent a sister from such an end. Pushing that thought away, she continued, "And then you were lucky with the wound you took."

"Aye, the scar kept me from marrying Adaira," he acknowledged. "I agree with ye there."

"I am not talking about that part now," she said solemnly. "Do you realize, had your attacker been standing even an inch or two nearer, you would not have survived the blow? Or, he could have been using a mace rather than a sword, or something else, which surely would have killed you. The very fact that you are alive is another instance of luck being on your side."

"I suppose it is," he acknowledged.

"And what is it but luck that you were blessed with such good looks that the injury barely detracts from them? Or that God graced you with an intelligence, kindness and chivalry I ken I am lucky to have encountered. Nay, husband, you are not unlucky. Or if you are, then your misfortune has been my good fortune, for had you not been injured and had your betrothed not refused to marry you, then I would not now get to marry you myself. And I know how lucky I am to be able to call you husband."

Seeing the doubt on his face, and determined to rid him of it, she said, "You are a good man, Aulay Buchanan. And that alone makes me lucky, but . . ." Closing her eyes, Jetta bit her lip briefly. She did not want him to have any doubt that she was marrying him for him, and not because she thought him a safe haven. But the only way she could think to do that was to admit . . . Straightening her shoulders, she opened her eyes and admitted what she thought he needed to hear. "I am very looking forward to the marriage bed, husband. In fact, I am sore disappointed the priest is not here and we are not already married, for your kisses fire my blood, and your touch makes me tremble and shiver with pleasure, and I should like nothing more than for you to take me in your arms and—"

Her words died as Aulay suddenly lunged up from the floor and covered her lips with his.

Chapter 14

*J*ETTA OPENED TO AULAY AT ONCE WHEN HIS MOUTH COVERED hers. She then gasped and clutched at his shoulders as he scooped her up and settled on the bed with her in his lap. Twisting her upper body toward him, Jetta kissed him back, meeting his thrusting tongue, and dueling with it as it invaded.

At first, all he did was kiss her. Long, deep, demanding kisses that had her moaning, and clutching at him as he clasped her face in his hands and tilted her head in the direction he wanted. Jetta went without protest, tilting one way and then the other as he kissed her thoroughly, and then one hand dropped along her throat to slide over her chest to one breast, where it stopped to squeeze and cup her, squeeze and cup in a slow, steady rhythm to match his kiss. She hardly noticed when his second hand slid away from her face, or that he was working on the fastenings of her gown, until part of it suddenly fell away. It now only covered one breast, held there by the hand squeezing her eager flesh. His other hand found the now naked breast and began to knead that one too. Jetta groaned as the rough skin of his palm and fingers added to her excitement and she arched into both hands, her kiss becoming a bit frantic. Aulay immediately removed his first hand long enough for the cloth to drop away and when he then continued to caress that breast too with his rough, bare hand she muttered a plea into his mouth that even she didn't understand.

In the next moment, she was crying out in protest when he broke their kiss, but then he leaned her back against his arm to allow his mouth to trail its way down her neck. By the time his mouth reached and replaced his hand at her breast, she was twisting her head and moaning in one long sound of need as he took as much of her breast into his mouth as he could fit and then drew his mouth away until only the nipple remained.

"Oh, husband," she groaned, clasping his head and shifting in his lap as need coalesced in her lower stomach and seemed to slide down between her legs.

"Aye, love," he growled against her skin and then eased her onto the bed and settled half on top, and half beside her. Shifting his attention to the other breast now, she felt his leg slide between hers and nudge against her core. Jetta instinctively closed her legs around his knee, riding it as he eased it back and forth against her.

Releasing her nipple a moment later, he growled, "I'm no' going to bed ye, lass."

Jetta blinked her eyes open and peered at him blankly, unable to speak or react. Her body was humming to the tune he was playing, and she was having trouble concentrating on anything.

Seeming to realize that, Aulay smiled crookedly and then said, "God, ye're beautiful like this."

Jetta glanced down the length of her body. The top of her gown was now tangled around her waist, the skirt pushed up almost as high and, as she watched, his hand released her breast and drifted idly down to slip between her legs as his knee shifted aside.

His first touch had her bucking beneath him and crying out. But he quickly covered her mouth with his to silence her as his fingers began to dance across her eager flesh, circling and nudging the center of her excitement there. Just when she thought she could not bear it a moment longer, Jetta felt something push into her. Since he was dressed and only his knee and hand were anywhere near the area, she thought it must be a finger, and then didn't care as it began to slide in and out while his thumb continued to caress the nub of her excitement.

"Oh, husband, please," Jetta gasped, breaking their kiss, and then frowned as she realized what she said. "I mean, Aulay."

"Call me husband. I will be soon enough and I like it," he murmured, nuzzling her breast. "It fires me blood."

"Aye, I'll call you husband then," she gasped as his tongue rasped across her nipple.

Aulay groaned as if the words truly did fire his blood and then claimed one nipple again with his mouth as his hand began to move faster between her legs, his finger plunging deeper.

"Oh, husband," Jetta cried, instinctively raising the knee not covered by his legs and pushing herself up into the caress.

"Oh please, husband, oh please, husband, oh please," Jetta breathed the litany, hardly aware she was doing it as she struggled toward what he was offering, and then a knock sounded at the door and they both froze. Jetta had to bite her lip to hold back her moan of protest when Aulay let her nipple slip from his mouth and lifted his head to glance toward the door. Surely whoever it was would have assumed them already asleep and left if he did not say anything, she thought as he called, "What?"

"Father Archibald just returned," Alick called out cheerfully through the door. "Dougall's gone down to the church to tell him ye want to marry first thing in the morn."

Aulay turned sharply to Jetta, took in her wide eyes, her erect nipples and his hand buried between her legs and growled, "Tonight."

"What?" Alick and Jetta both said with surprise.

"We marry tonight," he answered, withdrawing his hand from between her legs and pulling her from the bed as he got up.

"Did ye say ye want to marry Jetta tonight?" Alick asked, as if unsure he was hearing correctly.

"Aye," Aulay growled, beginning to tug Jetta's gown back into place. "Go tell him so he can ready himself. And tell Saidh to get everyone down to the church. Everyone. The people o' Buchanan will want to witness their laird claiming his bride. And tell Conran to see that lots o' ale, cider and uisge beatha are brought out. They'll want to celebrate after."

Alick grunted something that might have been an acknowledgment and then they heard his footsteps moving away.

"Are you sure you wish to marry tonight?" Jetta asked, her body humming with need. All she wanted was for him to strip her gown off and finish what he'd started. The wedding could wait, she thought, and said,

"We could always marry on the morrow. 'Twould give us more time to prepare and 'tis late now."

Finished putting her gown back in order, Aulay clasped her face between his hands and kissed her, a deep, hungry kiss full of need and passion. Moaning, Jetta melted into him at once, and went willingly when he backed her up. She was hoping he was urging her toward the bed, and he did, but not as she expected. He backed her up until the bedpost pressed into her spine, and then reached down behind her leg and lifted it up to pull around his hip, leaving her balanced on one leg as he ground himself intimately against her.

Breaking their kiss then, he pressed into her again and asked, "Can ye feel that I want ye?"

"Aye, husband," Jetta gasped, pressing back against the hardness rubbing against her.

"I want ye so bad it aches," he admitted, grinding against her again. "I want nothing more than to strip ye naked, toss ye on the bed and thrust into ye so hard and so deep ye scream yer pleasure fer all to hear."

"Oh aye, husband," Jetta almost sobbed, tightening her leg around him.

"But I want all who hear to ken yer me wife when I draw that scream from ye, love," he added, easing away from her a bit.

"Oh," Jetta breathed as disappointment crashed down on her at the realization that he didn't plan to pleasure her now.

Cupping her face, he said gently, "I'll no' take ye ere we're wed when the priest is here to do it." Kissing her gently on the nose, he smiled crookedly and assured her, "'Twill no' take long."

"Nay," she agreed weakly.

Smile turning wicked then, he slid his hand under her skirt and along the inside of her raised leg until his fingers brushed against her slick skin and he added, "And I'll enjoy kenning ye're still wet fer me when the priest asks do ye take me to be yer husband."

"Husband!" she groaned in what was supposed to be a shocked voice, but sounded more like a plea as he fondled her.

He ran his finger around the tight bud of her excitement and then plunged it into her and pressed firmly as he growled by her ear, "I promise, minutes after the priest finishes marrying us, I'll have yer skirt up and be thrusting into ye with the real thing. And I'll no' stop until ye're satisfied."

"Oh God," Jetta groaned when he eased his finger back out and let her leg drop. When he then caught her hand to lead her to the door, she followed docilely, but her mind was now spinning a bit. She was sorry at the interruption. She'd been so very close to finding the release he'd given her on the table at the lodge and could have wept at the interruption. On the other hand, she knew the wedding would only delay that release. She was going to be married and properly bedded tonight. Jetta had no doubt about that. And she had no doubt her husband would see to it she found her release once they were back here. The problem was, he would follow it up with the carrot and the bread loaf, and she wasn't at all sure she would like that.

Although, Jetta encouraged herself, he had pushed his finger inside of her and that had not hurt. Mayhap his carrot wouldn't either.

That was wishful thinking and she knew it. Jetta might be missing many of her memories, but there were certain things she wasn't and one of those was the church's claims that the joining was painful and meant to be a punishment for Eve's sins. At least that's what their priest had claimed.

Jetta recognized that she'd regained another memory, but didn't really care. It was one she could have done without. Besides, she was quite sure she'd heard that the joining was painful elsewhere too. At least the first time. She remembered those teachings as clearly as she recalled how to walk, talk and play chess, so suspected she was in for a night of sweet pleasure, followed by agony. It left her a little less than eager as Aulay escorted her out of the bedchamber.

"Alick says ye want to marry tonight."

Jetta glanced ahead at that announcement and spotted Saidh leading Edith, Murine and Jo toward them in the hall outside the bedchamber.

"Aye," Aulay said at once.

Saidh nodded. "Then we have to prepare Jetta."

Aulay scowled at the claim. "She does no' need preparing. She is fine."

"She is far from fine," Murine countered with dismay.

"Aye," Edith agreed. "Her caul is missing, her hair a mess and her dress wrinkled. She can no' be married and presented to the people o' Buchanan as their new lady like that."

When Aulay frowned and hesitated, Jo said soothingly, "With four of us working on her, we can have her ready in a matter of minutes. And you could do with a change of plaid as well, m'laird. You are a bit wrinkled too."

"And ye've wine or something on yer sleeve," Saidh added. "Jo's right. Ye should change."

Aulay glanced down at his sleeve, cursed, and then nodded and said with resignation, "Fine. I'll need to fetch a fresh plaid from me room first though."

"Ye can change in there," Murine said at once. "We can use the room Dougall and I are in. The dresses are in chests in the hall anyway, so we need no' go in the master bedchamber at all."

Nodding again, he paused long enough to squeeze Jetta's hand and offer her a smile before turning to head back the way they'd come.

"I think she should wear the pale green dress," Murine announced the minute the door closed behind Aulay.

"I think ye're right," Edith announced, moving away toward one of the half-dozen chests in the hall. The one she stopped by and opened was on the opposite side of the door to the master bedroom.

Jetta glanced from Edith to Murine and said, "But it is still in the chest. It will be wrinkled."

"Nay, it will no'," Murine said with a grin. "I took it out the minute the men brought up the chests. I suspected something like this would happen."

"Well, that explains why it's no' here," Edith said dryly and then frowned at the contents of the chest she'd just opened.

"What is it?" Saidh asked, moving toward Edith to peer down into the chest herself.

"The gowns are all crushed," Edith pointed out as Jetta, Murine and Jo joined them. "It looks like something heavy was lying on them."

"Aye," Saidh murmured and bent to pick up something poking out from under some of the material. Straightening, she held up a finely crafted knife with an ebony handle that had ornate carvings on it. "Something heavy like the person who dropped this, mayhap?"

"Hmm," Jo said, eyes narrowing. "Aye, mayhap even a certain archer who likes to push ladies down stairs?"

"'Tis a ballock dagger," Jetta said softly, staring at the two oval swellings on the guard and noting the figures carved into them. "I think I've seen that knife before."

"Can ye remember where?" Saidh asked, but when Jetta began to concentrate on trying to remember, she concealed the blade up her sleeve and squawked, "Nay, do no' try. 'Tis yer wedding night. The last thing ye need is a headache."

"But—" Jetta began in protest.

"Nay, Saidh is right," Jo interrupted, grasping Jetta's shoulders and turning her toward the room where Dougall and Murine were staying. "Tomorrow is soon enough to try to remember. For now, we need to— What the devil are you doing, Saidh?"

Jetta turned with a start at that comment to see that Jo was gaping at the other woman, who had stepped into the chest and was now dropping to crouch inside it.

"Seeing how big 'tis," Saidh said dryly and then crouched down and made herself as small as she could inside. Her voice was slightly muffled when she asked, "Is there a lot o' room left over? Could a man fit?"

"Aye," Edith said solemnly. "'Tis a big chest. There is at least a foot o' space above ye, no' counting the lid."

"And several inches in front, behind and on either side o' ye too," Murine added with a nod. "Even a man as big as one o' our husbands would fit."

"That's what I thought," Saidh said with satisfaction, straightening again. Stepping out, she muttered, "I suspected the men were wrong about the attacker using the passages. Only family members ken about them."

"'Tis hard to believe they did not check the chests though," Jo said with a frown.

"They probably did," Saidh said with a shrug, and then pointed out, "The dagger was under one o' the dresses. No doubt the attacker pulled out one o' the gowns, climbed in and pulled the gown o'er himself. Then when the men opened it—"

"They saw only gowns," Murine finished with a nod.

"They would no' ha'e thought to drag the gowns out to be sure that was all that was in the chests. They knew we'd packed them full."

"Aye," Edith muttered and then asked grimly, "But where are all the gowns from that chest?"

"Well, the pale green one is in me room," Murine pointed out. "And Jetta is wearing the dark green—" Pausing abruptly, she grimaced and said, "I am sorry. Would ye prefer Sorcha or Jetta?"

"In truth, I am more used to Jetta too now and prefer it."

"Good, then there will be less confusion when ye're visiting and our Sorcha is there," Saidh said with a smile.

"True," Jetta agreed with a grin.

They all smiled and then Edith cleared her throat and said, "Back to the dresses. I ken Jetta is wearing one, and the pale green one is in yer room, Murine, but that still leaves a number o' dresses missing from this chest."

"Aye," Jo agreed. "And when we sorted the gowns at the lodge, we put all the ones we thought looked best with Jetta's coloring in it."

"There are only two left in here now," Saidh said as she lifted out the top dress.

"The attacker must have planned ahead and removed most o' the dresses to prepare it as a quick hiding spot," Edith said thoughtfully.

"Aye, but where would he put the dresses when he removed them?" Jo asked with irritation.

They were all silent for a minute, and then Saidh dropped the gown she'd been holding and slammed the chest lid closed. "They must be here somewhere. He could hardly cart half a dozen dresses out o' the keep without someone noticing. We'll take a look around fer them tomorrow. Tonight we ha'e other things to tend."

"Aye," Jo agreed, turning to smile at Jetta.

"But what about the chest?" Edith asked as they ushered Jetta toward Murine's room. "Should we no' tell the men about it?"

"We can tell the men about it after the ceremony," Saidh decided. "But no' Aulay. He does no' need to worry about such and the like until tomorrow. We do no' want to ruin Jetta's big night."

"Aye." Murine nudged Jetta with an elbow and gave her a teasing grin. "Tonight he should only be concerned with pleasure."

"Ooooooh ayyyyye," Edith crooned on a laugh.

"Stop," Jetta said, half laughing at their teasing, but wholly blushing, and more than a little nervous about the night ahead.

Apparently noting her worry, Jo smiled sympathetically, and put a soothing arm around her. "'Twill be fine. It may hurt a little at first, but Aulay seems a kind man, and he definitely has tender feelings for you. He will be gentle with you."

"Do you think so?" Jetta asked hopefully.

"Of course he will. Aulay is a sweetheart. He'll definitely be gentle," she assured her and then added, "that linen Rory wrapped around yer ankle seems to be working nicely. Ye're hardly limping."

"Oh aye," Jetta muttered distractedly. "But I did not mean do you really think Aulay will be gentle with me. I already knew he would. I was questioning . . . Do you really think Aulay has tender feelings for me?" she explained. "I mean, I know he wants me, but he said he was not sure he loved me. Mayhap all he feels for me is desire and gratitude that I am not put off by his scar."

"And ye want his love," Saidh said quietly.

"Aye. I love him," she pointed out.

"Are ye sure ye do?" Saidh asked softly. "Or is it possible all you feel is desire and gratitude fer his saving yer life?"

"I—" Jetta began, and then paused and gave the question the consideration it deserved. Was it possible that she only loved him because she desired him and was grateful for all he'd done for her?

"Good God!"

Giving a start at that intrusion into her thoughts, Jetta turned to peer at Aulay with surprise. He was all finished getting ready. He'd changed, brushed his hair to a fine sheen and even had a quick wash in the basin in their chamber from what she could tell. The man was ready and they hadn't even begun to start on her. They hadn't even reached Murine's room yet.

"Ye've no' even started," Aulay squawked, as if he'd read her mind.

"We are going now," Saidh said firmly, catching Jetta's arm and ushering her the last few steps to the door to Murine and Dougall's room. Opening the door, she urged Jetta inside and called out to her brother, "Go on and head to the church. We'll be right behind ye. This will no' take a minute."

The other women had rushed into the room as she spoke, and the moment the last word was out, Saidh pushed the door closed.

Turning to Jetta, she smiled wryly and said, "It matters little if ye love him now or he loves you. Ye want each other, and more important, ye like each other and that's a good start. More than many begin marriage with."

"Liking is more important than wanting?" Jetta asked with interest.

"Oh aye," Jo assured her as the women set to work on removing the gown she wore. "Passion is like the waves, rising and falling with the hour, day and season. Friendship, though, is much more steady. It will get you through those days when passion is the last thing on your mind."

"Like when ye've a crying baby on your shoulder, and two chewing up yer teets, and ye're so exhausted ye can no' see straight, but he thinks to cheer ye with a little houghmagandie," Saidh said dryly. "Ye'll want to take a battle ax to his head then."

Jetta's eyes widened.

"But friendship will stay your hand," Jo said with amusement as the gown Jetta wore dropped to the floor and Murine approached with the pale green one she was to wear. As they lifted it over her head to put it on her, Jo continued, "And in a couple hours, days, or mayhap even a week, when you are well rested and recovered, you will again be interested in that houghmagandie he suggested earlier, and the sweet release he can offer."

"Aye, and 'twill be the same fer him," Murine assured her as the gown dropped into place and they set to fastening her stays. "He will have days where everything that can go wrong will, or that he is so blind with exhaustion that houghmagandie is the last thing on his mind and nothing ye do can raise his interest."

With the stays finished, they turned their attention to her hair as Murine admitted wryly, "Mind ye, those days are much less frequent fer the men. At least they are with Dougall."

"But yer friendship will see ye through those days too," Edith assured her.

"But that will no' be fer a while," Saidh assured her. "Ye and Aulay will be in yer room more than ye're out fer the next little while."

"Aye, so 'tis good we're here to help catch the attacker while ye're busy," Murine murmured, and admitted, "I can no' wait to tell the men that we discovered how the attacker eluded them."

"Aye," Jo said with a smile. "They will be so annoyed."

"No doubt," Saidh said cheerfully as they all stepped back to survey their handiwork.

"Lovely," Edith pronounced.

"Aye, perfect," Murine murmured and then turned Jetta toward the mirror on the wall so she could see herself as she added, "ye can no' even tell they cut her hair away."

Jetta peered at her reflection and blinked, barely recognizing herself. They'd made her look lovely.

"Thank you," she whispered.

"No thanks are needed," Saidh assured her with a smile. "Ye're a member o' the family now. Or will be once we get ye to the church."

"Speaking of which, shall we, ladies?" Jo said, heading for the door.

Jetta found herself hustled from the room and hurried down the hall by the four lovely, laughing ladies who were about to become her family.

Chapter 15

"CONGRATULATIONS, M'LAIRD! WE'RE ALL RIGHT HAPPY FER ye, and look forward to toasting to yer happiness together."

"Thank ye, Fergus," Aulay said, sincerely.

Jetta smiled and thanked the man too. She'd never met him before, but suspected he was one of her husband's soldiers. Many soldiers and servants had stopped to congratulate them since the ceremony had ended.

"We should go back and toast to yer happiness," Dougall said with a smile, slapping his brother on the back as the last of the people of Buchanan moved away and started back to the keep.

Jetta saw the frown that briefly crossed her new husband's face, and then he smiled, and nodded. "Aye. But first Jetta and I need to thank Father Archibald fer performing the service so late and after his long journey back."

"Oh aye." Dougall glanced toward the priest who was talking to people near the door to the church.

"You and the others go ahead," Aulay suggested lightly. "We'll be right behind ye."

Nodding, Dougall slapped him on the back one more time and then turned to gather the others and usher them back toward the keep, telling them that Aulay and Jetta would follow in a moment.

"Come." Aulay swept her up in his arms and turned, not toward the church or the keep, but away from both and ran through the darkness, straight into the stables.

"What are we doing here?" she asked with confusion as he entered the stables and slowed to a walk.

"Ere we left our room I made a promise to ye that within minutes after the ceremony, we'd return and finish what I'd started," he reminded her solemnly, carrying her past the stalls to the bales at the back of the stables. "Howbeit, if we return to the keep, I'll no' be able to honor that vow. Our people will insist on a toast, and then another, and it'll be hours ere we can retire to our room," he pointed out.

"Aye," she agreed, blushing.

"But do we stop here for a little bit," he added, lowering his head to nuzzle her ear, "I can keep me promise."

"Oh," she breathed as he raised his head again.

Aulay peered at her silently for a moment, as if memorizing her features, and then bent his head to kiss her.

Jetta's mouth opened on a gasp of surprise as he released her legs, and his tongue slid in to fill the open space at once. At first, she was too startled to respond, but then his hands drifted down over her body, massaging her back and pressing her closer before dropping to cup her bottom and lift her off the ground until he could press hard against the junction between her legs. His tongue thrust into her mouth in time with his grinding into her, and Jetta gave in with a groan and started to kiss him back. It seemed like she'd barely started to respond, though, when he tore his mouth away.

Shifting his lips to her ear, he nuzzled it as he growled, "I'm still hard fer ye, love. Are ye still wet fer me?"

"I—" She halted on a gasp as his hand shifted to the back of her thigh and drew her leg up and around his hip again as he had in their room earlier. He then slid his hand under her skirt and along her leg to find out for himself.

"Oh God, ye are," he groaned, and then covered her mouth with his own and kissed her passionately as he began to caress her.

Moaning, Jetta clutched at his shoulders and kissed him eagerly back, her hips moving into the caress. She broke their kiss on a gasping cry when he suddenly slid a finger into her, and Aulay returned to her ear, this time nibbling and sucking at the lobe as his hand worked its magic.

"Husband, please," Jetta whimpered, and sure her legs were about to give out, clutched at him desperately.

"Please, what?" he growled, thrusting harder. "Give me yer pleasure, wife."

"I—I, O—!"

Aulay cut off her cry with his mouth, kissing her deeply and continuing to thrust his finger into her as she convulsed and trembled in his arms. Jetta rode the wave he'd placed her on, expecting the lazy relaxed feeling to claim her again as it had that time at the lodge, but instead her excitement began to build again as he continued to caress her.

Tearing his mouth away, Aulay growled, "I want to taste yer pleasure."

Jetta blinked her eyes open with confusion at those words, and then gaped down at him in dismay when he suddenly dropped to kneel before her.

"Husband!" she hissed with horror, her gaze shooting to the open stable doors and back as he caught the hem of her gown. "What are you—Oh God," she gasped as he disappeared under her skirt. Trying to catch his head in the material, she whispered, "What if someone comes in?"

He pulled his head back out briefly to say, "The gates are closed and the bridge is up. No one will need the stables tonight, and Fergus is the stable master."

"Fergus?" Jetta echoed blankly as his head disappeared under her skirt again, and then recalled the last man to congratulate them. The man looking forward to drinking to their happiness, she recalled, and then fell backward as Aulay urged her legs apart. Fortunately, she fell onto the bales he'd stood her in front of. The moment she did, Aulay used his hold on her legs to shift her to his liking and then tasted her pleasure as he'd said he wished to do.

Covering her mouth with one hand to keep from screaming, Jetta reached for something to ground herself as he set to work on her. All she found was straw, but she dug her fingers in, tearing at it for all she was worth as Aulay seemed to try to devour her whole. His tongue moved up, down and around, and then he suckled at her tender folds before concentrating on the center of her excitement. He did that for what seemed like an eternity, urging her toward the release she craved, and then pulling her back by shifting his attentions until she thought she would go mad . . . or punch him if he did not stop driving her mad like that.

The thought nearly made her laugh as Jetta realized that, dear God, Saidh was right! And then Aulay suddenly slid a finger inside of her, and got serious with his mouth, and the combination sent her off. Screaming into her hand, she bucked on the bale as her release hit her, her mind drifting briefly loose as sensation overwhelmed it.

Jetta didn't know how much time had passed when she realized that Aulay hadn't stopped what he was doing. He was continuing to work on her with his fingers and mouth, though he'd eased away from the now-sensitive nub. And then his finger seemed to grow inside her. Which she knew was impossible, so could only assume he'd eased a second finger in to join the first. He was also moving them differently, she realized, spreading them slightly, spreading her, she realized, trying to prepare her for—

"Oh!" Jetta panted into her palm, losing interest in trying to figure out what he was doing as his tongue returned to the center of her excitement again. Dear God, she couldn't—He had to stop. She could not—

"Husband!" she cried out as she did find release again and her body began to shudder and jerk. Jetta was so caught up in the waves rolling over her that she hardly noticed when Aulay withdrew from beneath her skirt, stepped between her legs and clasped her hips. She definitely noticed, though, when he thrust into her. That was a little hard to miss, and that was when everything kind of stopped for her. It wasn't because it was excruciatingly painful as she'd feared it might be. In fact, Jetta wouldn't have described it as painful at all. It was more uncomfortable, like trying to squeeze into a dress that was too small. Or maybe the opposite of that. She was the dress that was too small, and he was the one trying to squeeze in. Although he'd already squeezed in. He was there, all of him, and unmoving as her body struggled to accommodate this new experience.

"Are ye all right, love?"

Blinking her eyes open, Jetta lifted her head to peer at him. His sword lay on the bale next to her, and his plaid was gone, his shirt the only thing remaining, but he'd pulled the front up and behind his head while leaving his arms in the sleeves so that it was more of a halter. A shoulder halter that left his beautiful chest and everything else on display. Well, everything but where he was joined to her, she thought.

"Love? Are ye all right?"

Raising her eyes quickly, Jetta met his gaze and frowned when she noted the pained expression he wore. His voice had been rather pained too when he asked his question, she thought, and instead of answering, asked, "Are you, husband?"

Presumably he took that for an "aye, I am fine," because he moved again then, easing himself back a bit, and then pressing back into her again.

Jetta bit her lip and waited, but there was nothing. No pain, but no pleasure either, just that strange, uncomfortable sensation.

"Am I hurting ye?" he growled, pausing again.

"Nay," Jetta assured him.

Nodding, Aulay eased out again, a little further this time, and then slid back in. He watched her face as he did this time, and not sure what he expected or wanted to see, Jetta tried a smile. She suspected it was the wrong expression when a breathless laugh slid from his lips. But then he moved one hand between them, to just above where they were joined, and began to caress her again.

Her eyes immediately widened incredulously as her earlier excitement instantly burst back to life. It was as if it had just stepped aside to allow her to adjust to this new experience, but was eager to return. The next time Aulay moved, the uncomfortable sensation was negligible and the time after that, Jetta found herself pushing into it. After the fourth move, she couldn't bear to not participate more, and rose up on the bale to wrap one hand around his neck and pull him down for a kiss.

Aulay complied at once, his tongue sliding between her lips to whip her excitement to a frenzy as he began to pound into her hard and fast.

This time when Jetta found her release and cried out, her husband cried out with her, although the sound he made was more of a roar. His legs must have gone weak as hers had earlier, because he then sort of collapsed against her, forcing her onto her back and following her down. He quickly rolled them both then, though, so that she rested on top of him instead of him crushing her. He also held her close and kissed her forehead, then ran his hands gently up and down her back.

Jetta sighed and snuggled against him, and then stiffened in surprise.

"What is it, love?" Aulay asked and she could hear the frown in his voice.

Tipping her head back, she peered at him uncertainly, and then said, "Ye're still—" She cut herself off with a blush, unable to say that he was still inside of her and still hard.

He had no compunction about saying it though. "Aye, I'm hard still and inside ye."

"Oh." She wasn't sure what to say. She had no idea if it was normal or not.

"I was aroused quite a while," he pointed out gently when she didn't say anything, but didn't relax against him again either. "Since before the ceremony. 'Twill take a while to go down."

"Oh," she repeated, and then asked, "Is it normal? I mean, you did . . . ?"

"Aye, I did," he said with amusement. "And aye, 'tis normal. Fer me anyway," he added wryly, his eyes closing.

Jetta considered that, and then asked, "Does that mean we can do it again?"

Eyes popping open, he jerked his head up and stared at her briefly, and then asked, "Do ye want to do it again?"

"Aye, please," she said solemnly.

"Well—oomph," he gasped when she placed her hands on his chest and pushed herself upright.

"Sorry," she muttered, realizing she'd knocked the wind from him briefly as she'd shifted to straddle him.

"'Tis fine," Aulay said quickly, reaching to tug at the neckline of her gown.

Jetta glanced down in time to see him pull the material under her breasts, leaving him free to cover them with his hands. Closing her eyes, she bit her lip and shifted on top of him as he cupped and squeezed and kneaded her breasts and then toyed with her nipples.

"Ye're so beautiful, love," he growled, and raised his knees behind her, tipping her slightly forward and more firmly into his hands.

"So are you," she whispered, opening her eyes and planting her hands on his chest to balance herself as she shifted over him, experimentally lifting herself slightly and then easing back down.

Aulay chuckled with disbelief at the claim, and pinched her nipples lightly as if punishing her for what he considered an untruth, but then said, "Touch yerself."

Jetta only realized her eyes had closed again when those growled words had her blinking them open.

"Go on," he urged, covering her breasts again and squeezing eagerly. "Slide yer hand down and touch yerself. Show me what ye like best."

Jetta swallowed uncertainly, her movements briefly ceasing.

"Please," he added solemnly.

Not wanting to disappoint him, Jetta reluctantly removed one hand from his chest and moved it down to touch herself tentatively.

"Close yer eyes and pretend 'tis me," he urged. "Only ye're directing me hand."

Jetta closed her eyes and pretended it was him caressing her . . . and was surprised to find it did make a little difference. Her fingers now pressed more firmly, and moved around her most sensitive area as he'd done, and then along either side of it and back to go around and round again.

"That's it," Aulay growled. "Aye, move how ye want, lass. Take yer pleasure from me. 'Tis yers."

It was only then Jetta realized she wasn't sliding up and down on him in the same kind of action as he had used with her. Instead, she was all over the place, moving up and down, from side to side, forward and back and her movements were no longer tentative. She was grinding herself into him, riding him willy-nilly, one hand between her legs and one now clasping one of his wrists for balance as he kneaded her breasts. She suspected she was giving him little pleasure with her actions, but damn, it felt good to her, and she was so close . . .

And then she crested the mountain she'd been climbing and her mouth opened on a long ululating sound. The moment that happened, Aulay released her breasts, clasped her hips and pounded up into her hard over and over, prolonging her release and then joining in it with a shout of triumph.

Jetta's heart was still thundering in her chest when she collapsed on top of Aulay, completely spent. She knew he said something to her then, she heard the rumble of sound in his chest under her ear, but she couldn't make sense of it. She was exhausted and drifting off to sleep.

"We should really join the others fer that toast," Aulay said reluctantly, once he had enough breath to speak. He wanted to get the suggestion out before Jetta asked to do it again. He wasn't sure he'd be able to walk again after another round. The lass had a powerful passion.

Realizing she hadn't responded, Aulay frowned.

"Lass?" he said, lifting his head to try to see Jetta's face when she still remained silent. His eyes widened incredulously when he saw that she was sound asleep on his chest. After a moment, the sight brought a soft smile to his face, but it was quickly followed by a frown as he recalled she was newly from her sickbed and still healing. Both from her head wounds, and now a turned ankle as well, he recalled, and silently cursed himself. They should have stopped after the first time, he thought, mentally kicking himself. Now he'd gone and worn her out.

Sighing, Aulay lay back and closed his eyes. He'd let her sleep for a bit, just a few minutes, and then he'd have to wake her, help her dress and urge her back to the keep. He'd probably carry her again, he thought, covering his mouth as a yawn claimed him. He'd noticed that her limp was more pronounced by the time the women had led her down to the church where he'd been waiting with the men, his people and Father Archibald. Aulay suspected the trek had been a bit much for her, and that for the time being she would do better to only walk short distances and rest her ankle as much as possible to allow it to heal.

The problem would be getting her to stay off her foot, he suspected. Or mayhap it wouldn't, Aulay thought, glancing down when she shifted sleepily on top of him and his cock responded with interest. Perhaps he just needed to distract her again like he had when he was trying to keep her from actively searching out memories. They were married now, and it was a chore he'd enjoy, Aulay thought as his eyes drifted closed.

IT WAS PAIN THAT ROUSED JETTA FROM SLEEP. LIFTING HER HEAD drowsily, she covered her mouth to muffle a cough and then peered down at her throbbing ankle. The firelight allowed her to see what the problem was. She had slid off Aulay's chest to sleep curled up against his side and her injured ankle had somehow got trapped under Aulay's leg. The weight on it was causing her excruciating pain.

Jetta had just started to try to slide her leg free of his when her brain woke up enough to question the firelight business. They were in the stables, which had been dark except for one torch by the door when they'd entered. There should not be firelight.

Jerking her gaze toward the source of light, Jetta stared blankly for a moment and then sat up with horror and smacked Aulay, hard. "Husband? Husband, wake up! The stables are on fire!"

"What?" Aulay sat straight up as if she'd poked him in the behind with a sgian dubh. Gaping at the flames climbing up the closed entrance doors, he breathed, "What the hell?"

Jetta didn't bother to answer. He could see what the hell. Besides, she was busy pulling the top of her gown back into place and pushing down her skirts.

"The horses."

Glancing up at those husky words, Jetta watched wide-eyed as Aulay scrambled off the bales and hurried to the nearest stall. The man hadn't done a thing about his own clothes. He was still only in his shirt, and that was still pulled up over his head like some kind of halter. Shaking her head, Jetta coughed again and slid off the bale, wincing as she put weight on her injured ankle. Ignoring the pain, she bent to pick up Aulay's plaid, and chased after him. He'd opened the nearest stall door and had moved on to the second.

"Husband, put yer plaid on," she said, shoving it at him as he swung the second stall door open and moved on to the third.

Waving away the offering, Aulay pulled this stall door open as well, but then turned to stare around with a frown. The horses were whin-nying in fear and banging about in their stalls, but not coming out of them. That didn't surprise her at all since it would merely take them closer to the fire.

Cursing, Aulay turned to head toward the back of the stables, barking, "Get the horses out of the back stalls, but stay away from the front ones and the fire."

Coughing again, Jetta glanced along the stalls and thought that they were all in terrible danger did they not soon get out of there, but the horses in the front were in the most immediate danger. The fire had not yet reached the stalls—they started ten feet in from the doors—but the flames were making their merry way toward them and frighteningly quickly.

Straightening her shoulders, Jetta did exactly what Aulay had ordered her not to do and ran to the first of the two stalls closest to the fire. The heat was unbearable at that end of the stables, and the smoke was build-ing up, becoming a black wall, but Jetta held her breath and felt her way and quickly opened the first stall. Unlike the animals at the back, this horse was eager to escape. The beast nearly trampled her in its panic to get away from the flames. Jetta managed to avoid its hooves, but was bumped to the side and slammed into the next stall with enough force that she swore she saw stars. Fortunately, she didn't have to direct the horse at least. It rushed to the back of the barn as if the hounds of hell were on its heels.

Giving her head a shake to clear it, Jetta pushed herself away from the stall she was clinging to and shouted a warning to Aulay so that he didn't get trampled. She then moved to the stall across from the one she'd just opened, and then to the second in line on each side, and then the third. But she was more careful after that first horse, making sure to keep out of the way as she freed the animals.

Jetta was approaching the sixth stall on the right before she heard the pounding. Glancing toward Aulay, she saw that he'd retrieved his sword from the bales and was hacking at the back wall of the stables with it, trying to make an opening for them all to escape. The crackle and rush of the fire must have muffled the noise he was making when she'd been closer to it, Jetta decided, because he'd actually made a sizeable hole already. One big enough for her to squeeze through, she was sure.

She'd barely had the thought when Aulay lowered his sword and turned to shout for her. Suspecting she knew what he wanted, Jetta waved him off and opened the next stall door. She would not crawl out and leave him alone to deal with all of this and that's what she suspected he wanted, for her to escape the exhausting heat, breathtaking smoke, and searing flames and wait outside while he battled on alone. Well, he could just forget about that, Jetta thought with disgust. She was no delicate flower in need of—

Her thoughts died abruptly when she was suddenly caught from behind, turned and swept off her feet.

"Husband!" Jetta protested, kicking her legs. "Put me down."

"I want ye out o' here. I'll handle the rest alone," he growled, striding back toward the hole he'd made.

"I am not leaving you alone in here," she snapped, kicking her legs again.

"The hell ye aren't!" he roared.

"The hell I am!" she roared right back, and then they both turned their heads sharply at the sound of pounding and stared at the quickly enlarging hole Aulay had started. Several swords, axes and other weapons were tearing away the back of the stables like it was made of cloth.

"Thank God," Aulay muttered, starting forward again. "Help has arrived."

"Aye," Jetta breathed, relaxing in his arms now that they would both soon be out of there.

By the time they reached the back of the stables, the hole was large enough for the already freed horses to escape. Aulay stood back to avoid being trampled as they rushed out, and Jetta took a moment to hope that the men outside had got out of the way in time to avoid being trampled as well, and then the last horse was out and the men began pouring in.

Leaving them to free the remaining horses, Aulay carried her quickly past them and out of the burning building. He didn't stop until they reached crisp, cool, smoke-free air.

"Aulay! Jetta! Dear God, what happened?"

In the midst of a coughing fit, it took Jetta a moment to glance around at that call. When she did, it was only to see that every member of her new family was now rushing across the bailey from the keep and barreling down on them. Truly, it was a beautiful sight, right up until the group drew up short several feet away, their mouths all dropping like fish out of water.

That was when she recalled Aulay's state of dress, or undress really. Other than his shirt, which was presently gathered at his shoulders and behind his head, she was his only covering. And he was holding her high enough that she suspected she wasn't covering much more than his chest. Even as Jetta thought that, Aulay lowered his arms so that her bottom covered his jewels. At least she hoped it did.

"I told you to put on your plaid," she said on a sigh.

Much to her surprise, rather than be annoyed at her *I told you so*, a bark of laughter slipped from Aulay. "Aye. That ye did, love. And next time I'll listen, I promise."

"Are ye both all right?" Rory asked, moving forward again and eyeing them with concern.

"I am, but Jetta swallowed a lot of smoke," Aulay said solemnly.

"I am fine," Jetta assured them in a hoarse voice. "Truly. We were very lucky."

"Aye, we were," Aulay said meeting her gaze. "Verra lucky."

"Well," Uncle Acair said, eyeing the pair of them. "Ye're covered in straw and soot and look like ye've been through a ragin' storm. I'd say ye've had one hell o' an exciting first night together."

While Jetta groaned again and turned her suddenly heated face into Aulay's neck, he merely started walking again and said, "That we did . . . until the stables burst into flames."

That brought about a burst of laughter that Jetta suspected was more relief that they were okay than anything. But the group remained behind as Aulay carried her toward the keep. Curious, Jetta leaned her head back and watched them around his arm, noting the serious expressions and gestures toward the stables and then toward her and Aulay. The conversation only took a moment or so and then Rory, Conran and Alick headed back to the stables while the rest of the group hurried to catch up to them.

Of course, their position behind them gave them a prime view of Aulay's rear. Jetta noted the way Jo, Murine and Edith were looking at it with definite appreciation, and curiosity made her look down. He was her husband, and she'd never actually seen his bare bottom. Unfortunately, she couldn't see it now really either. Well, she saw the curves from above, but it wasn't a good angle. Shifting her attention back to the women, she asked, "Are Rory, Conran and Alick going to help with the fire?"

"Aye," Saidh said. "Well, Conran and Alick are. Rory is checking to be sure no one was injured and in need o' his help."

Nodding, Jetta glanced ahead to see how close they were to the keep. She felt bad that her husband had to cart her about like a child, and briefly considered telling him to put her down and let her walk, but her ankle was throbbing like crazy. She supposed she shouldn't be surprised. It had been aching when she'd woken, and then she'd rushed about freeing the horses on it.

Muffled laughter drew her attention back to the women behind them, and she raised her eyebrows with curiosity.

Noting that, Murine smiled apologetically and explained, "We were just debating how the fire started."

"Aye," Edith agreed, and then with a teasing grin, asked, "so, was it yer passion that set flame to the stables?"

"Nay, wife," Niels said, sliding an arm around the woman. "Aulay probably knocked a lantern over in his eagerness."

Blushing, Jetta shook her head. "Neither is right. We were both sleeping when it started."

"Sleeping?" Cam asked sharply. "Aulay, is this true?"

"Aye," Aulay answered and paused to look back at the stables with a frown. "If Jetta had no' woke up . . ." He didn't finish the comment. He didn't have to. They were all now looking at the raging fire that had once been the stables. The building was fully engulfed now and men had formed a line from the stables to the well and were passing buckets of water along to be thrown on the flames. Jetta peered around at the horses milling about the bailey and hoped they had all escaped, and that none of the men who had rushed in as they left had been caught inside.

"What woke ye?" Aulay asked and she tore her gaze from the chaos and flames to see that he was eyeing her solemnly.

"Your leg was on top of mine, and my ankle was paining me," she admitted.

Her husband nodded, his gaze wandering to her legs and back before he asked, "Did ye hear or see anything when ye first woke?"

Jetta shook her head. "Just the flames burning. There was no one there."

"Ye think someone set the fire?" Dougall asked, turning away from the chaos to look at them.

Aulay shrugged and smiled wryly. "It seems more likely than that it started itself."

"Damn," Niels murmured. "Then the wedding did no' help at all."

Jetta did not miss the silencing look Aulay sent his brother. Offering her a smile, he said, "Mayhap no' in that way, but it did me a world o' good. Jetta is mine now. And archers, attackers and fires be damned, I'm a happy man."

Turning on that note, he continued on to the keep, but Jetta peered over his shoulder at the burning stables as they went and frowned. She knew he was just trying to keep her from getting upset or feeling responsible for this latest attack, and she appreciated the effort. But Jetta was very aware that this trouble had only started with her being fished from the ocean. She just didn't know what to do about it. She had no idea why it was happening or who could be behind it, and wouldn't until she had her memory back. She needed to try to remember.

Chapter 16

"*O*H, LORD LOVE US! WHAT HA'E THE PAIR O' YE GOT UP TO now? Are ye well? Ha'e either o' ye been injured?"

Jetta lifted her head off Aulay's shoulder and glanced around at that cry. They had entered the keep and started across the Great Hall and Mavis was rushing toward them, looking dismayed. Jetta offered the woman a reassuring smile, but it was Aulay who said, "We are fine, Mavis. No need to fuss."

"Ye're no' fine. Look at ye. Ye're both filthy with soot all o'er ye and straw sticking out o' yer hair and—Ye were in the stables!" she cried with realization. "Were ye in there when the fire started? What happened to yer clothes, Aulay? Good Lord, ye're bare as the day ye were born. Come along now, let's get ye above stairs. Ye both need a bath and fresh clothes," she said, leading the way toward the stairs, and then she slowed to shout, "Flora, put water on to warm and find some men to fetch the bath! Then have Cook fix a tray fer yer laird and his lady. And stop gawking at yer laird's bum, 'tis disrespectful. Goodness," she muttered and suddenly turned to rush around behind them.

Jetta stared wide-eyed as the woman moved up as close behind them as she could without tramping on Aulay's heels, and held out her skirts, trying to shelter his behind from view as they walked. Shaking her head, the old woman groused, "The maids'll be giggly all night after this show, m'laird. Ye should ha'e sent someone ahead fer a plaid and shirt ere entering. Oh, ye're wearing yer shirt. Sort of. What the devil ha'e ye done to yer shirt?"

Biting her lip to keep from laughing, Jetta leaned her head against

Aulay's shoulder again and listened to the woman mutter all the way upstairs to their bedchamber. She should have been amazed that the maid would talk so to her lord like that, but wasn't. First off, the woman wasn't a maid as she'd assumed at the lodge. While talking with the women at the tables after her fall, Jetta had learned that Mavis pretty much ran Buchanan, at least the keep itself. She oversaw the kitchen staff and maids, and saw to Aulay's comfort.

According to Saidh, Mavis was more like family than staff. She'd been their nursemaid when young, and tended to fuss over and reprimand them all still as if they were children. Jetta got the feeling that they all liked it, and suspected the woman's mothering them helped ease the loss of their own mother. Everyone needed mothering every once in a while.

"Here we are, just let me get the door." Mavis gave up covering Aulay's behind and rushed around them to open the door.

"Thank ye, Mavis," Aulay said affectionately as he carried Jetta inside.

"Yer welcome, m'laird. Ye just—Oy!" she suddenly cried with outrage. "What are ye doin'? Out o' here! Shoo!"

Jetta glanced around with surprise to see that the rest of their group had followed and Mavis was trying to push them back out into the hall.

"We need to talk to Aulay, Mavis. Someone set the stables on fire. We need to figure out what to do," Dougall grumbled.

"Ye put the fire out! Ye do no' need Aulay to tell ye that," Mavis said with exasperation, still trying to wrestle them out.

"Conran and Alick are helping with that. We are to be guarding Aulay and Jetta."

"And Geordie and Katie," Niels added.

Concern filled Mavis's face, but she stood firm. "Well, guards stay in the hall, no' the bedchamber. Now off with ye. They both need a bath, and Aulay needs clothes ere he receives company."

"We've seen him naked before, Mavis," Niels pointed out with exasperation. "And we're no' leaving Aulay and Jetta alone. Someone just tried to kill them. We need to protect them."

"What?" Mavis stopped trying to push the men out and turned to Aulay with dismay.

"We are fine," Aulay reminded her solemnly. "But aye, someone set the stables on fire while we were inside them, and aye, I suspect that killing us was the intention. However," he added quickly when she paled, "we were very lucky. We escaped unscathed, and I'm quite sure the horses and everyone else escaped without injury too. So other than the fact that we need to build new stables, all is well."

Mavis shook her head unhappily. "What the devil is happening? The fire, Katie shot with the arrow, and someone pushing Jetta down the stairs. I mean, Sorcha. I mean, m'lady," she added with a frown, and patted Jetta's arm. "I'm sorry, m'lady. I am just used to thinking on ye as Jetta. I'll remember to call ye m'lady or Lady Sorcha eventually."

"Jetta is fine," Jetta said gently.

"Truly?" Mavis asked. "'Cause I'll keep trying to remember to call ye Sorcha, do ye wish it."

"Nay. Truly, Jetta is what I would prefer to be called," she assured her, and then smiled crookedly and pointed out, "I do not even know who Sorcha is. I do not remember being her. I am Jetta now."

"Aye, well, if ye get ye're memories back, change yer mind and would prefer Sorcha, ye just let me ken," Mavis said, and then glanced to Aulay. "Put the lass down and cover yerself up. Ye've a room full o' people wanting to talk to ye. Besides, the maids'll be up here soon with food and water and do no' need to get another eyeful."

Nodding, Aulay turned toward the bed, and started to bend forward, intending to set Jetta down, but Mavis immediately squawked, "Nay! No' on the bed, Aulay! What are ye thinkin'? Ye're both filthy. I'd ha'e to ha'e the maids change the linens again and just had that done this morn. Set her in one o' the chairs by the fire."

Heaving a sigh, Aulay straightened and carried Jetta to the chair closest to the fire. He set her in it and then straightened, and they both saw that Mavis had grabbed a plaid and brought it over. The moment Aulay was upright, she wrapped it around his waist and quickly pinned it at his hip, muttering, "Reminds me o' when I used to change yer nappies."

Finished with covering him from the waist down, she shifted her attention to his shirt and frowned her displeasure. Reaching up, she began tugging on it, asking, "What the devil ha'e ye done to yer shirt? Why is it all caught up behind yer head? Who taught ye to dress yerself?"

"You did," Aulay said with amusement. Unfazed by her fussing, he reached up to pull the front of his shirt back over his head and let it drop down into place. Raising an eyebrow then, he asked, "Better?"

"It'll do," she said dryly and then turned to survey the group milling just inside the door. "Well, get over here and talk to him then. But once the bath is ready I want ye all out o' here so I can see these two cleaned up. They're filthy and smell bad. I do no' ken how they can stand it."

Eyes widening, Jetta raised her arm to sniff it and then grimaced. She smelled like smoked pork, a food her father loved above all others. The thought made her still briefly, and she almost told Aulay that she'd remembered that her uncle liked smoked pork, but then decided against it. That wasn't a very useful memory.

Sighing, she glanced up and managed a smile as her new family moved over to join them by the fire.

Greer was the first to speak, expression solemn he suggested, "Ye'll ha'e to arrange the guard ye mentioned ye wanted on Jetta now. I ken ye planned to wait until tomorrow morn because ye'd be with her, but—"

"Aye," Aulay interrupted. "As soon as the men finish up at the stables."

"Do ye ken who ye want?" Dougall asked with concern.

"I was thinking I'd have Cullen pick three other men he trusts and ha'e the four men guard her."

"Aye, Cullen's a good man," Dougall murmured.

"What about you?" Jetta asked as the men fell silent, and they all turned to look at her with uncertainty. Scowling at Aulay, she pointed out, "You were in the stables too. You should have a guard also."

Aulay shook his head. "Nay. I was no' the target. I just happened to be there."

"How can you be sure?" she asked at once. "First Katie was shot with the arrow, then I was pushed down the stairs, and now both you and I were locked in burning stables. It seems to me there is no real target. Someone is just rushing about trying to kill people."

Aulay smiled at her with approval. "Ye noticed that, did ye? That the stable doors were blocked?"

"The doors were open when you carried me in and you did not go back and close them, 'tis why I was so reticent at first. I wanted you to at least close the doors, and was going to ask you to, but then you distracted me," she admitted, and knew from the heat in her cheeks that she was blushing brightly. Rushing on, she said, "I know the doors were open when we fell asleep after . . . er . . ." Her face was positively on fire now. Unable to verbalize what they'd been doing, she skipped to, "Yet they were closed when I woke up to see the stables were on fire. That bothered me, so I looked back on the way to the keep and saw that not only were they shut, but pieces of wood had been jammed against them to keep them closed."

"The doors were jammed?" Dougall asked with surprise. "How did ye get out then?"

"Aulay hacked an opening in the back wall of the stables," Jetta told him proudly.

"It was only big enough fer Jetta to get out when I stopped to try to get her to leave, but the men arrived from the castle and started helping from the other side," Aulay said with a shrug. "They must ha'e approached just ere I stopped to fetch Jetta and try to get her to leave and heard me hacking away. That or something else made them look around back and see the hole I'd started."

"Ye were lucky," Dougall said, and then shook his head. "Sorry we did no' get to ye sooner, Aulay. We were at the high table waitin' on ye and Jetta to arrive, and joking about what might be delaying ye. By the time we realized something was amiss, half the men were already out the doors and the others were fighting to follow and blocking our way."

Jetta could almost visualize what Dougall said. Mealtime in a great hall was always a noisy affair with lots of movement. There were people constantly coming and going, and everyone was shouting along the tables to others. With the high table so far from the doors, the people at it were often the last to learn what was happening if someone ran in from the bailey with news.

"Here we are," Mavis said briskly as two men carted a tub through the door. They were followed by several maids all carrying pails of water. Jetta was vaguely surprised that the job had been left to the women, but then realized that the men were all presently busy. She supposed it was lucky that two had been found to carry the tub.

Jetta watched with silent amusement as Mavis hustled the others out of the room. The woman was as firm with them as if they were still children in her charge and they responded as such. Even Greer, Cam, Edith and Murine obediently left the room under her chivvying, and they had not been in her charge as children. But then, Jetta realized, she reacted the same way to the woman. Her motherly nature and take-charge attitude just made you instinctively want to please her and obey.

"Now." Mavis turned to survey them and then settled her gaze on Aulay and raised her eyebrows. "Did ye plan to share the bath, or shall I attend Jetta and then ye can—"

"We'll share," Aulay said at once with a grin, and the blush that had just left Jetta's face immediately warmed her cheeks again.

"Then I'll go see what's taking that tray from Cook so long," Mavis announced, reaching for the door. But then she paused and pursed her lips before saying, "I gather from what our Jetta said . . . and did no' say . . . that ye consummated the wedding in the stables?"

Groaning, Jetta lowered her head with embarrassment.

"I'll no' harangue ye, Aulay, fer doing it in the stable, o' all places," Mavis went on. "For if 'twas good enough fer Mary to birth Jesus, then I suppose 'tis good enough fer what ye got up to. But, Lord love us, lad, could ye no' ha'e at least taken a linen with ye so we'd ha'e something to show on the morrow?" she asked with exasperation.

Jetta glanced up with alarm as she realized there would be no bloody sheet as proof of her innocence when the priest came to collect it in the morning.

Sighing, Mavis shook her head. "I'll see if I can find ye some blood somewhere. I dare no' ask Cook. He'd suspect what it was for. I suppose I'll ha'e to kill a chicken or something to get it without anyone else kenning."

"There's no need, Mavis," Aulay interrupted gently. "I'll tend it."

Eyebrows rising, she asked, "Are ye sure?"

"Aye," he said and there was no mistaking the relief on the woman's face as she turned to open the door. It seemed she hadn't been looking forward to killing a chicken.

Jetta watched the door close and then smiled at Aulay as he walked toward her. "Mavis is . . ." Jetta hesitated and then picked the only word she could think of. "Special."

"Aye," Aulay agreed solemnly, reaching for her stays and beginning to undo them. "Our mother was wonderful, but with nine children and a castle to tend, she was always busy. Mavis stepped in and made sure we had what we needed and that none o' us felt left out when Mother was busy with the others."

"She was like a second mother to you all," Jetta said as he pulled her arms free of the undone gown.

"Aye, and when Mother died, she took over and still mothers us to this day," he said, letting her dress and the shift she wore under it drop to the floor. Scooping her up, Aulay carried her to the tub and bent to set her in it, and then quickly undressed himself and urged her forward in the tub so he could get in behind her.

"How do ye feel?" he asked, catching her by the waist and pulling her back to sit between his legs as he stretched them out.

"Fine. My throat hardly hurts at all anymore," she assured him and heard him chuckle.

Sliding his arms around her waist, he pulled her hair aside and pressed a kiss to her neck, and then murmured, "Ashamed as I am to admit it, I was no' thinking o' the aftereffects o' inhaling all that smoke when I asked how ye feel."

"Nay?" she asked with surprise. "What were you—oh," she breathed when he let one hand drift down between her legs.

"I was wondering if ye're feeling tender," he whispered by her ear as he began to caress.

"A little," she whispered honestly, and his hand paused at once. Leaning into him, she reached back between them and tentatively closed her hand around his erection, and then turned and tilted her head to look at him as she added, "But only a little. Please do not stop, husband. I like what you do to me."

"Oh, wife," Aulay breathed, closing his eyes as she touched him. "I like what ye do to me too."

The words had barely left his mouth when he opened his eyes, bent his head and claimed her lips as he began to caress her again.

"WIFE? ARE YE AWAKE?"

Jetta opened her eyes sleepily and peered at Aulay with confusion. "What?"

"Are ye awake?" he repeated with a smile, and then bent his head to catch her nipple lightly between his teeth and flick the tip with his tongue.

"I am now," Jetta moaned, her back arching and body stretching as it came to excited life. This was the second morning after their wedding. Or was it the third? She pondered the question briefly and then let it go. She simply didn't care. It didn't really matter. Nothing did but what Aulay was doing to her. They had not left their room since returning here after the fire. Everyone had come to the room the morning after to take away the blood-stained linen that was supposed to be proof of her innocence, but was actually blood from a cut on Aulay's hand. She'd been horrified when he'd done that to create the necessary stain, but he'd assured her that their time in the barn had been worth it. But other than that, they hadn't seen anyone, or gone anywhere. At least, she hadn't. Jetta suspected Aulay had slipped away to deal with matters a time or two while she slept. But she had remained in the room since their wedding night. Every time she woke it was to Aulay's kisses or caresses and they were soon consummating their marriage again. Not always in the bed. They had pretty much consummated it everywhere in the room—in the bed, on the floor, on the tabletop, in a chair, on a chest, against the wall . . .

Jetta had never realized the marriage could be consummated in so many different positions. It was a revelation to her. As was her response to him. It was almost automatic now. Aulay kissed, touched or caressed her and she was immediately aroused, her body humming and an ache starting between her thighs that demanded attention and release. Like now, she thought, and reached down to find the hardness that could give her that release.

Catching her hand to stop her, Aulay paused in suckling at her nipple and raised his head to claim her lips. Jetta kissed him back enthusiastically, and immediately wrapped her arms around his neck and then gasped in surprise when he suddenly sat up, taking her with him. Wrapping his own arms around her, Aulay then stood, bringing her along so that she hung in his arms, her feet dangling above the floor briefly before he bent slightly to set her down on her own two feet.

When he then broke their kiss and released her, Jetta opened her eyes with surprise to see him walking away from her. Frowning, she watched him open one of the chests along the wall and retrieve the top gown. Letting the chest lid drop, he walked back to offer it to her.

"Get dressed," he urged when she didn't immediately take the gown. "I want to take ye somewhere special to break our fast."

Eyes widening, Jetta accepted the gown and quickly pulled it on. Aulay helped her with the fastenings, and then fetched her brush and drew it quickly through her hair. He tried to be gentle, she knew he did, but after what she was guessing might be as many as three days without bathing or brushing and with a lot of rolling around on different surfaces, her hair was a terrible mess.

"I need a bath," she muttered, wincing as the brush got caught in the tangled mess of her hair.

"Ye'll ha'e one when we get there," Aulay promised her, and then cursed as the brush got stuck again. Giving up, he took her hand and led her to the door, assuring her, "We'll fix yer hair while we're there too."

"Where?" Jetta asked curiously.

"Ye'll see. 'Tis a surprise," he said pulling the bedchamber door open and urging her out into the hall.

Jetta raised her eyebrows at that, and then gazed around with surprise at the four men waiting in the hall. Two had been standing against the wall opposite their bedchamber door, while two had taken up a position on either side of it. They now all moved forward, almost circling them. One carried a basket, she noted curiously, and then two started up the hall, and two fell into step behind her and Aulay as he took her arm to escort her away from the room.

Jetta walked silently, sneaking glances at their guards. She'd forgotten all about Aulay's intention to arrange guards for her. But then this was her first time dealing with them. She wasn't sure she liked it. It made her self-conscious to have all these men around, and then they started down the stairs and she saw the Great Hall floor full of sleeping people.

"What time is it?" she asked Aulay in a whisper.

"Early," he whispered back, not very helpfully in her opinion. But Jetta didn't want to wake anyone, so didn't ask further, and concentrated on moving as quietly as she could as they reached the bottom of the stairs and she followed Aulay to the keep doors. The people sleeping in the hall had left a pathway to the doors, but it wasn't very wide, only allowing people to walk single file. With two soldiers in front and two behind, Jetta crept along behind Aulay, trying not to look at or step on anyone along the way. She breathed out a sigh of relief when they reached the keep doors, but peered about with surprise when they stepped out into the bailey.

Aulay's "early" had been a bit of an understatement. The sun wasn't even up yet. It was just peeking up over the horizon and it was still quite dark out as they made their way to the paddock where the horses were being kept. Still, Jetta could see that whatever had remained of the old stables after the fire had destroyed it had been torn down, and a new building was going up in its place.

"It should be done by week's end," Aulay said quietly, noting where her gaze was focused.

Jetta nodded but didn't comment, and they had soon reached the paddock. Aulay had definitely been up and about before waking her, Jetta decided when she saw that five saddled horses waited for them. At the very least he must have stuck his head out of their room to order one of the men to see to or arrange for the horses to be saddled.

With only five horses prepared, she wasn't surprised when Aulay mounted and then bent to lift her up before him. Once they were settled, he glanced around and nodded, and two men started away toward the castle gates and bridge, which even now were just opening. Aulay followed the men, and the other two members of their guard trailed them.

The ride to where they were going wasn't a long one. In fact, Jetta was actually surprised when the trees they were riding through suddenly gave way to a clearing and Aulay and the others reined in. Eyes widening, she sat up and peered around. The clearing was on the edge of a loch. The land on either side rose up into rolling hills, but here it was mostly flat, the land slanting just slightly down toward the beach and the water beyond.

Breathing out slowly, Jetta leaned back against Aulay and said, "'Tis beautiful."

"Aye," Aulay agreed. "'Tis me favorite spot at Buchanan. It always has been. I thought we could break our fast here and bathe."

"Bathe?" she asked, wide eyes shifting from the men with them to her husband.

"'Twill be fine," he said soothingly, and then lifted her down off his mount to stand next to it. Aulay quickly followed her to the ground and then tethered his horse to the low branch of a nearby tree. "Wait here just a moment."

Jetta nodded and then watched him walk to where the men had dismounted and gathered. Aulay spoke to them briefly, and then accepted the basket she'd noted earlier and a folded plaid and turned to walk back to her as the men disbursed to position themselves along the woods with their backs to the clearing.

Setting the plaid across the top of the basket under the handle, Aulay took her arm and walked her down to the shore.

The beach was much smaller here than it had been by the ocean, and there were rocky outcroppings reaching out into the lake on either side, forming a smaller bay. Jetta was glad that it was small, though. It meant less of a walk and little sand to traverse. She was stronger than she'd been when she first woke up more than two weeks ago, but was still pathetically weak in her opinion. She suspected she wouldn't have been out of breath after such a short walk before her head injury, and while she and Aulay had made love many times since the wedding, she had always been exhausted afterward despite his doing most of the work. She'd probably slept as much as she'd been awake these last couple of days.

"Do you come here often?" she asked breathlessly as they paused at the edge of the water.

"Aye. I usually come in the mornings and swim ere I break me fast," he admitted, setting down the basket and shaking out the plaid to lay it on the grass. "O' course, I did no' come here while at the lodge. 'Tis a longer ride here from the lodge and I would no' leave ye fer that long."

"Oh," Jetta said softly, touched by the admission.

"Do ye want to eat first or swim?" Aulay asked once he'd finished with the plaid.

Jetta hesitated, her gaze sliding from the basket to the loch. The sun was higher now, nearly free of the horizon, and the sky was lightening with its arrival, but the air was a bit chilly still. Soon it would be fully bright, the sky an azure blue with frothy white clouds, and the air would warm. Jetta knew from experience—though she didn't recall what experience—that cooler air made the water seem warmer more quickly. Besides, she wasn't really hungry at the moment.

"Swim," she announced, glancing back toward the men.

"They'll no' turn around," Aulay assured her solemnly and stepped closer to help her with the fastenings of her dress.

Jetta half expected him to take the opportunity to kiss and caress her, but he didn't. He helped her out of her dress, and then quickly stripped himself, and walked her to the shore's edge. As she'd expected, the water was cold, but the cool air soon made the water seem warmer than it was so that she kept as much of herself underwater as she could. They'd been in the water for several minutes before Aulay moved closer and slid his arms around her waist to pull her to him.

Eyes widening, Jetta glanced nervously toward the men, but Aulay smiled and said, "'Tis all right, love. Much as I'd like to, I'll no' start something with the men here. We'll ha'e to save that fer another time."

Relaxing, Jetta nodded and slid her arms around his neck, holding on as he drew her through the water, moving them in front of the rocky outcropping to the right of the little beach where the plaid lay.

Jetta bit her lip as they moved. He'd said he wouldn't start something with the men there, but she was beginning to wish he would. Her breasts were brushing against his chest under the water, her nipples hardening by the moment, and his leg kept sliding between hers and gently nudging her. Trying to distract herself, she asked, "Where are we going?"

"Just here," he murmured and then paused as soon as she could see the even smaller beach on the other side of the outcropping.

Except for the small stretch of sand, the land there was not flat. Instead it looked like this smaller bay was carved out of the surrounding hill, she noted.

"Do ye see that large bunch o' bushes on the left side o' the crag?" Aulay asked in a hushed voice as if trying to be sure he wasn't overheard.

"Aye." Jetta nodded, concentrating her gaze on the bush in question.

"Behind that is a cave, with a tunnel entrance in it that leads back to passages in the castle."

"Really?" Jetta glanced to him with surprise, and then found herself staring at his lips as he answered.

"Aye. I'll show it to ye sometime when we're here alone. Fer now, I just want ye to ken where it is."

Jetta nodded, but her gaze was still locked on his mouth. Now that they'd stopped moving, she'd drifted to rest against his front more fully and she could feel that he was hard.

Groaning, Aulay said, "Lass, stop looking at me that way."

"What way?" she asked, surprised to hear how breathless she sounded.

"Like ye want me to kiss and make love to ye," he growled.

"I am sorry, husband, but . . . I do," she admitted apologetically.

Aulay chuckled roughly at her words. "Ne'er be sorry fer that, love."

"We are not going to, though, are we?" she asked with disappointment as he eased her a little away from him.

"Nay," and now he sounded apologetic. "No' with the men here. Ye're no' the quiet type when it comes to lovin'. They'd hear."

"I could try to be quiet," she offered.

"Lass, if ye were quiet, I'd fear I was no' pleasurin' ye. Besides, yer cries and moans excite me. I'd no' enjoy it as much without it, and ye'd no' enjoy it as much trying to be quiet."

"Oh," she sighed.

Pulling her closer, he kissed the tip of her nose and then eased her back again. "I promise, we'll come alone the next time, and I'll love ye til ye scream so loud ye scare every bird in every tree for miles around into flyin' from their roosts."

Jetta chuckled softly at the promise and then shook her head. "Mayhap you should let me make my own way back to where we were, then, for I do not think I could bear the trip back otherwise."

He hesitated, but then nodded. Aulay didn't release her at once, however, but carried her closer to shore so that her head was above water when he let her go.

"Thank you," Jetta murmured, and then glanced toward the smaller beach again. As they started to move back through the water toward the larger beach, she admitted, "Saidh and the others mentioned something about passages in the keep."

"Did they?" he asked with surprise.

"Aye." She turned back to him. "They were talking about you thinking that whoever pushed me down the stairs must have known about the passages and used them to escape."

"Aye," he said grimly. "The problem is no one should ken about those passages but family."

Jetta noted his grim expression, and said, "Saidh does not think they used the passages."

Aulay's eyebrows rose at that. "Why not?"

"Most of the dresses were missing from one of the chests in the hall, and the ones that remained were crushed as if someone were sitting on them. Saidh thinks whoever pushed me hid in the chest afterward."

Aulay shook his head. "Niels checked the chests."

"Did he just open each one and move on? Or did he actually pull out a dress or two or press down on them?" Jetta asked. "Because Saidh found a ballock dagger under one of the gowns and thinks they must have pulled the gown over themselves to hide, and it must have fallen out while they did, so that when they got out and dropped the dress back in it partially covered it."

"A ballock dagger?" he asked with surprise.

"Aye. It was quite lovely with figures carved on the swellings of the guard."

Eyebrows rising slightly, he asked, "What did she do with it?"

"She has it. She and the other women were going to tell the men about it after the wedding ceremony. But she suggested you not be told until the next day so we could enjoy . . ." Pausing, she blushed and shrugged. "Despite her suggestion, I planned to tell you myself as soon as we were alone back in our room after the ceremony, but we did not go to our room, and then with one thing and another I forgot until just now."

Nodding, Aulay began to walk them back through the water the way they'd come. "We should eat and return. I should like to see this dagger."

"We can skip eating here and ride right back if you wish, husband. I do not mind and I know it will bother you until you get to talk to the others about it."

When Aulay hesitated, she added, "We can break our fast at the keep with everyone else while you talk to them."

Nodding, Aulay carried her out of the water.

Chapter 17

$\mathcal{T}$HE RIDE BACK WAS QUICKER THAN THE RIDE OUT HAD BEEN. IT seemed like just minutes before they were entering the keep. It was still early, though, and while the people who had been sleeping in the Great Hall were now up and about, Aulay's brothers and sister and their mates were nowhere to be seen and obviously still abed.

Aulay took that in as they entered, and then started to lead her to the tables, but Jetta drew him to a stop.

"Mayhap I should go above stairs and do something with my hair before I break my fast," she suggested, self-consciously feeling the back of her head. While the hair in front and on the sides was long and still a little damp, the short hair that had managed to grow in on the back was pretty much dry. She imagined it looked strange, though, and was eager to fix it with one of the cauls the women had given her.

Aulay nodded easily, handed the basket and plaid he carried to one of the men, and scooped her up into his arms.

"I can walk," Jetta protested as he turned toward the stairs, although not very vigorously. She was actually growing tired.

"I like carryin' ye," he said easily, and then added gently, "and ye're starting to drag yer feet, love. I keep forgetting that ye're still healing. I should ha'e dismounted at the keep doors and had one o' the men take the horses to the paddock rather than make ye walk all that way."

"Thank you," Jetta said, rather than argue further. Between the swimming, riding and walking she was knackered and grateful for his coddling.

Alick was coming out of his room, yawning and scratching the back of his head, when they reached the upper landing. Jetta spotted him as Aulay turned toward their room, and he obviously spotted them too. The younger man froze when he saw them, mouth open and arm raised, and gaped at them briefly. Although it seemed to Jetta he was gaping mostly at her, and then he gave his head a shake and let his arm drop, muttering, "It must ha'e been a dream."

"What must ha'e been a dream?" Aulay asked with amusement as they approached him, headed for their room.

"Oh." He smiled wryly. "I was thinking last night as I drifted off to sleep that ye'd ha'e to show Jetta the—"

"Show her what?" Aulay asked when he paused abruptly.

Rather than answer, Alick grimaced and let his gaze drift toward the soldiers behind them.

Understanding that whatever he was talking about was not something he wished to share with the men, Aulay said, "Come to our chamber with us."

When Alick fell into step with them, Aulay said, "Cullen, ha'e one o' the men go fetch Mavis, please."

"Aye, m'laird," Cullen said quietly, and then nodded to one of the soldiers, a strapping young ginger-haired man, who promptly turned to hurry back the way they'd come.

"I'll be out in just a minute," Aulay murmured as he carried Jetta into their bedchamber with Alick on his heels. Leaving Alick to close the door, he set Jetta down on the bed and then walked over to the table by the fireplace and turned to raise his eyebrows in question.

Alick hesitated and then joined him by the fire, and the two began to talk quietly enough that the men in the hall wouldn't hear. But Jetta could and listened unabashedly as she found her brush and began to pull it through her drying hair.

"So what were ye thinking I should show Jetta?" Aulay asked, dropping to sit in one of the chairs.

"The passages," Alick said in a low voice she barely caught.

"It must ha'e troubled ye greatly if ye were dreaming on it?" Aulay commented.

Alick grimaced. "Aye. The fire bothered me. Made me think she should ken about the passages so she could escape if anything o' the like happened in the keep. I mean, 'twould be just as easy to start a fire at a bedchamber door. 'Twould prevent anyone from rescuing her and prevent her escaping by the door as well."

"Aye, brother. Good thinking," Aulay said solemnly.

Alick nodded. "In me dream, I showed her the passage in me room and this room, told her how to open, close and lock them. I showed her the entrance to the stairs, and told her how to open the one at the bottom of the stairs that led into the tunnels as well, but just told her about the ones in the other rooms because people were sleeping in them." Smiling wryly, he added, "It all seemed real at the time, but me head was fuzzy, everything kept movin' on me, and Jetta had all her hair." Grimacing, he added, "I was glad to wake up this morn to find the room had stopped swaying and me stomach had settled. I felt quite sick during the dream."

"Well, ye can stop frettin'. I'll show Jetta how to open the passage to this room right now, and then show her the others when everyone is up and about," Aulay said, standing and walking Alick to the door. "Why do ye no' go down and break yer fast? We'll be along as soon as Mavis—Ah, here she is," Aulay said wryly. He'd opened the door to reveal Mavis on the other side with her hand raised. Stepping back and pulling Alick with him, they let Mavis enter and then Aulay urged his brother out the door, saying, "We'll be down shortly."

"You do not have to wait for me, husband," Jetta said, smiling at Mavis as the woman hurried to her side and took the hairbrush. "Two of the men can wait to escort me and you can take two of the men with you below."

"They are yer guards, wife. No' mine," he said moving over to sit on the end of the bed and watch Mavis work on her hair. "Besides, I want to see how Mavis puts the caul in. Then I can help ye with it the next time we ride out early."

Jetta couldn't hide her surprise at those words. He was willing to help her with her hair? Truly, he was a rare find.

"Do no' look so surprised, lass," Mavis said with amusement. "O' course he wants to learn how to fix yer hair. Aulay was always a smart lad. He kens ye'll be less likely to ride off with him fer some hough-magandie by the loch if ye're always returning with yer hair in the state it is now."

Eyes widening in alarm, Jetta pulled away from Mavis's ministrations and rushed to the mirror. Her jaw dropped in horror when she saw herself. The wind on the ride back had only half dried it, but it had left it in a flyaway mess.

Chuckling at her expression, Mavis walked up behind her and began brushing her hair again. "'Tis fine. I'll fix it. It'll no' take a minute."

"I'm sorry, Aulay. It did no' e'en occur to me to pull dresses out o' the chests or press down on them," Niels said for probably the sixth time since he'd come below some fifteen minutes ago.

Niels and Edith had been the last of their party to wake up and come down to the trestle tables this morn. By the time the pair had come below, everyone else had broken their fast and Jetta had returned to their bedchamber to lie down for a nap. He'd suggested it after she'd yawned for the tenth time. The ease with which she'd agreed told him just how tired she was. He shouldn't have woken her so early, Aulay supposed. But he'd known she'd want a bath this morning and he had wanted to show her the loch. He'd thought to kill two birds with one stone by taking her along for his morning swim.

"I should ha'e driven me sword into the bundles o' gowns," Niels muttered angrily, and then repeated, "I'm really sorry, brother."

"I ken. I'm no' angry with ye o'er it," Aulay said patiently, also for the sixth time.

"Aye, but if I'd just thought to do that, we'd already ha'e the culprit. The stables ne'er would ha'e burned, and—"

"Niels," Aulay interrupted, finally losing some of his patience. "Ye've naught to be sorry fer. I doubt I would ha'e thought to remove dresses or press on the material in each chest either. I probably would ha'e just opened each to be sure they were still full o' dresses and then moved on to the next. Stop apologizing. What's done is done."

"Aye," Niels mumbled. "I guess we should just be glad that is where they were hiding and no' the pass—elsewhere," he ended in a dull voice, remembering at the very last second not to mention the passages at the tables where anyone might hear. Aulay frowned at the man's sallow complexion and the way he kept slurring his words. "Ye're almost in worse shape than Alick this morn. What the devil did the two o' ye get up to last night?"

Niels grimaced. "Alick challenged me to a drinking game. I won."

Aulay smiled with amusement at the glum words. "Bored, were ye?"

Niels shrugged. "More like frustrated. The women had told us about the ballock dagger in the chest and their suspicions when we returned to the keep after the fire. We all discussed it, but wanted to talk to ye about it and see what ye thought, but ye did no' come below that night or the next, or—"

"Aye," Aulay interrupted. He had barely left his bedchamber since carrying Jetta up there. He'd slipped out a time or two, but only to talk to Cullen to find out if there was anything amiss. Cullen had passed on any grievances or issues that had cropped up with the normal running of Buchanan, but hadn't known about the knife and what his family members were fretting over. So Aulay had given the man orders on what to do about the issues he did know about and had slipped back to rejoin Jetta. Never once during that time had Aulay asked how Katie was doing, and it had been a conscious decision on his part. He'd wanted just to spend time with Jetta for a day or two and enjoy the fact that she was now his by law before rejoining the real world and addressing the waiting issues of murder attempts and whatnot.

That vacation from real life was over now, though, and he was neck-deep in theories and worries about the attacker who was plaguing them. If he weren't laird, Aulay would march right back upstairs now, climb into bed with Jetta and forget all of this by losing himself in her body. Despite being laird the idea was a tempting one, and he briefly considered doing just that, but then pushed the tempting thought away. He had responsibilities here.

"How long do ye think 'twill take Alick and Conran to find out which ship lost its mast?"

Aulay glanced up with a grimace at that question from Cam. After the first run of discussion about the ballock dagger, Aulay had sent Alick and Conran out again to travel to the various ports along the coast and ask around about the ship. This time, though, they would be looking for information on one that had lost its mast, rather than one that had sunk. The hope was that they would learn who might have been traveling on it, if not the name of the woman who had been strapped to it.

The pair had been leaving as Niels had come below little more than fifteen minutes ago, and since that was the only thing any of them could think to do at the moment, it would be a waiting game until they returned. Hopefully, one of them would gain the information they needed. Although Aulay wasn't sure what he would do with it once he had it. Tell Jetta her full name, that of the ship she was on, and where she was sailing to in hopes it would bring on the rest of her memories and shed some light on who might be behind the attacks? Or ride out to confront her family and this man they wanted her to marry to tell them she was a Buchanan now and would be protected, in hopes that would bring an end to the attacks?

The problem was, he needed more than just for the attacks to stop. While he and Jetta had survived the attacks on them, Katie still might not survive her own injury, and deserved justice.

"It depends on whether they get lucky, or no'," Aulay said finally. "If the boat launched from one o' the nearer ports and returned there as well, they may be back in a day or so. If it launched from further away, or limped into port further away, it could be as much as a week or week and a half."

"If the mast drifted up by the lodge, surely the ship would ha'e had to limp into a nearby port," Greer said quietly. "It could no' travel far without the main mast."

"Aye," Aulay agreed, but then pointed out, "howbeit the storm could ha'e pushed them a good distance along the coast ere dying out."

"Oh aye," Greer said with a frown.

"Then 'tis a waiting game," Dougall said solemnly. "There is little we can do until the lads return with an answer."

"Unless there is another attack," Aulay said grimly.

"That'll no' happen," Dougall assured him. "Ye ha'e men on Jetta now. And at the door to Katie's room as well. Only a fool would try to go after either woman with guards in the way."

"Mayhap," Aulay agreed solemnly. He'd decided on stationing guards on Katie's door the morning after the wedding when it occurred to him that it was unfair to use the lass as bait, even if he had someone in the passage watching over her. He had been in the stables with Jetta, and still she'd nearly died. They both had in that fire. He'd never forgive himself if something similar happened to the lass Geordie cared for.

A sigh from Niels drew his gaze, and Aulay frowned. His brother was being unusually quiet. As a rule the man had an opinion on everything, yet hadn't offered a single comment since his round of apologies. It was enough to worry him. That worry only deepened when he noted the way he was holding his head in his hands. Edith, he noticed, was watching her husband with deep concern too, which he understood completely. Aulay had never known Niels to suffer such a bad hangover. Even Alick hadn't been this bad when he came from his room. But then if Niels had won, it meant that after Alick had acknowledged himself the loser, or passed out—as was usually the case since none of them had been raised quitters—Niels had then had to gulp back whatever remained in the pitcher or pitchers they'd been drinking from. Still . . .

"Why do ye no' retire to yer room and rest awhile?" Aulay suggested.

"Aye. I think I will," Niels said with relief and stood up, only to sway a bit. When Edith rose as well, he waved her back down. "Nay. Ye do no' need to come, wife. I'm just going to sleep, and I'd feel bad fer ye missing out on visiting with Saidh and the others on me account. Besides, 'tis me own fault. I drank too much. Something I vow I'll no' do again."

"Why do we not move over by the fire and continue working on those gowns we were making for Jetta," Jo suggested suddenly, and Aulay turned from watching Niels walk away to see that Edith was staring after her husband with deep concern on her face.

Jo had apparently noticed that and hoped to distract the woman. Fortunately, Murine and Saidh seemed to realize that too and stood quickly.

"Oh aye, we should do that," Murine said with a good cheer Aulay suspected was feigned. "Come along, Edith. Niels'll be fine. A little rest and he'll be his old self."

"Aye," Edith whispered with little conviction as she stood to follow the women to the chairs by the fire.

"The women are making me wife dresses?" Aulay asked with surprise as he watched them move over to the chairs set up by the fire.

"Aye. They ha'e no' been able to find the gowns missing from the chest we think the attacker hid in. Since they were the only ones they thought would fit or look good on Jetta, they decided to use some of the fabric Jo supplied and make her a couple o' new ones," Greer answered.

Nodding, Aulay switched his gaze back to Niels, frowning at the way he was dragging his feet as he made his way above stairs. He wasn't the only one to notice.

"Mayhap Rory should take a look at Niels," Dougall suggested, watching their brother as well. "Drink does no' usually hit him this hard and I'm thinkin' . . ."

Turning a sharp eye on him when he paused, Aulay asked, "What are ye thinkin'?"

Dougall hesitated, and then shook his head. "I do no' ken what to think. 'Tis just that I ha'e never seen Niels like this, and with everything that has been going on here . . ."

"Did ye notice his eyes?" Greer asked suddenly.

"What about his eyes?" Aulay asked at once. Rory was always looking at his patients' eyes as if they could tell him something.

"The blacks in the center were almost pin-sized, they were so small," Greer said with a frown. "I do no' ken what that means, but they did no' look normal."

Aulay didn't know what that might mean either, but a glance at Cam, Greer and Dougall showed that the blacks of their eyes were bigger in the dim lighting of the Great Hall. Nowhere near pin-sized. Mouth tightening, he stood up. "I'll go ask Rory to take a look at him now."

Leaving them at the table, he moved quickly upstairs. He was stepping onto the landing when movement out of the corner of his eye caught his attention. Turning his head quickly, he caught a glimpse of Jetta slipping into Niels and Edith's room and paused abruptly. He watched with surprise as the door closed and then glanced the other way up the hall, wondering where the hell her guards had gone, but the hall was empty in both directions now.

Thinking he'd give the men who were supposed to be guarding her a good ballocking when he found them, Aulay headed toward Niels and Edith's room, thinking to see Jetta safely back to their chamber before he went to talk to Rory about Niels. He'd reached the door and had raised his hand to knock when he heard Niels's raised voice.

"God, woman, leave me alone. I do no' feel well."

Aulay's hackles rose along with his eyebrows at Niels's tone of disgust and the fact that he'd called Jetta woman as if 'twas an insult.

Jetta's answer when it came was too soft for him to hear more than a murmur of sound, but he heard Niels's response quite clearly again.

"Ha'e ye lost yer mind, Jetta?" Niels said, sounding more confused than angry. "He's me brother, and ye're his wife."

Aulay eased the door open a crack and this time heard Jetta's bitter words in response. "Open your eyes and look at me! I am beautiful! Do I not deserve a beautiful man? You are beautiful. All of you Buchanan brothers are . . . except for Aulay."

"But he loves ye, and you love him," Niels protested, sounding befuddled.

"Love?" she said with disgust. "He is a monster with that scar. It turns my stomach just to look at him. I could not bear his touching me. No woman would. Every time I see his face I think someone should kill him while he sleeps."

Aulay stiffened, his heart shriveling in his chest.

"But you would be different," she went on. "And I know you must want me too."

"All I want is to sleep until I stop wantin' to puke up me guts," Niels moaned.

Aulay heard some rustling sounds and opened the door further to see that Niels was reclined on the bed with his arm over his face. What little

Aulay could see of his skin looked green. That didn't seem to bother Jetta, however. She was climbing onto the bed and as he watched, she kissed his brother. Mouth tightening, and teeth grinding, he watched Niels turn his head with a start and tangle his hands in her hair to drag her face back away from him.

"The devil take ye!" Niels growled. "Go away and leave me alone."

"Nay. I want you to pleasure me."

Aulay started into the room, and then stopped and backed up instead, his hands clenching. He didn't dare intervene. In the state he was in, he feared he very well might beat his lying, faithless, whore of a wife to death for her perfidy.

Rustling drew his attention away toward the stairs, and much to his horror he saw Edith hurrying up the last few steps to the upper landing. He couldn't let her see this. Niels was doing nothing wrong, but Edith would still be hurt if she walked in on this and it was bad enough that he was suffering. Pulling the bedchamber door silently closed, he turned to rush back toward her.

"Aulay," Edith said with surprise when she reached the top of the stairs and he hurried forward to block her way. "I was just going to check on Niels. Is he—"

"Rory is with him," Aulay lied and took her arm to turn her back to the stairs. "Why do we no' let him examine him and see what he has to say?"

"Oh but . . ." Dragging her feet, Edith glanced back over her shoulder. "I want to see if he's okay."

"Aye. Rory will come below and let us ken once he's examined him," Aulay said, urging her along. "'Tis better if we no' distract him while he works, else he might miss something."

"Oh aye, I suppose," Edith said on a sigh and stopped fighting him.

"Good," Aulay muttered and walked her the rest of the way down the stairs and to the trestle tables. "Sit here with Dougall, Cam and Greer and I will just . . ."

He didn't bother finishing his sentence. He just had to get away from everyone for a minute. The scene he'd just witnessed upstairs was replaying itself in his head over and over. *"He is a monster with that scar. It turns my stomach just to look at him. I could not bear his touching me. No woman would. Every time I see his face I think someone should kill him while he sleeps."*

The words were like razor-sharp blades shredding his soul. To think Jetta, his Jetta, the woman he loved and whom he'd thought loved him felt that way . . . It was Adaira all over again. Only worse this time. Because he hadn't loved Adaira. He'd thought he had, but the pain he'd experienced when she rejected him was nothing compared to the agony ripping him apart now.

Aulay just didn't understand it. Jetta had never once visibly flinched from his scar. Not that he'd seen anyway, he thought, and then recalled that he had been asleep when she first woke up, and he had no idea how long she'd been awake before he'd opened his eyes. Perhaps she'd shown her revulsion then when he couldn't see it, and had managed to hide it afterward.

If so, what else had she hidden? Did she really not remember anything? Or had that been a lie too? Even her fear could be a lie, he supposed. Perhaps it all was. Perhaps it had all been lies and pretending to love him to hide at Buchanan from whatever truth she wasn't telling them.

And dear God, she was a good liar. He could still hear her sweet declarations of love in his head. Those and her fake moans of pleasure tortured him as he thought on how she'd pretended to pant for him, and feigned such an eager response to his kisses and touch. All lies. The woman was—

"M'laird?"

Aulay turned sharply and stared when he saw Cullen hurrying toward him. This was the man who should have been guarding his wife. If he had been, Aulay never would have witnessed that scene in the room, and would still happily believe his wife really loved him. His life would not now be turning to ashes around him.

"Where the hell were ye? Ye were to be guarding me wife!" he roared, furiously, taking out his pain and anger on the man. If he'd done his job, he would still be blissfully ignorant of Jetta's true nature, and if she'd killed him in his sleep as she'd threatened, at least he'd have died happy, thinking himself loved and cared for. Not destroyed by the knowledge that she had never wanted or loved him, and no one ever could or would. Thanks to this man, he'd die a lonely and bitter old man with no one at his side.

"I am. I mean I was," Cullen said with confusion. "And the men are with her still. Well, they're back out in the hall now and no' in the bedchamber with her as we ha'e been fer the past hour since we escorted her back to yer bedchamber. But they're there, guardin' her as we were ordered, and I would be too, only she sent me to fetch ye back."

Aulay stared at him blankly, trying to absorb his words. "What?"

"Shortly after she retired to yer chamber, she opened the door, poked her head out and asked would we help her move the bed," Cullen explained. "Well, o' course we said aye. But it was no' just the bed. She wanted rearranging o' the whole room, m'laird, and the room next to it too. We've done now and she sent me to fetch ye to see if ye like it." Grimacing, he added, "And I'm sure enough hopin' ye do. I do no' relish movin' everything back again if ye don't."

Aulay stared at him blankly for a moment, and then strode past him toward the keep. His mind was spinning. Nothing made sense. He'd seen Jetta in Niels and Edith's room with his own eyes. He'd heard her say those things. Yet Cullen was claiming he and the others had been up in the bedchamber with her since she'd gone above stairs? Maybe she'd slipped out while the men were busy, he thought. But that didn't seem likely. If there had only been two men, she might have managed to slip away, but four?

Ignoring the people at the table, Aulay strode straight upstairs and to his room. The other three guards were there now, positioned one on either side of the door and one against the opposite wall, facing the door. Aulay ignored them as well and stepped into his bedchamber and then paused abruptly when he saw Jetta standing on a wobbly chair next to the bed, fiddling with the drapes hanging from the canopy overhead. The bed, however, was now closer to the window. In fact, everything in the room had been moved as Cullen had said.

For a moment, all Aulay could do was stare as his mind tried to make sense of this morning's events . . . and then it occurred to him that Jetta was wearing a different gown. It was the same gown he'd helped her don in this room and at the loch this morning, but not the gown she'd been wearing in Niels's room, he realized. That one had been silver.

Jetta also didn't quite fill out her dress as well as the other Jetta had filled out the silver dress. That Jetta's clothes had fit snugly, this one's did not. The gown was a size or so too large at present, because she was underweight from her illness.

Cursing, Jetta tilted her head at a different angle as she tried to see whatever it was she was doing, and Aulay's gaze was drawn to the caul Mavis had fixed in her hair after they'd returned from the loch. He'd watched the woman put it on for Jetta, and suspected it wouldn't normally be that complicated a piece to put the average woman's hair up in, but it was more so on Jetta. Mavis had had to draw hair from the top and sides, and then braid and curl the strands to cover the large spot where her hair was missing before pinning the caul in place. It was something he was quite sure Jetta couldn't manage on her own. Yet she'd had the caul on when she left the table, hadn't been wearing it in Niels and Edith's room, but was wearing it again now.

Not only had she not been wearing it in Niels and Edith's room, he realized suddenly as a picture of Niels tangling his hands in her hair to pull her away from him rose up in his mind. That Jetta had had long black hair . . . everywhere. There had been no bald spot from where they'd shaved her head. In fact, it was her long hair at the back that Niels had caught at to pull her away from him.

It hadn't been Jetta, Aulay realized with relief, and then frowned. If the woman hadn't been Jetta, then who was she?

Chapter 18

"*O*h, husband! Cullen found you. Good. What do you think of the room?"

Aulay jerked out of his thoughts and focused on the woman who had spoken. His wife. Who apparently had a twin running about, trying to seduce his brothers and rip his heart out with both her words and act—

Aulay stopped abruptly as that thought ran through his mind. A twin. Jetta had remembered having a sister. Could she be a twin and the woman he'd seen in Niels and Edith's room? Other than having all of her hair, and a healthy weight, they had been identical.

No, he argued with himself. Even if Jetta did have a twin, the woman couldn't possibly know she was here. No one knew. He'd seen to that.

Still, what other explanation was there?

Frowning, Aulay opened his mouth, intending to ask her to try to remember if her sister was a twin, and then abruptly closed it again. Jetta never remembered anything when asked outright, and trying merely caused her pain. The only memories she'd regained to date had come to her "from the side," as Rory put it. He had to think of a way of getting the information without actually asking for it.

"Husband? Do you not like it?"

Aulay glanced toward her, a little distracted until he noted her expression. Jetta looked uncertain and even disappointed that he might not like what she had done, and he forced a smile and nod.

"Aye, 'tis nice," he assured her quickly.

"Oh good," she said with relief, and beamed at him before turning her attention back to what she was doing.

The moment she did, he turned his own attention back to trying to work out how to trick some memories out of her, or perhaps into her. Keeping her distracted would probably help, he thought, and asked, "What are ye doing now?"

"Oh, I am just trying to sort out how these drapes affix to the canopy around the bed. I thought with all the fabric Jo gave us, it might be nice to use some to make new drapes. These ones are old and a bit frayed."

"Hmm," he murmured, and not thinking of anything better to try, said, "Ye did no' mention yer sister was yer twin. She seems much different than you."

"Oh aye," she muttered, distractedly. "We are twins in countenance, not character, as Mother used to say."

"So she is no' like ye?" he asked carefully.

"Oh nay," she said on a laugh, tipping her head farther back to look at the cloth. "We are like night and day. Cat was always chatty and charming while I was quiet and more reserved. Mother used to say Cat was a peacock, and I more a—oh," she said softly.

Jetta stilled suddenly, her hands upraised, but no longer moving. Unfortunately, Aulay couldn't see her expression anymore since she'd tilted her head back a moment earlier. It wasn't until she drew a hand down to rub at her forehead that he realized the natural memories had stopped and she was now trying to force them.

Aulay started to reach for her, intending to distract her, but stopped before touching her, the other Jetta's words echoing in his head. *"He is a monster with that scar. It turns my stomach just to look at him. I could not bear his touching me. No woman would. Every time I see his face I think someone should kill him while he sleeps."*

Retrieving his hands, he said, "Jetta?"

"Aye," she murmured, lowering her head and continuing to rub it. Her expression was a combination of concentration and pain.

"Jetta," Aulay repeated with a frown, clenching his hands into fists to keep from touching her. "Ye have to stop, lass."

"I just . . . There is something important on the tip of my . . . I just need to remember . . ."

"Nay, lass. Ye need to stop," Aulay growled, his concerned gaze sliding from her to the door. He'd left the fake Jetta with Niels, who hadn't been in great shape. He shouldn't have left him, and now he couldn't leave Jetta until she stopped trying to remember. Turning his head back to his wife, he said, "Please, Jetta, ye ha'e to stop—Jetta!"

Crying out, he caught her as she wobbled and then fell off the chair. Aulay clutched her to his chest briefly, and then moved around to the other side of the bed and set her in it. Straightening then, he stared down at her with a frown. Her eyes were closed and he was sure she'd fainted, but her face was a picture of pain. It had followed her into unconsciousness. She'd pushed too hard again.

Aulay stared at her helplessly for a minute and then headed for the door, muttering, "I'll fetch Rory."

Opening the door, he stepped out into the hall and growled, "Do no' let Jetta leave the room, and no one goes in but Rory or me."

"Aye, m'laird," Cullen said solemnly.

Nodding, Aulay hurried up the hall to the room where Katie had been put. He nodded at the soldiers posted on either side of the door and opened it to glance in. A frown claimed his face when he saw that only Geordie and Katie were inside.

"Where's Rory?" he asked.

"He rode out to gather some more o' his herbs. Between Jetta and Katie, he's run low and needed more," Geordie answered, and then raised his eyebrows. "Why? What's about?"

Cursing, Aulay started to turn away, but then paused and said grimly, "If someone ye think is Jetta comes in here, do no' trust her, and under no circumstances leave Katie alone with her. She is no' Jetta."

"What?" Geordie gasped with dismay.

"I'll explain later," Aulay growled and pulled the door closed to continue on to Niels and Edith's room. Without Rory here there was nothing he could do for Jetta at the moment, and he had to get to Niels. He never should have left him alone with the wench. She'd already shot Katie with an arrow, probably poisoned the stew Mavis and Jetta were meant to eat, pushed Jetta down the stairs and set fire to the stables. He had no idea what she might do next. In fact, he had no idea why she'd done what she had so far. Katie had obviously been a case of mistaken identity. Jetta's twin—Cat, she had called her—must have thought her Jetta when she shot the arrow at her. But he had no idea why she was trying to kill her sister, or how she'd even discovered Jetta was still alive and here, or—

Aulay's thoughts died abruptly as he neared Niels and Edith's door and it opened. He stiffened, preparing to leap forward and grab Cat, but it was Edith who came out. The moment she closed the door, Aulay rushed the last few steps, caught her arm and drew her quickly away up the hall.

"Aulay?" Edith gasped with surprise. "What . . . ?"

Pausing by the stairs, Aulay hissed, "I told ye to wait below."

"Aye, but then Rory came below and headed out o' the keep, so I thought I'd check on Niels," she explained with a frown. "Rory has no' even been to see him yet."

"Nay. I had no' got to him yet, and then he headed out to get some weeds," he muttered, glancing toward the door Edith had just come out of. "What happened when ye entered the room?"

"Happened?" she asked with bewilderment.

"What were Jetta and Niels doing?" he asked more specifically.

"Jetta?" She raised her eyebrows with surprise. "She was no' there. Niels was lying in bed, holding his head. He is in terrible pain," she added with concern.

"Niels is alone?" Aulay asked, ignoring the rest of her words.

"Aye," she assured him. "Do ye ken how long Rory will be? Niels really needs one o' his medicinals. He's in agony."

"Nay," he growled. "Come with me." Taking her arm, he ushered her back to the door and then hesitated, before saying, "Ye'd best wait out here until I'm sure the room truly is empty."

"What?" she asked with surprise, but he was already opening the door and slipping inside.

Niels lay in bed as Edith had said, but appeared to be asleep. Leaving him for the moment, Aulay glanced around the room. It seemed empty, and there were precious few spots to hide. Under the bed and in the chests in the room were the only options. Recalling the chests in the hall and the women's theory that it was where the attacker had hidden after pushing Jetta down the stairs, Aulay walked to the first one, lifted the lid and then began to drag out the dresses it held.

"Aulay! What are ye doing?"

Glancing around at that cry, he frowned at Edith. "I told ye to wait in the hall."

"Aye, but—Stop that," she hissed with an anxious look at Niels as she rushed forward to snatch the dresses from him.

"Sorry," Aulay muttered and pressed down on the remaining gowns in the chest rather than pull any more out. Reassured that there was nothing but material in that chest, Aulay left it and moved on to the next. This one held plaids, linen shirts and weapons, he saw when he opened the lid. Niels's chest, he realized and scooped several items out, before dropping them back in and closing the lid.

"Ye think the attacker is here," Edith said with realization.

Aulay didn't comment, but moved to the bed and dropped to look under it. Nothing. Cat must have left before Edith entered. Cursing, he got back to his feet.

"Aulay?" Edith said as he turned to head for the door. When he didn't respond, she dropped the dresses and rushed to catch his wrist. "Aulay! What the devil is going on?"

Aulay pulled his arm away, and almost left without responding, but then paused and turned to face her and asked, "Did ye pass Jetta in the hall on yer way here?"

"Jetta? Nay," she said with a frown. "There was no one but the soldiers in the hall."

"The soldiers," he breathed and turned to the door again.

"Aulay, dammit!" Edith snapped, grabbing his wrist again.

It was the curse rather than her hold on his hand that stopped Aulay this time. Edith just was not the sort to curse, which told him how upset she was. Facing her again, he blurted, "I'm quite sure the culprit behind the attacks is Jetta's sister, Cat."

"What?" she gasped with dismay. "Why?"

"I do no' ken," he admitted grimly, glancing at his brother. "But she and Jetta are twins, and she was in here earlier. I thought her Jetta, but Jetta was in our room with her guards the whole time, and—" Taking a breath, he paused to order his thoughts and then said, "Jetta is in our room. She does no' ken Cat is here. I've told the guard no' to let her out o' our chamber to prevent any confusion. So, if ye see someone ye think is Jetta, it isna her. Be on yer guard, she's dangerous."

He glanced to Niels again and added, "Ye may want to stay here with Niels in case she returns. I'll tell the men in the hall to keep an eye on yer door as well."

"What are ye going to do?" Edith asked with concern. "How will ye find this sister?"

Aulay hesitated, and then decided, "I'm going to arrange a search."

Turning away then, he left the room before she could ask any more questions.

JETTA'S HEAD WAS POUNDING WHEN SHE WOKE UP. WINCING against the pain, she tried to lift her hand to her head and frowned when she couldn't. Confused, she opened her eyes and glanced around. She was on her side, with her hands restricted behind her back, tied up with something, and she was beside some kind of copper—

The tub, Jetta realized suddenly. She was lying next to the tub she'd had two of the men bring up and set in the small room off the master chamber. Mavis had said Aulay's father had built the room, taking up a portion of the master bedchamber and a portion of the bedchamber next to it, to make up this one. The wall between them had been torn down, and two more put up in its place to make the small chamber. It had been the baby's room, where the latest addition to their family slept so that the babe could be close to his wife, without having to be in the same room with them.

Jetta had thought it a good idea, but as they had no children yet, she'd decided it would make a good permanent spot for the bath. Well, permanent until they did have babies. Keeping the tub in here would save the servants from having to drag it up all those stairs when they wished to use it. The servants and soldiers apparently had a couple of large wooden tubs out behind the kitchens for their own use, and if guests or anyone else above stairs wished to use it, moving it from the little room to one of the others would surely be easier than carting it up the stairs.

She'd thought it a grand idea, and Mavis had agreed, so she'd put her guards to work helping her rearrange both the master bedchamber and this tiny room off of it. But she hadn't expected to end up lying next to it all trussed up like a turkey ready to go in a cooking pot.

"You are awake. Sorry. Good."

Jetta lifted her head and glanced around at the woman standing behind her and then rolled on her back to gape at her.

"Cateline." The name was a whisper on her lips as her memories were instantly all back. They did not suddenly come rushing into her mind like water into a cup. Instead, it was as if a veil had been lifted and everything was just there, where it had always been. And it wasn't the appearance of her sister that did it. It was the old nickname Cat had used. Sorry, a bastardization of her true name that she'd always hated. Probably because it was usually followed by the taunting, "Sorry Sorcha, such a sorry creature."

This time there was no aching head with the memories, but then she wasn't having to struggle to try to find them. They were all there: her full name, her home at Fitton, her childhood, her parents and this woman, her twin sister who was as different from her as darkness was from light.

Jetta also abruptly recalled how she'd come to be strapped to a mast, floating in the ocean. The memory made her scowl at her twin before she said coldly, "My apologies, Cat, but if you were hoping still to force me to France to marry your betrothed in your place, your plan will not work now. I am already married."

"Aye. I watched the wedding," Cat said with amusement.

Jetta stiffened in surprise. "You watched—? How long have you been at Buchanan?" she asked. It was a question she hadn't considered before this. She hadn't really considered anything since finding Cateline standing over her. Like why she was lying on the floor in the small anteroom off the master bedchamber? Why she was all trussed up? Where Aulay was? He'd been there when she'd got the memory back that Cateline was her twin, and that she differed from her greatly. He'd stood beside her as she'd tried to remember more, sure something important waited just outside her reach . . . and he'd attempted to get her to stop trying, she recalled. But she'd been determined despite the pain it was causing her, and then . . .

"I fainted again," Jetta said with a frown.

"I do not think fainting is the right word," Cateline said thoughtfully. "Nothing worked to wake you up after your husband finally left the room. Not slapping your face, not dumping water on you . . . You did not even wake up when I rolled you off the bed, and dragged you in here by your feet."

Jetta peered at her with disbelief, then glanced down at herself, noting that her hair was damp and she was now wearing only her shift, which was caught up around her waist. Scowling, she struggled to a sitting position and did her best to push her shift down with hands that were bound and could only reach her sides, and that with some pain as her bindings cut into her skin.

"Why am I tied up? And where has my gown—" She stopped mid-question as she looked at her sister and realized Cateline was wearing it now.

"I like it. So I took it," Cat said with a shrug. "I think it looks better on me. Do you not too?"

Straightening her shoulders, Jetta glared at her sister. "What are you up to now, Cat?"

"Finishing what I started," Cat said emotionlessly.

Jetta narrowed her gaze. "I told you, you and Father cannot make me marry your betrothed. I am already married."

"Father cannot make you do anything," Cat said idly, beginning to toy with a knife she held that Jetta hadn't noticed until she now began to turn it between her fingers.

"Why is that?" Jetta asked warily.

"Because he is dead," Cat said as if announcing that the sup was ready.

Jetta's eyes widened at the news. She waited for dismay or grief to claim her, but mostly all she felt was resignation and relief. Her father had been drinking himself to death for years now. From the day the healer had told them that Mother would never recover from the illness slowly ravaging her, that, unable to keep down food of any kind, she would simply grow weaker and thinner while suffering more and more pain, and then finally, mercifully expire. Unable to accept that, her father had retreated from life and hidden away in a flagon of ale. Although he'd alternated that with hiding in a flask of whiskey, or a cask of wine at times. It had depended on his mood and what was available to him.

"He finally drank himself to death," Jetta guessed quietly.

Cat gave a little huff of laughter, and said with disgust, "You always did think you knew everything."

"Am I wrong?" Jetta asked, watching her closely as she began to pick at the knots of the rope binding her hands. It had suddenly occurred to her that Cat may be behind the attacks here at Buchanan. She had no idea why that had not occurred to her before this. Perhaps because she had been too surprised that she was even here. She may even have been a little overwhelmed by the return of her memories. It was a lot to take. But the fact was, Cat was not only here, but apparently on finding her unconscious, had stripped her of her dress, dragged her into this small room off the bedchamber and tied her hands behind her back. That hardly suggested she was here to apologize for what she'd done in the past, and hoped for a closer relationship now that their father was dead.

Come to that, neither did her attitude, Jetta thought grimly. Cat had always been a selfish, spoiled brat, but at least prior to this she had tried to camouflage it somewhat behind simpering smiles and batting eyelashes. There was none of that now. The woman before her was cold and bitter and so filled with rage . . . Where Jetta had always just found her exasperating and even infuriating. The Cateline before her now was actually a bit terrifying. She could believe she was behind the attacks, and was here to try to kill her. That being the case, getting herself free so that she had half a chance at defending herself seemed a good idea. But she needed time to do it. She had to keep Cat talking.

"Aye, ye're wrong," Cat sneered.

"Then why do you not tell me what has happened since I left?" she suggested quietly. "I presume after you and Father saw me tied to the mast on the merchant ship, and on the way to marry your betrothed in your place, you rode back to Fitton in triumph?"

"Aye." She smiled crookedly. "I thought I had won. I was very happy that day. I grinned all afternoon and all the next day during the journey back to Fitton."

"All afternoon and the next day?" Jetta asked with surprise. "It took us only the one morning to make our way to the ship."

"Aye, but you would not allow Father to drink on the journey out."

"And you did on the way back," she guessed sadly.

Cat shrugged. "We were celebrating on the way back . . . and I was so happy I did not mind the travel or even that our having to stop to allow Papa to recover from his drinking made it take longer than the journey out, and you know how I hate travel." She grimaced.

"Aye. You always considered it torture."

"'Tis torture," Cat snapped. "Hours being bounced around on a horse's back, usually in rain or at least a cold wind, followed by relieving yourself in a bush, eating cold food or something charred almost to ashes over the fire, and then sleeping on the cold, hard ground." She shuddered with disgust. "There is nothing I hate worse than travel . . . but for that journey," she added, her voice softening. "'Twas sunny every minute of both days, the food was bearable, and even the ground did not seem so cold or hard for sleeping." Her smile faded and she sighed. "And then we got home, I slept snug in my own bed, and I woke up in the morning to find Captain Casey waiting below."

Jetta blinked. She'd forgotten the name of the captain of the ship she'd been on. But then she hadn't known him long, and he'd been a contemptible cur: unwashed, sour-smelling and more than happy to tie her to his mast and deliver her to her death for a couple coins. Aye, she remembered him now. He and the ship he captained, *Le Cok*, had been at the center of her worst nightmare.

"The ship had hit a storm, he said," Cat continued grimly. "And he had lost the mast and you along with it. His ship had been blown south, and he'd limped back into port the same evening he'd left. So, of course, once he'd finished seeing to the repair of his ship, he had rushed to Fitton to find out what Father wished to do about that."

Voice turning hard, she added, "Father apologized prettily to me, but explained everything would be lost if we broke the contract. We had done our best, but he had to send me. When I protested, he had me bound and gagged, and laid over the back of the Captain's horse to send me to the man you had managed to elude."

"He was *your* betrothed, Cat," Jetta pointed out angrily. "My own betrothed died in infancy."

"So?" Cateline cried bitterly. "What? That makes it all right that you escaped and fled, leaving me to have to marry him?"

Aye, Jetta thought, but said, "I did not escape and flee. In fact, I nearly died. The storm was horrible, Cat. The waves were as tall as mountains and at one point the ship got buffeted about so that it was sideways to the waves and trapped between two of them. The ship tipped, the top of the mast and part of the crow's nest dipped into the water of one of the waves, and the whole mast ripped free, taking me with it," she explained, recalling it as she did.

That storm had been terrifying, and one she had been sure she would not survive, even before the mast was ripped away. It had struck shortly after they'd left port, coming on quickly. It had seemed like mere minutes passed for it to go from a bit rough, to wind and rain lashing at them, and thunder crashing around them so loud she'd thought she'd go deaf. The size of the waves was like nothing she had ever seen, and had left her trembling in terror and awe. Just when Jetta had thought it could not possibly get worse, the mast she'd been strapped to had sort of vibrated, a loud creaking striking her ears, and she'd opened her tightly closed eyes to see the top of the mast had disappeared into the wave that had moments ago been beside them, but was now above as the ship tipped in the water.

Jetta had barely realized that when the mast had snapped just behind and a little above her knees with a thunderous crack that she'd felt in her very marrow. The next thing she knew, the mast was loose in the water, and her with it, being tossed about as the monstrous waves had crashed down, driving the mast under the water where she was sure she would drown before the mast bobbed back to the surface. Jetta would catch a quick, panicked breath, only to find herself driven down under the water with the mast again. And each time it had happened, her head had crashed against the hard wood behind her, eventually leaving her dazed, confused and aware only of pain and the struggle against drowning.

And then she'd woken to calm. The storm was over and she'd opened her eyes to see Aulay's face above her with a bright blue sky overhead. Jetta had thought him the most wondrous thing she had ever seen.

"Oh ballocks!" Cat snapped. "What did you promise him?"

"Who? Aulay?" Jetta asked with bewilderment.

"Nay! Captain Casey," Cat said furiously. "What did you give him? You had no coin. Did you let him bed you in exchange for his freeing you and claiming the mast broke off? Or was there really a storm and he freed you from the mast to allow you to find shelter in the cabin, but you escaped and leapt overboard in exchange for his kindness?"

Jetta stared at her with disbelief. "Nay, of course not. The mast tore away as I said. Did you not see that when he got you back to the ship?"

"*Le Cok*'s mast was intact and fine when he got me to the ship. In fact, the moment we arrived, he strapped me to it exactly as he had you just two days before."

"Oh aye. Ye said he'd repaired it ere traveling to Fitton," Jetta reminded her, but could tell Cat did not believe that. She had decided Jetta had somehow weaseled her way out of the fate Cat had manipulated for her, and was unwilling to believe otherwise.

They were both silent for a moment and then Cat shook her head. "I still cannot believe you outmaneuvered me and managed to escape marrying the marquis."

"Outmaneuvered?" Jetta asked bitterly, and then shook her head wearily. "I was not maneuvering at all, Cat. I was trying to save you right up until the moment I found myself strapped to the mast and learned that while I had been trying to save you, you had been plotting to see me sent in your stead." Shaking her head with hurt bewilderment, she asked, "How could you do that? I tried everything I could to save you. I used every argument I could think to sway Father from going through with the contract. And when none of my arguments worked, I even offered to help you escape and go with you to Mother's family to save you."

"Aye," Cat said with disgust. "That would have been fun. Would it not? The poor relations, depending on the charity of relatives? No betrothed, no prospects, no dower. We would have both ended up little more than unpaid servants, always having to give our thanks for being allowed to scrub their floors for our supper. Nay. I had no interest in that."

Jetta opened her mouth to respond, but then glanced sharply toward the doorway between this room and the next as they heard the door to the master bedchamber open.

"Jetta?" Aulay called.

She didn't get the chance to answer. Movement drew her gaze around just in time to see the hilt of Cat's dagger coming at her. Agony exploded in her forehead, bright and hot, and then just as quickly withdrew, leaving darkness behind.

Chapter 19

CONCERN BEGINNING TO CLUTCH AT HIM, AULAY GLANCED from the empty bed to the door to the little room off the master bedchamber, and started toward it as he called again, "Jetta?"

He had nearly reached the door when she came hurrying out and crashed into him.

"Oh, husband," she said on a laugh, clutching at his arms and leaning into him. "You startled me."

"Sorry, I was just coming to see if ye were in the baby's room." Sliding his arms around her, he patted her back distractedly.

"The baby's room?" She pulled back to peer at him with confusion.

"Aye. That is what me parents used that little room behind ye for," he explained.

"Oh." Relaxing, she smiled faintly, and lowered her head to watch her hands curl into the cloth of his plaid, as she asked, "Is there a reason you wished to see me?" Glancing up, she flashed her big green eyes at him and suggested, "Mayhap you wished to claim your husbandly rights?"

Aulay smiled faintly at the question, but shook his head. "Nay. In fact, I came to warn ye to stay in yer room."

"Oh?" she asked, her eyebrows rising.

"Aye," he said solemnly. "I believe yer attacker is in the keep and we are about to hunt them up, but I do no' want ye in harm's way. So ye're to stay here. I've told the guards no' to let ye leave the room," he added, fully expecting her to either insist on being allowed to help in the search, or to put up a fuss about being restricted to her room. This, after all, was the woman who had roared at him and even cursed in the stables when he'd tried to get her to go to safety and leave him to handle the horses and fire alone.

However, Jetta smiled sweetly and simply said, "Very well."

Aulay's eyebrows rose slightly, but he said, "Good," and started to release her, but she held on to his plaid and pursed her lips in a moue.

"Will you not kiss me before you go, husband?"

"Aye, o' course," Aulay murmured, wondering that he hadn't on his own and had needed the coaxing. Of course, he did have a lot on his mind just now what with everyone waiting out in the hall for him to start the search. He excused himself as he bent to kiss her.

Feeling guilty about her having to coax the kiss out of him, it was no light peck in parting. Aulay gave her one of his full-on, deep, hungry, devouring, suck the meat from between your teeth kisses. Apparently, Jetta hadn't been expecting that, for other than sag against his chest and wrap her arms around his neck as if he were the only thing holding her up, she didn't really respond.

However, she clung to him with both arms and lips, and moaned a protest when he broke the kiss and set her away.

Smiling at her dazed expression and heaving chest, Aulay turned her toward the door to the room she'd been busy in when he entered, and gave her a gentle push. "Now off with ye. I'll be back soon as I can. Hopefully, with news I've caught yer attacker."

"Aye," Jetta said breathily.

She'd filled in some, Aulay thought as he watched her bottom as she walked away. Pleased that she was regaining some of the weight she'd lost, and amused by her breathlessness and unsteady gait as she walked toward the door, Aulay teased, "Whether I ha'e or no' though, I'll be claiming those husbandly rights ye mentioned."

"I shall look forward to you pleasuring me," she breathed, and he saw her shoulders rise slightly toward her neck as a shiver slid down her back.

His smile a bit bemused, Aulay turned and left the room trying as he went to think why that had felt all wrong. He was perhaps halfway to the group of people waiting for him by the top of the stairs when it struck him and he froze in his tracks.

"Aulay?"

Blinking at that concerned voice, Aulay peered at the man leading the group toward him and immediately frowned. "Conran. What the devil are ye doing here? I sent ye out to—"

"Alick's horse threw a shoe ere we even got off Buchanan land. So I took him up on me horse and we led the beast back. We came in to tell ye what happened while we waited for the stable master to shoe his mount, and the others told us what was occurring here instead. We thought ye might want us to stay to help with the search fer Jetta's sister?"

"Aye," Aulay said nodding, and then shook his head. "Nay."

"Nay, ye do no' want us to help?" Conran asked with surprise.

"Nay, there's no need fer a search," Aulay corrected grimly. "I'm quite sure I've found me wife's sister. In fact, I believe I just kissed her," he said with a grimace, and wasn't surprised by the uproar that caused.

"Ye kissed her?"

"Ye kissed the attacker?"

"Ye kissed yer own wife's sister?"

"Are ye mad?"

Wincing at the cacophony of questions, Aulay said dryly, "Well, I did no' ken it was her at the time. I thought her Jetta." Glancing back toward the master bedchamber door, he frowned and suggested, "Perhaps we'd best move further along the hall to talk."

"I can no' believe ye could no' tell she was no' Jetta and kissed her," Saidh grumbled as they reached the far end of the hall and paused.

Aulay blew his breath out on a sigh and nodded. "I should ha'e kenned sooner, but in me own defense, she was in the room where I left Jetta with guards to prevent Jetta's leaving and anyone entering, and she was wearing Jetta's gown. The one she was wearing this morning and the one she was wearing when I left her earlier."

"Oh," Saidh said solemnly. "That is no' good."

"Aye," Aulay agreed. He had only realized that as he said it, and now pondered it with concern.

"Are ye sure 'tis Jetta's sister?" Alick asked. "Mayhap 'tis really Jetta this time."

"I am sure," Aulay assured him. "She is mayhap half a stone heavier than Jetta, which is about where Jetta was in weight when we found her."

"Aye, she lost a good stone while sick, and has gained perhaps half o' that back," Rory murmured.

Aulay nodded. "And the lass I just kissed, while wearing the right dress to be Jetta, was no' wearing her caul and had no bald spot."

"Ah." Everyone nodded solemnly. There was no mistaking her for Jetta if she had all her hair.

"Then this sister kens about the passages," Greer said solemnly.

Aulay nodded unhappily as he realized Greer was right. "She must. It is the only way she could ha'e got in the room with the guards at the door."

"Which means Jetta may no' even be in there," Saidh said with a grim expression.

"What?" Aulay turned to his sister with alarm.

"Well, you obviously did no' see her in the room," she said, and when he nodded that she was right, continued, "and the sister is wearing Jetta's gown. The only reason I can think that she would do that is so that she might move freely through the castle, which she could do if we thought her Jetta," she pointed out. "So, this twin may ha'e made Jetta take off her dress, donned it herself, and then forced her into the passages and out through the tunnel, and—" Mouth tightening, she avoided Aulay's eyes and instead of finishing, asked, "Why would the sister return? Why would she want to move freely through the castle once she . . . had Jetta?"

Aulay had no idea, and nothing was coming to mind . . . mostly because he was sifting through Saidh's words. Cat hadn't been trying to kidnap Jetta before now. She'd been trying to kill her, and he suspected that was what Saidh had not said. That Jetta had been made to strip, forced out of the castle through the passages and tunnel, and then killed.

Aulay turned abruptly, intending to head back to the master bedchamber. He was desperate to see if Jetta was in the baby's room. She couldn't be dead.

"Aulay, wait," Cam said firmly, catching his arm. "Ye can no' just go marching back in there. Ye might be jeopardizing Jetta. Ye said the sister came out o' the baby's room. Jetta may be in there. But she may not, and if she is no', then we might do better to pretend we believe the sister is Jetta and follow her to find where Jetta is."

"Cam is right," Greer said solemnly. "We need to see if Jetta is in there ere ye do anything. Is there a passage entrance in the little room as well?"

"Aye," Dougall said as Aulay tugged free of Cam's hold and started moving again, this time heading for the door just a few steps away. It was the door to Niels and Edith's room, and he didn't bother knocking, but thrust the door open and strode in.

"What the devil!" Niels barked, freezing in the middle of pulling on a fresh shirt. Yanking it down into place, he grabbed up a plaid to cover himself up and scowled at the lot of them. "Ha'e ye never heard o' knocking?"

"What has happened?" Edith asked anxiously, turning from the window to peer at them with concern. "Please tell me ye've caught the attacker, else Niels is determined to help ye find them."

"Nay, but I'm about to," Aulay growled as he continued to the passage entrance and quickly opened it.

"Yer eyes are back to normal," Greer commented behind him, presumably to Niels. "How are ye feeling?"

"Much better," Niels said quietly. "What's happening?"

"We're about to catch Jetta's sister," Alick said, directly behind Aulay, and the words made him freeze with one foot in the passage and one in the room. Turning back, he scowled.

"*We're* no' doing anything," he said firmly. "*I'm* going to sneak into the baby's room and see if Jetta is there. The rest o' ye will wait here."

"What if they are both in the baby's room?" Cam asked at once. "Ye can no' just go barging in. The sister could slit Jetta's throat ere ye got to them."

"Aulay's no' an idiot. He's no' going to just barge in," Saidh said with exasperation. "He'll check the know-holes first to be sure 'tis safe to enter."

"The what?" Aulay asked with bewilderment. He *had* been intending on just barging in.

"The know-holes," she repeated, her brow knitting as she took in his expression. "The spy holes? Ma called them know-holes when she showed them to me, because they let ye know what's happenin' in the rooms."

"We ha'e spy holes?" he asked with disbelief.

"Aye." Her eyebrows rose. "Surely ye kenned that?"

"Nay," he snapped and then glanced to his brothers. "Did any o' you?"

"Nay," they all said together, shaking their heads and looking rather put out themselves.

"Well, hell," he growled, turning back to his sister. "Why were we no' told about them? I should ha'e been told at least. I am the laird o' this keep."

Saidh shrugged unapologetically. "Ma told me. I just assumed she or Da had told the rest o' ye."

"I think I know why," Jo said thoughtfully, drawing all eyes her way.

Aulay's eyebrows rose. "How would you ken why our parents did no' tell us about the spy holes and only told Saidh?" he asked, more curious than anything.

"Because I have a son," Jo said wryly, and then asked, "I presume you were lads when you were told about the passages?"

They all nodded.

"How old?" she asked at once.

"Five or six," Aulay answered at once.

"Aye," Dougall agreed. "What has that to do with anything?"

Rather than answer, Jo asked, "If, as a lad, there had been a visitor to the keep, say a beautiful buxom blonde, or a curvy redhead you thought attractive. And if her maid sent for a bath within your hearing," she added. "Would you or would you not have slipped into the passages to peek through the spy holes at her?"

Affronted, Aulay opened his mouth to answer, but Jo held up her hand to forestall him.

"I am asking all of you Buchanan boys, and I do not mean now would you look, but when you were a young lad, of twelve or so, would you have tried to get a peek then?"

Aulay hesitated, and then exchanged glances with his brothers, before admitting on a sigh, "Aye," even as his brothers did. But he added, "'Tis the kind o' thing lads do."

Jo nodded as if that was exactly what she'd expected. "And that is why you were not told as children." Turning to Cam then, she added, "And that is also why we will not tell our sons about the spy holes in the passages at Sinclair until they are adults and can be trusted not to look unless necessary."

"There are spy holes in the passages at Sinclair?" Cam asked with amazement.

"Aye. Your mother showed them to me after we married," she announced.

"What?" he asked with disbelief. "Why did she or Father never tell me about them?"

When Jo shrugged her shoulders helplessly, Dougall suggested, "Mayhap they're waiting until yer an adult and can be trusted no' to look."

Cam stiffened, but then nodded solemnly. "Aye. And no doubt that is why yer parents ne'er told ye ere they died, and why ye're uncle still hasn't."

Aulay almost cracked a smile at the exchange of taunts, but in the end he didn't. No one did. They were all too aware that Jetta was in jeopardy . . . or possibly dead.

"Where are the spy holes?" he asked Saidh sharply, impatient to see if Jetta was all right.

"They are those small stones sticking out o' the wall," Saidh explained. "There are dozens o' them along the walls at all different heights. The stones pluck out easy as ye please, revealing a pinhole ye can see through into the room."

Nodding, Aulay turned to finish stepping into the passage, but paused again as someone bumped against him and he realized everyone had crowded forward, intending to follow him. Even Edith and Niels were moving toward the passage, he saw, and it was Alick who'd bumped into him.

"I am going alone," he growled. "The rest o' ye stay here."

"Ye might need help," Dougall argued at once.

"I'll be fine, and the bunch o' ye will make too much noise," he argued.

"We'll be quiet as mice," Alick assured him.

"Aulay," Saidh said quietly. "If she dies because ye refused help, ye'll never forgive yerself . . . and I may no' forgive ye either. I really like Jetta."

Aulay closed his eyes briefly, but then gave in with a sigh. "Fine. But ye can no' make a sound."

When every one of them nodded solemnly, Aulay turned and led the way into the passage.

IT WAS THE SPLASH OF COLD WATER THAT ROUSED JETTA. BLINKing her eyes open with alarm, she peered anxiously about, and then froze as she spotted Cateline and recalled her situation.

"Finally," Cat said, tossing aside the empty pitcher she held. "I thought you would never wake up."

Jetta eyed her with dislike. "I suppose it was too much to hope that your presence at Buchanan was just a nightmare."

"Oh my!" Cat's eyes widened in surprise and delight. "The kitty has developed claws. When did you find courage, sister? You never would have spoken to me like that at Fitton."

Jetta just shook her head and closed her eyes. She had no intention of getting into a battle with her sister. She had refused to do it when they were children growing up, and then as an adult, not because of a lack of courage, but because it upset their mother. She wouldn't do it now because she needed to think on how to escape. Getting her sister talking so that she could do that was more likely to aid her than wasting her thoughts on trading insults.

Determined to keep her talking, she asked, "Are you not going to finish telling me what happened after you and Father left me on the ship?"

There was a pause and Jetta began to worry her sister would not continue talking, but would move on to whatever she planned to do next, and then Cat said, "Aye. Where was I?"

"You were on *Le Cok*," Jetta said at once, and when Cat did not immediately begin speaking again, asked abruptly, "did you trade your body to the captain to escape marrying the marquis? Is that how you came to be here?"

"Nay. He was more interested in his first mate than me," she said with disgust.

"So you remained strapped to the mast all the way to the south of France?" Jetta asked, coaxing her along.

"Nay. The captain claimed he was afraid of another storm coming along and stealing his profits. Once we were far enough away from port that I could not possibly swim to freedom, he untied me from the mast, and tied me to his bed in his cabin instead."

Jetta stiffened, her head coming up. "His bed? He did not—?"

"Rape me?" Cat finished for her when she hesitated to ask. Sneering, she said, "Nay. Did I not mention he was more interested in his first mate?"

"Oh aye," she murmured.

"Anyway," Cateline continued. "The trip was uneventful and short. It only took five hours. There was not a whisper of a storm, but the wind was up. Mostly I was bored during the journey, and then we landed. The captain untied me, ordered me to clean myself up, and after informing me that he had stationed a man outside the window, and would stand guard at the door himself to ensure I did not escape, he locked me in his cabin."

"What did you do?" Jetta asked, her fingers working feverishly at the knots in the rope binding her, despite the certainty she had that it was impossible. The binding was too tight, making it hard to reach much of the rope to work at it.

"What could I do? I prepared myself to meet my doom," Cat said dryly. "By that point I had become resigned to my fate. I would marry the marquis, and become a marchioness, and pray he did not hurt me."

"Did he hurt you?" Jetta asked quietly.

Cat stared at her icily for a moment before speaking again, and when she did, it was not to answer the question. She simply continued with her story. "The marquis was not waiting at the docks as expected. But then, the ship was two days late thanks to the storm and your escape. So the captain hired a wagon, and a maid to accompany us for propriety's sake, and delivered me to the marquis personally."

She fell silent again and Jetta peered at her, wondering what she was thinking. Now that she had her memories back, Jetta suspected she had never really known her sister and that much had been hidden under all her fluff and flounce. Certainly, despite Cat's often selfish ways, Jetta had been completely flummoxed to find herself bound to *Le Cok*'s mast. And even that had not prepared her for finding herself in this situation. The woman before her was not the sister she'd thought she knew growing up. This woman was empty and cold and really rather scary.

"He was beautiful," Cat said finally and there was wonder in her voice. "Truly, I have never seen a more beautiful man. His hair was like spun gold, and his eyes as blue as a cloudless sky. When he smiled, it was enough to make a saint weep." Meeting her gaze, she added, "And he was so charming and kind.

"I expected the wedding to take place right away, but he told me it would not be for a week, that he had arranged it that way for my benefit. He wanted me to feel comfortable with him before we became man and wife." Meeting Jetta's gaze she asked, "Is that not the kindest thing you have ever heard?"

"It was kind," Jetta allowed, and did not tell her Aulay had shown her much more kindness saving her life, pretending to be her husband to make her feel safe and comfortable enough to heal, and in a hundred other ways since she'd washed up on his shores.

"That was truly the most wondrous week of my life," Cateline went on in an almost dreamy voice. "Compliments rolled off his tongue like honey. He proclaimed himself the most fortunate of men to have me to wife. I was the most beautiful woman he had ever seen. I would give him the loveliest children. He looked forward to our future together with excitement and wonder."

Smiling softly, she said, "I actually fell in love with him that week. I thought your death was fortuitous, that God had surely arranged it so that I would have to marry this man who had obviously been made just for me. I could see my life before me, and it would be just like a fairy tale. And the wedding!" she exclaimed with remembered delight. "The marquis had planned and prepared in advance. It was not rushed and tawdry like yours."

Jetta stiffened at that description of her wedding to Aulay. It may have been rushed, but there had been nothing tawdry about it in her mind.

"My wedding was beautiful," Cateline continued. "That week he arranged for a dress to be made for me, and it was the most glorious concoction I have ever seen. He spared no expense on the food and drink, and arranged for minstrels and entertainers to come from far and wide. It was like a dream," she breathed. "And then came time for the bedding. I was excited and nervous, but rather than bed me, he said he could see I was afraid, and would give me one more night to adjust to my new home and to him as husband. And then he cut his own hand and smeared the blood on the linens for the priest to find in the morning. But he did not leave the bed," she assured her. "He wrapped his arms around me and held me all night as if I was the most precious creature alive."

Meeting Jetta's gaze, she said solemnly, "I fell asleep feeling cherished and loved, and woke up thinking myself the most fortunate woman in the world." Cat paused as if to savor that feeling for a moment, and then continued, "Of course, the next day all our guests left. They had already stayed more than a week, longer than expected, so every one of our guests was gone by the sup. Frankly, I was happy to see them go. I was eager to spend time with my new husband. But eventually everyone was gone, we sat down to sup, and then my sweet husband escorted me up to our room and my true wedding night began . . . and my lovely dream turned into a nightmare."

Jetta blinked, but remained silent, leaving her to tell it in her own time.

"My beautiful marquis with the honeyed tongue vanished and a cruel, monstrous beast took his place. My wedding night became one long week of unending torture and depravity." Her gaze met Jetta's and for a moment the Cateline she'd known as a child was there, peering out of her eyes. Young, vulnerable, bewildered, she said, "He hurt me . . . and enjoyed the hurting. He did things . . ."

Shuddering, Cat turned her face away as she confessed, "At first, I tried to hide it from the servants and soldiers . . . that he was hurting me. But after the second or third night I could not hide the bruises and burns, they were everywhere, and the servants and soldiers began to eye me with pity. I bore that for a week, but then torturing me in our chamber was not enough. He dragged me naked down to the Great Hall, and beat and raped me on the trestle table for all to see."

Jetta gasped in horror, but Cat wasn't done. "When he was finished, he rolled me off the table to the floor to lie with the dogs as he said I deserved, and then he pissed on me."

"Oh Cat," Jetta breathed with horror, and Cateline's head whipped around like a striking snake, fury all that was left of her.

"Shut up!" she shrieked with rage. "It should have been you! It should have been you who suffered all of that disgusting . . ." She inhaled sharply, and turned away again. After a moment, she continued in a calm, uncaring voice, "Anyway, by that time I was . . ." Turning back, she gave a wry smile and said, "Well, frankly by that time I was so battered and bruised and appeared so weak, no one even imagined that I had anything to do with his falling down the stairs and breaking his neck on the way back to our room."

Chapter 20

$\mathcal{J}$ETTA STARED AT HER SISTER, HER THOUGHTS IN AN UPROAR AS what Cateline had revealed whirled in her mind. She could not begin to imagine what Cat had gone through, and didn't want to. No one deserved to go through that, and Jetta was very aware that she would have suffered that fate herself, had providence not intervened. So, she was not sorry that the marquis was dead. In fact, she took comfort in the knowledge that he could never again hurt Cat, or anyone else. For Jetta was sure a man such as that had not restricted his tortures to just his first wife and Cat, or even females alone.

However, Jetta was more concerned about Cat herself. She was just a ball of pain, buried under rage as far as she could tell. But the lightning-quick way her fury came on and just as quickly seemed to disappear troubled Jetta a great deal. She was certain she now understood Cat and what she was doing a little better. While her sister had been selfish and spoiled before, she was now broken . . . and she suspected very, very dangerous.

Taking a deep breath, Jetta released it slowly and simply said, "You pushed him down the stairs."

"Aye." Cateline's mouth twisted with bitterness. "And got absolutely nothing for my trouble. Everything was left to some cousin twice removed; the title, the castle, all that money, everything. Even my dower!" she added with outrage, and scowled as she continued. "The new marquis arrived to be titled four days later, and wanted nothing to do with me. As far as he was concerned I was an interloper. A week to the day after I killed my husband, the new marquis handed me over to Captain Casey."

Jetta gave a start of surprise and Cat smiled bitterly. "Aye, the very same captain who delivered me to France. Bastard," she added. "I shall have to pay him a visit when I am finished here."

Jetta forced herself not to react, but inside she was thinking, *Oh God, Oh God, Oh God.* Cat was more than broken. She was completely and utterly mad if she planned to go about killing everyone she even imagined had done her a wrong. Jetta had not liked Captain Casey either, but in the end, he had just been doing his job, delivering who he thought was a young girl to her betrothed. An unwilling young woman, but the betrothal contract had been real.

"I was still in bad shape," Cat went on. "But the new marquis could not be rid of me quick enough. He handed me over to the captain with nothing but a sack of coins. Even the jewels I was given as a wedding gift were taken from me. They were family jewels, and were to go to the new marquis's wife.

"I was still battered and bruised, but the marquis had arranged with the captain to have me returned home and we sailed back. Again, Captain Casey was to deliver me himself, but he had things to do first, so had one of his men go out and rent a wagon and put me in it. And then they just left me lying in the damned thing for hours with the sailor to guard me until the captain was ready.

"That is when I found out you were still alive," Cat said with a bitter smile. "I was lying in the bottom of the wagon, wrapped in furs, waiting impatiently for the captain to arrive, and a young man came along. He asked my guard if any ships had sunk in that storm a little more than three weeks back. My guard asked why he was asking, and he said he'd heard that a mast had been found floating about and thought perhaps a ship sank. My guard assured him he had not heard of anything of the like, and the young man went away."

"It was not long after that when the captain finally deigned to show himself. The guard told him what had transpired. They wondered if it was not their mast, and thought it must be, but decided you obviously had not been still on it or would have been mentioned. But I knew," she said with satisfaction. "I just felt it in my bones that that young man or someone connected to him had found you and you were still alive."

"But how did you know where I was?" Jetta asked at once.

"My guard recognized the man who had questioned him as one of the Buchanans. He told the captain they all look alike, but he thought it was the youngest one. Alick."

Jetta closed her eyes on a sigh, but then stilled as it suddenly occurred to her that Cateline had known all along that she hadn't bribed the captain, or escaped the ship. Cat knew the mast had ripped away, taking her with it. It seemed she needed to blame her for her woes in whatever way she could find.

"The captain delivered me home that evening," Cat continued. "Father pretended to be glad to see me alive and well. He claimed he had 'just known' I would come out all right. I smiled and nodded and suggested we celebrate my return."

Cateline offered her a smile that was all teeth. "He tried to say nay at first, but I insisted. We had to toast to my survival, after all. Eventually he agreed and I had the whiskey brought out. We toasted to my survival, and then I insisted we toast to your sad passing, and then Mother's, and so on. I did not drink my own whiskey, but made sure he drank his." Pausing, she glanced upward as if trying to remember and said thoughtfully, "I think it was probably the seventh or eighth whiskey that I put the poison in, and then I insisted on one final toast to his health and watched him die."

Jetta's head jerked up as if a string had been yanked. "You killed our father?"

"With pleasure," Cat growled.

"Why?" Jetta asked with amazement. Her father had given Cat everything she had ever wanted, including shipping Jetta off in Cat's place to marry the marquis at Cat's urging.

"I was very angry with him," Cat growled, her fury flashing briefly, and then it was gone again and she added mildly, "Besides, he was not drinking himself to death as I expected once you were gone. In fact, he was hardly drinking at all anymore. Where Mother's death made him drink, news of your so-called death seemed to sober him up. He stopped drinking altogether except for a stein of ale at the sup." Her mouth tightened, but her tone was still light when she said, "Until the night he died."

Jetta bowed her head. Her sister was more than insane. Killing the marquis was one thing, but their father was quite another. He had been her comrade at arms in the effort to ship Jetta off in place of Cat.

"Of course, the healer said it was the drink, and congratulated himself for being right when he had warned Father that drink would be the death of him. I just tried to look sad and nodded." Grinning, she added, "And suddenly I owned everything! I am the Lady at Fitton. Mistress of all."

"The king will appoint a guardian until a new marriage is arranged for you," Jetta predicted quietly.

"He already has—Father's brother, Uncle Albert."

Jetta gaped at her. "But Uncle Albert is—"

"Mad? Suffering woodness?" Cat suggested with a smile. "Aye, he is. Which works to my advantage. He is always off with his books, trying to prove that the devil exists, which leaves me to do as I wish." She shrugged. "So I am in control. He allows me my way in all things. In fact, he probably has not noticed that I am not at Fitton at present. That is the amount of freedom I now have. He cares not how I spend coin or what I do with my time."

"Then why are you here?" Jetta asked, suspecting she knew the answer, but seriously hoping she was wrong. "Why are you not at Fitton enjoying your new freedom?"

"Because there is still you," she said. "You are as much at fault for what I suffered as Father. If you had not escaped your fate and forced me to take your place I would not have suffered the marquis's abuse and depravities."

"It was not my fate. I—"

"So I decided I would come find and kill you too," Cateline continued. "The first morning I arrived I saw who I thought was you frolicking in the woods with whom I presumed was the laird here. She had the same

hair as us, and very similar features too. I can only think Father made
his way up here at some point fifteen or sixteen years ago and got some
maid with child. The lass looked a lot like us. At least, she did from a
distance. By the time I got close enough to see her, they were on horseback and riding for the castle. I followed and shot her just ere they went
through the gate."

Jetta swallowed. Cateline had always been an excellent shot with the
bow and arrow. "You shot a maid named Katie, not me."

"Aye, I found out later," she admitted dryly and grimaced. "Shortly
after I shot who I thought was you, a soldier came charging out of the
gates. I knew it had to have something to do with my arrow, so I followed
him. I was trying to think of a way to find out what had happened . . .
if you were dead or not. I had just decided that I would wait until he
stopped for the night and make him tell me at knifepoint, when he arrived at the lodge. An old woman was coming out and he talked to her,
told her the maid Katie was shot while riding with Geordie, and Rory
was needed.

"I was sore disappointed," she admitted on a sigh. "But then the old
woman said Rory and the master were down breaking their fast at the
beach with 'the young English lass.'" Cateline clucked her tongue. "I
had a feeling again, the same one I had when I heard young Alick asking around about any ships that sank. So I followed the messenger to the
beach and there you were!"

Shaking her head, she said, "You were terribly thin. Skeletal. And you
were wearing the most ridiculous outfit, too. But you were laughing, and
there was color in your cheeks and you looked like you were having a
grand time." Smile dying, she added angrily, "Like you had been having
a grand time the whole time I was suffering."

"I was unconscious for weeks, Cat. I had only woken up less than
two weeks before that, probably about the same time you were delivered
home. And that day at the beach was the first time I'd left the room since
I woke up in. I had no memories. I thought Aulay my husband."

"Hmm," she said dubiously and shrugged. "At any rate, the messenger
and Rory left at once, but you two packed up and headed back to the

lodge. Only Aulay left right away to follow Rory. After he left, I slipped inside while you and the old maid were still above stairs. There was a pot of stew boiling over the fire and I dumped some poison in, hoping that would do the trick. After giving it a good stir, I slipped back outside and went and found a nearby spot to camp and rest a bit while I waited for you to eat the stew. I returned later that night, expecting to find you and the old woman dead. Instead, there were men everywhere and the only thing dead was a dog," she said with disgust.

Jetta didn't explain that the stew had charred over the fire and been tossed out. Why bother?

"Of course, with Acair and the men there I did not dare stick around. I could hardly blend in with soldiers, so I retreated to my camp to try to decide what to do. And it was there I recalled the plaid you had dropped."

"The plaid?" Jetta echoed with confusion,

"Aye, ye dropped it on the beach ere leaving when the storm struck after yer picnic."

"Oh," Jetta murmured, recalling now. Aulay was actually the one who had dropped the plaid, and she'd almost thought he'd rush back for it when he realized, but the rain was coming down so heavy . . . She'd been relieved when he left it and they'd headed back to the lodge. Jetta had assumed he'd fetch it later, but then he'd left for Buchanan and she hadn't given it another thought. Now she asked, "What use was the plaid to you?"

"Well, I could hardly slip into Buchanan in my expensive gown, could I?" she asked dryly. "That plaid is how I managed to slip in without notice. I made an arisaidh of it, gathered some rushes, lavender and other plants on my way back to Buchanan, and then left my horse tethered in the woods and simply walked into Buchanan with my weeds as if I belonged there. No one gave me a second glance, not even the men on the wall. And why would they? I was just an innocent young lass."

Suddenly tired beyond words, Jetta decided to speed this along and said, "You pushed me down the stairs."

Cat shrugged. "It worked with my husband."

"You hid in a chest in the hall afterward to avoid discovery."

Startled, she scowled and asked, "How did you know that?"

"You dropped Father's ballock knife while you were hiding in there. We found it later."

"Ah. I wondered where that had gone. I brought it, hoping to use it on you. I lay awake each night here, imaging what I would do to you with it."

"We are sisters, Cat," Jetta said desperately. "More than sisters— twins—and yet you hate me and—"

"Of course I do!" she bellowed. "You escaped *Le Cok*, forcing me to marry the marquis!"

"He was *your* betrothed!" Jetta bellowed right back. "And I escaped nothing as you very well know. I was tied to the mast and it was ripped from the ship as if God himself reached down and tore it off."

"God," Cat sneered. "Now you will try to claim God saved you? Where was he when I needed him, then? Why did he not kill my husband ere I had to marry him? Or ensure I was betrothed to someone else to begin with? Someone young, strong, handsome and virile?"

"Perhaps he did try to give you a husband who was young, strong, handsome and virile," Jetta argued.

"What?" Cat asked with confusion, and then snapped impatiently, "What are you driveling on about now?"

"It occurs to me that had you not connived to make me marry the marquis in your place, and had you been on *Le Cok* the first time instead of me, it would have been *you* on the mast that tore from the ship and floated up to shore near Aulay's lodge. And had that happened, it might now be *you* married to him and enjoying the benefits of a young, strong, very handsome, and incredibly virile husband who is also kind and would never even think of hurting you.

"Come to think of it," she added now, "mayhap I should thank you for your perfidy. For I owe every happiness I have enjoyed to date to your conniving and convincing father to send me to the marquis in your place."

Cat's eyes narrowed, and then she gave a hard laugh. "Your husband is far from handsome. I may have married a man who was monstrous in deed, but yours is monstrous to look at. Frankly, I do not understand how you can bear to let him touch you."

"I like his face and find him handsome," Jetta said unperturbed. "To me he is the most beautiful man I have ever met."

"Of course, you would think so," Cat said with derision. "You always preferred the flawed to the flawless. I once told Mother I was sure you were blind, but she said nay, that you found beauty in imperfection." She rolled her eyes to show her opinion of that, and then her mouth compressed and she seemed to struggle briefly before admitting, "Although, I will concede that he seems very virile. The things he did to you in the stables . . . The way you moaned, cried out and thrashed about as he did them . . ." She gave a little shiver at the memory and said, "It made me think mayhap the bedding did not have to be so painful and humiliating. It made me want to experience that pleasure myself."

"You watched us in the stables?" Jetta gasped with horror.

"Where do you think I was sleeping up until then?" she asked tightly. "I could hardly sleep in the keep and risk you seeing and recognizing me. Others might have been fooled by the dirt I smeared on my face, and my covering my hair, but I knew you would not. So I slept up in the hayloft, and had a perfect view of both your wedding and the two of you consummating it afterward."

"And then you locked us in and set the fire," Jetta said, her own voice a little cold.

"Aye." Cat made the admission with no remorse. "The moment you fell asleep, I crept down, started the fire and blocked the doors so you could not escape." Mouth twisting bitterly she added, "But of course you did. Again."

When Jetta just glared at her, she eyed her back for a moment, and then smiled cruelly and said, "But perhaps that has worked out to my advantage in the end. Because, I have to say, sister, I think I will enjoy having yer Aulay pleasure me before I kill him."

"What?" Jetta asked sharply.

Cat shrugged. "It is not as if I need rush home after killing you. I still want to kill Captain Casey, but there is no rush. I can dally here a day or two and taste that pleasure ye've been enjoying before I slit the Buchanan's throat while he sleeps."

"What?" Jetta asked with amazement. "Why would you kill Aulay?"

"Because he gave you pleasure while I suffered," Cat said furiously, and then shrugged that fury away like it was a pesky fly that had landed on her shoulder, and added, "It only seems fair that he gives me some of that pleasure too before I punish him."

Relaxing suddenly, Jetta shook her head. "Nay. You will not. You said he had a monstrous face and you did not understand how I could let him touch me," she reminded her.

"Aye, I did. And 'tis true, which is why originally, I intended to try it on with one of his brothers," she admitted. "Of course, I did not want them to remember it, so I dropped a few weeds and herbs in a pitcher of ale, covered my hair, muddied my face and took it out to set it in front of Conran. Unfortunately, Alick grabbed it and challenged Niels to a drinking contest and the two of them drank it all. Conran did not even get a sip of the concoction," she said with irritation.

Smiling again, she announced, "But I have since decided that might have been fortuitous. Unfortunately, Edith was in bed with Niels so I went to Alick first. I tried to get him to bed me, but even drugged and brainless, he had too many scruples and would have naught to do with bedding his brother's wife."

"O' course I would no'," Alick muttered with disgust beside Aulay in the dark passage, and he punched him in the arm for speaking. Although he was surprised at how quiet they had all managed to be. Aside from the occasional horrified gasp, or disgusted tsk, everyone had remained silent. Enthralled by the tale told. Even he was. It was the only reason he had not yet slid along the wall to the entrance to the passage from the bedchamber and gone to save his wife.

"You tried to seduce Alick?" he heard Jetta ask with dismay and turned back to his spy hole as she protested, "He is just a boy."

Knowing his brother as he did, Aulay quickly covered Alick's mouth with his hand, muffling the outraged squawk that followed that comment. When Alick's furious eyes swiveled his way, he whispered, "Quiet as mice, remember?"

Unable to speak, Alick nodded.

Sighing his relief, Aulay turned back to the hole as Cat continued, "'Twas probably for the best. I do not think it would have worked anyway. I learned from the few kisses I managed to coax out of him that he is a sloppy kisser. I did not feel even a touch of the passion you seemed to experience with Aulay."

Aulay turned sharply on Alick, but this time Dougall had acted more swiftly and covered their brother's mouth.

"Ye kissed me wife?" he demanded in a hiss.

"He kissed Cat, no' Jetta," Dougall said soothingly. "And most like no' willingly. Ye heard her say he refused her."

Aulay growled low in his throat, but turned back to the hole again.

"But the night was not a complete waste," Cat commented. "I got him to show me the entrance to the passages. He was very gullible, or perhaps the weeds made him tractable. I told him Aulay said he should, and he did. He showed me the one in his room, and then took me through the passages to the entrance to the stairs, and then the tunnel and all the way out to the cave and back, and then he told me how to open the passage to each room as we passed." She grimaced. "I had to shush him a time or two, for fear he would wake those in the rooms, but we got away with it.

"And then there was Niels," Cat continued, and Aulay tore his eye from the hole to glance worriedly along the line of dark shapes, trying to see Edith. He suspected she would be the one upset by what was coming and hoped to God Niels had the good sense to silence her when that happened.

"It was morning ere I could get Niels alone." Cat's voice drew his attention back. "He and Edith went below to break their fast, but it was not long before he returned without her." Cat's mouth tightened. "The drink I had given him had obviously mostly worn off by then, for he would not even kiss me. He was most upset for Aulay, and disgusted by what he thought was your behavior," she said with irritation. "And that is when

I realized the only chance I probably have of experiencing that pleasure Aulay gave you was with Aulay himself."

"You are not sleeping with my husband," Jetta said grimly.

Cat laughed and taunted her, "Oh come now, sister, do not be so greedy. Mother always admonished us to share our toys."

"Aulay is not a toy. He is the man I love and my husband."

Aulay swallowed. It felt like his heart was swelling. He would never again doubt her love for him.

Cat shrugged. "Which means he is the one man in this castle who will not reject me when I come to him as *you*. Instead, he will work hard to please me." She gave a little shiver of anticipated pleasure, and then added, "And, who knows? If he is very very good at it, as I suspect he will be, I may let him live a while. At least until I tire of him."

"But you said you could not bear to look on his face," Jetta almost howled.

"I will snuff out all the candles and torches," she said simply. "And if that does not work and the fire reveals too much of his face, I will close my eyes. Besides, I doubt you saw much of his face when he was under your skirts." Laughing at Jetta's expression, she added, "Actually, now that I have decided on it, I am looking forward to his pleasuring me. Ugly or not, I enjoyed his kiss earlier."

"He kissed you?" Jetta asked, sounding wounded, and Aulay clenched his hands, wishing he could throttle his wife's sister.

"Aye, and it was . . ." Cat shivered happily, and breathed, "Oh aye. I am eager for more."

Aulay's mouth tightened at the very thought. It would be a cold day in hell before he would even touch the woman. Well, other than to apprehend her.

"Speaking of which," Cat said now. "He and the others should soon finish their search, and then he promised to return to claim his husbandly rights, so . . . we really need to move this along so I can send one of the soldiers to fetch him back here. From what I have seen, I expect I will be naked, on my back and moaning and groaning minutes after he comes through the door."

"Over my dead body," Jetta growled.

"That is the plan, sister. Literally," Cat said on a laugh. "I plan to kill you first and, since I cannot move you until things settle down, shove your dead body under the bed. Your husband will literally be giving me pleasure right over your dead body."

When Cat started toward Jetta, brandishing her knife, Aulay's heart nearly stopped in his chest.

Chapter 21

*H*E HAD LEFT IT TOO LATE, AULAY REALIZED WITH DISMAY. Instead of intervening the moment he saw both women in there, he had allowed himself to be distracted by the tale his wife's sister told. Cursing, Aulay pressed on the lever to open the passage entrance to the small room and rushed inside. But he didn't get to Cat before she got to Jetta. She must have heard him. Perhaps the rustle of his clothes or a footfall gave him away. He didn't know, but before he could reach Cat, the crazy wench rushed to Jetta and moved behind her. In a heartbeat, she had dropped to her haunches so that Jetta hid most of her from view, and placed her knife at Jetta's throat.

Aulay froze at once. Trying not to show the alarm coursing through him, he growled, "Put down the knife, Cat. Ye're caught."

"I am not caught yet," she assured him grimly, her gaze sliding from him to the passage entrance.

Aulay glanced toward it, relieved to see that the passage looked empty. Alick had had the good sense not to follow him and was nowhere in sight. Turning back to the women, he said, "Ye're right, and ye do no' ha'e to be. Let go o' Jetta and—"

"I am not a fool," she interrupted dryly. "The minute I let her go you will attack." Her gaze slid to the passage and back again and she urged Jetta to her feet as she said, "So . . . I think I will just take her with me."

"I'm no' a fool either, wench," Aulay growled. "I ken do ye leave here with Jetta, she's as good as dead."

"Jetta," Cat said with disgust. "Her name is Sorcha, or Sorry, as I like to call her. But it is not Jetta."

"It is now," Aulay said unperturbed. He'd noticed Jetta's wince at the unkind nickname, and vowed if he ever heard anyone call Jetta that, he'd beat them into the ground himself. Returning to the subject at hand, he said, "Ye can take Jetta with ye as far as the passage entrance. If ye let her go there, ye're free to flee through the passages. I'll no pursue ye."

Cat looked toward the passage and back to him, as if considering, and then said, "Move away from there then."

Aulay nodded, and took a moment to glance to Jetta. He hadn't dared before this, but now he met her gaze and offered her a reassuring smile, trying to convey that all would be well. His heart nearly broke when Jetta peered back at him with apology in her eyes, of all things. To him that meant she'd already given up.

Mouth tightening, he eased to his left, moving closer to the tub, but on the side opposite the two women. Cat watched him narrowly as if expecting a trick, but did urge Jetta to move along the other side of the tub in the direction of the passage. When she gestured with her head that Aulay should move further to his left, he took a couple of short steps along the tub toward the back wall of the room.

Once he had, Cat moved Jetta another few feet the opposite way and then suddenly paused.

Noting the way her eyes narrowed as she looked through the opening into the passage, Aulay felt his heart sink.

"Who's in there?" she barked suddenly. "Come out."

There was a pause and then Alick stepped into the opening, looking chagrined.

"Get over there with Aulay," Cat snapped.

Muttering an apology, Alick moved up beside him, and they both watched Cat tilt her head to get a better look into the darkness. A moment passed, and Aulay was quite sure she didn't see anything else. His brothers weren't stupid. They would have moved back to ensure they didn't give their presence away until she was in the passage. Aulay was positive she didn't see anything. Unfortunately, the lass was smart and said, "I know you are there. You might as well come out."

When silence reigned and no one appeared, she said, "Or should I just slit Jetta's throat and be done with it?"

Aulay saw Jetta wince, noted the bead of blood that appeared as

Cat pressed the point of her knife harder against his wife's skin. Hands clenching helplessly, he barked, "Come out!"

Dougall appeared, followed by Murine, Uncle Acair, Conran . . .

Mouth tight, Aulay shifted his gaze to see how Cat was taking this development, and she snapped, "Over by Aulay. Now."

The room wasn't a very big one, and they'd all been kind of gathering in front of the passage opening, blocking it somewhat from view, but now they moved as a group toward him and Alick, allowing Niels, Edith, Greer, Cam, Rory and Jo to follow.

Cat scowled at the group of them now clustered across from her. She'd drawn Jetta back several steps to stay out of reach as the crowd grew, and now stood in the door to the master bedchamber and eyed them all with irritation.

"What about the other one?" Cat asked sharply. "The one who was with the maid when I shot her?"

"Geordie is with her still. He has no' left her bedside since she was injured," Aulay assured her solemnly, trying to keep her calm. She seemed to him to be getting agitated.

"You probably have soldiers in there, waiting to grab me," she muttered to herself.

Before Aulay could assure her there were no soldiers, Jetta said, "You cannot get away, Cat. It is finished. Please, just give yourself up before you get hurt."

"You would like that would you not? Me being in your husband's dungeon for the rest of my days so you could visit me and flaunt how you outmaneuvered me?"

"I would never—" Jetta began.

"I do not think so," Cat spat, interrupting her. Digging her knife in again, she placed her mouth by Jetta's ear and added, "And you had best hope it is not finished for me. Because if it is, I shall make sure 'tis finished for you as well, Sorry."

"Cat," Aulay said quickly.

Much to his relief, Cat shifted her attention to him and at least didn't put further pressure on the knife at Jetta's throat.

"Surely we can come to some kind of arrangement?" he suggested in bored tones. While he was desperate, it wouldn't do to let that show. Predators fed on fear.

Cat eased the knife out of Jetta's skin, but Aulay didn't feel relief as he watched the line of blood rolling down her throat to soak into the neckline of her shift.

"What kind of an arrangement?" Cat asked warily.

"What do ye want?" he asked, and then holding his hands out to indicate his entire domain, he said, "Ye can take whatever ye want in exchange fer Jetta."

She considered him with interest, and then her gaze shifted from him to Jetta and back. A slow smile began to curve her lips, and Aulay had a bad feeling even before she said, "I want you."

"You cannot have him," Jetta said at once. "He vowed himself to me in front of a priest. He's mine. He cannot give himself to you."

"Oh, please," Cat said on a laugh. "My husband vowed to love and honor me in his marriage vows. Those vows mean nothing. Besides, mayhap Aulay would rather have me than a sorry creature like you, Sorry Sorcha. I was always the prettier of the two of us and more interesting by half than you with your stained gowns, always running about fetching Mother this, and getting Mother that like a faithful dog."

"She was dying and in terrible pain," Jetta said angrily. "Of course I did all I could to comfort her."

"And made yourself a dull little wren in the process." She smiled coldly, and added, "And a nag. You were forever locking away the whiskey and wine so Father could not drink. 'Tis why it was so easy for me to convince him to send you to the marquis in my place. I promised to let him drink all he wished." Raising her eyebrows, she asked, "Do you lock up Aulay's whiskey too?"

"Of course not," Jetta said with a frown. "Aulay is not drinking himself to death. You know the healer said if Father continued to drink as he was it would be the death of him."

"At least he would have died happy," Cat said with a shrug.

"And did he die happy when you poisoned his whiskey?" Jetta asked grimly.

Cat's eyes narrowed, but she shifted her gaze to Aulay and said, "I am the better of the two of us. Surely you can see that? I am prettier, smarter and more fun. 'Tis the reason Mother always said I was the golden hawk and Sorry Sorcha a goose. Would you not rather have me to wife than a sorry old goose?"

Aulay stared at the woman with disbelief. They were identical twins. It was impossible for her to be prettier. Their mother probably hadn't been describing their looks so much as their personalities when she called Jetta a goose and Cat a golden eagle. Neither bird was black, but the goose *was* a nurturing bird, looking after and loyal to everyone in their gaggle, while a golden eagle was a vicious predator. He'd once seen one drag a goat off a cliff to fall to its death and then land on it and start eating it while it still lived. Aye, he was quite sure the mother had been thinking of their personalities. From what he could tell, Jetta appeared to have gotten all that was good when it came to character, while Cat was a bitter, angry, murdering bitch. Of course he preferred his Jetta.

"Tell her," Cat said confidently. "Tell her you want me more than her. I know you do. I could tell when you kissed me."

Aulay almost said "aye," just to please the woman, and hopefully, use the lie somehow to save Jetta, but then his gaze slid to his wife and he saw the worry and uncertainty in her expression. She truly feared he might prefer her sister, and for a moment he was flummoxed at the thought. How could she not know her value? How could she not know he loved her?

That last was a bit startling.

Love.

Did he love her? The answer was easy: aye. He loved her with both his body and soul. Of course, he'd never told her that. As for her not knowing her value . . . She had her memories back, and her sister had just told him how she could be unsure of her value. Her words had painted a perfect picture for him of Jetta's past.

Jetta, quietly doing what she could to ease her mother's suffering and prevent her father from drinking himself to death while Cat, he was sure, concerned herself with little more than fashion and flirting with the soldiers. Oh, and tormenting "Sorry Sorcha." Aye, he could see where her insecurities came from, and he would not add to them or hurt her by lying to her bitch of a sister.

"Nay," he said firmly. "I do no' want ye more than Jetta. In fact, I do no' want ye at all."

"Liar!" she accused furiously.

"Aulay ne'er lies," Alick assured her.

"But—" she began and then paused and smiled suddenly. "You did not know it was me. The last time you entered the room, it was me you kissed. You had come to tell Jetta that you were going to search the castle and had ordered the guards to keep her in here. Do you remember?"

"I remember," he assured her solemnly. "And I remember walking away, wondering why kissing who I thought was the woman I loved felt so lacking."

"No!" she shrieked. "That kiss was amazing. You wanted me. We could be good together. Better than you and Sorry."

"I do no' love Sorry," he snapped, sick of hearing her use that name. "I love Jetta. As for me and you . . . ye're just a mad, murderous bitch who looks like the woman I love."

Aulay knew at once he'd just been a little too honest. Because Cat released an animalistic shriek of fury, and then she pulled the knife back from Jetta's neck and started to plunge it downward, aiming for Jetta's heart. He didn't even have time to try to leap across the space dividing them and prevent the blow. He was sure he was watching his love die, and then Cat jerked to a halt midmovement with the knife blade less than an inch from Jetta's heart.

As Aulay watched in surprise, Cat's eyes widened incredulously, and then she dropped like Jetta after she'd tried too hard to remember something. She fell flat on her face on the rush-covered floor, revealing Saidh standing in the center of the master bedchamber beyond, her expression grim.

For a moment, Aulay was confused. Saidh was too far away to have knocked the woman out. But as he rushed to Jetta, he spared a glance for Cat and one look clarified matters. There was a ballocks dagger sticking out of her back. He had no doubt it was the one Saidh had found in one of the chests of dresses in the hall. Jetta had said his sister had kept it. Well, she'd just given it back, Aulay thought and nodded at his sister over Jetta's head as he wrapped his wife in his arms.

"Felled by her own dagger," Aulay muttered as Rory rushed forward and knelt to check on Cateline.

"My father's dagger," Jetta corrected him, watching Rory. "She wanted to torture me with it before she killed me. Apparently, she fantasized about that a great deal before she lost the dagger."

Aulay's arms tightened around her at the thought, and then Rory glanced up and shook his head, telling him that Cat was dead. It seemed to him to be justice that she died by a dagger that had belonged to the father she'd killed.

"Ye'd best let me see yer neck," Rory said, straightening to approach them.

Aulay eased his hold on Jetta and watched his brother urge her hand away from the wound she'd been holding. His mouth tightened when he saw the cut. It wasn't terribly deep, but would leave a scar and she had been very lucky. Cat had just missed hitting the vein.

"I need bandages, hot water and my medicinals," Rory said firmly.

Alick, Conran and Dougall all headed out of the room to fetch what was needed.

The moment they were gone, Rory suggested, "Mayhap we should move out to the master bedchamber."

Noting Rory's slight gesture toward the body on the floor, Aulay nodded at once and scooped Jetta into his arms. He carried her out of the little room and to the bed in their own chamber. The moment he set her down, he found himself pushed back out of the way so that Rory could get to Jetta again.

"Ye've a new knot on yer forehead, lass. What happened there?" Rory asked, leaning close to look at the swelling bruise.

"Cat hit me in the forehead with the hilt of her knife to knock me out when Aulay came to the room," Jetta explained with a grimace.

"Did she hit ye anywhere else?" Rory asked, peering at the swelling knot.

When she said nay, Aulay relaxed and then became aware of movement and glanced around. The women had all moved up alongside him, forming a sort of wall. He knew at once they were trying to block Jetta's view of the little room next door, and glanced that way to see Cam and Greer picking up Cat by her hands and feet.

"They're going to move her body to the dungeon until ye decide what to do with her," Saidh said quietly.

"The dungeon?" Aulay asked with surprise. The dungeon had not been used in ages.

Saidh shrugged. "All the bedchambers are taken."

Aulay looked to Saidh and said sincerely, "Thank you. Ye saved Jetta's life when I could not."

"Ye would ha'e thought o' something," she assured him solemnly. "But I'm glad I could help." Shifting her gaze to Jetta, she smiled and added, "As I told ye earlier, I like her. I think she'll make ye a fine wife, and is a grand addition to the family."

Aulay thought so too, but said dryly, "Nice to ken I ha'e yer approval."

"Ye do," she said lightly.

The door opened then and his brothers returned with the items Rory had requested. Aulay watched Rory clean the wound on Jetta's neck, relieved when he decided stitches would not be needed. Rory spent a moment poking at Jetta's newest head wound, asking if it hurt, but then nodded and stepped back. "I think ye'll be fine, but let me ken if ye start feeling poorly."

"Aye," Jetta murmured, glancing toward the door as Greer and Cam returned from their own task.

Aulay nodded at the pair in thanks, and then distracted Jetta by brushing his fingers gently down her cheek. When she turned to him, he asked solemnly, "Do ye want to rest after your excitement?"

"Nay," she murmured, and then, meeting his gaze, said sadly, "I am sorry, husband. This was all my fault. My sister—"

"It was no' yer fault," he interrupted firmly.

"Aye. It was," Jetta insisted. "She was after me, and in the process burned down your stables, shot poor young Katie with an arrow and killed Robbie's dog."

"Wife—" he tried to interrupt, but she continued.

"And she killed my father, too," Jetta finished, her face crumbling.

"Oh, lass." Aulay caught her hand and tugged her to her feet and into his arms, murmuring, "I'm sorry."

"I thought I would never forgive him for agreeing to send me to the marquis in her place when it happened. But when she said she had killed him, I just . . ."

"I ken," he said, rubbing her back as she wept against his chest.

"I am sorry. On top of everything else, I am getting you all wet. I am nothing but trouble. Ye must hate me," she mumbled, straightening away from him and sniffling miserably.

"Never be sorry, love," he growled. "Ye've done nothing wrong. And nay, I could ne'er hate ye. I love ye, lass."

"You do not have to say that, husband." She sniffled. "I know you are just being kind."

Aulay pulled back to scowl at her. "I'm no' being kind. 'Tis true."

Shaking her head, Jetta protested, "You cannot possibly love me. How can you love me when I have caused you nothing but unpleasantness and worry since you pulled me out of the ocean?"

Aulay had to bite back a smile at the question. She had almost howled it with despair.

"I do no ken," he said with a smile. "Mayhap because ye're brave, and smart, and bellow at me like a fishwife when I try to get ye to do something fer yer own good. Or mayhap because I see ye everywhere I look. I see yer skin in the clouds, yer eyes in the grass and yer hair in me horse's tail."

"Oh, Lord love us," Uncle Acair muttered, reminding him that they were not alone. "Aulay, lad, I ken yer no' a minstrel, but could ye no' at least ha'e said yer horse's mane?"

Tossing him a scowl over his shoulder, he snapped, "Nay. Me horse's mane is dark brown." Turning back to Jetta, he added, "The hair o' his tail, though, is the same midnight black as yer hair and 'tis beautiful."

Eyes wide and watery, she managed a choked, "Oh."

"Which is beautiful?" Niels asked sounding confused. "Ye're horse's tail or her hair?"

"Her hair," he barked, turning to glare at the man.

"Ignore him," Edith said, smacking her husband. Offering Aulay an encouraging smile then, she added, "Go on. Ye like her hair and eyes."

"How do ye ken he likes her eyes?" Dougall asked with amusement. "All he said was he sees them in the grass."

"Husband," Murine hissed.

"Well, he did."

Aulay turned back to Jetta, and closed his eyes briefly as he breathed out a sigh, and then said, "I'm sorry, lass. I wanted to tell ye I love ye using the flowery words I ken you women like, but instead I'm mucking this up horribly."

"Oh, husband," Jetta said, her arms tightening around him. When he opened his eyes, it was to see her smiling through her tears. Raising a hand to caress his cheek as she had the first time he saw her, she blinked her tears away and said softly, "I do not need flowery words. Your love is all I need. 'Tis all I want. You truly are a gift from God to me, husband. You are my own personal angel, a savior sent for me to love."

Aulay closed his eyes again, savoring the words. He'd never thought to have a woman feel that way about him, not since he'd been scarred so horribly. But his sweet Jetta did. She might think him her savior, but the truth was Jetta was his savior. She'd saved him from a long, lonely, and no doubt bitter life thinking of himself as a monster too ugly to be loved by any but his siblings.

Opening his eyes again, he met her gaze solemnly and said, "I'll keep ye safe and love ye till me dying breath, Jetta. I promise. And ye ken I keep me promises."

"Aye, I do," she assured him solemnly and reached up on her tiptoes to press a kiss to his chin. At least, he suspected that was her intent, but he lowered his head at the last minute, giving her his lips instead. Jetta hesitated when their mouths met, but then gave him a short sweet kiss before settling back flat on her feet.

Noting the smile now curving her lips, he tilted his head with curiosity. "What are ye grinning about, lass?"

"I was just recalling the last promise ye kept," she admitted.

Recalling it too, and how it had led to their consummating their wedding in the stables, he smiled back, but said, "And now I am recalling a promise I made and ha'e yet to keep."

Jetta looked thoughtful for a moment, but apparently couldn't recall the promise, because she shook her head and asked, "What promise is that?"

"Ye'll see," Aulay said with a grin, and scooped her up into his arms. Maneuvering his way around the large crowd in their room, he carried her to the door and paused. Realizing he couldn't open it, Jetta reached out and did it for him. Aulay started forward once it had swung open out of the way, but slowed when the four men in the hall immediately came to attention and moved forward to surround them.

"My wife no longer needs a guard, Cullen. You and your men are dismissed," he said firmly.

"Aye, m'laird," Cullen murmured, and nodded at the men. The moment they started away up the hall, Aulay began to move again, carrying Jetta toward the stairs.

"Where are we going?" Alick asked suddenly, on his heels.

Aulay glanced around with a start, a scowl claiming his face when he saw his entire family as well as Jo and Cam were following them.

Shaking his head, he started walking again. "*We're* going nowhere. *I'm* taking me wife to the loch fer a little rest and some relaxin'."

"Would that be fishin' relaxin' or relaxin' relaxin' . . . ?" Alick asked in a teasing voice.

"It'd be a man with the woman he loves relaxin'," Aulay said firmly. "And the rest o' ye are no' welcome."

Much to his relief, they stopped following him then, leaving him alone as he headed down the stairs.

"I just realized what promise you have not yet kept," Jetta admitted with a slow smile as they reached the Great Hall floor. "Ye promised to take me back to the loch alone the next time."

"And to love ye til ye scream so loud ye scare every bird in every tree for miles around into flyin' from their roosts," Aulay finished.

"And you always keep your promises," Jetta said with a grin, and then, her expression becoming serious, she said, "I believe that is one of the things I love best about you, husband."

"God, I love ye, wife," Aulay said fervently, his arms tightening around her.

"I love you too, husband," she assured him solemnly.

"Then I'm a lucky man."